"Computer, take us to Vic Fontaine's current location."

"No!" Nog yelled as he leaped back to his feet.

Around them, the scene shifted, wavering as the holo-program reshaped the setting. Their shabby surroundings vanished, replaced by opulence. They suddenly stood in a corridor wider than Vic's tumbledown hotel room. Bright crystal chandeliers hung from a high ceiling, illuminating wainscoted walls and beautifully patterned carpeting.

"Computer —" Nog rushed to say, but if he intended to reverse Candlewood's command or end the program, he never got that far. "Vic?" Candlewood didn't recognize the lounge singer from behind, but Nog clearly did.

Vic turned at the sound of his name. So did the two large men walking on either side of him. Candlewood would later think that Nog had taken a step forward, and that Vic had called out to him, but everything happened so quickly that he couldn't be sure. Before the science officer could process what he saw—a captive being led somewhere by his abductors—the two burly men reached into their jackets and drew weapons.

The two big men strode forward as they began firing. The loud report of their weapons filled the corridor, and brief flashes of orange-yellow light accompanied each shot. An acrid scent filled the air. Candlewood instinctively raised his arms to protect himself.

STAR TREK
DEEP SPACE NINE®

THE LONG MIRAGE

DAVID R. GEORGE III

Based upon *Star Trek* and
Star Trek: The Next Generation®
created by Gene Roddenberry
and
Star Trek: Deep Space Nine
created by Rick Berman & Michael Piller

POCKET BOOKS

New York   London   Toronto   Sydney   New Delhi   Mericor City

Pocket Books
An Imprint of Simon & Schuster, Inc.
1230 Avenue of the Americas
New York, NY 10020

This book is a work of fiction. Any references to historical events, real people, or real places are used fictitiously. Other names, characters, places, and events are products of the author's imagination, and any resemblance to actual events or places or persons, living or dead, is entirely coincidental.

This book is published by Pocket Books,
an imprint of Simon & Schuster, Inc.,
under exclusive license from CBS Studios Inc.

First Pocket Books paperback edition March 2017

POCKET and colophon are registered trademarks of Simon & Schuster, Inc.

For information about special discounts for bulk purchases, please contact Simon & Schuster Special Sales at 1-866-506-1949 or business@simonandschuster.com.

The Simon & Schuster Speakers Bureau can bring authors to your live event. For more information or to book an event, contact the Simon & Schuster Speakers Bureau at 1-866-248-3049 or visit our website at www.simonspeakers.com.

Manufactured in the United States of America

10 9 8 7 6 5 4 3 2 1

ISBN 978-1-5011-3297-1
ISBN 978-1-5011-3321-3 (ebook)

I dedicate this book to a great friend;
he stood beside me
as a best man at my wedding,
he bats third,
he plays shortstop,
and his name is
Mark Gemello.
(There's always room for Gemello!)

Historian's Note

The primary story of this novel commences in late January 2386, immediately following the final events of the *Star Trek: Deep Space Nine* novel *Ascendance*.

We are all independent vessels
sailing the seas of life to and fro
oft meeting among the tides and swells,
but each how full, we alone can know.

—Akorem Laan
The Book of Sighs, "Songs and Silence"

Prologue

Collateral Damage

As the waitress approached the booth where the stranger sat, a curl of suspicion twisted in her gut. The man wore casual clothes—a dark striped cardigan atop a collared pullover shirt, tan slacks, and loafers—but he bore a serious manner. Mister Cardigan had smiled at her when she'd taken his order, but as she'd stepped back behind the counter, the good cheer had drained from his face. Something significant plainly occupied the man's mind, and the waitress could only hope that the subject of his thoughts did not mean trouble for the diner. They'd already had enough excitement around there recently: a fight had broken out in the parking lot just the previous week, and a month before that, the place had been robbed at gunpoint.

The waitress walked across the checkered linoleum floor, over patches of midafternoon sunlight slanting in through the front windows of the diner. Though past the traditional hours for lunch and still well before dinnertime, a number of customers—many of them regulars—sat scattered about the eatery. Mister Cardigan had chosen the booth farthest from the door, down by the other end of the counter, away from the main dining room and all the other customers. When the waitress arrived at his table, she reached up to the circular tray perched on her splayed fingers. She took hold of the tall, fluted soda-fountain glass and set it down before the man. Her hand came away slick with condensation.

"Thank you, Joy," Mister Cardigan said, glancing up and reading her name from the tag affixed to the strap of her bib apron. His lips curved upward at the ends, but his expression seemed like a façade erected for her benefit, rather than something genuine.

"You're welcome, sir," Joy said. "I hope you enjoy it." She waited a few seconds, trying to gauge the man's true temperament, and thereby his intentions. She thought about the slip of paper beside the telephone in the tiny, windowless room that served as the manager's office. She pictured the series of digits written there, the main number for the local sheriff's office.

The man must have thought Joy lingered for a response because he reacted to her scrutiny. He pulled the glass toward him and sipped from the straw sticking out of the frothy white head crowning the chocolaty drink. "Not bad," Mister Cardigan said. "Not quite like they make them on Passyunk Avenue, but pretty good for out West."

Joy didn't know how to reply to the man—she'd never heard of the street he'd mentioned—but then his eyes shifted and he looked past her. She followed his gaze and glanced back over her shoulder. Another man had entered the diner, and Mister Cardigan offered him a quick wave. Joy watched as the new customer lumbered along beside the counter and toward the booth. Thick-armed and barrel-chested, he had a long, frowning face and only a few wisps of hair on his dappled bald head. He acknowledged the waitress with a nod, then slid ponderously into the booth, directly across from the first man.

"Good afternoon, sir," Joy said, and she reached across the table to where they kept the menus propped up between the sugar pourer and the salt and pepper shakers. Mister Cardigan stopped her with a touch to her forearm. It required a conscious effort for her not to flinch away from him.

"Just bring him one of these," Mister Cardigan said, tapping the side of his glass. The waitress looked to the second man for confirmation. He shrugged.

Joy took a pad and pen from the wide front pocket of her apron and jotted the order down, then headed back behind the counter and retrieved another soda-fountain glass. As she poured a couple inches of milk into it, she looked over at the booth to see the second man open the bulky vest he wore and extract a large manila envelope from beneath it, which he then deposited on the table.

"This is it?" Mister Cardigan asked, his tone mixing disappointment and disbelief. Though he spoke quietly, Joy could still hear him. He picked up the envelope and held it vertically on the table. The mustard-colored packet had a thickness to it, though it did not appear overfilled. "This doesn't look big enough to hold all the cash, or small enough to contain just a check." The second man shook his head, an action that set his shoulders wobbling back and forth.

The waitress plopped a long-handled spoon into the glass, then walked to the other end of the counter to get a seltzer bottle. She aimed the siphon at the bowl of the spoon and filled the glass almost to the rim, giving the mixture a foamy top. By the time she moved back to the far end of the counter for the chocolate syrup, she saw that Mister Cardigan had pulled a sheaf of papers partially out of the envelope.

"This won't fly—not as repayment for your credit line," he said as he examined the documents. "I mean . . . if you intend to use this as a form of security . . ." Mister Cardigan let his words trail off, as though considering the idea to which he had just given voice. The second man held up his arms, hands open and apart, as if to suggest that there could be no other reasonable interpretation of the envelope's contents. It did not surprise the waitress to hear the two men talking about money or about what sounded like an ill-conceived debt. Such subjects arose a great deal—not just at the Deauville Diner, but all around town.

Joy unscrewed the cap on the bottle of chocolate syrup and began pouring it into the glass. Though she watched what she did, she continued to listen, waiting for the two men to go on with their conversation. Finally, Mister Cardigan spoke again. "Maybe," he allowed. "I can try to sell this as surety for your losses, but I don't know how far I'm gonna get touting water rights in the desert."

Joy stirred the concoction she'd just made. The spoon clinked against the glass, drowning out the big man's reaction. When the waitress finished, she plucked a straw from the dispenser on the counter and stuck it into the effervescent chocolate drink. As she placed the glass on a tray and started back out onto the floor, she heard Mister Cardigan sigh heavily.

"Dealing with things like this makes me think again about getting outta here," he said. Joy hoped that meant that he would soon leave the diner and never return, but as she set down the second glass, Mister Cardigan smiled at her again. The second man added a grateful nod, an action that, because he essentially had no neck, caused his entire body to dip forward. The sluggish movement made him seem far from formidable—even as strong as he looked, Joy figured that she could easily outrun him. She realized that she didn't really fear either of the two men, but the dubious nature of their commerce still gave her pause.

Carrying her empty tray back toward the counter, the waitress heard Mister Cardigan say, "What? Don't gimme that look. I know I can't go anywhere, but this—" Joy visualized him holding up the large envelope with the bundle of papers protruding from it. "—isn't gonna make my life any easier around here. I hope you have a backup plan."

Before the second man could respond, a customer at the other end of the counter motioned with his empty cup to the waitress. Joy quickly put down her tray and grabbed the coffeepot from the brewing station. She crossed the diner to fill the man's mug, then seated a middle-aged couple who strolled in through the front door. She spoke with them for a few minutes until they eventually decided what they wanted to eat. She scribbled their choices—meatloaf for the husband, fried chicken for the wife—on the top sheet of her pad, then went back behind the counter to the pass-through, where she hung up the order for the cook to see. Several other plates had been completed, and so she delivered those meals to other customers.

When Joy finally peered back across the diner toward Mister Cardigan, she saw that he and his colleague had risen from their booth. She quickly looked down and searched through the pocket of her apron to find their bill, but by the time she pulled it out, Mister Cardigan had already reached her. "I have your ticket, sir," she said, holding the small piece of paper out to him.

"Thank you, Joy," the man said. In one smooth motion, he took the bill from her hand and replaced it with several dollars. Joy thought she heard the second man say something behind him, back at the booth, but she could not make out the words.

"I'll be right back with your change," she told Mister Cardigan, but he generously told her to keep it for herself. He curled her fingers closed around the money, smiled, then stepped past her and over to the front door. When he opened it and walked outside, Joy smelled the parched desert air. Then the door closed and she looked back toward the second man.

He wasn't there.

Joy whirled around, searching for him. The diner had only a single entrance accessible to customers, as well as a rear door for employees, but the second man could not have reached either without making his way past her. The waitress spun back toward the booth, which still sat empty.

Joy did not see the technological arch that had appeared

and stood beside the table because she had been specifically programmed not to see it. She could not observe the second man passing through the arch, nor the Cardassian architecture of the corridor he entered beyond it. For Joy, the Deauville Diner existed, and Las Vegas around it, but the holosuite in which her life unfolded did not. She had never heard of Quark's Bar or of Deep Space 9.

In the next millisecond, the software overseeing holoprogram Bashir 62 loaded a memory into Joy's matrix, alleviating the disconnect of the second man's inexplicable disappearance. The waitress suddenly recalled him passing her and leaving the diner through the front door. Nothing any longer seemed out of the ordinary.

Still, as she headed back behind the counter to resume her work, the waitress hoped that neither Mister Cardigan nor his burly colleague would ever return to the diner. Though she had concluded that she needn't fear either man, Joy hadn't liked what she'd seen and heard. Though she did not know the details of their business, she had nevertheless perceived danger in its character.

On that score, she would prove prophetic.

One

High-Risk Investment

Captain Ro Laren strode into the hangar with a sense of purpose, eager to confirm or refute the alleged identity of the pilot who had just landed a vessel aboard Deep Space 9. Doctor Pascal Boudreaux, the starbase's chief medical officer, walked beside her, with Crewmen Barry Herriot and Torvan Pim behind them on either flank. By the captain's order, the two security officers kept their phasers holstered.

With a gesture, Ro positioned Herriot and Torvan inside the door to the hangar, then continued on with Boudreaux toward the ship. Above, the stars winked out as the overhead hatch glided closed. A band of emitters around the opening shined electric blue, signaling the operation of the hangar's force field that maintained the compartment's internal atmosphere.

Ro and the doctor came to a halt half a dozen meters from the ship. The whine of antigravs receded as the vessel powered down. The ship sported a lusterless, mottled hull that probably lent itself to camouflage in particular environments. Not quite the size of a runabout, it readily fit within the hangar's designated landing zone. Its relatively compact size and simple configuration suggested that it might not function autonomously, but as an auxiliary craft attached to a larger vessel.

Working as the beta-shift duty officer in the Hub that day, Ensign Allasar had reported no match for the ship in any of the relevant databases. Ro did not recognize its architecture, leaving her unable even to conjecture about its world of origin. Of course, it had just entered the Bajoran system through the wormhole, meaning that, theoretically, it could have come from any number of unknown planets in the vast, largely unexplored expanse of the Gamma Quadrant.

"Don't look familiar to me," Boudreaux offered, echoing the captain's thoughts, albeit in words flavored with his rich Creole patois. "I'm detecting a single set of life signs," he said, consulting the tricorder he held out before him. "Definitely reads as Bajoran." Ro had informed the doctor of the identity claimed by the ship's lone passenger.

"Make sure to run a blood sample," the captain ordered. "With everything that's happened recently, I want to be certain we're dealing with the genuine article and not an Ascendant or Founder or some other shape-shifter."

"Understood."

As Ro reached for her combadge, the overhead hatch shot home with a reassuring clang. She waited a moment for the thick reverberation to quiet. The bright blue of the emitters around the hatch faded to black as the force-field generator automatically deactivated.

Ro tapped her combadge, which chirped beneath her touch. Before she could open a channel to the vessel sitting in front of her, though, a panel in the ship's hull withdrew inward. Ro heard the whisper of equalizing pressure. A moment later, the panel opened laterally, revealing a single individual standing just inside the ship.

It was Kira Nerys.

Despite several changes in the vedek's appearance since last Ro had seen her, the captain knew her at once. After all, they had served together aboard the old Deep Space 9, day in and day out, for two years, until Kira had left Starfleet to join the Bajoran clergy. Standing in the entryway of the alien vessel, the vedek did not wear the traditional robes of her position, but a dark-green tunic with matching pants, an outfit that trod the middle ground between utilitarian shipboard wear and a uniform. Kira's hair had grown down well past her shoulders, longer than the captain had ever seen it. The vedek also looked older to Ro, and thinner.

But I've seen her carry herself with that bearing before, Ro thought. *I've seen that expression on her face.* Kira had always worn her determination like a second skin. Indeed, it had been with such resolve that, more than two years prior, the vedek had stolen a runabout and absconded with it into the wormhole. There, she had helped to defeat the rogue crew of a Romulan warbird, and to save Captain Sisko and *Defiant*, but she had been believed lost when the great subspace bridge had collapsed with her inside it.

But obviously she wasn't lost, Ro thought. Although she would wait for Doctor Boudreaux to draw a firm medical conclusion, the captain did not doubt that Kira Nerys had returned. As a Resistance fighter, as a Bajoran Militia member, and as a Starfleet officer, the vedek had defied death on numerous occasions, but Ro's confidence about her identity came borne less by Kira's resilience and more by the increasingly impressive series of recent events centered around the Prophets.

As Ro and Boudreaux approached the ship, the vedek stepped down to the deck. The captain felt the urge to embrace her former commanding officer, suddenly returned after missing for so long, but before Ro could react in any way, Kira spoke, her manner matter-of-fact. "Captain, Doctor," the vedek greeted them. "I assume you want a sample of my DNA." Without waiting for a response, she held her arm out, her hand open, palm facing upward. "You should also test my blood for morphogenic properties." Having served aboard the old DS9 for nearly a decade, Kira clearly understood Starfleet's security imperatives.

"Thank you," Ro said. She nodded to Boudreaux, who immediately extracted an instrument from the medkit hanging at his side. He collected a selection of epidermal cells from Kira's outstretched hand, then fed the sample into his tricorder. He then swapped out the medical tool for a second device and raised it to the vedek's upper arm, where he filled a phial with her blood. It required less than two minutes for Boudreaux to corroborate Kira's identity.

"Thank you, Doctor," the vedek said. Then, of Ro, she asked, "How long have I been gone?"

"More than two years," Ro said, wondering about the perception of time passing within the Celestial Temple. "The wormhole collapsed shortly after you entered it. You were presumed lost—" The captain stopped herself in midsentence. "The Vedek Assembly declared you missing and presumed to be in the care of the Prophets." As desperate and unlikely as the official statement had always sounded to Ro, it all at once made perfect sense. "Was that the case? Have you been inside the wormhole all this time?"

Kira glanced from Ro to the doctor and back again. "We need to speak in private, Captain."

Ro looked to Boudreaux, whose eyebrows rose, whether with amusement or indignation, the captain could not tell. She didn't need to consider the request for long; she trusted Kira's judgment. "Pascal, return to Sector General and report your findings to Commander Blackmer. When Vedek Kira and I are done here, I'll bring her down for a full workup."

"Aye, Captain." Before departing, the doctor addressed Kira directly. "It's good to see you again, Vedek." Kira nodded but said nothing, and Boudreaux headed for the hangar door.

After he'd gone, Ro pointed to the vedek's ship. The captain had questions about the vessel—*Had the Prophets created it Themselves, and if not, then where had it come from?*—but for the moment she would wait to ask them. Ro perceived an urgency in the vedek's manner and in her entreaty for a confidential conversation. "Can we find privacy aboard?"

Kira nodded again, then led the captain up the steps and into the main cabin. Ro found the space cramped. Six chairs on either side of the small compartment faced each other, leaving little room to maneuver. Peering aft, Ro saw that the bulk of the interior had been given over to a large transporter platform and what looked like a cargo hold.

Ro sat down in one of the two forward chairs, located at the vessel's main console. Kira remained standing. "I'll be happy to answer all of your questions, Captain, but there are some things I need to know first," the vedek said. "What can you tell me about the Ascendants' attack and what happened on Endalla? And what about the fate of Taran'atar?"

The questions surprised Ro. Had somebody informed Kira about everything that had taken place over the past couple of months? Had she somehow been a witness to those events? All of the incidents to which she referred had taken place during the vedek's absence . . . unless— "Did you encounter the Ascendants inside the wormhole? Did you visit their world there?"

The vedek blinked. "What?" she finally said, plainly confused by what Ro had asked. "Are you saying that there is an Ascendant world . . . *inside* the Celestial Temple?" Kira looked almost as though she'd been struck. She sat down heavily in the other chair at the front panel. She gazed off to one side, through the forward port, but Ro thought she actually looked inward, searching for some form of understanding. At last, she peered back at the captain and leaned toward her. "What are you talking about?"

ii

Kira listened in silence as Captain Ro related an account of what had transpired over the previous two months in the Bajoran system—and in the wormhole. The vedek attempted to process the implications of what she heard, a task rendered more difficult by the tumultuous impact of her own circumstances. Only moments before—at least by Kira's reckoning—she had been working in the Gamma Quadrant with Taran'atar to fend off an Ascendant attack on Idran IV. They sought not only to protect the planet's Eav'oq population, but to safeguard Kai Pralon during her visit there. They succeeded, and the vedek then followed Taran'atar as he pursued the Ascendant fleet through the wormhole and into the Bajoran system.

Except that when Kira had exited the Celestial Temple in the Alpha Quadrant, she'd detected no ships ahead of her. Instead, she spied an enormous space station occupying the coordinates of the old Cardassian ore-processing facility that had eventually become Deep Space 9, and which had ultimately been destroyed. Although Kira had never seen a base like the one she encountered upon leaving the wormhole, she still recognized its Starfleet design. A magnified view revealed the skewed chevron that represented the space service, as well as the words UNITED FEDERATION OF PLANETS marching down the outer edge of one of the station's vertical rings. The vedek concluded at once that, during her transit through the Celestial Temple, the Prophets had moved her temporally, from the past, when Bajor first faced an offensive by the Ascendants, back to her own time.

Kira felt beset as the captain unspooled the story of recent events. It angered the vedek to hear of another Ohalavaru assault on Endalla, then confused her when she learned about their discovery deep beneath the moon's surface of what they described as a falsework. The return of the Ascendants did not entirely surprise her—Raiq had remained convinced that some of her people had somehow survived the conflagration above Bajor—but their collective metamorphosis into a link of shape-shifters did. Kira did not know what to make of Taran'atar's presence among them, or of the revelation that they had all entered the Celestial Temple and formed into a malleable world there, apparently to stay.

The vedek could not help but speculate about her own time spent within the wormhole. She had walked along the surface of a world there, had witnessed events from the past that had seemed to unfold directly before her. More than that, she had lived as another person, evidently sometime deep in Bajor's history, and though she could no longer fully recall the details of that experience, it occurred to her that it all could have been an elaborate simulation created in an environment that could readily alter its form. Once she had sorted it out in her mind, she knew she would have to reveal all of it to the captain.

When Ro finished speaking, the vedek remained quiet. Kira tried to collate what she had been through with what the captain had just told her, searching for meaning in the flow of events. She wanted to understand the will of the Prophets, but she also recognized the folly in trying to do so. Still, the contours of how it all fit together seemed tantalizingly close.

"So you didn't have anything at all to do with what's happened," Ro finally said, breaking the silence. "You didn't even know about any of it." She offered the observations as statements, not as questions.

"No, I didn't."

"But then why would you ask specifically about those incidents?" the captain asked. "How could you even know to ask about them?" For the moment, her attitude seemed more a matter of curiosity than of suspicion, but Kira knew that would change quickly if she chose anything other than complete disclosure with Ro.

"I wasn't asking about anything you just told me," the

vedek said. "I was asking about the Ascendants' attack on Bajor, and Taran'atar triggering Iliana Ghemor's isolytic subspace weapon."

"But all of that happened eight years ago . . . and you were there," Ro said. "You witnessed everything that took place."

"Not everything," Kira said. "I didn't see what happened on the other side of the wormhole before the Ascendants traveled through it."

"Of course not," the captain agreed. "How could you?"

"Because I was there," Kira said. "Because after the wormhole collapsed, I lived some sort of alternate life within it—or I *imagined* that I did—and then the Prophets sent me deep into the Gamma Quadrant . . . and into the past."

Ro nodded slowly, and Kira could see her putting the pieces together. "So while you faced the Ascendants as the commanding officer of Deep Space Nine, a future version of yourself existed on the other side of the wormhole?"

"Yes," Kira said. "And I thought . . . I thought that maybe I could change what happened. I thought that I might be able to prevent the scientists on Endalla from being wiped out, that I could keep Taran'atar from getting killed. I tried but . . ." Kira did not finish her sentence. Ro did.

"But even after whatever actions you took," the captain said, "everything transpired the way it had originally."

"Yes," Kira said, the admission painful. *I thought I was the Hand of the Prophets.* Had she imagined her encounters with Them? Or had she misinterpreted Their intentions for her?

No, neither, the vedek realized. The Prophets had communicated with her, They had meant for her to act on Their behalf. She had simply failed.

"Except . . . maybe that's not what *originally* happened,"

Ro proposed. "Maybe, before your future self intervened, all of Bajor was destroyed by the Ascendants."

Kira considered the possibility. As she understood it, temporal theorists believed that, in typical situations that involved time travel—if ever travel through time could be considered typical—such unknowable discontinuities abounded. In the vedek's own experience with the Prophets, though, her awareness of historical changes remained. When Akorem Laan—a poet who had been lost with one of his greatest compositions left unfinished—returned to his own time and concluded his work, Kira retained memories of the incomplete poem. The vedek said as much to Ro.

"Then maybe the Prophets sent you into the past specifically so that your actions would result in what happened," the captain suggested.

"The destruction of Endalla's ecosystem and the deaths of all the scientists there?" Kira said. "That doesn't sound like something the Prophets would do."

"But if, without your involvement, Endalla *and* Bajor would have been lost, it makes sense," the captain went on. "And if the Prophets put you in place to influence those events, then it stands to reason that you impacted what followed: the merging of the Ascendants and Taran'atar in a shape-shifting link, their establishment of a world inside the wormhole, and the discovery of the Endalla falsework."

Kira's mind reeled at the implications. Had the Prophets sent her into the Gamma Quadrant in the past specifically so that she could ensure that Taran'atar traveled through the wormhole aboard *Even Odds*, where he would employ the peculiar alien ship to prevent the Ascendants from decimating the population of Bajor? Where the Jem'Hadar's actions would result in him then physically joining the zealous aliens and forming a world within the Celestial Temple, apparently with the will of the Prophets?

And was that where I landed inside the wormhole? Kira asked herself. Could she have alit on that variable world *before* it had been created? She knew well the Emissary's declaration that the Prophets did not exist linearly in time, and certainly she had witnessed evidence of that herself. It would mean that she had interacted with the Prophets in a place that would not exist until she subsequently set in motion events that would lead to the formation of that place.

"Maybe," she finally allowed, and she immediately discovered that she wanted Ro's explanation to be true. Kira could not pretend that the actions she had taken in the Gamma Quadrant had undone the terrible damage to Endalla or the deaths of the scientists there, but she could see how what she had done had set in motion the later events that Ro had described—events that could be characterized as momentous.

"Maybe," the vedek said again, and she heard more conviction in her voice. For the first time, Kira sensed that she might actually have fulfilled the role the Prophets had given her when They had designated her Their Hand.

iii

Nog sat by himself at a small table in a rear corner of the Replimat. His dinner—actually just an appetizer of *relotho* larvae—went untouched in a covered dish set off to the side. A slew of personal access display devices lay spread across the tabletop, most of them activated. He looked from one to another, studying images, reading text, interpreting data, trying to formulate some sort of a plan, but he had trouble even determining where to begin.

"Evening." Nog looked up to see Lieutenant Commander John Candlewood, DS9's primary science officer, standing on the other side of the table. He carried a tray with several dishes and a tall glass of water or some other transparent beverage. "Mind if I join you?"

"Um," Nog said, unsure how best to decline. He and Candlewood had become friends over their years of service together, first becoming acquainted almost a decade earlier, during *Defiant*'s historic three-month exploratory mission in the Gamma Quadrant. Though Nog didn't want any company at that moment, he also didn't want to hurt the science officer's feelings. "I'm sorry, John," he said. "I'm really busy right now and need to be alone."

Candlewood nodded, then leaned over and set his tray on the other chair. "If you truly wanted isolation," he said as he collected up several of the padds, stacked them, and pushed them aside, "you'd be in your very private quarters right now." Nog started to protest, but Candlewood retrieved his tray and set it down on the table in the freshly cleared space. The science officer's meal consisted of a bowl of sickeningly green soup, a small plate containing a leafy salad, and a larger dish of variously colored vegetables and cheeses.

"John, listen," Nog said, still meaning to ask his friend to allow him solitude, but Candlewood leaned in over the table to glance at the padd atop the pile he had just gathered together. Nog looked at it himself and saw a land map displayed there.

"Are you going prospecting for treasure on some far-flung world?" Candlewood asked. Despite that Nog had served as a Starfleet officer for more than a dozen years, several of his friends still teased him about the Ferengi penchant for profit.

"No, I'm not on a treasure hunt," Nog said, a little more sharply than he'd intended. "No," he said again, softening his tone. He regarded his friend across the table, and Nog realized that he really did want to talk about what had happened. To that point, he had told nobody about his success in uploading Vic Fontaine's program to a holosuite—not even Ulu Lani, the beautiful Bajoran woman who worked as a server for Quark, and who had recently taken to flirting with Nog.

The operations chief looked around to ensure that nobody in the Replimat paid any attention to him and Candlewood, then lowered his voice to a conspiratorial level. Nog filled in his friend about Vic's matrix and the dramatic, unexplained changes to it. That included the lounge singer living at a seedy hotel, from which he had just the previous night been abducted at gunpoint.

"So is that what all this is about?" Candlewood asked, waving a hand over the padds on the table.

"Yes."

"What are you planning on doing?"

Nog shrugged. "I'm going to do the only thing I can do," he said. "I'm going to reenter the program and rescue Vic."

"Rescue him from what?"

"That's just it: I don't know." Nog sighed in frustration. "That's what I'm trying to figure out."

"Why don't you just reinitialize the program?" Candlewood suggested. Nog opened his mouth to protest, but the science officer quickly held up his hands to stop him. "Wait, wait. Sorry," Candlewood said. "I forgot that Vic is 'special.'"

Nog could hear the mild disdain in his friend's voice. Back on the original DS9, Candlewood had visited Vic's a few times. While he claimed to enjoy those experiences, and admitted that the character possessed a certain virtual charm, the science officer also revealed that he found it a bit strange that Nog could profess friendship with a simulation comprising computer code and holographically projected light.

"Vic *is* special," Nog insisted. "And you know that if I

reset his holoprogram, his memories would be completely erased. I'd effectively be killing the Vic Fontaine I know."

"Yes, I realize that, I'm sorry," Candlewood said. "It's just that . . . until you were able to upload his matrix again, you hadn't even seen him since the destruction of the old station. That was a long time ago. How much would you really be losing?"

"I know you think it's peculiar, but Vic is my friend," Nog said. "Deleting his memories would be like deleting our friendship."

"All right, all right. I shouldn't judge." Candlewood dipped a spoon into his soup and raised it to his lips. After taking a few such sips, he stopped and asked, "Didn't you tell me once before about having to save Vic inside the program?"

"That was a long time ago too, but yes, a group of us helped Doctor Bashir do that," Nog said. "That was a well-defined problem specifically included in the code, though, with recognizable parameters and a clear resolution."

"A 'jack-in-the-box,' " Candlewood said.

"Right," Nog said. "Which is why I've contacted Felix Knightly, the man who created Vic's code, to find out if this is just another surprise he hid inside the program. I haven't heard back from him yet." Nog shook his head. "I hope that's what this is, but it feels different from that. Part of it's that Vic has been trapped in the simulation tester for so long." Quark had prevented the lounge singer from being lost when the first Deep Space 9 had been destroyed; Nog's uncle had installed Vic's matrix inside a testing device, but circumstances had prevented the singer from being uploaded to a holosuite until just recently.

"Do you think Vic not having any interaction outside his own program could have caused this?" Candlewood set down his spoon in favor of a fork and began picking at his salad.

"Maybe, but I don't know," Nog said. "That's the biggest problem I have right now: I don't have any idea what's going on. I only know that Vic's been kidnapped. I don't know who's taken him, where they're holding him, or for what reason, all of which means I don't know how to find him and successfully free him without putting him in danger."

"I hate to ask this," Candlewood said as he speared a radish, "but how do you know if Vic's even still alive after his abduction?"

"Because if he wasn't, I'm pretty sure the program would either reset with another main character or shut down," Nog said. "Either way, Vic's holomatrix would be permanently deleted."

Candlewood appeared to consider this. As the science officer continued his meal, Nog glanced at the covered dish of relotho larvae. He thought about eating, but he really didn't have much of an appetite. Ever since he'd witnessed the three armed thugs forcibly remove Vic from the hotel where the lounge singer had been staying, Nog had felt sick to his stomach.

"So how can I help?" Candlewood asked.

"What? I thought you didn't think much of Vic."

"It's not that I don't think much of him; it's just that . . . well, he's a hologram," Candlewood said. "But you're my friend and in obvious distress, so I'd like to help however I can."

"Thank you," Nog said, grateful for the offer. While Candlewood served as the starbase's primary science officer, he had begun his Starfleet career as a computer specialist. Nog knew his way around an isolinear core, but he thought that Candlewood could provide invaluable assistance. "Once I hear back from Knightly, we can figure out how to proceed."

"Or maybe we don't have to wait that long," Candlewood said. "Maybe we can enter Vic's program and start searching for clues about what's happened to him."

"You would do that?"

Candlewood set his fork down on his plate and stood up. "Let's go," he said.

Nog didn't need a second invitation.

iv

Odo waited as patiently as he could while the doctor waved her scanner over his faux-Bajoran form. Lying on a diagnostic pallet in Newton Outpost's otherwise-empty infirmary, he strived to keep still. He normally eschewed such examinations. The non-Changelings with whom he had lived—first the Cardassians, and then the Bajorans—had always wanted to study him to learn about his physical nature, but when he'd begun serving alongside Starfleet personnel, the UFP's space service had tried to insist that he undergo regular medical checkups as part of their preventive-care regimen. Odo had occasionally relented—Captain Sisko had sometimes been particularly persuasive—but more often than not, the shape-shifter had demurred as a simple issue of maintaining his dignity and privacy.

Since Doctor Girani had informed him that the situation with the strange new shape-shifting life-form had been resolved peacefully and without further casualties, Odo felt less urgency to depart Newton Outpost. At the same time, it reinforced his decision that the time had come for him to return to his own people. He had no idea what he would discover back in the Dominion—how many Founders had returned, how the Vorta and the Jem'Hadar had fared in his absence, and what had become of Laas, Weyoun, and Rotan'talag, among others—but he wanted to find out.

Odo felt the impulse to move—if not to alter his structure, then at least to stand up and walk about the compartment. He didn't, though, nor did he protest the continued poking and prodding by Girani Semna. The Bajoran physician had not only nursed him back to health after his nearly lethal encounter with the Ascendant link, she had gone out of her way to do so. She had traveled all the way to Newton Outpost from her home on Bajor specifically so that she could tend to his compromised mental and physical condition. He very well might owe her his life, and he felt that it would be unjust for him to deny her the final ministrations of her care.

Of even greater importance, Odo believed that he actually needed to be examined. Not since he had contracted the morphogenic virus during the Dominion War had his corporal well-being been in such doubt. His explosive contact with the Ascendant link had left him in the Changeling equivalent of a coma, with no internal cognition and no sensory awareness. He regained consciousness weeks later, only to find himself in an amorphous state and unable to alter his form. He did perceive Girani attempting to help him convalesce, and with her aid and the passage of more time, he eventually regained his shape-shifting abilities.

Odo began to squirm atop the bio-bed, and with an effort, he stilled his movements. "That's all right," the doctor said with a gentle touch to his shoulder. The hum of the scanner ceased, and the doctor secured the device in her tricorder. "I see nothing that indicates that you're in any medical danger." She peered up over Odo's head at a display of diagnostic readings. "But I am still a little concerned about your metabolism."

"I am tired," Odo admitted, "but besides that, I feel fine."

"I don't think it's anything to be concerned about," Girani said. Odo pushed himself up on the pallet, and the doctor stepped back so that he could swing his legs down and bring himself up to a sitting position. "After what you've been through, it's to be expected. It will probably be a few more days, if not weeks, before you regain your full strength. Until then, I wouldn't spend too much time changing your form. Even holding one shape for too long will probably exhaust you."

"I understand," Odo said. "I presume that you've already made the same report to Starfleet."

"I have," Girani told him without hesitation. In the time they had served together aboard the old Deep Space 9, Odo had always appreciated her forthrightness. "This is their facility, at least in part, and even though I'm not a member of Starfleet, I am functioning here under their auspices."

Odo harrumphed. "As a courtesy, I informed Admiral Herthum's office this morning that I would be leaving Newton Outpost and returning to the Dominion as soon as I received your medical clearance." Odo did not mention to the doctor that he considered his adhering to her recommendations also a matter of civility.

"I take no issue with you departing the outpost," Girani said, "unless you intend to shape-shift into some sort of spacefaring creature in order to travel any significant distance."

"That is precisely what I intended to do," Odo said. "Instead, based on your report, Starfleet Operations has . . . offered . . . me passage aboard a shuttlecraft to Deep Space Nine, and to have a starship ferry me through the wormhole and to the Dominion. In deference to your medical advice, I've agreed."

"That's good to hear, Odo," the doctor said. "I wouldn't want all my efforts to go to waste."

Odo grumbled again, and Girani met his crosspatch response with a smile. She reached forward and tucked the

tricorder into a storage niche built into the side of the bio-
bed. When she straightened, she said, "I'll sign orders for
your release from the infirmary. I'll speak to Doctor Norsa
and Commander Selten so that they can assign you quarters until the shuttlecraft is cleared to depart."

"Thank you, Doctor."

Girani smiled again, then headed for the door. Before she
reached it, Odo hopped off the pallet and called after her.
She stopped and turned just as the door glided open. "Yes?"

"Thank you, Doctor," he said again, but with a greater
sense of gravity. "I . . ." He wanted to tell her that he didn't
know if he would have survived without all that she'd done
for him, but propriety prevented him from uttering words
he feared would sound mawkish. "Thank you," he repeated.

"You're welcome," Girani said. Before the moment could
grow sentimental, she turned and continued out the door.
The panel slid closed behind her, leaving Odo alone with
his thoughts.

V

"I can't believe my ears!" Quark said, gesturing at the sides
of his head. "And when a Ferengi says that, it means something." Sitting in his office, Quark brought his hands down
hard on the freestanding companel console he utilized as a
desk. He considered severing the connection—not just the
comm channel, but the business relationship he'd forged
over nearly four months with Mayereen Viray. He looked
down at his hand, so close to the control that would ban-
ish the private investigator's image from the display, but he
allowed a beat to pass in which to calm himself. He recited
the 101st Rule of Acquisition in his mind—*Profit trumps
emotion*—then reviewed the lie he'd been telling himself
for nearly a year, when he'd first hired a different detective

to track down Morn. During the Lurian's long patronage of Quark's, the barkeep had often joked that he considered the monthly remittance of Morn's tab a long-term business asset—which the Ferengi then used as justification to pay somebody to locate his friend.

"I am doing what you engaged me to do," Viray said. The Petarian had a wide, flat nose, dark eyes, and flesh tinted a warm, golden hue. *"If you wish to terminate our agreement, you need only say so."*

"What I wish is that you would finally find Morn," Quark said. "I've already paid for you to travel all over the quadrant—to Micsim Four, Ardana, Janus Six—and now you want me to provide even more funds to send you to a planet you won't even identify."

"It's not that I won't *identify the planet,"* Viray said. *"It's that I* can't—*at least not yet. It could be one of several different worlds, and I need resources not just to travel wherever I'm going, but to secure the information I need."*

"Meaning that you need latinum to bribe somebody at the Geopolis spaceport to tell you where Morn headed." Quark could appreciate the nature of the disbursement, but he resented continually having to pay for Viray's expenses. He'd attempted to hire her on a flat-rate basis, but she'd declined, and so he'd had to remunerate her both for her time and for her working costs.

"You know that I decline to discuss my operational methods," Viray said. *"My research tells me that the subject is on his way either to Mericor, Portas, or Delta Leonis. I need to determine which of those is his destination and secure passage there as quickly as possible, before his trail grows cold."*

Quark shook his head. "I've heard this before," he said. "I've already paid you more than I ever expected to. At some point, what started out as a legitimate investment can turn bad."

"I understand," Viray said. *"It's your decision. If you choose, we can dissolve our professional relationship at once."*

Quark hesitated. He wanted to find his old friend, and if he told himself the truth, not just to bring him back as a reliable customer; he wanted to make sure Morn was safe, and that the Lurian had overcome the grief and the guilt he felt after the destruction of the old Deep Space 9. But Quark had already spent a small fortune on Mayereen Viray, largely because she had come highly recommended, but also because the two cut-rate investigators he'd hired prior to the Petarian had demonstrated an old *hew-mon* maxim: You get what you pay for.

Forget Earth adages, Quark chastised himself. *I'm better off sticking with the Rules of Acquisition.* With disappointment, he realized that he found himself on the wrong end of number 19: *Satisfaction is not guaranteed.*

Quark made the decision to dismiss Viray from his employ, but before he could tell her so, she spoke up. *"I know it's been a long road, but I'm making progress,"* she said. *"I'm not just getting closer; I'm getting* close.*"*

Quark gazed around his office, as though he might find the answer hidden somewhere around him. Images played out across the rows of silenced but active screens lining the bulkhead, displays that carried information to him and his robust data-mining programs from all across the quadrant. Quark took in none of it, thinking that he very much wanted what the detective told him to be true, but that same desire also made him leery of assigning her words too much credence. Still, he needed to do something—either to proceed ahead with Viray or to discharge her and go in another direction.

"All right," Quark said. "Stand by." He paused their comlink, then fetched a padd from the shelf behind him. He accessed the Ferengi Central Reserve's current interest rates, then set them in service of the Bank of Luria's fractional-moment compounding rules. Once he calculated a projected value for his account balance, he accessed the Lurian Commerce Net on a secure connection and, with a sigh of relief, verified the sum there. With the two amounts in agreement, Quark then flagged a portion of his assets for transfer to the coffers of Mayereen Viray and set the transaction in motion.

Heat drained from his lobes, but he had committed to a course of action, at least for now. He set the padd to one side and resumed his comlink with Viray. "It's done," he told her.

"I will collect the funds at once," Viray said. *"I don't think you'll regret this."*

"I *already* regret it, considering all the latinum I've spent," Quark said. "I just hope you can pinpoint Morn's location before too much longer."

"You should be prepared that finding the subject may be the easy part of your endeavors," Viray said.

"What does that mean?"

"It means that I've traced the last year and a half of the subject's movements across the quadrant, into and out of Federation space," the investigator said. *"He's made circumspect inquiries of and about some questionable characters. It seems apparent that he is pursuing some sort of extralegal, possibly nefarious agenda."*

"I trust that you won't disseminate any information you've gleaned while working for me," Quark said. He immediately cursed himself for the thought. *Trust,* the 99th Rule of Acquisition taught, *is the biggest liability of all.* Nevertheless, he appreciated Viray's response.

"Along with an attention to detail," she said, *"discretion is at the heart of my business."* She paused, then added, *"But once I track the subject down, if you're hoping to bring him*

back to the Bajoran system, to meet with him in some other location, or even just to contact him, you may find all of that far more difficult than you expect."

"What do you base that on?" Quark wanted to know.

"I take it as a consequence of his actions," Viray said. *"The subject does not appear to know that his movements are being traced, and yet he is behaving in a manner so as to avoid detection. You want to find him, but he does not want to be found."*

"I'll take that into consideration," Quark said, having no intention of doing so. He had hired Viray for her investigatory abilities, not for her opinions. "Once you ascertain which planet—"

The companel picked up a high-pitched squawk, interrupting Quark. Viray snapped her head to one side and obviously saw something startling in the accommodations she'd taken somewhere on Janus VI. An instant later, the room went dark. Viray briefly turned back toward the companel, the grim expression on her face illuminated by the glow of her screen. She quickly punched at a control and was plunged into shadow. Quark could just make out her figure as she rose and backed away from the companel. Another shape came into view from the direction in which Viray had looked. Barely visible in the darkened room, the intruder closed on the private investigator.

Quark checked his readout and saw that Viray had blanked the display on her end, but she'd also clearly left the channel open. *She wants me to see what's happening,* he thought. *She wants me to see, but she doesn't want the intruder to know there's a witness.*

"Who are you?" she asked loudly. Quark heard a reply, but too far from the companel for even his sensitive ears to make out.

Viray continued to back away until she disappeared from view. Suddenly, the intruder lunged after her. Quark waited for something to happen, and then a second tres-passer appeared. He crossed in front of the screen and out of sight. Quark heard voices he could not make out, and what sounded like a tussle. The two intruders then reappeared, hauling the private investigator along between them. They headed back in the direction from which they'd entered, but then they glanced over at the companel.

Quark froze. He knew he couldn't be seen, but the at-tention of the intruders unnerved him. When the second figure rushed toward Viray's companel, Quark flinched. Panicked, he quickly reached for his own console, fumbled to find the appropriate control surface, and at last suc-ceeded in terminating the subspace connection.

Quark sat motionless for a few moments, staring at the blank screen. He didn't know what to think about what he'd just witnessed, much less what, if anything, he should do about it. It did not seem at all unlikely to him that, plying her trade as a private investigator, Viray could have made enemies. Quark had no interest in getting involved, but he also concluded from what he'd seen that his hunt for Morn had been disrupted.

Feeling his lobes begin to burn, Quark reached for his padd. He once again accessed his account at the Bank of Luria, knowing that it would be too late to recall his pay-ment to Viray. When he inspected his balance, he saw that the funds he'd earmarked for the investigator had already been withdrawn.

Absently, Quark reached across his panel and tapped at a control. Both the door to his office and the inner, sound-proof panel slid open. An olio of noises greeted him: the voices of customers and employees, the ring of glassware, the cheeps and twitters of the *dom-jot* table, and best of all, the swirling hum of the *dabo* wheel.

"Shorting the double-ride," said Orcam, the dabo boy

working the table. Quark closed his eyes and listened as the latest spin wound down. Despite that his revenues from gaming had far outpaced his expectations since the starbase had opened for business, he braced himself for the inevitable cry of "Dabo!" and a roar of excitement from the crowd; he had learned from bitter experience that when latinum abandoned you, it tended to do so in droves.

But when the beeps of the wheel slowed and finally quieted, he heard Orcam call out, "Thirty-one *gork*. No winners." Some customers groaned, but others excitedly called out their next bets: "Link plus," "Bastion through," and Quark's personal favorite, "Triple over."

It sounded like another good night for the proprietor. Quark allowed himself a small smile, his slantwise teeth comfortingly sharp against the inside of his lips. But as he stood up and headed out into his consistently profitable Public House, Café, Gaming Emporium, Holosuite Arcade, and Ferengi Embassy to Bajor, he could only think about the fact that Morn had never set foot in the place.

vi

Kira rose from the bed where she had lain as Doctor Boudreaux had completed his physical examination of her. The energy and emotion that had coursed through the vedek over the past few hours of her life had drained away, leaving her wholly enervated. More than anything, she craved sleep, but she also knew that Captain Ro likely still had many questions for her.

Resisting the urge to sit on the edge of the bed—from where it would be a simple matter to lay her head back down on the temptingly soft pillow—Kira crossed to the bedroom door, to where the captain stood. Ro had offered to leave during Boudreaux's workup, but the vedek had declined, not feeling the need for that level of privacy. On the other hand, she did appreciate that the captain had granted her request to undergo the exam somewhere other than in the infirmary—in the *hospital*, Ro had called it. For the time being, Kira wanted to keep her return confidential, until she could personally contact her friends and colleagues, both on the new Deep Space 9 and on Bajor. Ro had obliged by transporting the vedek directly from *Even Odds'* dropship to guest quarters.

"I appreciate your forbearance," the captain said as Kira reached her.

"Not at all," the vedek said. "When I took over after Captain Sisko, I remember the long list of standard procedures Starfleet forced on me. It made me think that, considering how many processes they followed and reports they required, it was amazing that the Federation ever managed to expand beyond Andor and Vulcan."

Ro chuckled. "I think it's gotten worse," she said.

Across the room, Boudreaux collected the portable diagnostic scanner from the bed and carried it over to a small, square table in the corner. "It'll take a few minutes to review these results," he said.

"I understand," Ro said.

As the two women waited for the doctor, Kira took stock of the guest cabin she'd been assigned. The accommodations did not seem larger than those on the old station, but they still felt like a considerable upgrade. The dark, sharp-edged, almost reptilian character of the original DS9 had been replaced by a brighter, softer ambience. Kira didn't think she drew that determination out of any residual antipathy for the Cardassians that might still linger within her, but from an objective assessment. On the new starbase, at least in her guest quarters, she did not have to step over any raised thresholds, she did not mistakenly think she'd spotted movement in a shadowy corner, she did not experience an abiding sense of discomfiture.

When Boudreaux finished his work with the portable scanner and his other equipment, he walked over to the women. "From what I can see, Vedek, you're in good health," he said. "I do read indications of recent stress, and you're showing signs of both mental and physical fatigue, but it's nothing that an uninterrupted night of sleep won't relieve."

"I could have predicted that result," Kira said with a weary smile.

"I'm waiting on the lab to complete more involved tests for me, but only regarding longer-term health matters," Boudreaux continued. "Based on what I've seen so far, I don't expect those analyses to turn up any issues. You're in good physical shape and your artificial heart is functioning well within normal parameters. I have no concerns about your immediate medical condition."

"What about any evidence of time travel?" Ro asked. The captain must have informed Boudreaux about Kira's journey into the past, both because he gave no outward sign of surprise at the question and because he'd obviously known to run the relevant tests.

"I detected no chronometric radiation," the doctor said. "Normally, that would indicate that an individual has *not* traveled in time, but we have evidence that's not necessarily the case when the wormhole is involved." Kira assumed that he referred to an incident Ro had mentioned to her, when a visitor recently emerged from the Celestial Temple and apparently out of Bajor's past, much like the poet Akorem Laan had done a decade and a half earlier. "It might be that the wormhole's own properties—the significant neutrino activity and proton counts, the subspace distortions, the asymmetric wave intensities—it might be that all of that dampens or masks the residual effects of chronitons."

"Or it might be that traveling in time within the wormhole is achieved by some means that doesn't involve chronitons at all," Ro conjectured.

"Possibly," Boudreaux said. "You'd be better off talking about that with Commander Candlewood. I have enough trouble figuring out how to make it in one piece from the morning to the afternoon."

Ro smiled. "Thank you, Pascal."

"One other thing," Boudreaux said. "I compared Vedek Kira's physiological age with her chronological age. They more or less match. In the twenty-eight months she's been missing, she's lived roughly the same amount of time."

"Understood," Ro said. Kira understood the implication as well: the fact that her physiological age had advanced the same amount as the calendar since she'd disappeared inside the wormhole provided no independent evidence of her travel through time. If she'd lived only a year in the intervening period, or if she'd lived five, the mismatch would have gone a long way to substantiating her temporal displacement.

Boudreaux returned to the table in the corner, gathered up his medical equipment, and headed from the bedroom out into the main living area. Ro followed along after him, as did Kira, her concerns about what she'd just heard growing in her mind. Once the doctor had departed, she addressed the issue.

"Captain," she said, careful to keep any hint of accusation from her voice, "do you doubt my report about traveling in time through the wormhole?"

"I don't doubt you at all," Ro said. "But as we just discussed, Starfleet has its rules. I'm actually pleased by your medical results. If Doctor Boudreaux's exam had turned up any chronometric radiation, that would have provided concrete scientific proof that you'd time-traveled. In that case, I would have had no choice but to file a report with the Department of Temporal Investigations."

The vedek heard exasperation in Ro's tone, and she empathized. Kira had dealt with DTI personnel on a few occasions during her tenure on DS9, and they had universally proven to be humorless, self-important, and fractious. "So you won't have to report this?" she asked.

"No, unfortunately I will," Ro said. "But without verifiable proof of time travel, I have some leeway on how soon I have to report it. Better than that, I might be able to stave off an actual visit from the clock-watchers."

"May the Prophets smile upon you," Kira said, offering a familiar blessing.

"Let's hope so."

Kira felt a yawn coming on, and she raised a hand to cover her mouth. "Forgive me, Captain," she said. "It's been a long day. I need to sit down." Kira paced toward the sitting area.

"Of course," Ro said, trailing after the vedek. "I'd like to talk more with you about your experiences in the past, but that can wait for right now." Kira settled into the first seat she reached, an overstuffed chair arranged with several others and a small sofa around a low, oval table, but the captain remained on her feet. "You obviously need to get some rest, so we can meet tomorrow. Do you have any idea when you might want to head back to Bajor?"

Kira hesitated. She hadn't given the matter any thought. Fresh from enduring the Ascendant attack on Idran IV, she'd come racing through the wormhole intent on engaging the zealots, not anticipating that she'd end up at a time when the battle she'd envisioned joining had been fought eight years earlier. Even so, she still bore the aftereffects of entering a combat zone, something she hadn't experienced in a long time. Since trading in her Starfleet uniform for the attire of the Bajoran clergy, such experiences had become a rarity in her life.

More than all of that, though, Kira felt drained—even almost traumatized—by everything else that Ro had told her. Although it appeared as though the vedek might well have fulfilled the role given to her by the Prophets, the loss of the scientific community on Bajor's largest moon weighed on Kira as if it had just happened—because for her, it had. It also shocked her to learn about the assassination of the Federation president, part of a conspiracy orchestrated by a power-hungry Bajoran.

"Everything's happened so quickly and so unexpectedly that I haven't had time to think about what comes next," Kira told the captain. "I know I need to contact the kai and the Vedek Assembly before long, but I'm not prepared to do that just yet." She anticipated that her return from the Celestial Temple after such a lengthy absence—longer even than that of the Emissary—would likely incite a tempest, especially considering the emotional and spiritual upheaval already in progress on Bajor thanks to the discovery of the Endalla falsework.

"You've been missing for more than two years," Ro said. "I don't suppose that waiting another day or two before announcing your reappearance will make any difference."

"Thank you, Captain," Kira said. She appreciated Ro's consideration, but she also noted that the DS9 commanding officer hadn't offered to keep her return secret for more than a couple of days. Given everything that Ro had told her had taken place recently, and taking into account the captain's responsibility for more than twenty-five hundred crew and ten thousand civilian residents, it made sense that she would want to ship Kira off to Bajor as quickly as possible, if only to avoid further complicating life aboard Deep Space 9.

"I'll let you get some rest," the captain said. The vedek

stood up and approached Ro. "We can talk again tomorrow. In the meantime, if you need anything, you can contact me directly, or my first officer, Commander Blackmer." Kira did not know Blackmer well, but she had met him during some of her visits to the old DS9; back then, he had served as chief of security.

Kira watched the captain leave. She thought about ordering something to eat from the replicator—she'd begun to get hungry during Doctor Boudreaux's exam—but then decided to head straight back into the bedroom. She collapsed onto the bed without even removing her clothing, thinking that she would close her eyes for a few minutes and then get undressed. As tired as she felt, she worried that she wouldn't be able to sleep because of all the matters clamoring for attention in her mind, from her travels through time to everything that had happened in the Bajoran system since she'd been gone, from the people she would have to contact to how she would handle whatever furor her return might cause.

Within minutes, though, Kira drifted into a deep and dreamless sleep.

vii

"Computer, run program Bashir Sixty-two."

Candlewood waited quietly beside Nog as the holosuite about them faded from view, overlaid with the drab tones of a cheerless, begrimed hallway. Dim light filtered in through a cloudy window up ahead, revealing cracks in the plaster walls and deep scratches in the wooden floor. The air tasted of something sour, like a piece of fruit that has spoiled.

"This place is terrible," Candlewood said.

"Shhh," Nog hissed, as though he worried about rousing the attention of any holographic characters that might be behind the closed doors lining the hall on either side. "This is where I found Vic when I finally uploaded his program," he whispered. "This is where I saw him get abducted." He pointed to one of the doors, and the two men walked over to it. A single tarnished metal number—*3*—hung there, beside the outline of a second digit—*2*—that had once preceded it. Candlewood saw a sizable chunk of wood missing from the jamb.

"It doesn't look like it's been repaired since you saw those thugs kick it in," he said.

"No," Nog agreed, and he reached for the knob. "It's locked."

"How can it be locked?" Candlewood asked. "It's not even securely in the frame." He sidled past Nog and tested the knob himself, which refused to turn in his hand. He leaned forward, placed his shoulder against the door, and pushed. Nothing happened, so he set his thigh against the bottom half of the door, which immediately lurched inward. The latch pulled free of the strike plate, and the lower hinge from the jamb. Candlewood awkwardly swung the door around and propped it against the interior wall.

As Nog entered behind him, Candlewood looked about. The squalid room contained little in the way of furniture. A small bed, its drooping mattress set in a rusting iron frame, almost filled the entire space. A tattered piece of fabric straggled across the floor beside a flimsy rod that Candlewood suspected had once held it up as a curtain in front of the lone window.

The science officer took a step forward and felt something beneath his foot. He reached down and picked up a metal *2*. Candlewood thought that the number had probably come off when the door had been kicked in, but given the hotel's state of disrepair, it wouldn't have surprised him to learn that it had fallen onto the floor long before that.

"This was where Vic was living?" he asked.

"Yes," Nog said. "I don't know if it was permanent or temporary, but he was definitely staying here when I saw him."

"That just doesn't make any sense," Candlewood said, turning in place to take in their dilapidated surroundings. "I know Vic is just a hologram, but he's a pretty well-defined character. He would never live in a place like this."

"Not under normal circumstances, no," Nog said. "But I told you that something must have occurred inside the program."

"Right, right," Candlewood said, but something else nagged at him. "Why is the holomatrix entry point here? I only visited Vic's a few times, but whenever I did, I entered a large, well-run hotel and casino. Before you successfully reloaded the program, did it ever bring you here?"

"No," Nog said. "It always brought me to the same place it brought you. I just supposed that when Vic took up residence here, the program must have automatically reconfigured the entry point."

"But Vic's no longer here," Candlewood said. "If the program resets to Vic's location, why isn't it bringing us to him now?"

"I . . . I don't know."

Candlewood shook his head, trying to puzzle out the situation. Not since his days attending the University of Mumbai had he coded any holographic software, and only once had he crafted an open-ended narrative program. Still, his training as a computer specialist provided him with more than just a rudimentary understanding of the field's fundamental principles. He knew that Bashir 62 represented a departure from some of those standards—chief among them Vic Fontaine's awareness of his own nature as a holographic character—but that didn't mean that attributes like the program's entry point would change randomly.

Candlewood looked down and saw that he still held the metal *2* he had picked up. He tossed it onto the bed. "We can't help Vic unless we know where he is."

"I know," Nog said. He stepped over to the bed, lowered himself to his knees, and peered beneath it. "I was hoping that we could find some clues here that'll help explain who kidnapped Vic and why."

"I don't know if any of that matters as much as *where* he is," Candlewood said. "Computer, take us to Vic Fontaine's current location."

"No!" Nog yelled as he leaped back to his feet.

Around them, the scene shifted, wavering as the holo-program reshaped the setting. Their shabby surroundings vanished, replaced by opulence. They suddenly stood in a corridor wider than Vic's tumbledown hotel room. Bright crystal chandeliers hung from a high ceiling, illuminating wainscoted walls and beautifully patterned carpeting.

"Computer—" Nog rushed to say, but if he intended to reverse Candlewood's command or end the program, he never got that far. "Vic?" Candlewood didn't recognize the lounge singer from behind, but Nog clearly did.

Vic turned at the sound of his name. So did the two large men walking on either side of him. Candlewood would later think that Nog had taken a step forward, and that Vic had called out to him, but everything happened so quickly that he couldn't be sure. Before the science officer could process what he saw—a captive being led somewhere by his abductors—the two burly men reached into their jackets and drew weapons.

In the back of his mind, Candlewood knew that he and Nog could not be harmed inside the holosuite, that the safety protocols would protect them from whatever fictional perils they faced. But he also could not help conjuring up the image of Nanietta Bacco standing on the stage of DS9's auditorium. Like most of his DS9 crewmates, he had watched as three shots had brutally torn through the Federation president, ending her life. Afterward, he had also been called upon to perform a ballistics analysis. Projectile weapons might be considered antiquated and seldom used in the twenty-fourth century, but Candlewood did not doubt their capacity to inflict damage on living beings.

The two big men strode forward as they began firing. The loud report of their weapons filled the corridor, and brief flashes of orange-yellow light accompanied each shot. An acrid scent filled the air. Candlewood instinctively raised his arms to protect himself. He felt multiple impacts on his body, the holosuite producing sharp taps in place of what would have been hot metal piercing his flesh. He felt himself pushed backward by the impacts, another part of the program's illusion. He reached back to brace himself as he fell to the floor, but the holosuite encoding cushioned his impact.

By the time Candlewood looked over at Nog lying beside him, the corridor had disappeared, along with Vic Fontaine and the two armed men beside him. The flat environment of the holosuite, featureless but for the door and rows of embedded emitters, had returned. "What just happened?" Nog said.

"I'd say we found the people who abducted Vic," Candlewood said. The two Starfleet officers climbed back to their feet.

"No, I know that," Nog said. "I mean why did the program shut down?"

"I'm not sure."

"Computer," Nog said, "run program Bashir Sixty-two, with the entry point at the Fremont-Sunrise Hotel."

Candlewood assumed that had been where they had first found themselves in the program. Nog clearly wanted to ensure that they didn't end up right back in a hail of bullets.

A discordant hum sounded, followed by the voice of the computer. *"Unable to comply."*

Nog's brows knit. "Computer, run program Bashir Sixty-two," he said, omitting the specification of the entry point.

The off-key drone signaled again. *"Unable to comply."*

"What—" Nog said, and then his eyes went wide. "Oh, no. Computer, was Vic Fontaine killed in program Bashir Sixty-two?"

"Negative."

"Then Vic is still alive?" Nog said, as though he needed reassurance.

"The character of Vic Fontaine continues to exist in program Bashir Sixty-two."

"Computer, then run program Bashir Sixty-two," Nog tried again.

Buzz. *"Unable to comply."*

"Computer, why?" Candlewood asked. "Why can't you execute the program?"

"Participants are not authorized to run Bashir Sixty-two."

"What?" Nog said. "How can that be? We were just running the program."

"Computer," the science officer ventured, "reauthorize Commander Nog and Commander Candlewood to execute Bashir Sixty-two."

Buzz. *"Unable to comply."*

"Computer, override all program lockouts," Nog tried again. "Run in diagnostic mode, authorization Nog Beta Three Five Five Three."

Buzz. *"Unable to comply."*

The confusion Nog wore on his face mirrored what

Candlewood felt. Experience told him that software errors could prove intricate, difficult to diagnose, and therefore challenging to correct. He didn't know what had gone wrong with Bashir 62 and Vic Fontaine, but something clearly had.

Two

Transition Management

The fist-sized stone struck the lighting scaffold at the rear of the stage, sending out a loud ringing over the crowd. Vedek Solis—tall and regal in his long white robe, with thinning hair that betrayed his advancing years—whirled toward the sound, then peered back out at those who had assembled to listen to his address, as though he could pinpoint whoever had hurled the rock. In the foreground on the display, attendees at the front of the gathering also turned to search for the culprit. Suddenly, the image shifted, rushing around to focus on two men shoving each other. Several other people tried to step in and put a stop to it, but then one of the men leveled a roundhouse punch at the other. The picture shook, then canted to one side before the recording went black.

From where he sat in front of the captain's desk, Commander Jefferson Blackmer spun in his chair, away from the viewscreen on the opposite bulkhead and toward Ro. "I know that looked bad," he said, "but it could have been worse." He had been telling himself that since Dellasant had contacted him at the end of delta shift to inform him about the incident, which she had picked up from the Bajoran communications network. It did not escape his notice that on his first full day as Deep Space 9's official executive officer, Bajor appeared on the verge of descending into sectarian conflict. As the former security chief of the starbase, Blackmer automatically thought about what measures could be put into place onboard to ensure that any such violence did not spread to DS9. Of the nearly thirteen thousand full-time residents, a majority hailed from Bajor.

"Was anybody hurt?" Ro asked.

"I spoke with one of my contacts in Hedrikspool law enforcement," Blackmer said. "She told me there were a dozen fistfights, some minor injuries, and a number of arrests, but they're more concerned about what might lie ahead."

"I can understand why," Ro said. "Solis Tendren is a well-respected vedek, but he's also the most prominent supporter of the Ohalavaru. If he's facing threats of violence, it means that some mainstream Bajoran adherents are willing to cross the line between peacefully protesting and taking up arms."

"And if some are," Blackmer said, "more could follow."

Ro nodded her head, then picked up a padd from her desk. "Part of the problem," she said as she activated the device, "might be that, in the last few weeks, the ranks of the Ohalavaru have swelled." She handed the padd across to Blackmer. He studied the chart on the display, which showed that the number of Bajorans who identified as Ohalavaru had increased by a third since the falsework had been discovered.

"That's got to make the establishment nervous," Blackmer said. The Ohalavaru believed that what they found beneath the surface of Endalla supported their view that the Prophets were not gods.

"I think it might be more unnerving for the laity," Ro said. "I spoke with First Minister Asarem yesterday, obviously before all of that took place in Ilvia." The captain gestured toward the viewscreen on the bulkhead behind Blackmer. "She firmly believes that once the scientists and engineers begin their research efforts on Endalla, under the watchful eyes of both traditional and Ohalavaru vedeks, tempers will ease."

"I'm not so sure," Blackmer said. It seemed to him that the more attention the falsework drew, the more tensions would mount on Bajor. He said as much, and the captain agreed. "The good news is that Vedek Yevir stood up in the

Assembly this morning and condemned the violence aimed against the Ohalavaru."

"Yevir, not the kai," Ro said. "I guess that Kai Pralon is attempting to stay above the fray. I think she wants both sides to view her as *the* spiritual leader of Bajor, regardless of their beliefs or hers."

"That might be difficult to accomplish with the Ohalavaru," Blackmer said. "She's part of the traditional religious establishment. Her fundamental conviction that the Prophets are divine completely contradicts the primary tenet of the Ohalu texts."

"That's true," Ro said, "but the kai also supports the Ohalavaru's desire to study the falsework. That goes against the wishes of many of Pralon's traditional followers, who want the site secured and closed to visitors of any kind."

Blackmer set the padd down on the captain's desk. "It sounds like they're scared of learning the truth about the falsework . . . and maybe about the Prophets too."

"Of course they are," Ro said. "Look at what it did to Desca." Six weeks earlier, his faith shaken to the core in the wake of the Ohalavaru discovery, Colonel Cenn Desca, DS9's first officer, had resigned his position in the Militia and departed not only the starbase, but the Bajoran system.

"I know," Blackmer said. "But I don't think most people are as devout as Cenn."

"Believe me, there are plenty of pious Bajorans," Ro said. "But I'm not even sure you have to be that deeply religious to oppose seeking out the truth."

"That doesn't make much sense to me."

"Doesn't it?" Ro asked. "The truth isn't always a positive thing to people. Just imagine finding out that something you've held dear in your life, something around which you've organized your existence—and it doesn't even have to be religion—imagine finding out that it's a lie."

"I'm sure it would be difficult."

"That sounds like an intellectual assessment," Ro told him. "Try envisioning it from an emotional perspective."

Blackmer thought about it. "Honestly, I'm not sure I can."

"I'm not sure I can either," Ro said. "Maybe that's just who we are. But we both saw firsthand how it devastated Desca. He might have been orthodox, but he wasn't stupid or mentally unbalanced. He was a product of his upbringing, which took place at a time when Bajorans desperately needed to believe in the Prophets as gods. When your home is invaded, when your lands are occupied by a brutal enemy . . . when you don't know where your next meal is coming from, or if, when it does come, that there will be enough food for everyone . . ." The captain stared past Blackmer, the look in her eyes distant, her voice growing quieter. "When you and the people you know, the people you love, are pressed into servitude . . . when people are tortured or killed . . . the belief in a higher power, the hope that faith engenders, can be a very powerful thing." Ro blinked, then met her exec's gaze once more.

"I don't know what to say, Captain. I never really thought about the Bajoran faith in those terms."

"It's not just the people of Bajor," Ro said. "Similar stories range across worlds. And it wasn't the Occupation that brought the worship of the Prophets to Bajor. My people have believed in Them, in Their divinity, for a long time. Like in many places, there was a need for people to explain the world, to understand life, to cope with suffering and seek a better tomorrow. I lived through the Occupation, so I know how much it impacted Bajor, how great the need for the Prophets was."

Blackmer understood, but something confused him. "You say Bajor needed the Prophets, but, if you don't mind me saying so . . . you're not a believer."

"I try not to label myself, not to limit myself," she said, a bit forcefully. She took a moment to carefully fold her hands in front of her and place them on the desk. When she continued, she had reined in her agitation. "No, I haven't always held to the divinity of the Prophets. I suppose I still don't, even though I've been coming to appreciate Them and Their abilities, no matter how They're characterized. My point is that many people don't want their beliefs tested, and some, no matter what the scientists conclude on Endalla, still won't change their minds."

"So the mainstream Bajoran faithful and the Ohalavaru have that in common," Blackmer said, not without a sense of irony. "How long will it be before the examination and analysis of the falsework can begin?"

"Just a matter of days, I think," Ro said. "It shouldn't take long to establish a shirtsleeve environment on Endalla." Blackmer knew that the Bajoran Militia had already started efforts to seal the subterranean chamber on the moon, and to establish both an atmosphere and full artificial gravity within it—practical considerations that did nothing to reduce the societal stresses on Bajor. The first minister had also taken the unusual step of requesting that the Federation government and Starfleet refrain from offering assistance; Asarem wanted such a sensitive issue resolved solely by Bajorans, specifically to avoid any suspicion of outside influences.

"Should I include the unrest on Bajor in the report?" Blackmer asked. As the new first officer, he would be drafting the monthly status for Starfleet Operations.

"Definitely. What happens there can have an impact here," the captain said. "Vel has comm briefings scheduled for this afternoon with Gandal Traco and Ranz Vecta. Make sure to include whatever he learns." Like Blackmer, Lieutenant Aleco Vel had just been promoted to his new position; he would serve DS9 as its official liaison to Bajor. As a part of those responsibilities, he would be speaking on a regular basis with Minister of State Gandal, Minister of Defense Ranz, and their subordinates.

"Aye, Captain."

"Is there anything else?" Ro asked.

"Just Doctor Boudreaux's final medical report on Vedek Kira," Blackmer said. "The lab tests have been completed and he's given her a clean bill of health."

"Good," Ro said. "Include her arrival in the report, but mark it classified for now. We'll keep her return confidential until she's had a chance to inform the people close to her."

"Aye." Blackmer stood up and headed toward the door that led to the Hub, but as the panels parted, he slowed. He had served as Ro Laren's interim executive officer for the past month and a half, but he realized that when he stepped into DS9's command-and-control center, he would for the first time do so as Cenn Desca's permanent replacement.

"Jeff," the captain said from her desk. He stopped and glanced back at her. "You're ready for this."

"Aye," Blackmer said. He allowed himself a small smile, grateful for Ro's encouragement. "Thank you, Captain." He continued into the Hub, ready to assume his new position on Deep Space 9.

ii

When the door signal in her office chimed, Ro had made it only halfway through *Dalin* Slaine's report on the deficiencies of Deep Space 9's weapons and defensive systems during the crew's encounter with the shape-shifting Ascendant life-form. The strategic operations officer had spent the past five weeks studying the sensor logs collected during the incident, when the starbase's phasers and quantum torpedoes had failed even to make contact with the attacking force, much less stop it or slow it down. Likewise, DS9's standard shields had proven incapable of impeding the shape-shifting entity's advance, as had the thoron shield, despite that the latter had been designed specifically to prevent the incursion not just of energy weapons, but of physical objects.

Zivan Slaine had not only investigated those inadequacies, she had consulted with engineers, tactical and security officers, physicists, chemists, materials scientists, and other of the crew in an attempt to design modifications to improve the effectiveness of those systems. Although the attack had resulted in no casualties and no damage to DS9, that had been the choice of the communal Ascendant lifeform. Since that shape-shifting amalgam had subsequently taken up residence in the wormhole, that meant it remained a potential threat to the starbase—even though Ro believed that the Ascendants had found the place they belonged and would not stray from there.

The captain had made it only halfway through Slaine's recommendations because she'd needed to read several sections multiple times. Ro had passed the basic engineering and physics courses at Starfleet Academy, and she'd successfully completed the rigorous Advanced Tactical Training, but the technical nature of the report exceeded her ability to easily understand it. The work impressed her, and if the second half matched the first in quality—and she had no reason to think that it wouldn't—she decided that she would include a special note about it in the packet of review materials that the Cardassian Guard had requested her to complete.

Slaine had served under Ro's command for almost three years, but technically remained on detached assignment from the Cardassian Union's military. On a recent visit to DS9 aboard his ship, *Trager*, *Gul* Macet had informed Ro that Slaine had probably earned an elevation in rank from dalin to *dal*—the Starfleet equivalent of lieutenant commander to commander—but that such advances typically accompanied a rise to second-in-command of a starship or a space station, or even to the command of a smaller vessel. Ro would hate to lose her strategic operations officer, but if life had taught her anything, it was that people moved on. *And until I ended up on Deep Space Nine, that was always true of me too.*

The door signal sounded a second time, stirring Ro from her thoughts. She checked the time on her padd and saw that more than an hour remained before her next appointment. Captain Marcel Javier, the commanding officer of the *Achilles*-class *U.S.S. Diomedes*, which had docked at DS9 earlier that day, had asked to meet with Ro during his crew's leave on the starbase. Thinking that either she or Javier might have gotten the time of their meeting wrong, she said, "Come in." The door that led out into the turbolift corridor opened, but the *Diomedes* captain had not yet come to call on her.

Quark had.

As soon as the door opened, he entered, clad in a crimson moiré jacket, its two breast panels clasped together by a circular gold medallion. Just looking at him, Ro knew why he'd come, and she felt immediately guilty. It had been months since she and Quark had spent any time alone with each other, though he had invited her to do so on several occasions. Ro's affection for him hadn't changed, but the demanding responsibilities of making the *Frontier*-class DS9 operational and then commanding it had left her little personal time to spare.

But I've made time for Dans. More than a month earlier,

Ro had begun a romance with Doctor Altek Dans, a man who had emerged from the wormhole in an evanescent Orb of the Prophets, evidently from some period deep in Bajor's history. She hadn't had all that much time for Dans either, but their relationship had progressed enough that she'd resolved to tell Quark about it—particularly before he learned about it from somebody else. Somehow, though, Ro had so far failed to speak with him.

"Captain," Quark said as he stepped up to her desk. While he never called her by her given name in public, he usually did so in private. His use of her rank in the privacy of her office might signal his disappointment, perhaps even his anger, at her recent aloofness.

"Hello, Quark," Ro said. She girded herself not only to apologize for essentially ignoring him of late, but also to tell him of her budding relationship with Dans. He sat down in a chair in front of her desk, but when he spoke, it had nothing at all to do with her.

"You know that I've been trying to locate Morn," he said. Quark proceeded to tell her about what had happened the previous night during his conversation with the private investigator he'd hired. Ro thought he might want her to intervene with the authorities on Janus VI to help find out what had happened to Mayereen Viray. Instead, he grumbled about his lost investment, which the captain found callous, even for a profit-driven Ferengi, and especially for Quark, who had revealed to her a far more caring side.

"You have my sympathy," Ro said, trying to give him the support he seemed to need.

"I don't want your sympathy, Captain," Quark said, sounding offended. "I want your help."

"Oh," Ro said. "Well, I can contact law enforcement in Geopolis and report the incident to them so that they can try to find Viray and make sure she's all right."

"What?" Quark said. He cocked his head to one side in apparent confusion. "Don't you see what's happened?"

"I know what you just told me," Ro said. "Is there more to the story than that?"

"That's what I asked myself last night," Quark said. "I kept thinking about all the payments I made to Viray, about how she kept telling me she was on the verge of catching up to Morn. I paid for her time—a *lot* of her time—and for her to travel all over the quadrant."

Ro didn't quite see Quark's point. "You spent your profits in the service of a good cause," she said. "Morn's your friend, and I know you're concerned about him."

"I am," Quark said, "but now I'm concerned about my latinum: Mayereen Viray has been duping me."

"What?" Ro asked. "What are you talking about?"

"I've been anxious for a long time about paying that woman," Quark said. "She kept sending me vague reports about Morn's whereabouts and movements, always asking me for more and more latinum so that she could follow him to the next planet. She did the same thing last night, telling me that Morn had just left Janus Six, and that she needed funds immediately so that she could pursue him."

"And that's not good information?" Ro asked.

Quark grabbed the edge of the desk and leaned forward. "I did some checking of my own last night," he said. "I couldn't find any indication at all that Morn was ever in Geopolis."

"But does that prove anything?" Ro asked. "I mean, you hired a private investigator specifically because you couldn't find Morn on your own."

Quark bared his misaligned teeth, and Ro realized that she glimpsed an anger in him that she had never before seen. "I couldn't find Morn," he snarled, "but I found this." He reached into his tailored jacket and pulled out a Fe-

rengi padd. He expertly tapped out a series of control movements, then set the device down on the desk. It emitted
rays of light that formed into a three-dimensional image
directly above the padd. Ro couldn't quite make sense of
what she saw, but then a form moved into the field of view.
Quark stabbed at the controls and the image froze. It displayed a figure walking alone down a pedestrian pathway.
A marbled blue-gray sky hung overhead.

No, not a sky, Ro realized. *The interior walls and ceiling of
a vast underground excavation.*

"This is Mayereen Viray," he said, and he worked the
padd once more. A second copy of the image appeared beside the first, and then its perspective changed, focusing in
on the subject's face. Her wide, dark eyes and gold-hued
skin revealed her as a Petarian. "I collected these images
from a surveillance station near the main transportation
hub in Geopolis." Having once visited Janus VI, Ro knew
that banks of high-speed turbolifts ferried travelers between the subterranean city and the domed spaceport on
the surface.

"I don't see the significance," she said. "You just told me
that Viray was in Geopolis."

"The significance is that I captured these images two
hours *after* I thought I saw her get abducted," Quark said.
"Do you notice any kidnappers here? Do you see her trying to get away from anybody? Do you detect any sense of
panic on her face?"

Ro examined the two still images. Viray did appear to be
alone, and she displayed no outward signs of stress. Still—
"Just because we can't see anybody with her doesn't mean
that she wasn't abducted. Maybe she's being blackmailed or
otherwise manipulated in some way."

"I'm the one who's been manipulated," Quark said, clap-
ping a hand against his chest. He jumped to his feet, gestic-

ulating wildly. "I should have known better." He marched away from the desk and toward the rounded rectangular port at the far end of Ro's office. He muttered to himself, asserted that he should have paid heed to the 119th Rule of Acquisition—the captain had no idea what that might be—then turned back toward the desk. "Viray's been lying to me, falsifying her reports about Morn in order to extort latinum from me. She faked her own kidnapping to complete her fraud. She gauged that somebody like me would never contact law enforcement or attempt to identify and deal with her abductors."

"Which leaves her free to make off with your profits," Ro said, following Quark's thinking.

"Which leaves her free to make off with my profits," he said, his voice rising and arms waving. Ro had seen him animated before, particularly over the subject of profits, but she had never seen him vent such spleen. She couldn't help wondering if the distance she'd let grow between them had something to do with that.

"What is it you think I can do to help?" Ro asked.

Quark paced back over to Ro's desk. He didn't sit, but stood with his fingertips brushing against her desktop. "I want my latinum back, so I'm heading to Janus Six to track down Viray. I need you to provide me with the assistance and protection I'll need. I know Chief O'Brien has engaged in similar investigations before, but I'll settle for whichever senior security personnel you can spare."

Ro stared at Quark for a long moment. She recognized his determination, even understood it, but she found it astonishing that he thought it even a possibility she would assign any members of her crew to join his personal crusade. "Of course," Ro said. "You'll no doubt need a runabout as well—or maybe even the *Defiant*."

Quark reacted as though she had physically slapped

him. Ro at once regretted how brusque and dismissive she'd been. She wondered if her poor behavior had been motivated by the shame she felt for not yet having told Quark about her feelings for Altek Dans.

"I've already hired a ship," Quark said, clearly affronted. "It will be here tomorrow morning. And you can mock my request for assistance, but even though Mayereen Viray never set foot on this starbase, my transfer of funds to her under false pretenses *did* occur on Deep Space Nine, which gives you jurisdiction."

"I'm not so sure Starfleet would agree with that assessment," Ro said, and although she had not intended the words harshly, they sounded that way. In an effort both to mollify Quark and to sooth her own conscience, she added, "But I'll bring the matter to Commander Desjardins for his legal interpretation." Stationed on DS9 but not under Ro's command, Gregory Desjardins headed the judge advocate general's office for Bajor Sector.

The peace offering had its intended effect. Quark calmed down. He took a seat again and thanked Ro.

"Regardless of what Commander Desjardins says, you really should report the incident to the authorities on Janus Six," the captain told Quark. "And you definitely should not pursue Viray on your own."

"I won't contact law enforcement in Geopolis because I don't want to alert that swindler that I know what she's done, and that I intend to get my misappropriated funds back," Quark said, his voice beginning to rise again. "I don't want to chase down Viray by myself, which is why I came to you." He stood back up. "But if you don't want to help me, I'll have to do it on my own." He started for the door, but stopped and looked back at her before reaching it. "It's not like I haven't been doing things without you anyway."

"Quark—" Ro began, standing up. She didn't know what she could say to him, but she also didn't want him leaving when he was so upset.

It didn't matter. Quark didn't hesitate. He headed out into the corridor, and the door closed behind him.

iii

Kira sat at the companel in the living area of her guest quarters, speaking with Kai Pralon. After a good night's sleep, the vedek felt rested and ready to resume her "normal" life. To that end, she had earlier that day asked Captain Ro to inform both First Minister Asarem and the kai of her emergence from the Celestial Temple. Kira also asked to speak with Pralon at her earliest convenience. The vedek would have gotten in touch with the first minister and the kai herself, but she wanted neither to shock them nor to talk with any of their staff and risk word of her return spreading before she'd contacted those to whom she'd been closest.

"It truly is good to see you, Vedek," Pralon said, not for the first time. Kira felt the same about the kai, but also couldn't help noticing that the Bajoran spiritual leader seemed as though she had lived longer than the two years since last they had seen each other. Only recently turned sixty, she still did not look her age, but streaks of silver had begun to twine their way through her short blond hair, and her sharp features hosted deeper lines around her eyes and mouth than Kira remembered. She also appeared haggard, as though she hadn't slept well in recent days, and the reason seemed obvious: the religious crisis plaguing Bajor.

"I'm very glad to see you, Kai Pralon." The vedek had already learned from Captain Ro that Pralon had survived the attack on Idran IV—an attack during which Kira had led Taran'atar on a mission to protect the kai and her legation on their visit to the native Eav'oq—but it still felt satisfying to actually see her.

"*When the Celestial Temple closed with you inside it, I believed that the Prophets would keep you in Their care,*" Pralon said. "*I must confess, though, that I never expected that you would return to Bajor.*"

"I didn't either," Kira said.

"*It is a beneficence,*" Pralon said. "*I have in my life consulted all nine of the Tears, and I have twice been blessed with a pagh'tem'far, but I must tell you that I have trouble contemplating what you have experienced.*" Her reaction did not seem one of skepticism or of envy, but of sincere curiosity.

"It is difficult to discuss," Kira said. "Not just for me to find the words to convey my experiences within the Celestial Temple, but to find enough coherence in my memories just to think about them." Indistinct impressions remained with Kira from her time inside the wormhole—flashes of observing the Emissary's first meeting with the Prophets, and of her living an existence as an abolitionist sometime back in Bajor's distant past—but those recollections continued to blur at the edges, fading like long-ago dreams. The notion that she might have alit inside the Celestial Temple on a shape-shifting world comprising Taran'atar and the surviving Ascendants confused her, and she wanted to reflect on what such an intersection could possibly mean. She could have revealed to the kai the few details she remembered, or spoken in nebulous terms about the texture of what she had gone through, but she chose not to do so. The Prophets had called Kira Their Hand, and whether or not she had discharged that responsibility, it belonged to her alone, and at least for the time being, she wanted to keep it that way.

The vedek had also debated about whether or not to

tell Pralon about her travels through time in the Gamma Quadrant. Kira had confided in Ro primarily in order to learn whether her efforts aboard *Even Odds* and at Idran IV had succeeded in altering the past. The vedek understood the reasoning behind Starfleet's Temporal Prime Directive, and so she had decided not to tell anybody else.

"Whatever your experience, Vedek, I am pleased that you are back," the kai said. *"Your presence has been missed in the Vedek Assembly. Now more than ever, the combination of your depth of faith and your practical honesty is in short supply."*

Practical honesty? Kira thought. *Practical honesty? What does that mean?* She could only surmise that, given the growing religious turmoil, Pralon referred to the vedek's decision a decade prior to release the writings of Ohalu to the Bajoran people, even though Kira did not subscribe to them herself.

"Captain Ro told me about the events on Endalla," Kira said. "What can I do to help?"

"Your dedication to service is admirable," said Pralon. *"Your return to Bajor will be a benefit to our people. It will mean much for them to see a vedek thought lost has now come home."*

Kira valued the simple sentiment, but she also detected subtext in the kai's words: positive news on the religious front could help ease the rising stresses on Bajor—especially given that Kira had a reputation for treating the Ohala-varu fairly, despite their differing beliefs. Another thought crossed the vedek's mind as well—namely that some might frame Kira's return from the Celestial Temple as tacit evidence of the divinity of the Prophets.

Is that unreasonable? the vedek asked herself. She didn't think so, and yet the idea disturbed her on some level. She couldn't say why, but it felt like trying to recall a fact long forgotten.

Unable to fill in the detail of her intuition, Kira told the kai, "I'll speak to Captain Ro. I'm sure her crew can help me arrange transport back to Bajor."

"There's no need for that, Vedek," Pralon said. *"I will dispatch a ship at once to collect you."*

Kira offered the kai a tight-lipped smile. She appreciated Pralon's gesture, but accepting any sort of privilege always made her uncomfortable. "That's not necessary, Eminence," she said, employing the honorific to remind the kai of their relative positions. "I can find passage to Bajor on my own."

"Vedek Kira," Pralon said, *"you survived the Occupation as a member of an active Resistance cell, you served as a vital link between Bajor and the Federation, you enjoyed the friendship of the Emissary, you commanded Deep Space Nine, and you lived for more than two years within the Celestial Temple. I have no doubt that you could find your own way home. That's not the point. I insist on sending a vessel with members of my staff aboard to accompany you back to Bajor."*

Pralon exuded both strength and sincerity. "Of course," Kira said. "Thank you."

"I will make the arrangements immediately," the kai said. *"I look forward to seeing you in person."* Pralon tapped at a control on her companel, and Kira's display went black, the image of Pralon Onala replaced by the bisected oval of the Bajoran emblem. The vedek stared at it for a moment, until it too disappeared.

She continued to sit at her companel, still bothered by something she could not name. Kira served her people as a vedek, and so it made sense for the kai to support her return to Bajor. *Is it important that some might point to my coming back from the Celestial Temple as evidence of the Prophets' godhood?* It might matter, she supposed, but she had no wish to persuade people to her personal beliefs. As a vedek, she sought to conduct the rites of their faith, to provide comfort and solace when needed, and above all, to guide adherents on their own paths.

I want to go back to Bajor, Kira thought, *but I don't want my return used as a weapon in the spiritual divide of our people.* Did the kai intend to do that? Kira didn't think so; that did not sound to her like the way Pralon Onala conducted herself.

It sounds more like Kai Winn.

Just the thought of Winn Adami chilled Kira. Her machinations, her hunger for power, her jealous self-interest had brought Bajor to the precipice during her term as kai. The suggestion of any meaningful similarity between Winn and Pralon seemed absurd to Kira, and she dismissed it out of hand.

The vedek rose from her seat at the companel, turning her thoughts to what she needed to do prior to departing for Bajor. Ro had told her of some major events that had occurred in and around the system during her time away, but Kira wanted both to fill in the details of those events and to learn more about what had taken place in the rest of the quadrant. As for preparing to actually leave DS9, she certainly had no belongings to pack, but there were people she wanted to contact, to let them know that she had not been lost when the wormhole had collapsed around her. She had almost no family—an uncle and two cousins—but even though they had never been close, she wanted to tell them that she had not perished. Kira would wait until she reached Bajor to inform her friends and colleagues there, but with such a significant civilian population and such a large crew on the new DS9, she guessed that there must be people aboard with whom she would want to speak.

"Computer, this is Kira Nerys," she said. "Compare the current crew manifest and the directory of residents to those of the previous Deep Space Nine station. Provide a list of individuals common to both."

"Evaluating specified data," the computer responded.

"Route the results to the companel." Kira sat down again as the display winked back to life. Names and faces immediately began appearing. Some she recognized and some she didn't, but it took a few moments before she saw people she wanted to contact: Keiko and Miles O'Brien, Nog, Prynn Tenmei, and a few others. She waited for particular individuals to appear, but when the computer had completed its task, they were conspicuous by their absence: Julian Bashir, Cenn Desca, Sarina Douglas.

Kira picked a name. "Computer," she said, "locate Prynn Tenmei."

"Lieutenant Tenmei is in her quarters."

Kira took a deep breath. "Computer, open a channel to Prynn Tenmei."

iv

The man did not actually smile, but the expression on his face nevertheless looked wry, as though it amused him that he knew more than Nog—which Nog felt certain he did about the subject at hand. *"Two years?"* the man asked. He had contacted Nog from aboard *R'Novia*, a civilian transport registered out of Vulcan.

"It's been a little longer than that," Nog said. The operations chief stood in his quarters aboard DS9, in front of the companel, too anxious to sit down. It took all of his willpower to keep from pacing. He scrutinized the man on the display, trying to take his measure in the way he'd been taught from a young age to do, as a salesman appraising a customer. It didn't matter that Nog needed something from the man rather than the other way around; as the 151st

Rule of Acquisition preached: *Even when you're a customer, sell yourself.*

"That's a long time for a self-aware holographic program to execute without external stimuli," the man said. Nog had detailed for Doctor Bashir's friend the journey that Vic Fontaine had taken in getting from the old Deep Space 9 to the new starbase, as well as the dramatic and unexplained developments that had occurred within the holoprogram in the interim. *"It sounds like a fascinating experiment."*

Nog didn't much care for the idea of considering Vic some sort of test subject, any more than he liked thinking of him as "just" a hologram. No matter his origin, no matter his nature, Vic had been a good friend. Some people might not countenance such a relationship, they might even ridicule it, but none of that mattered to Nog. "Mister Knightly—"

"Please call me Felix."

"Felix," Nog corrected himself. He had heard Doctor Bashir talk about the programming savant, the man who had breathed life into Vic in the first place, and who had coded the setting in which the lounge singer lived, but Nog had never before spoken with him. A human, Felix had dark-brown skin, with high cheekbones and a broad, smooth nose. His voice held a deep, resonant timbre. "So you think that the drastic changes I witnessed are the result of the program running in isolation for so long?" Nog asked. "Could it be another jack-in-the-box?"

"I only included one surprise subroutine in the code," Felix said, *"and it sounds as though you already know about that one. Julian contacted me about it when it sprang up. That was a long time ago."* As Nog recalled, the sudden introduction of Vic's childhood nemesis—who had turned into an adult mobster—had taken place before the end of the Dominion War, which meant more than a decade earlier.

"I helped Doctor Bashir resolve Vic's problem and set the program back to its normal operating mode."

Felix folded his arms across his chest and leaned back in his chair. Behind him, through a small, round port in the bulkhead of *R'Novia*, stars streaked past. *"The thing that's interesting to me about this is that I wrote the program to be expansive,"* he said. *"That means that the code is able to incorporate era-specific social and environmental details as needed. Under normal circumstances, especially if the program has been running with no user participation, I'd hypothesize that it might have been influenced by the historical record of nineteen-sixties Earth, a period of considerable upheaval. But since it's been executing in a stand-alone simulation tester, that's not possible; without a connection to a larger database, there would necessarily be a limitation to the number of outside details that the program could bring in."*

"What about the change in the entry point?" Nog asked.

"That's probably just a function of the program's main character relocating," Felix said.

"When I first uploaded the program to a holosuite from the tester, the entry point was still in the casino," Nog said. "That must mean that Vic relocated recently."

"Not necessarily," Felix said. *"You told me that when you first reloaded the program, you saw only a small swath of the holographic setting. That means that the code could have been executing in a testing or safety mode. It might not reflect the current state of the program at that time."*

Nog had considered that possibility himself. "But why hasn't the entry point changed again?" he asked.

"You told me that Vic was abducted," Felix said. *"That obviously wouldn't count as voluntary relocation, and so it wouldn't have any effect on the program's entry point."*

That made sense to Nog, but it did not answer a more

significant question. "Could any of that have to do with why I can't restart the program?"

"Oh, no, not at all," Felix said. *"In your account of what happened your last time in the program, the people who kidnapped Vic fired weapons at you. It's likely that, as far as the code is concerned, you were flagged as fatalities. It's probably not that the program can no longer be run in a holosuite; it's that you personally can't reenter it."*

"What?" Nog said, though he understood precisely what Felix had just told him. The operations chief stepped forward and leaned heavily on the front of his companel. "I can't *ever* enter the program again?" He dreaded the answer. It meant that he couldn't help save Vic from his current troubles, and also that, even if the lounge singer managed to resolve the situation on his own and resume his normal existence, Nog wouldn't be able to interact with him.

"I wrote the code as a real-world emulation," Felix explained. *"You can't include genuine physical jeopardy for users in holoprograms—at least not legally or ethically—but I wanted to give Julian a piece of code that had some weight to it . . . where his actions would have consequences."*

"Is there any way . . ." Nog began, but a terrible sense of despair washed over him. He stopped, then started again. "Can I modify the code?"

"You can try, but I doubt you'll have much success," Felix told him. *"I programmed it in such a way that any attempts to alter it causes its immediate deletion."*

"Isn't there anything I can do?" Nog heard the desperation in his voice.

"You can always just reinitialize the program and start all over again," Felix said.

"It's not the program that's important," Nog said. "It's Vic. Resetting the code would mean erasing his memories . . . effectively ending his life. Even if I could be his friend again, it wouldn't be the same—*he* wouldn't be the same."

"No, he wouldn't," Felix said, *"and not just because his memories would be deleted. Everything about him would be gone: his physical parameters, the composition of his mental and emotional processing. When the program started the first time, it created Vic's character from several specified constants—his age, his profession, his talent—as well as a random selection of attributes."*

With every word, the news worsened. In theory, Nog could request some of his crewmates to help Vic, but even if they succeeded in doing so, it would have no impact on Nog's inability to reenter the singer's Las Vegas habitat. He didn't even know whom he could reasonably ask, since so many of those who'd been closest to Vic did not live on the new Deep Space 9: Doctor Bashir and Lieutenant Commander Douglas, Vedek Kira, Captain Sisko and Kasidy Yates, Captain Dax, Odo. Chief O'Brien resided on the starbase, but his wife and children had only recently joined him from Bajor, filling most of his off-duty hours with family.

Nog pulled out the chair in front of the companel and slumped into it. "Isn't there anything I can do to reenter the program?" he asked.

"Not in the usual manner, no," Felix said. *"But . . . there is a back door."*

"A back door?" Nog asked, his voice rising along with a sudden sense of hope.

"I always leave myself a way back into my work in case of emergency," Felix said. *"I can give you a set of commands that will allow you to bypass the program's regular checks. That would allow you to go back in, but it will only work once, so if you use it, you'll have to remain in the program until you reestablish your identity."*

"How can I do that?"

Actually, the main character can do it," Felix said. *"Vic probably doesn't even know he has that capability, but as soon as he sees you alive, that should trigger the procedure."*

"That's great," Nog said. Yes, he would have to rescue Vic from the thugs who had abducted him, but he was going to have to do that anyway. "That's what I'll do."

"There's one other thing," Felix said. *"Once you utilize the back door, you'll have exactly one week to reestablish your identity."*

Nog didn't think it would take that long to determine Vic's situation and deal with it accordingly, but he also needed to know the strictures under which he would be operating. "What happens if I can't find Vic and reestablish my identity in a week?"

"Then the program will automatically reestablish your identity for you," Felix said. *"And to do that, it will completely reinitialize itself."*

Nog slipped back down into his chair. "And that means . . ."

"It means that if you can't recover Vic in that time," Felix said, *"he will cease to exist."*

V

In the living area of her quarters, Ro lifted a platter of sliced *hasperat* from the replicator and carried it over to the dining table. She set it down between the two place settings laid out there, alongside a bowl containing braised *lorpa* beans and another with *decapus* salad. The food looked and smelled delicious—a consequence not just of the traditional Bajoran dishes she'd chosen from the replicator, but from her renewed appetite. Over the past month or so—really from about the time she had left the Ascendant link living peaceably inside the wormhole—life had mostly settled down for the captain aboard Deep Space 9. She still spent multiple shifts each day fulfilling her responsibilities as the commanding officer of the busy, highly populated starbase, but she had begun to find a rhythm in it. She had actually shortened her workdays a bit and she'd started to give more attention to her off-duty hours.

"This all looks wonderful," Altek Dans said of the food—although as he glanced across the table at Ro with a warm smile and a gleam in his eyes, she thought that he might be referring to more than just their dinner. She sat down across from him and reached for a bottle of Andorian red wine she'd found at Celestial Spirits on the Plaza. She poured out two glasses.

Ro lifted her wine to sip from it, but she stopped when Dans raised his glass toward her. "To Ro Laren," he said.

"And why are you toasting me?"

"There could be many reasons," Dans said. "Your beauty, your strength, your intelligence, your honesty—"

"All right, all right," Ro said, interrupting him. "You're clearly not appealing to my sense of humility."

"I said those *could* be the reasons, but they're not," he told her playfully. "I'm saluting you for everything you've done on my behalf since my arrival."

"I'm just doing my duty," Ro said, more out of reflex than anything else. Although she had never cared for the considerable criticism she'd endured on many fronts throughout her life, she had also never been comfortable accepting approbation.

"You're being modest, and that's fine," Dans said, "but I want you to know that I appreciate all you've done for me—particularly in trying to get the Bajoran government to allow me to go home."

"If they ever do."

"That's what I'm saluting," Dans said, and he eased his glass forward to tap it against Ro's. The contact produced a melodic ring. "The minister of state's office contacted me today."

"Congratulations," Ro said. She sipped from her wineglass, and Dans followed suit. Although she felt conflicted about the news, it did please her for his sake. More than two months prior, Dans had indicated his desire to return to Bajor, and the captain had set about trying to make that happen. She had run into resistance, initially because of the political turmoil following the assassination of President Bacco, and later owing to the complicated unrest fomented by the discovery of the Endalla falsework and the Ohalavaru claims about it. Ro eventually met in person with Kai Pralon and helped convince her that she should actively support Dans's request. Just the previous day, the kai's office alerted the captain that First Minister Asarem finally agreed to direct her government to issue identity and travel documents to Dans. "What did the minister's office tell you?"

"Nothing definitive," Dans said, "but Minister Gandal wanted me to know that his people are working toward drafting the necessary documents to allow me to head to Bajor."

Ro couldn't be sure, but it sounded like another delaying tactic. She served herself a helping of hasperat as she considered what to say. She didn't want to spoil Dans's optimism. "Did they give you a timeframe?"

"Not a precise one." Dans scooped some lorpa beans onto his plate, then used a pair of serving spoons to add some salad. "They told me that it should happen within a week, perhaps as soon as three or four days from now."

"That at least sounds more convincing than what we've heard before." Ro passed the platter of hasperat to Dans, who took two helpings, then served herself the beans and salad.

"I'm hopeful, anyway," Dans said.

They lapsed into comfortable silence for a few minutes as they started eating. Ro contemplated how quickly she had become accustomed to having Dans in her life, and how much she enjoyed his company. Although he didn't seem especially backward, as one might expect of a man who had lived hundreds—perhaps even *thousands*—of years in the past, Ro could not quite picture him living in modern society—at least not without her nearby presence and counsel. "What are your plans once you reach Bajor?" she eventually asked, and another question rose in her mind. "Where do you even plan on going?"

"I've been thinking about that," Dans said between a bite of hasperat and a forkful of beans. "You know that I've been reading a lot about contemporary Bajor. I was looking at first for familiar place names, but I didn't have any luck. There were occasional similarities here and there, but nothing that truly matched up with locations from my time. So if I really want to learn about Bajor and its people today, I thought I might best be served by starting out in the capital."

"That sounds like a good idea," Ro said. "You'll be able to immerse yourself in Bajoran culture—much more so than here. Deep Space Nine may be in the Bajoran system and largely inhabited by its citizens, but this is still a Starfleet facility. I think you'll have an entirely different experience in Ashalla than you've had here."

"I think so too," Dans said. "Your crew have all treated me well in my time here, but I'm hoping that I can sort of get lost in the capital . . . not draw too much attention to myself."

"I think that may depend on the first minister and the

kai," Ro said. "I suspect that they're going to want to announce your arrival to Bajorans. I know you don't think it's
significant, but your being sent through time by the Prophets will interest a lot of people."

"I can understand that point of view," Dans said, "but
there just doesn't seem to be any reason for me to be here.
I'm more inclined to think that what's happened is just a
matter of chance. I might not understand how I came to
be here, but there doesn't seem to be any particular reason
behind it."

"Believers claim that the Prophets work in mysterious
ways."

"I'm one of those believers," Dans said. "I just have a
difficult time imagining that the Prophets have singled me
out for some reason."

"I'm not sure it will be hard for others to make that
leap," Ro said. "People will want to speak with you, listen
to your views. With the rift regarding the falsework, both
sides will want to recruit you to their way of thinking."

"I'll try to avoid anything like that."

"I hope you can, for your sake," Ro said. "Do you have
any idea what you might want to do in the longer term?"

Dans took his glass and drank the last few sips of wine
from it, then poured himself another. He held the bottle
up to the captain's nearly empty glass, but she stopped him
with a gesture. Dans drank again before answering. "I guess
I just want to get a feel for Bajor, for its people—and I want
to find my place among them."

"You want to go *home*."

Dans nodded, but Ro detected a melancholy about him.
"I know I can't go home, not really, I know that," he said.
"But I'd like to approximate that as best I can, and I think
there's a way I can do so . . . by returning to the practice of
medicine."

"Do you think you can do that?" Ro assumed that Dans's experiences as a doctor must have differed greatly from those of present-day Bajoran physicians.

"I do," Dans said. "There have obviously been advances since my time, both technologically and in terms of knowledge, but I can learn all of that. I'll go back to school."

"That's commendable," Ro said.

Dans shrugged. "It's selfish," he said. "I want to belong. I want to feel useful. I've been a lot of things in my life—a son, a brother, a colleague, a friend, a lover. Of all those roles, the most important were a liberator of slaves and a physician. As far as I know, today's Bajor has no slaves, but there will always be sick and injured people to care for."

"The Bajoran people will be lucky to have you back."

As they continued their meal, they talked more about Bajor. Ro shared with Dans some of her favorite places on the planet, including the Endestre Wilderness Preserve, Borvalo Falls, and the Tannatuk Colony, a small settlement of artists in Tozhat Province who focused both on their creative endeavors and on maintaining a way of life less dependent on technology. They spoke about various forms of entertainment, and Ro learned that Dans enjoyed attending the theater. He also talked about his younger days playing a ball-based team sport called *renfor*, which the captain had never heard of; when he tried to explain the rules, they left her thoroughly confused.

Dans wanted to know how Ro's day had gone and what lay ahead for her in her command of DS9. After a while, as they moved on from their meal to dessert—they shared a slice of Terran apple pie—Ro became increasingly aware that they both danced around the *kulloth* in the room: what would become of their budding relationship?

It had been a long time since Ro had needed to deal with such matters. She had shared a close bond with Quark for years, first connecting with him over their mutual sense of being outsiders aboard the old DS9, and then finding in each other a romantic partner. Ro could not deny the love she felt for the barkeep, but as a close and special friend. She knew that Quark thought of their relationship as something more than that—and Ro knew she would have to address his feelings before too much more time had passed—but she considered them casual lovers. By contrast, she was falling in love with Altek Dans.

After dinner, as they sat on the sofa with cups of *raktajino*, Ro finally broached the subject. "I'm going to miss you," she said.

"I'll miss you too," Dans said, "but not for long, I hope." Ro felt her eyebrows lift in surprise at what sounded like something between an insult and a dismissal. "No, no," Dans rushed to say, clearly reading her reaction. "What I mean is that I won't miss you for long because we'll be seeing each other—at least, I hope we will be."

"I would like that," Ro said. She felt earnest in her desire to continue spending time with Dans, but awkward in her declaration. It seemed ridiculous, but she—

The door chime sounded.

"Are you expecting a visitor?" Dans asked.

"No," Ro said, but she immediately suspected that Quark had come to pay her a visit. A knot formed deep inside her. *It's my own fault,* she thought. *I've been meaning to talk to him for so long now.* Ro glanced across the compartment at her companel, which displayed the time. She saw that gamma shift had begun a short time prior, which made her think that perhaps Quark *hadn't* come to see her. At that time of the evening, he could almost always be found in his establishment on the Plaza.

"No, I'm not expecting anyone." She stood up and headed toward the door. "Come in," she called. The door panels split apart and withdrew into the bulkhead as she approached. Relief rose within her when she saw somebody other than Quark standing in the corridor. Taller than the barkeep, the figure wore an old-fashioned robe with its hood pulled up, obscuring the face within. As Ro watched, the person reached up and pulled the hood back, revealing a familiar face.

<u>vi</u>

As inviting as she found the pictures of the greensward adorning the outer portion of the residential deck, Kira chose an inner corridor to reach the captain's quarters. The vedek selected the less open route because she didn't want anybody she knew to see her. She had spent much of the afternoon contacting friends and colleagues, letting them know that she hadn't been lost inside the wormhole, that she had returned. Those conversations had been emotional, and Kira needed a respite. She hadn't been able to reach everyone. In some cases, as with the O'Briens and Nog, they hadn't been available when she'd tried to contact them. In other instances—like that of Cenn Desca—they had left DS9 permanently, and Kira had been unable to find a way to contact them.

Wearing a conservative clerical robe with its hood raised, she reached the captain's cabin without being recognized. She activated the visitor's signal and waited. Kira could simply have reached out to Ro via the comm system, but she wanted to speak with her in person, both to inform her that she would be departing for Bajor in the morning and to thank her—for listening to her story, for believing her, and for helping her to contact the kai and the first minister.

The door opened. The vedek saw Ro approaching. Kira detected no sign of recognition on the captain's face, and so she reached up and lowered her hood.

"Vedek," Ro said.

"Captain," Kira said, "I'd like to speak with you for a moment, if that's all right."

"Of course," Ro said, glancing off to the side. "Please come in." The captain took a step back and Kira followed her into the cabin. "What can I do for you?"

"Well, to begin with, I wanted to let you know that, thanks to your efforts, both First Minister Asarem and Kai Pralon contacted me today," Kira said. "I'll be traveling to Bajor tomorrow and—"

"Anora?"

The single word triggered an instantaneous response in Kira. Both the word and the voice that expressed it elicited an immediate sense of displacement. The moment disoriented her as she snapped her head around to seek out the speaker. She saw a man across the compartment stand up from the sofa while he stared at her, his mouth agape.

"Keev Anora?" he said, his tone one of incredulity.

"No," Ro said, though her voice sounded far away. "This is Kira Nerys."

The man seemed to pay no attention to the captain's statement. Kira studied him, and she knew that she had never before laid eyes upon him. In the next moment, though, an image of the man racing through a dense wood, and then out into a clearing, rose in her mind. "Dans?"

An avalanche of memories tumbled over Kira. She saw the man—*Dans,* she thought, *Altek Dans*—walking through a city, digging in a cave, sitting by a campfire. She saw him, and yet she held on to her recollections only tenuously, as though they might be swept away by the next spill of remembrances.

The man took a step away from the sofa, and then another. Kira's own mouth dropped open, and though benumbed and confused, she suddenly became certain that she had—somehow, somewhere—shared something strong and deep with the man before her. He must have seen the look of recognition in her eyes, because he sprinted the rest of the way across the cabin and threw his arms around her.

Kira returned his embrace. His body felt wholly foreign pressed against hers, and completely familiar. She held the man, and then she let him go. Kira stepped back and looked to the captain, who stood beside the pair, watching and obviously startled by what she saw.

"This is Kira Nerys," Ro said again.

"No," Kira said, but then she shook her head and started again. "I mean, yes, I'm Kira Nerys, but . . . I am also Keev Anora." In her mind's eye, the vedek saw other faces and recalled the names associated with them: Veralla Sil, Jennica Lin, Renet Losig, and others. *The gild*, Kira thought, almost as though she gathered information by eavesdropping on somebody else's memories.

"Are you or are you not Kira Nerys?" Ro demanded.

"Yes," the vedek said. "Yes, I'm Kira, but—" *But what?* she asked herself—and then she knew. "But when I was in the Celestial Temple, for a time I also became a woman named Keev Anora."

"And as Keev Anora, you knew Dans?" Ro asked. "But he's from Bajor's past, so how is that possible?"

Kira looked from the captain to Dans. The answer seemed evident. "It's possible," the vedek said, "because the Prophets made it possible."

vii

Nog strode into Quark's wearing a dark-gray suit, white button-down shirt, and blue patterned tie, all of which he had just replicated. John Candlewood walked alongside him, similarly attired, in pinstriped navy-blue garb. Earlier that afternoon, after his conversation with Felix Knightly, Nog had visited Candlewood in his quarters to brief him on what the programmer had told him, and to see if the science officer still wanted to help in rescuing Vic and returning the singer's life to normal. He did. Together, the two men then approached the captain, each asking for a week's leave. Ro raised an inquisitive eyebrow—Nog knew that Candlewood had once had a crush on him, which might have stirred the captain's curiosity—but she quickly approved their requests.

For the remainder of beta shift, the two officers holed up in Nog's quarters, where they attempted to plot out how they would proceed once they reentered Bashir 62. They pored over land maps of Las Vegas from the 1960s and 1970s, discussed potential strategies for finding Vic, and mulled over what they would do—what they *could* do— once they located the lounge singer. Nog knew that, after what had happened previously, he probably didn't need to exact a promise from Candlewood not to issue any orders to the holosuite computer, but he did so anyway; the science officer appeared suitably sheepish and agreed at once.

After a dinner that Nog suspected might be their last decent meal for days, the two men headed for Quark's. Gamma shift had begun, and customers packed the place. Along with commingled voices and the ringing of glasses, the sounds of gaming bombarded Nog's powerful hearing: the whir of the dabo wheel, the shuffling of playing cards, the thumps and chirrups of the dom-jot table.

With Candlewood in tow, Nog headed for the bar, but as they neared, to his surprise, he did not see his uncle. Instead, Broik and Ulu Lani mixed and served the drinks. Nog threaded his way through the throng of customers until he finally reached the spectacular silvern bar that Quark had acquired from a Saurian craftsman. As though she had been waiting specifically for him—a conceit Nog would have loved to indulge—Lani came right over to him.

"Hi, Nog," she said easily, her voice like music. "What can I get you tonight?"

"Nothing to drink right now," he said. "I'm looking for my uncle."

Lani nodded knowingly. "You're heading back into the holosuite, aren't you?" she said. "You're still trying to restore Vic's program."

"That's right," Nog said. He regretted lying to Lani—he doubted that she would view deceit as a proper prologue for what he hoped would eventually be a romance—but he didn't want anybody to know what had happened within Vic's holoprogram for fear that Quark would shut it down or reinitialize it.

"I haven't seen your uncle since I started my shift," Lani said. "I'm sure he must be in his office."

"Okay," Nog said. "Thanks." He pushed off from the bar, but before he moved away, he felt a touch on his hand. He looked back to see that Lani had draped her delicate fingers over his. She gave him a quick, sly smile, then headed down the bar to take a customer's order.

"I think she's after your latinum," Candlewood whispered in Nog's ear. Given his abandonment of traditional Ferengi values when he entered Starfleet, the operations chief understood the nature of his friend's raillery.

Nog and Candlewood made their way around the end of the bar and back past the open-riser staircase that led up to the second and third levels. He anticipated finding the door to Quark's office closed, but it stood opened wide. Even more unexpected, he did not see his uncle inside, but Treir. The Orion woman had worked for Quark for nearly ten years, and as far as Nog knew, she currently managed his establishment in Aljuli, on Bajor.

"Where's Uncle?" Nog asked from the doorway.

Treir looked up from where she sat at the office's free-standing companel console. "I'm fine, Nog, thank you," she said. "And how are you?"

"Oh . . . uh . . . I'm well," Nog stammered. "Sorry. I just wasn't expecting you to be here."

"I wasn't expecting to be here either," Treir said. Tall and lithe, she wore a formfitting white dress that reached all the way down to her calves and beautifully complemented her lustrous green skin. "Quark contacted me this morning and insisted that I come to Deep Space Nine at once."

"Why?" Nog asked.

"Quark is preparing to depart the starbase tomorrow morning," Treir said, "and he wants me to run the place while he's away."

"Where is he going?" Candlewood asked from over Nog's shoulder.

"Hello, John," Treir said. "He didn't tell me, but I gather that he's going to be gone for at least a few days, maybe longer."

It concerned Nog to learn that his uncle intended to leave DS9 without telling him. *Maybe he plans to let me know.* Under different circumstances, Nog would have sought out Quark just to check on him, but he saw the opportunity he'd been afforded and he didn't want to waste it. "Uh, we need to use a holosuite," he told Treir.

"Sure." She consulted the companel, tapped at a few controls, then said, "Take number seven. It's free until midnight."

"We're going to need it for longer than that," Nog said, grateful that he didn't have to make the request of his uncle. "We need dedicated access for at least a few days . . . maybe as long as a week."

"I see," Treir said. "I'd heard that there might be a new installment of *Vulcan Love Slave.*"

"No, it's not that," Candlewood quickly said.

"Either way, it doesn't matter to me," Treir said with a shrug. She worked the companel again, then said, "I've reserved number eleven for you for the week."

Nog immediately became suspicious. Where he would undoubtedly have had to argue with his uncle about using a holosuite for such an extended period, Treir had been extraordinarily accommodating. Nog wondered if her easy acquiescence to his request marked an attempt to curry favor with Quark by treating his nephew well, or if she intended somehow to take advantage of her boss, or if she just wanted to vex him. *Or maybe she doesn't even care,* Nog thought. He quickly decided that her motivations didn't matter, that he needed to exploit the situation.

"Thank you, Treir," Nog said. "We appreciate it." He waited just long enough for her to acknowledge his thanks, and then he hurried away, leading Candlewood toward holosuite number eleven.

viii

Night had fallen in the holoprogram, leaving the dim illumination of a single bulb to light the hallway. Candlewood saw that the sallow glow softened details, but also that it could not obscure the neglect and filth of the surroundings. The door to room 23—Vic's room, according to Nog—stood open, just as they'd left it.

Candlewood watched as the operations chief stepped inside and peered around. "It's empty," Nog said. Something inside the room, or maybe outside its window, glowed red, throwing an unnatural radiance across half of Nog's face.

"Then there's no reason for us to stay here," Candlewood said. Before reentering the holosuite, they had discussed how to proceed. It seemed clear to both of them that in order to rescue Vic, they first needed to know where he was being held, but they would likely need more information than that, such as who had abducted him and why they had done so. Nog made it clear that breaking the singer out of captivity would provide only one part of the solution. For Vic to be able to return to his ordinary existence, whatever complications had led to his kidnapping would also have to be resolved. It would be of little use to free Vic if the danger to him could not be eliminated.

"Let's go," Nog said, motioning toward the far end of the corridor. Candlewood trailed him in that direction, toward the hallway's single window, then followed him to the left and down a narrow staircase. They descended one flight that doubled back, to a small, roughly square lobby. Chipped and scuffed black and white tiles covered the floor. A door in the center of one wall looked as though it led outdoors, while opposite, a short hallway ran off the lobby. Ahead of them, visible through a lattice of metal bars, a man of indeterminate age sat in a walled-off compartment. A tangle of dark hair nested atop his head, and stubble coated his face. He did not look up.

Candlewood headed for the door, but Nog stopped him. "Hold on," the operations chief said, sotto voce. He motioned toward the man in the compartment. "Maybe he knows something."

"Maybe," Candlewood said tentatively. He regarded the man, whose eyes remained downcast. "He doesn't look like somebody inclined to offer assistance to strangers." Candlewood paused, then added, "He doesn't even look like somebody who'd be much interested in helping his *friends*."

"I tried to speak with him once before," Nog said, keeping his voice low. "Right after I uploaded Vic's program from the tester."

"You 'tried' to speak with him?" Candlewood said. "I

take it that means he wasn't a valuable source of information."

"I was called to the Hub before I really got to ask him anything," Nog said. "Maybe I'll have better luck this time." They walked over, and Nog said, "Pardon me. I'm trying to find an old friend who used to stay here."

"Good for you," the man said, still not looking up. Closer to him, Candlewood could see the object of the man's attention, a paper tabloid on his lap. When he turned a page by first closing and then reopening the broadside, the science officer spotted the words *Racing Form* splashed across the front.

"My friend was here until two nights ago," Nog continued. "He was staying on the second floor, but three large men abducted him—"

At last the man lifted his gaze. "I don't know nuthin bout that."

"Listen," Nog persisted, "I'm just trying to find my friend."

The man swept the *Racing Form* to one side and dropped it in a rustle on a small table beside him. "You cops?" he asked. He stood up from his chair, leaned in close to the metal bars protecting him, and peered sidelong into the lobby.

"We're not law-enforcement officers," Candlewood said. "We're just concerned about our friend."

The man pulled back and glared at Candlewood and Nog. "No, you don't look like cops." He bent slightly and reached down, out of sight. Candlewood knew what would happen even before the man stood back up with a pistol in his hand.

"Hey," the science officer called out. He grabbed for Nog's arm and pulled him toward the door. As Candlewood turned in that direction, he ran into a circular wire rack. His feet tangled with it, and he fell on top of it as it toppled over, spilling its contents—pamphlets of some kind—across the floor. He quickly tried to scramble to his feet and slipped, but then he felt Nog's grip around his upper arm, helping him up. Candlewood reached the door and pulled it open, and he and Nog rushed out into the night. They raced along the sidewalk for about a block before it became clear that they were not being pursued. A ground vehicle passed, but neither the driver nor the passenger paid them any attention.

"What's happened to this program?" Candlewood asked. "We were shot at yesterday and we almost got shot at again today."

"And we can't afford to get killed again," Nog said. "We used a back door to enter the holoprogram this time, but Doctor Bashir's friend was clear: if we get killed again, the code will automatically reset—and, as a consequence, completely delete the character of Vic Fontaine."

"I know that this time period and location is a bit rough-and-tumble," Candlewood said, "but something must have gone very wrong for Vic to stay in a place like that." He looked back down the block to the building from which they'd just bolted. He saw that the brick structure rose four stories above the dark street, the tallest among its ramshackle neighbors. An anemic red neon sign hung from the side of the building and read FREMONT-SUNRISE HOTEL—or it would have if four of its letters hadn't been dark. A streetlamp across from the building sparked on and off inconsistently, as though somebody was attempting to use it to send a coded signal.

"Maybe our fortunes are changing," Nog said. He held up a rectangle of paper, what looked like a tract of some kind, but Candlewood couldn't read what it said in the murky light.

"What's that?"

Nog unfolded the paper once, twice, and then he pulled at its ends, expanding it like an accordion. "It's a map," he said. Candlewood had spent part of that afternoon in Nog's quarters studying the layout of 1960s and 1970s Las Vegas, in particular because they could not bring any maps with them. Bashir 62 permitted users to enter the program with little more than the clothes on their backs.

The two men quickly moved farther down the street, into a circle of light thrown by a functioning streetlamp. After examining the map for a moment, Nog said, "It has hotels and casinos on it."

"Do you still want to go to the lounge where Vic used to sing?" Candlewood asked.

"I think it's the best place to start our search," Nog said. "Here's where it is." He pointed out a line drawing of a building adorned with palm trees and a stylized sun.

"And we're on Sunrise Avenue, right?" Candlewood asked. Back in Nog's quarters, the operations chief had shown him a map of the area. Candlewood glanced around, saw a street sign where the road intersected another at an acute angle, and walked over to it. "We're at the junction with Fremont Street."

"Right," Nog said, studying the map. "Got it." He pointed out what seemed like the most direct route for them to take: just over to Bruce Street from Fremont, down to Charleston Boulevard, and from there to South Las Vegas Boulevard.

"All right," Candlewood said. "Let's see what we can find out."

ix

During the many hours Nog had spent in Vic's holoprogram, he had almost never ventured outside the hotel and casino where the singer lived and worked. As he and Candlewood walked along what Vic called the Strip, the densely packed gambling center evoked certain similarities to Ferengi culture. The city appeared to exist expressly for the purpose of divesting visitors of their capital, and it made only the barest pretense otherwise. Great lighted signage everywhere advertised big payouts and improved odds, but Nog had observed and played the various games in Vic's casino—craps, keno, roulette, slot machines, wheels of fortune, and others—and it didn't require much analysis to realize that, in almost all cases, the probabilities were stacked heavily in favor of the house. By the same token, visitors to the city sought their own fortune, hoping to cash in on random chance rather than on hard work or well-crafted financial deals. Nog had traveled all over Ferenginar, had traveled throughout the Alpha Quadrant and beyond, but rarely had he seen such an obvious monument to avarice as the Las Vegas of Vic Fontaine.

"This is really something," Candlewood said as they neared yet another set of connected buildings fronted by a large, well-lighted marquee. A second sign blazed atop the tallest of the structures, embellished with a glowing cactus. Both announced the name of the establishment: Desert Inn. Already, they had passed numerous other hotel-and-casino complexes, with names like Sahara, Thunderbird, Riviera, Stardust, Silver Slipper.

Despite the lateness of the hour, Nog watched as a stream of automobiles turned from Las Vegas Boulevard onto the grounds around the Desert Inn. He surveyed people as they strolled toward or away from the casino, not expecting to spot any familiar faces, but looking anyway, just in case. In the distance, farther along the Strip, a tall letter *S* shimmered in the night. "Sands," he read. Below the single word, in smaller block type, the sign read A PLACE IN THE

SUN. The names of entertainers performing there filled the marquee below. "Vic's hotel should be—"

Nog halted abruptly, and a man and a woman walking arm in arm nearly stumbled into him. They weaved around and continued on their way. A few paces ahead, Candlewood stopped and looked back. "Nog?"

The operations chief pointed. "We're here," he said. Just up ahead, amid the crowded run of signs and buildings, a wide marquee in the shape of sand dunes featured palm trees with gleaming fronds on one side and a sparkling yellow sun on the other. The words SHINING OASIS ran across the top of the sign. Below marched a list of performers currently playing there: Faith Shay, Mick Frey, the Alison Armanza Singers, Comedian Frankie Nedboy. Nog hadn't expected to see Vic's name, but its absence still disappointed him.

"We're here," Candlewood said, "but Vic isn't."

"Come on," Nog said, and he started toward the nearest driveway that led into the Shining Oasis Hotel and Casino. Unlike its immediate neighbors with their tall buildings— the Desert Inn complex contained a rectangular nine-story structure, while the Sands's round tower rose five additional floors—the Shining Oasis only sprawled. Its highest building reached just three stories.

As Nog and Candlewood approached the entrance to the casino, the science officer said, "I really wish we had our own weapons. Not phasers, I don't mean modern weapons, but something appropriate to the period."

"I'm glad we don't," Nog said. "We've already seen enough firearms in this program. The holosuite safety protocols will protect us, but that's not true for Vic. What we need are ready funds."

"Funds?"

"They're often a much more useful weapon," Nog said.

"Fortunately, I should be able to access some capital here."

"Here? How?" Candlewood asked. "You're not going to gamble, are you?" The science officer seemed to think about that possibility for a few seconds, then said, "No, of course you're not. You only have minimal stakes to bet with." Users of Vic's holoprogram always entered it to find themselves with the modest financial resources necessary both to enjoy the lounge, where they could pay for food and drink, and to gamble in the casino, where they could wager on various table games and machines. Some visitors to Bashir 62 managed to accrue greater funds through gambling, which they could bank with the casino for future visits.

"I don't need to gamble," Nog told him. "I have a substantial account at the Shining Oasis." When Candlewood gave him a questioning look, Nog shrugged. "I used to come here a lot." Nog had enjoyed some success playing blackjack, which could be beaten by using skill, rather than relying on chance.

Inside the casino, it pleased Nog to see that it didn't look any different from the last time he'd been there. Familiar noises buffeted his ears, dominated by the spin of slot machine wheels, the jangle of coins, and human voices. People communicated not just in words, but in myriad other sounds, from groans to laughter, from exclamations of defeat to shouts of victory.

Nog led the way directly to the lounge where Vic used to sing. At the moment, nobody performed there, the entertainment for the night clearly ended. A placard placed in the entrance to the lounge showed a picture of the headliner onstage, a dark-haired songstress named Faith Shay. Nog leaned in close to the image and studied it, seeing something that encouraged him. "We'll come back tomorrow," he said.

Together, Nog and Candlewood wended through the

late-night gamblers to a bank of cashiers. An older blond woman with a well-lined faced greeted Nog with a thin-lipped smile. Her name tag read MADGE. "How can I help you, sir?"

"My name is Nog," the operations chief said. "I have an account here that I'd like to access."

"Very good, sir," Madge said. She collected a piece of paper from a stack set off to one side, along with a pencil. "May I have your account number?" Nog provided it and Madge dutifully copied it down. She then excused herself to check the casino's records, crossing the cashier's compartment to a cabinet comprising numerous small drawers. She opened one and riffled through the cards inside.

"You remember your account number?" Candlewood asked. "When you haven't been here in more than two years?"

"I may be in Starfleet," Nog said, "but I still have the lobes for business."

"I guess so," Candlewood said. "Remind me to play dabo with you next time we're in Quark's."

Nog chuckled. "There's a sucker born every minute."

"Which Rule of Acquisition is that?"

"It's not one of the rules," Nog said. "It's a human saying I learned from Jake Sisko."

Madge returned carrying a card in her hand. "Mister Nog," she said, her smile considerably brighter and cheerier than it had been when she'd first addressed the operations chief. "I see that you haven't been with us in some time. I'd like to welcome you back to the Shining Oasis."

"Thank you."

"How can I help you tonight?"

"I'm in town for a few days and I'd like to have some cash while I'm here," Nog said. "A thousand dollars should suffice."

"Yes, sir, right away," Madge said. She set down the card and made a notation on it, then slid it over to Nog for him to sign. As he did so, Madge asked, "Will you be staying with us this week, Mister Nog?"

"Uh . . . yes," Nog said, deciding that since they needed to stay somewhere inside the program, it might as well be the Shining Oasis. "My colleague and I haven't checked in yet, though."

"Let me call over to the hotel and speak with the concierge for you," Madge said. She accepted the card back from Nog, examined it for a moment, then opened a drawer in front of her. From it, she withdrew a stack of green-hued bills, counted out ten hundreds, and pushed them over to Nog. "By the time you get over to the hotel," she said, "your suite will be ready."

"Thank you, Madge." Nog scooped up the bills, folded them, and tucked them into an inside pocket of his suit jacket.

"My pleasure, sir." As Madge picked up the receiver of a telephone, Nog and Candlewood started away.

"Now what?" the science officer asked.

"Now we check in to our suite and get some sleep," Nog said. "Tomorrow, we find Vic."

X

Ro stood in front of one of the ports in the living area of her quarters, her arms folded across her chest as she stared out across the spread of natural grass that bordered the residential deck. She spotted two of her crew—Ensigns Amélie d'Arnaud and Betulio Becerra—strolling along one of the footpaths that curled about beneath the transparent bulkhead circling the middle of DS9's main sphere. Becerra looked in the captain's direction for a moment, as though he sensed her attention, but Ro knew that the one-way ports did not allow visibility into the starbase's cabins from outside.

Beyond her two crew members, beyond the clear bulk-head, the stars shined in the night sky. From her vantage, Ro could see several vessels docked along DS9's wide *x*-ring, including *Diomedes* and a number of civilian ships. Past them, unseen in the firmament, the Alpha Quadrant terminus of the Bajoran wormhole lurked, waiting to open, either to admit or expel travelers as part of a journey of seventy thousand light-years that almost miraculously lasted just minutes. Ro's mind returned to the great subspace bridge again and again, and to its mysterious and powerful denizens, even as she tried to concentrate on all that her visitors had to say.

After the vedek had shown up at her door, Kira and Dans had taken easy chairs in the sitting area, facing each other across the low table there, while the captain had remained standing. Driven by Ro's many questions, as well as their own, the two time-travelers spoke of their shared experiences in Bajor's past, with the vedek recalling more details as the discussion wore on. None of it made sense to Ro, and yet she could not deny that what she heard felt like it bore the imprimatur of the Prophets.

More questions spun through the captain's mind, none of them admitting of any obvious answers. Assuming that the events of which Dans and Kira spoke had actually taken place, that they were not phantom memories left by some mutual Orb experience or pagh'tem'far or the like, then for what purpose had the Prophets sent the vedek into history? Had Keev Anora been a real person, and if so, had Kira somehow taken over the woman's life? Why? And why had Dans been brought forward in time? Was it a coincidence that the vedek had returned from the Celestial Temple just as Dans was about to travel to modern-day Bajor for the first time? The captain also wondered if their separate arrivals on Deep Space 9 had anything to do with the discovery of the Endalla falsework.

After her initial spate of questions, Ro had mostly listened as Dans and Kira talked, occasionally interjecting to ask for clarification on some point or another. The captain did not raise the issue of the relationship between Altek Dans and Kira Nerys—or between Dans and Keev Anora—and neither did they. It didn't matter. Ro did not need the details spelled out for her; she had seen the emotion on Dans's face, and the sense of recognition on Kira's: in their time together in Bajor's past, the two had been not merely lovers, but in love. The captain did not lie to herself that the observation didn't hurt her, but she chose to push it aside in favor of trying to comprehend and deal with what seemed like larger issues.

As Dans spoke of Kira in the person of Keev Anora, as the two of them recalled the intensity of their time together struggling to free slaves from servitude, they attempted to piece together the tapestry of the Prophets' plans for them, individually and together. It seemed like a fool's errand, with multitudes of uncertainties and an even greater number of possibilities, but no ready answers. Ro feared that, even if they somehow developed a theory that explained all that had happened, they would have no means of determining its veracity.

The captain heard the sound of somebody rising, and she turned from the port to see Kira on her feet. Dans rose as well. "It's late," the vedek said, and Ro glanced at the companel to see that the time had passed midnight. "It can be a powerful and illuminating experience to explore the will of the Prophets, but it almost never results in any sort of definitive understanding."

"I've found that, even without answers, asking questions can still bring us closer to the Prophets," Dans said.

"Of course," Kira agreed, "and it can lead to personal revelations as well."

Such sentiments did not impress Ro. Even as recent observations and experiences had motivated her to reconsider her evaluation of the Prophets' divinity, the language, rites, and trappings of the formal Bajoran religion had become no less objectionable to her. She listened without comment.

The vedek looked to Ro. "I hope we can talk more, Captain," Kira said, "but I'll be departing early tomorrow morning, so I need to go. Thank you again for everything."

"Of course," Ro said. "Have a pleasant trip back to Bajor."

Kira turned her attention to Dans. "It was good to see you," she said, her manner awkward. Ro imagined that the vedek didn't know if she could be, or should be, or even wanted to be with a man she had known well, but when she'd worn a different persona.

For his part, Dans seemed uncomfortable as well. He skirted the table and walked over to Kira. Ro thought for an instant that he might embrace the vedek once more, but instead, he offered his hand. She took it in both of hers. "It was good to see you too." He did not say the name *Anora*, but it seemed poised on his lips. Despite the lack of demonstrative affection at that moment between Dans and Kira, Ro sensed the emotional undercurrents at play.

The vedek raised the hood of her robe as she crossed the compartment, and left. After the door closed behind her, a laden atmosphere descended on the cabin. Ro chose to break the silence before it could extend too long. "That was . . . unexpected," she said. She crossed from the port over to the sitting area.

"It was," Dans agreed, "but maybe it shouldn't have been."

He sat back down on the sofa, and Ro took a place next to him.

"Why do you say that?"

Dans shrugged. "We've been questioning why I'm here ever since I arrived," he said. "*I've* been questioning it. None of it has made sense to me . . . being ripped from my time and deposited here. I've been adapting—what else could I do?—but it would still help to know that this hasn't been random."

"And your experience with Vedek Kira, and now seeing her here, tells you that." Ro could see how that would be the case, even if the reasons for what Dans had been through remained inscrutable.

"Yes, I guess so," he said, though he sounded less than convincing to Ro. Dans appeared pensive, and it seemed to her that even if his seeing Kira—or Keev—helped him in some way, it also provided an entirely new set of challenges.

Which undoubtedly includes his relationship with me.

"I'm sorry," she told Dans. She reached over and placed her hand atop his. He didn't move—neither pulling away nor taking her hand in his. "I know how difficult all of this has been for you, and now seeing Kira . . ." She didn't really know what else to say.

"Yeah," he said, the word barely audible. "It's . . . it's hard." Without warning, he stood up, breaking the physical contact of their hands. "I'm sorry. I need to sleep too." Ro interpreted his declaration to mean that he would not be spending the night in her quarters. "Maybe after a good night's rest, I'll be able to find some clarity tomorrow."

"I understand," Ro said. She anticipated him telling her that nothing had changed between them, that he still wanted to see her, but he didn't say anything. Instead, he headed for the door to leave. Ro accompanied him, and for her, the moment felt fraught with suppressed emotion and things unsaid.

At the door, Dans turned to her. Ro waited, unsure what to do. At last, he said, "Good night." He leaned in to kiss her, but his lips did not find hers; instead, they brushed along her cheek. Then he turned and left.

Ro stood and stared at the closed door for a long time.

xi

The night, already long, grew longer.

Ro lay in the darkness of her bedroom, unable to get comfortable. She adjusted her position, moved from one side to the other, onto her belly, onto her back, but sleep eluded her. Worse than simple insomnia, uncomfortable thoughts and images crowded her mind. The love she felt for Dans gave way to the unmistakable expression on Dans's face when he first saw Kira Nerys, and later, when he said good-bye to her.

Those thoughts led Ro to think of Quark. *I've seen that look on his face, haven't I?* The question came as a prickly reminder that she had failed to live up to her personal responsibilities with respect to their relationship, no matter its casual nature.

In some ways, everything Ro felt lately in her day-to-day life seemed new to her—her romance with Dans, her neglect of Quark, her deliberations about faith, all of it. New, and unexpected. *What's wrong with me?* In many regards, Ro believed that she remained the person she had always been: strong, focused, principled. *But maybe not as rebellious,* she thought. *Maybe not as contrary . . . not quite as willing to overlook rules and regulations.*

Ro whipped the covers from atop her body and threw her legs over the side of the bed, sitting up in the darkness. *Am I the same person I used to be?* she asked herself. *Am I the person I want to be?* She wondered if her ascent through the ranks of Starfleet had suppressed the more independent parts of her nature. She preferred to believe that her rise to the command of Deep Space 9, to her captaincy, had stifled those aspects of her personality out of necessity. *But that's a lie,* she had to admit. The same traits that had gotten her in trouble throughout her life and in her career had also contributed considerably to every promotion she'd ever received.

So then what's changed?

"Computer, lights up one-quarter." The overhead panels eased on, and Ro got up and crossed to her closet, where she pulled out a thigh-length lavender robe and put it on. She walked out of her bedroom and into the living area of her quarters, for no other reason than the need to move her body.

I've had to keep moving my whole life, she thought as she paced to and fro, and all at once, the answer to what had changed seemed obvious. It surprised her in its simplicity: she had called one place—essentially one place—home for the longest time in her life. She spent almost eight years on the original DS9, then two at Bajoran Space Central on Bajor, and the last five months aboard the new starbase, and all of that decade-plus among many of the same people.

Have I become complacent? she asked herself. *Do I need to move on?*

The question startled her. Her transition from the defeated Maquis to the Bajoran Militia had been a boon to her, a life-affirming decision that had presented her with the opportunity to play a positive role in her people's society. Her assignment to DS9, and then her transfer into Starfleet when it had absorbed the off-world duties of the Militia, had both been bumpy. Even her posting to first officer of the station, and then to commanding officer, had not been smooth, the result of resistance to her advancement by several admirals in Starfleet Command, most notably Starfleet's current commander in chief, Leonard James Akaar.

But I fought to stay here, Ro thought as she leaned against the sill of one of the ports that looked out on the grassy sweep of the residential deck. Because of the lateness of the hour, the footpaths wound emptily through the space. *For the first time in my life, I didn't move on. Is that why I'm feeling what I'm feeling? Because I've been in one place for too long?*

Despite the peculiarity of her rootedness on Deep Space 9, the slew of negative emotions coursing through Ro possessed an air of familiarity, from her disappointment to her loneliness, from her sense of failure to her feelings of abandonment. Memories from all across her life percolated upward. She had never been able to bury the recollection of her father's torture and eventual death at the hands of a Cardassian occupier. She remembered the little boy in the refugee camps who turned her in to the Cardassian overseers for hoarding paltry scraps of food. She could easily visualize the last time she saw her mother, shipping off the young Laren to be raised by an older and ill-equipped uncle. She recalled her life on the streets and the girlfriend who pledged to stick by her side no matter what happened, but who bolted the first time a Cardassian caught them attempting a con.

What good is thinking about all this? Exhaustion took hold of her and threatened to drop her where she stood. Ro pushed away from the port and crossed back to her bedroom, where she flung her robe to the deck and threw herself onto the bed. She didn't know if she would be able to sleep, but she at least needed to rest. She had to try to clear her mind, even if she lay awake for hours.

Ro thought to concentrate on the darkness, but even

before she could order the computer to black out the lights in her cabin, slumber found her. While her body rested, her mind did not. Dreams descended on the captain, bringing with them bittersweet memories of a youth best left in the past.

Three

Market Exposure

Ro sat in the command chair in the Hub and listened to the overnight status report from Ensign Leo Lubitsch, the delta-shift duty officer that week. Mercifully, the watch had been quiet and nothing required the captain's attention. Ro copied Lubitsch's report from his padd to her own, then dismissed the ensign. She waited for Commander Blackmer to arrive, and when he did, she handed over the reins of the Hub to him and withdrew into her office.

Bleary-eyed, Ro dropped heavily into the seat behind her desk. She had slept fitfully, visited by dreams she could no longer recall, but which had done little to allow her unsettled mind to rest. She had awoken that morning still troubled, and by the time she'd made it to her office, anger had joined the emotional mix.

Ro directed her ire neither at Altek Dans nor at Kira Nerys, but at herself. It bothered her to feel jealousy, but she also found it disturbed her that she had let herself become vulnerable to such emotions in the first place. *I know better, don't I?* She had never been averse to love or commitment, to finding the right person to stay with for the long term—even if she doubted that she ever would—but in the absence of that, she had still striven to live a full, active, and mostly satisfying life. *Isn't that why I've had many of the relationships I've had—those that were more than a friendship, but less than a commitment? Isn't that why I haven't gotten more deeply involved with Quark?* Ro hated having to ask herself such questions.

The captain also ruminated about the Prophets apparently delivering Kira into Dans's life deep in Bajor's past, and then summoning both of them forward to the present. The circumstances made the time-travelers' relationship seem fated—even literally gods-given. *Which also means*

that Kira knew him first, Ro thought, and then she casti-
gated herself for what sounded like an idea more suited to a
lovesick teen than to the commanding officer of a starbase.

I don't want this, Ro told herself. *Living with this sort of
melodrama is not who I am.*

That quickly, Ro made a decision. "Captain to the Hub,"
she said.

"Blackmer here, Captain," her first officer replied at once.

"Jeff," she said, "I'd like to see you in my office."

ii

Quark stood amidships and pointed to the aft section of the
small but fleet scoutship he had contracted out of Nexvahl
IV. "Load that into the sleeping quarters," he told Flink, one
of the many Ferengi he employed as a waiter in the bar, but
who could also function as a stevedore when necessary. Quark
stepped aside as Flink used an antigrav to push aboard a
trunk—mostly filled with the barkeep's flamboyant clothing.

"I've programmed our course to Janus Six, boss," called
Zirk from up ahead, from inside the vessel's cockpit.
Though Zirk was another of Quark's waiters, his skills as a
pilot sometimes came in handy. "I've got the warp engine
powered up in standby mode."

Quark entered the cramped cockpit, which featured
only two seats, one forward and one rear. Zirk occupied
the chair at the main control console, and Quark sat down
behind him. "How long will the trip take?" he asked.

"Depends if this ship can maintain its advertised cruis-
ing speed," Zirk said. "I ran a diagnostic when it arrived this
morning, and the warp drive checks out, so I'd estimate
something just shy of two hundred hours." Quark hated to
be away from the bar for that long—at least a week to Janus
VI and another week back, plus however long it would take

him to deal with Mayereen Viray—but he hated having his latinum stolen even more.

Flink poked his head into the cockpit. "All done, boss," he said. "Is there anything else?"

"Just keep your ears on Treir while I'm gone." Quark didn't actually worry much about Treir stealing or otherwise betraying him in some way—she'd been working for him for almost ten years—but he also didn't fully trust her either. He based that not just on the 190th Rule of Acquisition, but on his own life experience; he had been disappointed more often than he cared to recall. "In fact, keep your ears on all my employees."

"Okay, boss." Flink ducked out of the cockpit and headed back to the starbase. Quark returned his attention to Zirk.

"You ran a diagnostic on the warp engine," he said. "Did you check out the rest of the ship's systems?"

"I tested the computer, life-support, the navigational system, the deflectors, the transporter, the emergency pod, and the sublight drive," Zirk said. "All matched or exceeded your requirements in the contract."

"Really?" Quark said, surprised. Despite the success he'd enjoyed with his establishment on Bajor, and how well business had gone aboard the new DS9, he usually anticipated setbacks. "How long will it be before we can get under way?"

"We can depart immediately," Zirk said. "I just need to coordinate with the dockmaster and—"

Quark interrupted Zirk by holding up a hand toward him, palm out. The barkeep thought he'd heard something—footfalls, arranged in a familiar gait. He listened closely, but they'd stopped. *But do I hear breathing? Is that—*

"Hello?"

The single word elicited a complex mix of emotions within Quark. He quickly stood up and looked out the cockpit doorway. In the external hatchway stood Ro Laren.

A rush of heat surged through Quark's lobes at the sight of her. The romance that they had nurtured for so long had in recent months begun to slip away. He tried to curb the plunge in the amount of time they spent together, he wanted to reverse the downward trajectory of their relationship, but despite his efforts, that hadn't happened. The loss of their intimacy saddened him, but the way she treated him the day before, the way she dismissed him when he sought her aid, made him angry.

"Captain," he said, his voice flat. "Are you here to apologize for not wanting to help me? Maybe by lending me a security officer for my trip?"

"Not exactly," Ro said. "But I did speak with Commander Desjardins in the JAG office. While you might have witnessed a crime from Deep Space Nine, and while you initiated a transfer of funds here under false pretenses, Viray's presence in Geopolis puts Janus Six's law enforcement squarely in charge of the matter."

Quark nodded. "Of course it does," he said with as much disdain as he could muster. "So you won't send one of your crew with me?"

"Not one of my crew, no," Ro said. She reached back through the hatchway and hoisted a travel duffel onto her shoulder. "*I* am going with you." Quark's mouth dropped open, and he made a conscious effort to close it. "If that's all right with you."

The prospect of spending any time at all with Laren thrilled Quark, and the idea of taking a journey with her that would last a minimum of two weeks sounded better than winning the Lissepian Lottery. He called back over his shoulder, "Zirk, I found another pilot. Go back to the bar and help Frool and Grimp with doing the inventory."

"Are you sure, boss?" Quark turned and glared at Zirk, who shrank back in his seat. "Okay, sorry, sorry."

He got up, squeezed past Quark, hied through the main compartment—which spanned the middle half of the vessel—and ducked into the sleeping quarters. He reappeared a moment later carrying his own travel bag. "Is there anything else you need?" he asked. Quark felt a quick surge of pride at how well he'd trained his employees.

"There's nothing else," Quark said. Zirk excused himself to the captain, who moved to one side so that he could exit.

Once he had gone, Ro said, "So when do we leave?"

"Right away," Quark said. He had actually intended to return to the bar and take care of some unrelated last-minute business, but he didn't want to risk something arising that could provoke Laren to change her mind.

"All right," she said, setting her duffel down inside the hatch. "Let's go."

Quark stepped out of the way so that Laren could enter the cockpit, then followed her inside and sat down behind her. He watched her as she executed a series of systems checks, her hands moving nimbly across the main console. "Would you close the hatch?" she asked as she worked, and he found the proper control on the auxiliary panel beside him.

Laren continued to work, until at last she spun in her chair to face him. "I have something for you," she said.

Quark didn't see anything in her hands, and she certainly didn't carry anything in her Starfleet uniform, but he liked the prospect of receiving a gift from Laren. He waited, and she lifted her hand and tapped on the main console. Quark craned his neck and saw a navigational display, which listed their destination not as Janus VI, but as Mericor. The change distressed him. As highly as he would value time alone with Laren, he still wanted to track down the duplicitous Mayereen Viray and retrieve the latinum she'd swindled from him.

"I have a friend at the spaceport in Geopolis," Ro said.

She stood up and left the cockpit, but raised her voice and continued talking. "I contacted her to confirm that your private investigator and possible thief was still there." Quark heard Ro rummaging through her duffel. "It turns out that Viray boarded a flight out of Janus Six yesterday." She quieted for a moment, then returned to the cockpit with a padd, which she handed to Quark. On the display, he saw a paused image of Viray. He touched the screen, and a clip played of the Petarian woman boarding a ship. "My friend secured this sequence from spaceport surveillance," Ro said as she sat back down at the main console. "That ship is a Mizarian transport headed for Mericor. Depending on their route and speed, we might be able to get there before Viray. We should be able to reach the planet in two days or so."

Quark took in what he heard and tried to process it. Beyond the obvious value of the information he'd just received, it also touched him that Laren had gone out of her way to help him track down his lost profits. Unfortunately, a journey to Mericor rather than to Janus VI would mean considerably less time alone with her. Still, Quark would take it.

"The sooner we leave, the sooner we'll get there," he said.

Ro swung back to the console and operated the controls. "Nexvahl vessel to Deep Space Nine," she said. "Requesting exit vector and immediate departure."

Five minutes later, the scoutship raced away from the starbase on a heading for Mericor. Quark was alone with the woman he loved—a Starfleet captain—on a quest for latinum. It seemed like a fantasy.

If this is a dream, Quark thought, *I don't want to wake up.*

iii

The space had been decorated with a simplicity and soft beauty that Kira found welcoming in the most unobtrusive way. Understated yellow lighting suffused the air like early-morning sunlight, just before dawn. Brighter beams picked out several pieces of hanging abstract artwork. A number of chairs and curved benches offered comfortable seating, and a lazy stream of water seeped from a fountain in one corner. The setting put Kira in mind of a Bajoran temple.

Which makes sense, Kira thought, *since it's the kai's ship.*

Though unnamed—Pralon Onala did not care much for pomp—the ship belonged to a group of vessels permanently at the kai's disposal. The transport had arrived at DS9 during the night, and its master—a man named Beren Togg—had left Kira a message that she'd received upon rising that morning. The ship would depart for Bajor at ten hundred hours.

"This is the passenger lounge," said Jamay Pal, who had introduced herself as an aide to the kai, and who'd barely been able to contain her wonderment at Kira's return from being MIA in the Celestial Temple. Pralon had not made the voyage to DS9, Jamay explained, because she preferred to remain on Bajor while the controversy surrounding the Endalla falsework continued to unfold. "You may relax here during the trip, or if you prefer, I can offer you a private cabin."

"This will be fine, thank you." Alone in the passenger lounge, Kira would have all the privacy she needed.

"Would you care for something to eat or drink, Vedek?" Jamay asked.

"No, thank you."

"If you would like something later, you may contact me, or there's a replicator in an alcove down the next corridor." Jamay motioned to the passage, which ran aft from the lounge. "You'll find a refresher down that way as well."

"Thank you."

"We will be departing shortly," Jamay said, "just as soon as our other passenger arrives." Before Kira could ask who would be joining her on the way to Bajor, a figure appeared in the forward doorway: Altek Dans. Kira felt something like an electric charge jolt through her. She had yet to overcome the shock of seeing him the previous night, of realizing in what context the two had known each other—known each other, and more.

Jamay greeted Altek with the same information she had provided Kira. The kai's aide offered him refreshments and the option of traveling in a private cabin, both of which he declined, and then Jamay pointed out the locations of the replicator and refresher. "Now that you're both here," she said, "we will be leaving Deep Space Nine and heading for Bajor at once. If either of you require anything at all during the trip, please let me know." Jamay exited the lounge, leaving Kira and Altek alone. The moment felt immediately awkward.

"It's good to see you again," Altek said. An inactive padd dangled from his right hand.

Kira regarded him, unsure what she should say. She opted to ask the most basic question of all. "What are you doing here?"

"Here in the future? I have no idea," Altek said with a smile, apparently trying to make a joke. "As far as being on the ship, I was contacted by Kai Pralon this morning. She told me that she had spoken directly with the first minister and the minister of state, and that I finally have full clearance to go to Bajor. The kai said that she'd sent a ship to bring you home, and she invited me to come along. I took the opportunity because . . . well, because I wanted to go to Bajor, but also because I wanted to see you again . . . to speak with you."

Kira nodded, then slowly paced away from him across the lounge. She realized that she not only didn't know what to say to Altek, she didn't know what to think or feel either. After seeing him again the prior night, after recognizing him, she'd concluded that his journey out of history, like her own travels through time, must have been effected by the Prophets, but that didn't mean that she understood why she and Altek had been brought together, either in the past or in the present.

When Kira reached the gently burbling fountain, she turned back to face Altek. As she formulated what to say to him, he spoke first. "I didn't get much sleep last night. My mind kept racing through the time we spent together, back during my life on Bajor." He started toward Kira, but stopped halfway across the lounge and sat down on a bench, setting his padd down beside him. He leaned forward and placed his arms on his knees, his eyes focused on his steepled hands, his manner suddenly serious. "When I first ended up here, on Deep Space Nine, my recollections were confusing and not as sharp as they had been previously, and in the months since, they've been dulling even further. It's harder and harder to visualize the faces of the people I once knew, to recall the places and events that made up my life prior to coming here. But when I saw you last night . . ." Altek looked up, and Kira saw hope in his eyes. "When I saw you, a lot of memories came flooding back . . . memories of you . . . memories of *us*."

"I know," Kira said. "I mean, I remembered you too. That period of time came back to me, or some of it did, anyway. A lot of it's still foggy, but I do recall the gild . . . our efforts in Joradell . . ." Her voice trailed into silence. She did not want to reveal how the emotion of that time had welled up within her. Those old feelings seemed genuine, but also peculiar: she had grown to know Altek, and to love him, while in the identity of another person, another life—and yet, somehow, she had still looked the same, had still been herself.

"I know that this is a strange situation," Altek said, perhaps reading Kira's low-level anxiety. "It hasn't been easy trying to believe what's happened to me; I would have had less trouble thinking that I'd gone mad. I've had to accept that I traveled far into the future, and I've had to accept the astonishing reality of my new circumstances." He sat up and held his arms out wide, palms up. "I'm in a ship, flying from a starbase, through space, to a planet where I once lived hundreds or thousands of years ago, where everybody I ever knew lived . . . and died."

Altek dropped his hands down into his lap. He looked defeated. Kira walked forward and sat down beside him on the bench. "I'm sorry," she said. "It must be incredibly difficult for you."

"It is," Altek said. "But it's also been getting better, getting easier . . . but then when I saw you last night . . ." He shrugged. "It's all so confusing. All that's happened has left me in awe of the Prophets, but I also want to understand what it all means, and I don't. Why have the Prophets brought me here and now? And what do They expect of me?"

"I understand," Kira said. Her designation by the Prophets as Their Hand had come with no list of expectations, no instructions on what she should do or how she should do it.

"Since seeing you again last night, I've also been wondering about your part in all of this," Altek said. "What was the purpose of you living as Keev Anora?"

"I don't think it's reasonable to think that we can comprehend the will of the Prophets," Kira said. "But maybe the answer is simple: maybe I was there just to help free Bajorans from slavery."

"Maybe," Altek said, though without conviction. "How much do you remember?" He looked at her beseechingly, revealing without words what he truly wanted to know.

"I recall things in waves, but so far, my memories haven't been able to withstand my examination of them. It's like an image you can perceive in your peripheral vision, but that you can't see if you look directly at it. I do have a sense of our time together, even if I can't bring many particulars to mind." Kira hesitated. Another explanation had occurred to her, but she knew that Altek would resist it. She had to tell him anyway. "I can't even be certain that what I experienced didn't happen only in my mind—in our minds—or as some sort of simulation, rather than in reality."

"That's not how it was," Altek said, rejecting the possibility outright. "We met after I chased you through a wood outside Joradell. You raced to the gild, and I ran directly into their midst. If not for Veralla Sil's composure, I probably would have been killed right then . . . possibly by you."

As Altek spoke, images flashed across Kira's mind. "I remember at least some of that," she told him, "but I can't tell if I'm remembering actual events or something that took place in my mind—an Orb experience, or a pagh'tem'far, or even just a dream."

"Our time together wasn't just a dream," Altek said definitively.

Kira could see that he believed that, and in truth, so did she. But she also couldn't dismiss the other possibilities without cause. Her own life experience had taught her that obvious explanations, no matter how compelling, did not always mesh with reality. And after what Ro had told her about the shape-shifting Ascendant life-form that had taken up residence within the wormhole, she also had to allow for the chance that what she and Altek remembered could have been events in a setting created by that link— like a living holosuite. She could have explained that to Altek, but for the moment, she chose not to, for fear of agitating him even more.

They sat together quietly for a few moments. Kira considered contacting Jamay and requesting a cabin for herself, just to give Altek some space, to allow him to work out the emotions clearly roiling within him. *Or maybe to make it easier on me,* Kira thought. She did not find the present situation particularly comfortable, but she didn't think she should allow such a consideration to outweigh Altek's obvious distress. "What can I do to help?" she asked.

Altek met her gaze. "I loved Anora," he said. "I loved *you.*"

The declaration inspired both joy and fear in Kira. She decided to tread carefully. "Anora loved you too," she said, "but that was a very long time ago."

"It hasn't been a long time for me," Altek said. "I last saw you just a few months ago." It had been longer for Kira, she thought, but after her time in the Celestial Temple and in the Gamma Quadrant, she couldn't precisely pinpoint the interval for her. "I never thought I'd see you again, but I . . . I still love you."

Kira's heart quickened with Altek's words, but she also felt the conflicting impulse to dash from the lounge. Before she could settle on how to respond, Altek leaned toward her and slowly, gently pressed his lips to hers. Kira recognized the feel of his kiss, and the sensation rekindled the emotions she felt for him.

Or that Keev Anora felt for him.

Kira felt wildly uncomfortable with how quickly and unexpectedly she and Altek had gotten to that point. Only the night before, it had been startling to see him again, a man pulled from her hazy past and unexpectedly reintroduced into her present. When they pulled back from each other and gazed into each other's eyes, Kira decided to say something to slow down the situation. She could not even consider her feelings for Altek until she returned to the life she had built for herself on Bajor, until she had fully acclimated back into her vedek's existence. Before she could say anything, though, Altek spoke.

"We should move forward carefully," he said. "We should

get to know each other again. We've both been through so much . . . we need time to get used to our reunion."

Kira didn't know if he voiced his actual thoughts on the matter, or if he simply wanted to tell her what he thought she wanted to hear, but she agreed with him, and she told him so. He smiled at her, a forlorn sort of expression that appeared to capture both his ardor and his uncertainty. Those emotions reflected Kira's own frame of mind.

In an attempt to get past the moment, Kira pointed to the padd sitting on the bench beside Altek. "What are you reading?" she asked. Altek picked up the device and activated it. The display showed a conformal map projection of Bajor.

"I've been studying both modern and historical Bajor for months," he said. "I've been trying to find even the slightest correspondence with the Bajor of my time."

"Any luck?"

"No," he said, then pointed at the map. "The oceans and land masses are essentially the same, and the mountain ranges and rivers seem right, at least from what I can remember, but that hasn't really helped. All it tells me is what I already know: I've traveled into Bajor's future." He paused, then added, "I just wish I knew why." He sounded anguished.

"I know you do," Kira said. "Remember that I'm in a similar situation: the Prophets have sent me backward and forward through time, with no roadmap for what I should do." She did not mention that she believed she had fulfilled her role as Their Hand by facilitating Taran'atar's arrival at Bajor, aboard *Even Odds*, in time to thwart the Ascendant attack led by Iliana Ghemor. "I worried about how I could determine what They wanted me to do, but I think now that all I needed to do was to have faith—in Them and in myself—and to believe I would rise to the occasion without trying to put myself in the mind-set of the Prophets."

"So when I get to Bajor . . . what?" he asked.

"Just do what feels right," Kira said. "The Prophets have laid out a path for you. You may not know where it's headed, but all you need to do is keep walking."

Altek appeared to think about that for a few seconds. "Maybe you're right," he said at last. Kira didn't know if he believed what he said, or if he wanted to convince himself of it, but then he smiled. "I'll try."

iv

Candlewood pulled on the control arm, sending the wheels in the slot machine spinning. He watched contentedly as the pictures hummed past, surprisingly satisfied playing the game of chance. He'd thought that his having no discernible effect on the outcome would necessarily hinder his enjoyment of the diversion. Instead, he found a thrill in the randomness, of the nonzero possibility of winning with no help from skill or strategy. The effort required in hauling down the mechanical arm, the purr of the rotating drums, the blur of the figures—cherries, bells, horseshoes, and others—as they spun past, all contributed to the experience. Anticipation gripped Candlewood as the reels one by one thumped to a stop: Cherry. Bar. The number 7. A loser.

It didn't matter. The failure to win just strengthened Candlewood's desire to play, to attempt to recoup his losses. The money, which Nog had provided, meant nothing to him, not just in terms of his living in the twenty-fourth-century Federation, but because his capital existed only holographically.

"Would you care for something to drink, sir?" The waitress carried a circular tray with a troop of empty glasses atop it. She wore a sequined red blouse above a pleated black skirt. A nametag identified her as DONNA.

"Yes, I would," Candlewood said. "I'd like a ginger ale, please." The waitress repeated his request and made a notation on a pad on her tray, deftly handling her load of glassware. As she began to walk away, Candlewood called after her. "Oh, Donna," he said, and she looked back over her shoulder.

"Sir?"

"Do you know who's singing in the main lounge tonight?" Candlewood asked.

"The headliner is Faith Shay," Donna said. "Her show starts at nine."

"Thanks," Candlewood said, and then, as nonchalantly as he could, he asked, "Didn't you used to have a man singing in the main lounge?"

"Yes, but that was a year or two ago. Miss Shay's been with us for a while now."

"I look forward to hearing her." Candlewood waited just long enough to make his next question appear an afterthought. "Whatever happened to Vic Fontaine?"

"You know, I'm not sure," the waitress said. "He must be singing somewhere else in town."

"Okay, thanks," Candlewood said, not wanting to push the issue and draw attention to his questions. He and Nog had spent most of the day in the hotel and casino, occasionally playing various casino games as cover, and casually speaking with employees in an effort to collect information about Vic. They hoped to learn some detail that would help them figure out who had abducted the singer, where they had taken him, and how the two Starfleet officers could free him. To this point, they'd had little success, other than to find out that Vic had probably stopped performing at the Shining Oasis not long after the original Deep Space 9 had been destroyed. Nog wondered if the loss of the station and the subsequent loading of Vic's program into a simulation tester had caused something within the code to go wrong, but Candlewood had no idea why that would be the case.

The science officer loaded another coin into the slot machine, then pulled down on its arm. The wheels whirled into motion. Candlewood watched as a set of cherries thumped into place, and then a second set. For an instant, his excitement built, but then a horseshoe appeared in the final position. Still, the machine dropped two coins into the payout tray with a pair of pleasing *clink*s.

"Dabo," said a voice behind him, as though he had just won a jackpot in the Ferengi gambling game. Candlewood looked up to see that Nog had rejoined him.

"Don't laugh," Candlewood said. "This place probably has better payoffs than your uncle's dabo wheel."

"Don't be too sure," Nog said. "Have you found out anything?"

"Not much," Candlewood said. "The people I've spoken with say that Vic stopped singing here within the last couple of years. They don't know why, and they don't know where he's gone."

"I got the same information."

"So now what do we do?"

Nog pulled up the cuffs of his shirt and jacket and examined a timepiece he had purchased earlier. "We've got a little while before the show starts," he said. "Let's try Vic's apartment again." Throughout the day, they had knocked on the door to the hotel suite the singer had once called home. They'd received no response, and the corridor had been busy enough that Nog hadn't wanted to risk breaking in; in their quest to help Vic, they did not need to be detained for any period of time—or worse, end up in jail.

Candlewood retrieved the cup holding his coins, stood up, and started to walk with Nog, then remembered his last minor victory. He darted back to the slot machine and retrieved his two coins. Before dropping them into the cup, he held them up for Nog to see. "Any profit is good profit," Candlewood said. "Is that a Rule of Acquisition?"

"It's more of an axiom."

The two men made their way through the flash and clatter of the casino, until they reached the enclosed walkway to the hotel complex. When they made it to the proper building and suite 107, they found the corridor empty. Nog looked in both directions, then whispered, "If he's not here, I'm going to pick the lock and let myself in." Candlewood agreed, then knocked on the door. To his surprise, it opened immediately.

"Yes?" asked a statuesque redhead.

Nog's eyebrows lifted in an expression of possibility. Candlewood assumed that Vic had been known to entertain, and that the operations chief hoped that the woman was one of the singer's guests.

"We'd like to see Vic, please," Nog said.

"Sorry," the woman said. "You got the wrong room, fellas." Candlewood peered past her into the suite. He saw a wall of pink curtains opposite, and a selection of furniture dressed in similar reddish tones, some lighter, some darker, but all distinctly feminine. The woman started to close the door, but Nog stamped his foot down to stop it.

"Wait," he said. "Vic Fontaine doesn't live here?"

"I told you," the woman said, annoyance in her tone, "you got the wrong room."

"Nog," Candlewood said quietly, "look." The science officer pointed past the woman. "Does that seem like Vic's décor?"

Nog ducked his head to the side, to gaze past the woman. After a few seconds, he looked up at her. "Do you know Vic Fontaine?" he asked her. "He used to live here."

"Never heard of him," the woman said. "Now, if you don't mind, I need to get ready for a date."

"Excuse the interruption, ma'am," Candlewood said. He reached over to Nog and tapped him on the shoulder, urging him to withdraw. Nog stepped back, and the woman closed the door. "I'm sorry," Candlewood said, "but that didn't look anything like a place Vic would live."

"No, you're right," Nog said. "I've been here before, when he did live here, and it didn't look like that."

"You shouldn't be surprised or disappointed," Candlewood said. "You saw Vic get abducted, and we know from everybody we've spoken to that he hasn't been here for a while."

"I know, I know," Nog said. "I was just hoping that this might still be his apartment, and that we might be able to find some clues about what's happened." He sounded disconsolate.

"Look, we really didn't expect to learn anything today," Candlewood reminded him. "Tonight is when you thought we might be able to finally find out something."

"Right," Nog said. "You're right." He checked the timepiece on his wrist again. "The show's about to start."

"All right," Candlewood said. "Then let's go."

V

The woman on stage—long and lean in a sultry wine-colored dress, with wavy dark hair that tumbled down to the small of her back—belted out a song in a way that her predecessor never had. Nog loved Vic's smooth voice, his velvety tones and punchy phrasing, but Faith Shay delivered her music with impressive power. The operations chief hadn't really been able to enjoy her singing, though, because he looked forward throughout the show for that first set to come to a close.

When Shay finally sang her last note, took a bow, and

announced that she would return after a short break, Nog moved quickly. "Come on," he told Candlewood. Nog stood up and led his crewmate over to the right-hand side of the curved stage. Nog watched as the musicians set down their instruments. He recognized only one of them, the bassist, whom he'd seen in the background of the poster advertising Shay's appearance at the Shining Oasis. "Cool Papa," Nog called in a stage whisper.

A couple of the musicians peered over, including the bassist. The man had dark, leathery skin, and a dusting of gray colored his close-cropped, curly hair. He looked first at Candlewood, and then at Nog. When he saw the operations chief, he finished placing his instrument in a stand, then made his way over to the side of the stage and stepped down to the floor of the lounge.

"Nog," he said in a raspy voice. He always sounded as though he might have just swallowed a handful of gravel. "Been a while." He held out his hand, which Nog gripped in his own, feeling the roughness of the man's long, callused fingers. An angry scar the operations chief didn't recall creased the man's left temple.

"Quite a while," Nog agreed. "Do you have a few minutes to talk?"

"How come I think I know what this is about?" the man asked, though the question seemed rhetorical. He nodded toward Candlewood. "Who's your friend?"

"This is John Candlewood," Nog said. "John, this is Vernon Owens."

"Only my mama calls me Vernon. I've been 'Cool Papa' just about as long as I can remember." He reached out to the science officer. "Good to meet you."

"Nice to meet you," Candlewood said, shaking Owens's hand.

"So what can I do for you, Nog?" Owens asked.

"I was hoping I could ask you some questions about Vic."

Owens reacted by peering around the lounge, as though checking to see who might be observing their conversation. He kept his manner casual, but Nog perceived a nervousness about him. "Haven't seen the man," Owens said. "Don't know where he might be these days."

Despite the disclaimer, Owens's manner conveyed a different message. Nog dropped the volume of his voice so that he would not be overheard. "We know Vic's in trouble," he said. "That's why we're here. We want to help him."

Owens hesitated. "I know you're friends with Vic," he said, "but I'm not sure you can do anything for him."

"Then you do know what's happened to him," Nog said, excited at the chance of finding out something that would lead them to Vic. "What can you tell us?"

Owens took a long time to respond. Finally, he said, "I don't know nuthin'."

Nog's eyes narrowed. It didn't require the instincts of a Ferengi to see that Owens *did* have information about Vic. "You clearly do know something."

"Sorry, man. I gotta get ready for the next set." Owens started for the steps leading up to the back of the stage.

"Cool Papa," Nog said, his voice still low, but carrying the urgency he felt. "You said you knew I was Vic's friend, so please let me help him. Tell me what you know."

Again, Owens looked around, then walked back over to Nog. "Not here." He reached into a pocket of his suit jacket, didn't find what he wanted, then reached into another pocket. He pulled out a packet of matches, followed by a stub of pencil. He quickly scribbled something on the matchbook cover and pushed it into Nog's hand. "Meet me there," Owens said, his eyes once more scanning the lounge. "Two thirty."

Before Nog could respond, Owens climbed back up onto the stage. He paced over to his bass and took a moment to examine something there. Then he walked offstage, disappearing into the wing opposite the two Starfleet officers.

"What did he write?" Candlewood asked.

Nog inspected the matchbook. "It's an address and an apartment number."

"Is it Owens's address?"

"I don't know, but I guess we'll find out," Nog said. "Let's go back to the suite and find it on the map."

As the two men started out of the lounge, Candlewood said, "I wonder why he was so wary of talking about Vic."

"I don't know," Nog said. "But I don't think he was just wary. He was also scared."

vi

Ro studied her cards carefully. She didn't often play tabletop games. For that matter, she didn't much care for sports, other than solo events in which she could challenge herself. In her experience, competition mostly brought out the worst traits in people—not just in Bajorans, but in Ferengi, humans, Klingons, and numerous other species. Of course, most Ferengi men lived in a perpetually competitive state, striving virtually every moment of every day to "win" by accumulating more wealth.

And yet despite all that, she thought, *here I am playing cards with a Ferengi man and having a good time doing it.*

Seated in the passenger cabin of the Nexvahl vessel, Ro selected two of her cards—a green *2* and a blue *8*—and set them faceup on the table in front of her. "Collecting value," she said, trying to sound surer than she felt. Although she and Quark had occasionally played various games over the years, including the current one, Ro had never quite gotten accustomed to Antarean decks, which consisted of round cards of various colors based on a hexadecimal numbering system.

Quark quickly reached forward and tapped at the padd sitting beside the cards on the table. "I'll double the bet." On the display, the number *6400* became *12800*.

"Again?" Ro said.

"What are you complaining about?" Quark asked. "You keep winning."

"You can relax, you know. We're not playing for actual latinum."

"Which is a fortunate thing for me," Quark said, "considering the paltry finances of Federation citizens. I'd never be able to collect."

"What we lack in funds, we make up for in charm," Ro countered.

"I don't know about the rest of the Federation," Quark said, "but *you* certainly do." He picked up his cup of snail juice—she'd ordered it extra smooth for him—and toasted Ro. "Of course," Quark added, "we Ferengi have both finances *and* charm."

Ro smiled, picked up her glass of *pooncheenee*, and raised it toward Quark. "I don't know about other Ferengi," she said, "but *you* certainly do."

Quark threw his head back and laughed, a hoarse, guttural sound that nevertheless delighted Ro. It had been a while since the two of them had spent any real time with each other, and it pleased her that they could so easily find their way back to joking and having fun together. She realized that, despite whatever else had taken place in her life, she genuinely missed Quark.

"Kind words," he said around his sharp, skewed teeth, "but do you accept the wager?"

"Why not?" Ro said, hitting a control on the padd to

confirm the bet. "By the time we get back to Deep Space Nine, you'll probably own the whole starbase."

"If I do, I'll leave you in command."

"Aren't I the lucky captain?" Ro said, also smiling. "But I think you're stalling, which means you were trying to bluff me."

"Ferengi never bluff," Quark said, putting on a serious expression. Ro couldn't help but howl in laughter.

"Ferengi *always* bluff. Now go." Quark chose a card from his hand and tossed it atop Ro's green *2*; it was an orange *2*. "I knew it," Ro said, and she swept up the pair and added them to her pile. "What else have you got?"

"Nothing on the eight," Quark said, and he dutifully pushed it into the discard patch. Then he took two of his own cards and played: a *4* and an *E*, both of them blue. "Collecting color."

"Nothing on blue," Ro said quickly, then she scarfed up the *4* and put it in her hand. She arranged her cards and laid them down. To one side, she set her discards, but directly before her, she placed two *B*s, a *C*, and the *4* she had just acquired from Quark. "*Fizzbin!*"

"Fizzbin?" Quark groused. "You need a *D* and a two, not a *C* and a four."

Ro hiked a thumb over her shoulder, pointing at the port in the starboard side of the ship. "The stars are out, so it's night," she said. "That means I have a fizzbin."

"But it's probably daytime on Beta Antares Four," Quark argued.

"But it's night on Deep Space Nine, and that's where this voyage originated."

"All right, all right, you win," Quark said, tossing his cards down and holding his hands up in supplication.

"Which means it's your turn to check the ship's status."

Quark leaped to his feet. "Yes, Captain," he said, offering up some convoluted gesture with his hand that might've passed for a salute somewhere in the galaxy. Ro snickered as he marched into the cockpit. As she waited for him to return, she picked up her glass of pooncheenee and sat back in her chair. "The autopilot reads optimal," Quark called back to her. "The ship is on course and maintaining velocity. Navigational deflectors are up full." If any of that hadn't been the case, the onboard computer should have notified them, but it always paid to verify the performance of an unfamiliar vessel, even one with a valid operating certificate.

Ro sipped at her fruit juice. As Quark came back from the cockpit, a thought popped into her head. "We don't have a name for this ship," she said.

Quark walked over to the external hatch and pointed to a small plaque beside it. "Technically, it's Nexvahl Scoutship Seven-Eight-One-Eight dash Seven-Three."

"That's not really a name so much as a designation," Ro said. "We can do better than that."

"All right," Quark said. "How about . . . *Laren*?"

"That's a little dull, wouldn't you say?"

"All right, then, how about *Laren's Latinum*?"

"Which would mean it didn't exist," Ro said, though she found Quark's attempt to name the ship after her sweet. "It should have something to do with the reason we're aboard."

"*Tracking Down Quark's Stolen Latinum* doesn't exactly sound like poetry."

"No, but what about *Quark's Quest*?" Ro watched his reaction: a grin from ear to ear. *Which has to mean more when you say it of a Ferengi.*

"I like it," Quark said. He walked over and settled himself back in his chair. "Shall we play another game?"

Normally, Ro would have demurred, but she could not deny how much she had so far enjoyed their journey. She shrugged. "I'll be happy to take all your virtual latinum before we get to Mericor," she teased. She scooped up her winning cards and mixed them in with the spread of discards, aligned them, and reached for Quark's hand. As she gathered up his cards, it surprised her to see red and yellow among them . . . and also a *4* . . . and— "Hey," she said. "You knew I wasn't playing for green or blue, so why didn't you try for the other colors? And why did you throw down a four when you had another one in your hand?" She peered across at him.

"I guess I'm not on my game tonight," he said, but Ro could see a flush crawling up his lobes.

"You let me win," Ro said, astonished. She would never expect a Ferengi, even among friends, to willingly lose a game, whether playing for genuine stakes or not. "I can't believe it."

"I wouldn't say I 'let' you win."

"You did," she said, the mealy character of his denial confirming her suspicion.

"It's not as though we're playing for real latinum," he said, but something in his manner told her that the nature of the stakes had nothing at all to do with his decision to throw the game.

"You can't fool me, Quark," she said, pointing at him across the table. "You *wanted* me to win, and that wouldn't have changed even if were betting actual latinum." She shook her head. "I can't believe you would forfeit profit like that."

"I wouldn't count it as forfeiting profit," he said.

"Of course it would be."

"No," Quark said, his tone defensive. "Not if I hoped that, one day, we would commingle our finances—" He abruptly shut his mouth, as though to prevent himself from saying something he shouldn't.

Except he already said too much, didn't he? Ro realized that Quark had essentially revealed his plans at some point to essentially propose a romantic commitment between them—not just an extension of what they'd shared, off and on, for the better part of a decade, but more than that.

"Quark," she said, "I don't know how to react."

"There's nothing to react to." He waved his hand dismissively through the air. "Forget I said anything. Deal the cards."

"I can't forget," she said. "I won't forget." Ro could have stopped speaking at that point—she *wanted* to stop. She could have dealt the cards and let the conversation move on to another subject. Instead, she set the deck down on the table. She owed Quark more than that. "I'm sorry," she said quietly. "I don't see us ever—"

Ever what? Making a long-term commitment to each other? Getting married? Ro found it difficult to choose her words, and so she opted to use his. "I don't see us ever commingling our finances."

"I have enough reserves now for both of us," Quark said, a statement that, for a Ferengi, amounted to a declaration of love. "We have so much in common, and we obviously enjoy being together."

"I know," Ro agreed. "Already, this trip has been a tonic for me. I can't tell you how much our time together means."

"You can try," Quark said meekly.

"You're right, I can," Ro said. "But you already know because we've been doing this for a long time. But as close as we are, as much as we do have in common, we're still very different people."

"Every pair of people in the universe are different," Quark said. He stood up and paced away, though he couldn't go far in the small compartment. Near the aft doorway, which led to the sleeping quarters, he said, "Our distinctions make us who we are, and what does it matter if the people we are care for each other?"

"All of that's true, Quark," Ro said, but she knew that she needed to be wholly honest with him. She'd known that all along. She never wanted to hurt him, but Ro had to admit that she didn't avoid doing so solely for his sake; she selfishly wanted to avoid the distress that comes along with breaking somebody's heart.

I took the easy way out, she thought. *I took the coward's way out.* She told herself that she had to stop doing that, and she had to stop at once.

"You must know how much I care for you," she said.

"I used to know," Quark said, "but not for a while now."

"I can understand that," Ro said. "But I still care for you. That hasn't changed." She tried to steel herself for what she knew would come next. "What has changed is that I developed feelings for somebody else."

"For somebody else," Quark said, his tone accusatory. "You mean for Altek Dans."

Ro felt ashamed that Quark already knew about her relationship with Dans. "I'm sorry," she said. "I should have told you sooner. You should've found out about it from me."

"I did find out about it from you," Quark spat, disgusted.

"What? I never said anything to you."

"Not to me, no," Quark said. "But I have ears. I hear things."

"What things?"

"Things like your tone of voice when you talk to him."

"I'm sorry," Ro said again. "I should have told you sooner, but even if I had, it wouldn't have changed our situation."

"It would have for me."

"Yes, of course, you're right," Ro said. "But whatever I had with Dans is over now. The point isn't that I'm carrying a torch for somebody else; it's that I could develop an emotional attachment to another person while I was involved with you."

"So it's my fault?"

"No, no, I'm not saying that at all," Ro told him. "The pain you feel is because of me. Part of it's because of my negligence in not being open with you about Dans, but part of it is about my feelings for you. I love you, Quark, and I value you being in my life, but not in a way that will allow me to make a long-term commitment to you."

"You already said that."

"Quark, I really am sorry," Ro said.

"Yeah," Quark said. "So am I." Without another word, he stalked off to the aft section of the vessel, leaving Ro alone with her guilt.

vii

Kira sat on the floor, her back against the wall, her knees up, a padd propped on her thighs. She felt comfortable— no, not comfortable, but *normal*, as though the fabric of her life, torn into shreds, had finally been stitched whole. Her existence had been a patchwork of sorts, but the one thread sewn through all the pieces—through the Resistance, Deep Space 9, the Dominion War, the clergy, the Celestial Temple and the past, Taran'atar and the Ascendants—the one thread unifying it all had been Bajor. Even before reaching an age when she could understand about the Prophets, before faith blossomed within her, she accepted the idea of *home*. Growing up under the yoke of Cardassian oppression, she could not tie the concept to a residence of any kind, and the refugee camps were places to stay, but often became inhumane prisons, or worse, killing fields. Throughout her teenage years into her twenties, during her years battling the Occupation, she lived on the run. But through all that time, she held fast to a free Bajor, birthplace to her people, and the objective for which they risked their lives.

In the large but sparingly furnished room she had been provided in the Shikina Monastery, Kira closed her eyes and breathed in deeply. The evening air smelled rich, heavy with the scent of summer blossoms—*kidu* and *esani* and *nerak*. She could taste the metallic tang of ozone from a thunderstorm that had passed through Ashalla late that afternoon. In the cool touch of the stone floor beneath her, in the silence and stillness permeating the cloister, a familiar tranquility nestled her in its folds. Kira accepted it, allowed it to fill her, cherished what her years in the clergy had taught her to think of as a more mature sense of home: inner peace.

Minutes slipped past. Kira concentrated on her breathing, focused her attention on the emptiness of the void and the fullness of time. Her lips remained closed, but by degrees, she began in her mind to hum the ancient, wordless music of clerical meditation.

At last, Kira opened her eyes, prepared to carry on—with her day, with her calling, with her life. After arriving on Bajor from DS9 that afternoon, she and Altek had been transported to the monastery, where they'd parted ways, each taken to their own accommodations in the hostelry. Although Kira had yet to see the kai, Pralon's staff had visited throughout the day, at first bringing greetings from Her Eminence, and then sustenance, and finally information.

Kira reactivated her padd so that she could continue studying the materials that the kai's staff had provided. She read through Starfleet accounts about the assault on Endalla and the discovery of the falsework. She watched members of the Ohalavaru—including such highly regarded vedeks as Solis Tendren and Garune Sysha—deliver spirited oratory to public gatherings of their followers. She saw engineering efforts to fashion a working environment on Endalla, and heated debates in the Vedek Assembly. More than anything else, though, she focused on the incidents of unrest that had plagued her homeworld over the past seven weeks, and which appeared to be escalating.

As Kira read a troubling report about the discovery of an explosive device at an Ohalavaru sanctuary, a distant sound infiltrated her awareness. She looked up from her padd and listened, but could not identify what she heard. She set the padd down, rose to her feet, and, following the sound, crossed the high-ceilinged room to an open archway that led to a balcony. Outside, she peered over the waist-high balustrade toward the tall main gates at the front of the monastery grounds—gates that, until that moment, Kira couldn't recall ever before seeing closed. A large crowd had gathered outside the entrance. The vedek couldn't discern much detail among the people milling about, their individual voices lost in the collective hum of the assemblage. She supposed that it could be a demonstration by the Ohalavaru, but something— perhaps the considerable size of the throng—suggested to her that people of her own faith had congregated.

"They feel lost," Kira heard somebody say behind her. She turned, not startled, both because she recognized the voice and because she had intentionally left her door standing wide, just as she often had during her years at the Vanadwan Monastery. Many vedeks engaged in the practice, a symbolic gesture meant to signify the openness of the clergy. "Forgive the intrusion," Kai Pralon said. "Your door was not closed."

"Please come in, Eminence." Kira stepped in from the balcony as the kai walked into the room from the entry hall. The vedek stopped when she reached Pralon, and she bowed her head before the Bajoran spiritual leader in a show of respect. The kai reached for Kira's ear and grasped her lobe between thumb and forefinger. The vedek felt a gentle warmth overtake her, like the effect of a summer breeze.

"Your *pagh* is strong," Pralon said after a moment. "Somewhat scattered, but settling."

"Yes, Eminence," Kira said. "Scattered from the last time I was here to my time here now, into the Celestial Temple and out of it, from the Gamma Quadrant to the Alpha Quadrant to Deep Space Nine."

"And finally back to Bajor," the kai said. "Welcome home, Vedek Kira."

"Thank you, Eminence."

Pralon released Kira's ear and gazed past the vedek toward the balcony. When the kai padded in that direction, Kira accompanied her. Outside, they stood together and observed the milling crowd in the distance.

"I don't think I've ever seen the gates of the monastery closed," Kira said.

"From time to time, there is a need," Pralon said. "In most cases, as in this one, it is troubling."

"I assume the gathering is about the falsework."

"These days, I'm afraid, that is just about all that concerns the people of Bajor," the kai said. "The discovery on Endalla is consuming public discourse, and not for the better. Debates are loud, and sometimes shrill, with a great deal of talking and very little listening. People demonize each other for differing beliefs. It is both turbulent and disquieting."

"I understand that there have been acts of violence," Kira said.

"A few isolated incidents so far," Pralon said, "but there have been recent hints of coordination and threats of escalation."

"I was just reading about a bomb placed in Rimanabod," Kira said.

"At the Ohalu shrine there, yes," Pralon said. "Fortunately, the perpetrator, or somebody aware of their efforts, contacted authorities in time to prevent any casualties or damage. I was notified just before coming here that an arrest has been made."

"It's very troubling," Kira said.

"It is indeed," the kai said. "In the decade since the Prophecies of Ohalu were released to the public, the threat of extremism has almost always come from a handful of the Ohalavaru." Pralon did not mention that Kira had been the one to upload the Ohalu texts to the Bajoran comnet, but the vedek remained keenly aware of her role in bringing those works to light. "Since the discovery on Endalla, that has changed, and the Ohalavaru have found themselves targeted as well."

"What about those demonstrators?" Kira asked, gesturing toward the crowd beyond the front gates.

"I am sorry to say that they are people of our own creed," Pralon said. "Their protest is a direct response to the announcement late today by First Minister Asarem that engineers have successfully erected a working artificial environment about the location of the falsework. With the site secured, the government intends to carry out its stated plan to send scientists to study what the Ohalavaru have uncovered."

"They're protesting against the *study* of the site?" Kira asked

"They are," the kai said. She turned away from the view of the milling crowd and walked back inside. Kira followed. "A significant number of Bajoran traditionalists decry any such plans, and they are speaking out vociferously in an attempt to forestall such efforts. Some have even gone so far as to suggest that the first minister should be recalled from her post."

"Surely that won't happen," Kira said. "Minister Asarem has been an effective and wildly popular leader for Bajor. When she stood for reelection, she won convincingly."

"And a majority of the populace still support her," Pralon said. The kai motioned to a table and chairs arrayed along one wall, and she and Kira sat down there. The large room did not contain enough furnishings to fill it: a daybed provided a place to sleep, a small shrine stood in one corner and a companel in another, with several potted plants dotting the floor and a few hanging tapestries adorning the walls. "But make no mistake," Pralon continued. "The political and religious realms are in flux on Bajor. Fanatics on either end of the spectrum are in the minority, but theirs are the voices that are being heard. The question is how long the center can hold."

"May I ask what your public response to all of this has been?"

"I am trying to be the voice of reason," the kai said with a half-smile. "I have tried to accommodate those on both sides of the issue by working out a compromise with the first minister. Scientists and engineers will soon make their way to Endalla to investigate the falsework, but they will do so under the watchful eyes of vedek observers, which will include mainstream and Ohalavaru adherents."

"How has that plan been received?" Kira asked.

"The reaction has been mixed," Pralon said. "It has appeased many of the dissenters on both sides, but there are traditionalists who are demanding I be removed as kai."

The news shocked Kira. Pralon's predecessor, Winn Adami, had been a self-serving political schemer whose popularity had waned over time, but even she had not inspired a public outcry for her removal from office. "Are you concerned?" she asked.

"About my own position?" Pralon asked. "Not at all. Even were circumstances severe enough to motivate me to step down as kai, or for the Vedek Assembly to censure me and demand that I vacate the Apex Chair, I would do what is needed to be done for the good of the people's collective spirit. That is the path that the Prophets have laid out for me. I will not deviate from my course just because it becomes difficult to traverse."

"Those are inspiring words, Eminence," Kira said. The vedek could not help but draw distinctions between Pralon and Winn. It pleased Kira that the people had such a positive and dedicated spiritual leader.

"To be honest, Vedek, I do not feel inspired," the kai said. "I feel saddened."

"Because of the dissension among the people."

"No," the kai said. "Differing views and the controversies they arouse do not overly concern me. I am sad because of what all of this turmoil reveals—namely that there are many believers whose faith is so weak that they fear the falsework because they perceive it as a threat to the foundations of their lives. There is no room in their worldview for growth. They cannot abide change, whether for better or worse."

"I wonder if there's not more to it than that," Kira said. "Might it not be that people with strong faith find it hard to maintain their beliefs in the face of facts that contradict them?"

"Are you such a person, Vedek?"

Kira resisted answering the kai's question out of reflex. Instead, she considered what she'd been asked, and how she felt about the Endalla falsework. She had only had a couple of days to think about it. Finally, she said, "No, I don't think I am such a person. I've felt firsthand the presence and the power of the Prophets in my life. I cannot imagine crediting somebody's interpretation of a physical construct so much, even if corroborated by prophecy, that it could demonstrate to me that I have not had personal experience with the divine."

"I am pleased to hear that," the kai said. "You are obviously newly returned from the Celestial Temple, but I wonder if you have had time to form an opinion about the falsework, beyond its inability to disrupt your faith."

"I don't know really know," Kira admitted. "Captain Ro informed me about it, and I learned more on the comnet, and today I've been going through all of the information your staff provided. I actually think it's fascinating, and puzzling, but we're going to need the scientists to examine it in detail before we can draw any conclusions about it."

"It is a shame that not everybody feels as you do," Pralon said. "People are so quick to judge, based not on facts, but on what they wish reality to be."

"It is a mentality driven by fear," Kira noted. "I've done it myself, but I think it's important never to run from the truth. As long as people feel that they're represented in the efforts to explore the falsework, they should embrace it, no matter the end results. I think you're right to send traditional and Ohalavaru vedeks along with the scientists to Endalla. Perhaps it would also be wise to include a neutral third party as well, such as Starfleet."

"You have a high estimation of Captain Ro and her crew." Though she offered her remark as a statement, the kai clearly wanted confirmation of Kira's opinion.

"I have a high estimation of Captain Ro, yes, and those of her crew that I know," the vedek said. "I'm sure that she and her people would be up to the task."

"She has offered her assistance," Pralon said. "The first minister and I are considering it. Regardless, I hope that you will be disposed to help try to defuse the uproar on Bajor."

"I would be happy to do my part, of course," Kira said, "but I'm not sure what I can do."

"After I have announced your return from the Celestial Temple," Pralon said, "I'd like you to address the people of Bajor."

"About the falsework?" Kira said. "I don't think I'm qualified to do that."

"No, not about the falsework," Pralon said. "I'd like you to speak about your experiences in the Celestial Temple."

The suggestion made Kira immediately uncomfortable. To begin with, she had spoken exclusively to Captain Ro about her travels in time. Altek Dans knew about his apparent inter-action with her in her guise as Keev Anora, but Kira had told only Ro about her time in the past with Taran'atar aboard *Even Odds*. More than that, the vedek had not yet fully ex-amined everything she had been through since the wormhole had collapsed around her more than two years prior, and the notion of talking about it in a public setting unnerved her. To the kai, she said, "I do not recall all the details of my time in the Celestial Temple." True words, but still a prevarication.

"Do not speak in details, then," Pralon said. "You should still be able to convey your perception of the divinity of the Prophets."

"I can do that," Kira said cautiously, though she did not at all like the idea of proselytizing to her fellow Bajorans. *Or to anybody else, for that matter.* "I'm not really sure that anything I have to say will help matters."

"Vedek Kira, you are well known among our people," the kai said. "Your efforts in the Resistance, your Militia ser-vice aboard Deep Space Nine alongside the Emissary, and your time in the Bajoran clergy all confer a certain authority upon you. Returning to Bajor after spending more than two years in the Celestial Temple will only reinforce that."

"There may be truth to that, Eminence, but I should re-mind you that I was also Attainted by the Vedek Assembly."

"You do not need to remind me," Pralon said. "I voted against your Attainder, and later, for your reinstatement. It was a stain upon the Assembly that a majority of such an august body followed the narrow-minded lead of Vedek Yevir in expelling you from the faith."

"Thank you for saying so, Eminence."

"In this case, though, your Attainder suits the needs of our people," Pralon said. "It was short-lived and not enough to undermine the weight of your considerable record as a champion of Bajor. At the same time, because it resulted from you making the Ohalu texts public, it lends you significant credibility with the Ohalavaru." The kai pushed away from the table and stood up, and so Kira did as well. Pralon stepped forward to stand directly before the vedek. "You may be the perfect person to deliver a message of unity to all the people of Bajor."

Kira felt the strength of the kai's gaze upon her. "I will bear such responsibility as best I can, Eminence."

"I am sure of it," Pralon said. "If one were particularly religious," she went on, the slightest of smiles dancing across her features, "one might think that the Prophets have sent you back to Bajor specifically for that purpose."

Kira didn't know what to say in reply. She did not wish to disagree with the kai's assessment, but concurring with such a characterization would have been arrogant. Kira chose instead to say nothing.

"I will make a public address tomorrow, during which I will announce that you have returned from the Celestial Temple," the kai said. "We will wait a day for the significance of that to take root, and then you will speak to Bajor."

"Yes, Eminence."

"Thank you, Vedek," Pralon said. "I had intended to extend an invitation to you for dinner so that we could discuss all that you have been through, but I'm afraid that other urgent matters have arisen that require my immediate attention. Perhaps we can speak tomorrow."

"Of course," Kira said. The kai strode toward the entry hall and the door, but Kira called after her. "Eminence."

Pralon stopped and turned. "Yes?"

"I would like to contact Opaka Sulan to let her know

that I've come back to Bajor," Kira said. "I was also hoping to let my fellow clergy at the Vanadwan Monastery know, as well as Raiq. I thought I should check with you first."

"I understand your desire to share your good news with friends and colleagues," Pralon said, "but I would ask you to wait to do so. I think it would be best for that to happen after my announcement of your return."

"Of course," Kira said, though she did not entirely understand why the kai thought that way. "Whatever you think is best."

Pralon gave a single nod, then continued on her way. Once she had gone, Kira went back to where she'd been sitting on the floor, bent down, and picked up her padd. She reactivated its display, but something bothered her. She set the padd down on the table and walked back out onto the balcony, where she regarded the demonstrators out beyond the monastery gates. For some reason she could not identify, she thought Pralon wanted her to wait to tell people she knew on Bajor that she had come back from the Celestial Temple specifically so that she wouldn't speak with Opaka until after the kai's announcement.

But why? Kira wondered. She couldn't think of any justification for Pralon wanting to prevent her from talking to Opaka. *It makes no sense, and on top of that, it's not really in keeping with the kai's character.*

Kira thought about it for a few moments more, but she could not parse her hunch into a coherent notion. With a shrug, she dismissed it. She glanced out at the protestors once more, then walked back inside.

viii

Candlewood trailed after Nog as they skulked among the collection of two-story buildings, deadening their footsteps by walking not on the concrete path, but on the grass. Earlier, after studying the map of Las Vegas, the two Starfleet officers had hired a taxicab out of the Shining Oasis. They rode past more hotels and casinos—Flamingo, Caesar's Palace, Aladdin, Dunes, Tropicana—but once they turned off the Strip, the great neon signs had grown scarce, and then nonexistent. The towers, sprawling complexes, and brilliant lights of the gambling mecca's raison d'être gave way to low-rise buildings and darkened neighborhoods.

Nog had suggested that they not take the taxi all the way to their destination, instead making the final part of their journey on foot. In that way, they could tell whether they'd been followed from the Shining Oasis, and also avoid drawing attention to themselves when they'd gotten where they were going. Candlewood went along with the plan, but he didn't actually see the need for the subterfuge. Overall, Nog's efforts to find and help his holographic "friend" seemed excessive. As a diversion, experiencing a week's holiday in a historic locale, essentially living out the plot of an old-fashioned detective novel, made sense to Candlewood, even if such a holosuite program would not have been his first recreational choice. But Nog did not treat their time in Bashir 62 as entertainment; rather, he viewed it as a life-and-death effort to preserve the programming and memory state of a computer-generated simulacrum. In some ways, it felt like struggling to save a padd or a companel.

Don't be jealous, Candlewood told himself as they slinked through the shadows of the residential structures. It had been a long time since he had developed—and then overcome—his infatuation with Nog. They ended up becoming friends, but it felt as if the operations chief cared more about a conglomeration of computer algorithms and three-dimensional lighting displays than he did about flesh-and-blood people.

Which means I'm resentful of a hologram, Candlewood realized, *and that's even more ridiculous.* He reminded himself that friendship did not come packaged as a zero-sum game. Nog could have other people in his life—whether real or virtual—and still have a strong bond with Candlewood. The science officer just needed to accept the situation, regard it as an interesting adventure, and enjoy the time with his friend.

Candlewood shook off his errant thoughts and refocused on the task at hand. When he did, he espied a small sign hanging on the end of one of the buildings. "There," he whispered to Nog, pointing past him. "Number three."

Nog looked toward the sign. "Good," he whispered back. "Come on." They made their way to the front of the building, to where an outdoor staircase led up to the second level. They mounted the steps slowly, minimizing the noise they made. They stopped at the first door they came to, on which hung the apartment number Cool Papa Owens had given them: *321.*

Nog reached up to knock, but before he could, the door swung open. Owens stood there, still in the suit he'd worn at the Shining Oasis, though he'd removed his tie and unbuttoned his collar. Without saying anything, he lunged forward, took hold of Nog by the arm, and pulled him across the threshold. Candlewood hurried inside after him. When he did, Owens quickly stepped past him, peered around outside for a moment, then returned and closed the door.

"We made sure we weren't followed," Candlewood assured Owens.

"That's good," Owens said.

"Actually, somebody did tail us from the hotel," Nog said.

"What?" Candlewood said.

To Owens, Nog said, "We took a taxi from the hotel and had the driver let us out a few blocks from here. Somebody followed us in another taxi. They passed us when we stopped and turned down another street, but the passenger got out shortly after that. Fortunately, we traveled quickly and quietly on foot, and we managed to lose ourselves in the darkness."

"How do you know all that?" As soon as Candlewood asked the question, he realized what the answer would be.

"I heard them." Nog assured Owens that they had lost their tail, and that nobody had seen them arrive at his apartment.

"Well, if you didn't lose them," Owens said, "we'll know soon enough."

"Who is 'them'?" Candlewood asked.

"I don't know exactly," Owens said, "but we'll get to that." He crossed the room to an open doorway. "Get you boys a drink?" Both Candlewood and Nog demurred. "Well, I'm gonna need one for this conversation." He disappeared into a space decorated mostly in shades of white that Candlewood took to be a kitchen. "Have a seat," he called back.

Candlewood and Nog looked around the neat but wellworn apartment. Clearly a living space, the front room, covered in a neutral beige carpet, contained a sofa covered in dark-green velour; a low, rectangular wooden table before it; several filled bookcases; and a low console of some sort. Curtains of a lighter green covered the front windows, and a standing lamp in one corner offered the only light. A broken music stand lay on the floor against the far wall. Nog moved to the far end of the sofa and sat down, and Candlewood took a seat on the other end.

"Where you been, Nog?" Owens asked as he came back into the living room. In one hand, he carried a bottle three-quarters filled with an amber liquid, and in the other, his fingers gripped the insides of three plain, round drinking glasses. He set the bottle on the table, then made a point of holding the glasses up before also putting them down. "Just in case you change your mind," he said. He pulled a cork from the mouth of the bottle, then splashed a measure of its contents into a glass. Block printing on the bottle's label read GOLDSILL RYE.

"I left town a couple of years ago," Nog said, "and I haven't been able to get back here until now."

Owens put the bottle down on the table and moved to one of the bookcases. There, he selected not a book, but a thin paper envelope perhaps thirty centimeters square. From it, he withdrew a black disc, which he then carried over and appeared to install in the low console opposite the sofa. A song began to play, a stringed instrument joined by a low, mournful voice.

Owens ducked back into the kitchen for a moment. He returned with a wooden chair, which he placed on the other side of the low table from Candlewood and Nog. He sat down, picked up his glass of rye, and asked, "What is it you boys need to know about Vic?"

"Whatever you can tell us," Nog said at once. "We heard he was in some sort of trouble, and we wanted to help him."

"I really don't know what kind of trouble he's in," Owens said. "I haven't seen him in a while."

"When was the last time you did see him?" Candlewood asked.

"Maybe bout a year or so ago," Owens said. "But he disappeared before that."

"When was that?" Nog asked.

"Had to be more than two years ago now," Owens said. Nog glanced over at Candlewood, obviously taking note that Vic's disappearance more or less coincided with the destruction of the old DS9. The science officer still didn't see how or why the two events would be connected. "Truth be told, though, he started acting kinda strange in the months leading up to that."

"What do you mean 'strange'?" Nog wanted to know.

"Not strange like peculiar, but strange like different than how he usually acted," Owens said. "He sometimes showed up late for rehearsals, and a couple times, he left early. One night, he even showed up to the Shining Oasis late for a set."

"And he'd never done any of those things before?" Candlewood asked.

"Never," Owens said. "Up to then, he was the most professional cat I ever met. But there were other things too. A couple times outside the casino, I saw Vic with bad guys."

"'Bad guys'?" Candlewood asked, looking for clarification of the term.

"Hoods," Owens said. "Known criminals. Not connected guys, but petty crooks. I once saw Vic walking down the street with one, and then having lunch over at Vinny's Desert Steakhouse with another. You know Vic usually avoided those guys like the plague. I mean, they sometimes chatted him up after a show, but that's as far as it went."

"Vic stayed away from the criminal element as much as he could," Nog told Candlewood.

"There was that business with Frankie Chalmers that one time," Owens said, "but that was just a guy he grew up with making life hard on Vic." Candlewood recognized the character name from what Nog had told him about the jack-in-the-box subprogram.

"So when did Vic disappear?" Candlewood asked.

"One night—this is maybe two years ago, maybe a little longer—he never showed up for our regular gig at the Shining Oasis," Owens said. "He didn't call, either. The band just figured he got sick, but when Bill Coogan—that's the manager of the lounge—went to Vic's suite, he wasn't there, and the place was ransacked."

"Did anybody contact the authorities?" Nog asked.

"The cops came in, but they couldn't find out what happened to him," Owens said. "Vic didn't show up the next night, either, and Coogan didn't have any choice but to hire another singer. Me and a couple of the guys in the band convinced him to make it temporary, which he did for a week, but after that, it was obvious Vic wasn't coming back. Coogan had to replace him for good."

"But you saw Vic again after that," Candlewood prompted.

"I did, but not for a while—months, at least, maybe six or more," Owens said. "But I did ask around a bit, and from time to time, I heard things."

"What things?" Nog asked. Despite the indeterminate description, what Owens had said still sounded ominous to Candlewood.

"I heard rumors here and there that Vic had run afoul of the hard guys."

"Men involved in organized crime," Nog said, part statement, part question.

"That's right," Owens said.

"But you said it yourself," Nog noted. "That's not like Vic."

"It didn't used to be, no," Owens said, "but before he went missing, I did see him with hoods those couple of times I mentioned, and after he disappeared, the rumors kept up about him getting in deep with mobsters. Eventually, I know a few folks who figured that he ended up out in the desert in a shallow grave."

"Is that what you thought too?" Nog asked.

"I didn't know," Owens said. "When he didn't show

up at the Shining Oasis and then got replaced, I started to think so." The musician gazed down at his glass. He swirled around the small amount of rye left, and he seemed lost in thought. Candlewood was about to pose another question when Owens looked back up. "Of course, then I ended up seeing him again."

"Where?" Nog asked. "Where was the last place you saw him?"

"Right here," Owens said. He pointed to a darkened hallway that ran off to the left between the living room and the kitchen. "Well, in there, actually, in the back bedroom."

"What was he doing here?" Candlewood asked.

Owens leaned forward in his chair. "He was running for his life."

ix

Vernon "Cool Papa" Owens sat bolt upright on the couch, his heart pounding hard in his chest—except that the knocking he heard didn't originate in his chest, but at the front door. It reminded him of the raids he occasionally had to endure in his days playing Chicago speakeasies back in the thirties. That had been a long time ago, in a different place; booze was legal again in the U.S. of A., and in Vegas, so was gambling.

On top of that, Owens wasn't at the casino, but in his apartment. He must have dozed off on the couch, and the drumming on the front door had woken him. All had gone quiet, though, and so Owens listened. When the knocking came again, it didn't sound loud after all, but more like tapping. He checked his watch and saw the lateness of the hour: just past three in the morning. He'd gotten home from a late-night set not long before, and he assumed that one of the boys in the band must have come calling for a drink—or, just possibly, Darlene had undergone a change of heart after their recent breakup.

Owens got up from the couch and ambled over to the door. He unlocked and opened it, hoping to see Darlene, but anticipating one of his fellow musicians. Instead, he saw a face he hadn't in quite a while.

"Vic," he said, surprised. "I thought you was dead."

"Not yet," the singer said. "Can I come in, Cool Papa?" Vic looked back over first one shoulder, then the other. He seemed on the verge of panic.

"Course," Owens said, stepping aside to let Vic enter. Owens closed the door and locked it, then eyeballed the singer. He looked disheveled, his clothes wrinkled, his hair mussed, his eyes sporting dark circles beneath them. It also appeared as though he'd lost weight. Owens had never seen Vic look so bad; quite the opposite, Vic had always been the picture of nattiness.

"I hate to impose on you, Cool Papa," the singer said, "but I need a place to hide out for a while."

"Who you hiding out from?" Owens asked. "You gonna get me killed?"

"I wouldn't have come here if I thought that," Vic said. "But you're better off not knowing anything."

"If somebody's looking for you, they'd sure as hell check your friends' places," Owens said. "Including the guys in the band."

"They've been keeping eyes on your place, and on the other guys' too," Vic said. "I know because I've been watching them look for me. Tonight's the first time in months that nobody's out there."

"You think they'll be back?" Owens asked.

"I want to tell you no," Vic said, "but the truth is that, yes, I think they'll probably be back. If you let me stay here, I promise to keep outta sight." He reached into the pocket of the nondescript jacket he wore and pulled out a wad of cash. "I can pay you, Cool Papa."

Owens beheld the twist of bills with suspicion, suspecting its provenance. "Do I wanna know where that money come from?"

"Probably not," Vic said, "but I can tell you that it's not stolen—at least not by me."

"Yeah, well that's something, I guess," Owens said. He walked past Vic to the other side of the living room, considering what he should do. At last, he said, "You can stay, but you can keep your money. Friends do for friends." Owens believed that, and he would have let Vic stay there regardless, but he also had self-preservation in mind in wanting to keep from tying himself to what he assumed to be the singer's ill-gotten gains. "I got some extra sheets and blankets. I'll get em and you can make up the couch."

"Thanks, Cool Papa," Vic said. "You're a lifesaver."

On his way into the hall, Owens stopped and looked back at Vic. "From the looks of you," he told the singer, "I believe it."

X

The instant he heard the crash, Owens knew what had happened. He tossed off the sheet and blanket atop him, leaped from his bed, and raced in his underwear out into the living room. Dim light spilled into the apartment through the open front door, which had been thrown wide. Pieces of wood had splintered from the jamb and lay scattered on the carpeting.

A large man stepped forward into the doorway, silhouetted against the glow of a streetlamp outside, his height and the broadness of his shoulders nearly filling the space. He entered the apartment casually, as though arriving for a friendly visit. His hand went up to the inner wall, presumably feeling for a light switch. When he didn't find one, he stepped forward and reached for the lamp on the end table beside the couch. He turned it on and light streamed through the top of the lampshade, illuminating his face, but the glint of the gun in the man's hand caught Owens's attention. Then a second bruiser entered the apartment, also wielding a weapon.

"Where is he?" the first man asked. He had squarish features and a deep voice.

Owens pointed back the way he had come, into the short hall that ran between the apartment's two bedrooms. "That way," he said. "In the back bedroom." He stepped out of the way as the first man sprang forward and raced past him. It startled Owens that somebody of such considerable bulk could move so quickly.

A doorknob rattled. Owens knew that Vic locked it at night. In the months he had been staying there, the singer had taken to sleeping on the floor in the back bedroom. Owens used the space during the day as a rehearsal room, where he practiced new pieces on his bass. He'd also recently taken up the violin.

Early on, Vic had spoken of the possibility of men coming after him. He believed that they might force their way in and make threats. Vic made Owens promise that, if that should happen, he would give up the singer immediately.

A second crash reverberated through the apartment. Owens peeked into the hall to see that the first man had kicked open the door to the back bedroom. The window in the far wall stood open, its screen gone. So was Vic.

Owens watched as the first man hurried to the window and leaned outside. The sound of running footsteps echoed up from behind the building. Owens imagined Vic climbing out the window, hanging down as far as he could, and dropping to the alley below.

Then the big man turned from the window and set his attention on Owens.

xi

"They beat me," Owens said, and Nog winced at the idea of the older man being set upon by the two thugs. The musician lifted his glass to his lips and upended it, downing the last of his rye. "They left me with this—" He pointed to the ugly scar that crossed his temple. "—but it could've been worse. I told them everything I knew about Vic, but that wasn't much. I used to think Vic kept quiet when he stayed with me in order to protect himself, but now I think it was to protect me. Those guys hit me, but they realized pretty quickly that I couldn't help them."

"What *did* you tell them?" Nog asked.

"Basically what I just told you," Owens said. "I haven't seen Vic or heard from him since that night, probably right around a year ago."

"What about rumors?" Nog asked. "Has anybody else said anything about him?"

"People always talk, whether they know anything or not," Owens said. "Most of the rumors about Vic are at one extreme or the other: either he found his way down to the sunny beaches of Acapulco, where he's living the life of Riley, or he's six feet under." Accustomed to the argot of Vic's program, Nog understood the meaning of Owens's idioms from their context. "Me, I'd like to think the first is true, but seeing the guys who are after him, I'm more inclined to believe the second."

"Neither one of them is true," Nog said. "I saw Vic three nights ago."

"Here?" Owens asked. "In Vegas? Alive?"

"Yes, here in Vegas, alive," Nog said. "But I'm not sure

for how long." He told Owens about witnessing Vic's abduction from a third-rate hotel. "Do you have any idea who the men were that broke in here?" Nog asked.

"No, and I haven't seen em since," Owens said. "But this town's got more hoods in it than decks of cards."

"Your description of the man who kicked in your door sounds a lot like the one who led Vic's abduction," Nog said. "Tall, big, square jaw."

"Did you see what kind of car they took Vic away in?" Owens asked.

At the time of Vic's abduction, Nog had made a point of committing to memory as many details of the incident as he could. "It was long and black—black on the outside and on the inside. It had two doors, and the wheels were mostly silver on the side with a white circle around them. It had a shield emblem and the name ELDORADO on it."

"A black Caddie," Owens said reflectively. "There are a lot of those driven around Vegas these days, by a lot of big-time mobsters. Joey Conterelli's boys got em, and Bugsy Calderone's, and Big Jimmy Flanagan's."

"So you think it could be one of those criminal organizations?" Candlewood asked.

"I dunno, could be," Owens said, but then he seemed to think better of his response. "Probably. I mean, who else would dare to kidnap somebody like that?"

"But why?" Nog asked.

"I dunno, but remember, I saw Vic with some bad people even before he disappeared the first time," Owens said. "Not mobsters, as far as I know, but still crooks."

Nog shook his head. He couldn't sort out the situation in his mind. He could have understood it as the product of another jack-in-the-box hidden in Vic's holoprogram, but as a consequence of the person he knew Vic Fontaine to be, it made no sense.

"Nog, do you think Vic knew his abductors?" Candlewood asked.

"I don't know," Nog said. "Maybe."

"He told me that he'd been keeping an eye on the people looking for him," Owens said. "That tells me he probably knew."

"But he didn't tell you?" Nog asked. "Or mention anything that suggested their identity?"

"Nope," Owens said. "I doubt he would've told me if I'd asked. Like I said, I think he was trying to protect me if anybody came around looking for him." Owens picked up the bottle of rye and poured another measure into his glass.

"And obviously, when you saw Vic get abducted, he didn't say anything to you," Candlewood said to Nog.

"No. He only told me not to get involved," Nog said. "And that the fat lady was about to sing."

"The fat lady?" Owens said, peering quizzically over the rim of his glass.

"It's from an old saying," Nog told the musician. "I looked it up: 'It ain't over till the fat lady sings.' The way Vic said it, I think he meant that whatever he was involved in was almost over. I think he feared for his life."

"I never heard that saying," Owens replied, "but I might just know who the fat lady is."

"What?" Nog said. "Are you saying the fat lady is an actual person?" *Or in this case, a* virtual *person,* he thought.

"There's a lady of ample proportions performing in town these days," Owens said. "Her name's Naomi Smith and she sings over at the Silver Lode. It's the casino run by Bugsy Calderone."

"That's it," Nog said, springing to his feet. "Vic was sending me a message."

"Are you sure?" Candlewood asked.

"Why else would he say that?" Nog asked. He extended

his hand above the table in the traditional human custom. "Thank you, Cool Papa."

Owens set down his glass, stood up, and shook Nog's hand. "You're welcome," he said. "I just hope you can find Vic and help him before . . . well." Owens didn't need to finish his statement to make his intention clear.

Candlewood rose beside Nog. "We'll do our best," the science officer said. "Thanks to you, we now know where to look."

"Are you heading there right now?" Owens asked.

Nog glanced up at Candlewood. "No, I don't think so. It's late and we need to get some sleep, but we'll go there tomorrow."

Nog and Candlewood moved away from the sofa, over to the front door, which Owens unlocked and opened for them. The two Starfleet officers walked back out into the Las Vegas night. As they descended the stairs, they heard Owens call after them.

"Good luck," he said.

Nog thought that they would need it.

Four

Transactions

A triadic tone sounded in the Hub, accompanied by a visual notification on one of the tactical station's displays. Zivan Slaine toggled a control surface on her console, acknowledging the alert and bringing up the details of its cause. "We're receiving a signal from the CAS buoy," she announced. The DS9 crew had recently anchored a communications-and-sensor buoy on the Gamma Quadrant side of the wormhole, just beyond the Idran system. "According to long-range sensors, a single vessel is approaching the wormhole on a direct course." She worked to refine the readings.

"Can you identify it?" asked Commander Blackmer from where he sat in the command chair. With Captain Ro on leave, the exec acted as commanding officer of the starbase.

"Attempting to," Slaine said. She tried to tune the CAS buoy's sensors. "It's too distant to determine its configuration, but it is traveling at high warp."

"Assuming a constant trajectory, can you extrapolate its course backward?" Blackmer asked.

"Calculating." Slaine activated the holographic display above the situation table, causing a field of stars to appear. Blackmer stood up from the command chair and descended one of the sets of steps down into the Well. "Here is the Gamma Quadrant terminus of the wormhole," Slaine said, tapping a control to highlight the reference point in blue. "And here's the approaching ship." She operated her panel to make a flashing red light appear in the holographic display. Slaine computed the formula for the path of the vessel, then solved it for earlier values. Above the sit table, a red line extended backward from the ship's current position.

"Do we know where it's coming from?" Blackmer asked. Slaine adjusted the holographic display to shift perspective and follow the rearward course of the unidentified vessel. She froze the three-dimensional image when the red line intersected a labeled volume of space. It said DOMINION.

"There's a ship headed here from the Dominion?" Chief O'Brien said from his position at the main engineering panel. "That's all we need."

"Curious, isn't it?" Blackmer said, though Slaine could think of other ways to describe the situation. "The Dominion has essentially remained in isolation since the war. They've sent almost no ships beyond their space that we know of, and they've declared their borders closed to outsiders."

"It's just one ship?" asked Lieutenant Ren Kalanent Viss from the communications station. The helmet of her Alonis environmental suit translated her underwater speech into Federation Standard. "Should we try to contact its crew?"

"Not yet," Blackmer said. "Since it's just shown up on long-range sensors, we have some time before it reaches the wormhole."

Slaine studied the numbers on her console. "At its present velocity, it will take three days."

"Before we start talking to our visitors," Blackmer said, "let's find out who they are. Dalin, keep the buoy's sensors trained on the ship. Let's see as soon as we can if it really does belong to the Dominion, and if so, what type of ship it is—Jem'Hadar, Karemma, T-Rogoran, or somebody else."

"Aye, sir." Slaine issued a command to the CAS buoy to maintain a sensor lock on the unknown ship. She waited for a return signal confirming the order. "Sensors are locked."

"Very good," Blackmer said. He touched a control on the sit table, deactivating the three-dimensional display above it. Then he mounted the steps to the outer ring of the Hub and returned to the command chair.

Slaine followed the forward motion of the approaching vessel on sensors for a few minutes. Given its path from the Dominion, it seemed to her that the ship had indeed originated there. She could only hope that its crew came in peace.

ii

Kira heard the clomp of shoes on the stone floor. In her room in the hostelry, she opened her eyes and turned from the shrine, where she had been offering prayers to the Prophets. A robed figure stood in the entry hall. An older man of slight build, he had thinning silver hair and pale skin. "Vedek Kira, I am Ranjen Linsa Noth. I serve as an aide to Kai Pralon."

"Please come in, Ranjen," Kira said. "What can I do for you?"

Linsa took only a single step into the room. "The kai wished me to let you know that she is about to deliver her address to the Bajoran people," he said. "It is being carried on the comnet."

"Thank you."

Linsa bowed his head, then withdrew. Kira made her way over to the companel in the corner, sat down, and activated the device. She navigated to the Bajoran comnet. Although she had no interest in the notoriety that would doubtless attend the public announcement of her return from the Celestial Temple, she looked forward to resuming the routine of her everyday life. If she'd had her preference, she would already have gone back to Releketh Province, to her position at the Vanadwan Monastery. While Kira did not consider herself a prisoner in Ashalla, Kai Pralon made it clear that she preferred the vedek to remain there until after the announcement. Since arriving the previous afternoon, Kira had essentially remained sequestered, seeing only the kai and members of her staff.

On the companel, a view of the Great Assembly appeared. Sitting atop the highest elevation in the capital, the circular structure had been refurbished after the Cardassians had finally left Bajor. Ironically, the building had survived intact and in good repair for most of the Occupation, with the oppressors utilizing it as their own planetbound command post. When the Cardassians had finally left Bajor, though, they had done so with contempt, wreaking devastation everywhere, leaving cities in ruins and farmlands contaminated. The Great Assembly had been a casualty, but under the leadership of Shakaar Edon, the first minister at the time, it had been among the initial reconstructions undertaken. With its broad, shallow dome held up by a ring of ornate columns, the building had quickly become a vibrant symbol of Bajor's renewal.

The image on the display shifted to a view inside the Great Assembly, to the main hall. The large semicircular room featured rows of seats rising from a proscenium. The hall could hold every member of the Vedek Assembly and the Chamber of Ministers, both of which appeared represented in full.

The scene surprised Kira. Although she had not spoken with Pralon about it, she had expected the kai to address the Bajoran people outdoors, in a public space, such as the Taluno Lawn at the Shikina Monastery or the Crescent Courtyard outside the Great Assembly. It seemed more fitting to the vedek that Pralon stand not before Bajor's leaders, but before its citizens. Large gatherings of true believers could certainly be found all over the planet. Kira could only surmise that security concerns—doubtless magnified by the recent outbursts of violence—had won the day and forced the kai to talk to the people of Bajor from a secure location. It made the vedek vaguely uneasy.

It doesn't really matter, Kira told herself. Via the comnet, Pralon would reach virtually all of Bajor.

On the companel display, the lights above the audience darkened, and those on the stage came up. A podium stood in front, and at the rear, two lavish cathedrae: the Premier Chair, usually occupied by the highest ranking member of the secular government present, and the Apex Chair, for use by the kai. Asarem Wadeen sat in one cathedra, and Pralon Onala in the other.

As Kira watched, the soft murmur of the vedeks and ministers in the Great Assembly faded to silence. In a break from tradition, the kai rose from the Apex Chair without introduction and approached the podium. At once, a vedek in the front row stood up and applauded, and three-quarters or more of the Vedek Assembly followed his lead. Numerous ministers then got to their feet as well and joined in.

To the casual observer, the kai's reception probably would have appeared spontaneous, but Kira sensed planning in the effort. The first vedek to his feet had been Yevir Linjarin, a high-profile religious leader who had once seriously considered seeking the Apex Chair himself, and who had always stood in vocal opposition to the Ohalavaru. Though Kira had since made peace with Yevir, he had been the driving force behind her Attainder.

He's trying too hard, she thought. *They all are.* The choice by other vedeks to remain seated during the ovation for the kai seemed just as considered. They all plainly wanted to show a unified front with their side in the ongoing controversy over the discovery on Endalla and the surrounding claims by the Ohalavaru.

"Good afternoon, First Minister, ministers, vedeks, people of Bajor," Pralon intoned at the podium. She looked elegant in a layered red robe and matching headpiece of swirled fabric. *"I have come to stand before you today to deliver not*

just good news, but inspiring *news."* Again, Yevir jumped up to clap, though that time, fewer of his fellow vedeks did so behind him, and almost none of the ministers. Asarem sat motionless in the Premier Chair. The kai gestured for those standing in the audience to sit, and once they had, she continued. *"In recent days, we have not been united as a people. Differences of opinion have arisen among us, and while that is neither cause for alarm nor reason for neighbors to pit themselves one against another, it has led us to difficult times.*

"I will not need to convince any of you when I say that we Bajorans are no strangers to difficult times," the kai went on. *"But we are strong, and resolute; and just as we have worked hard in the past to find our collective way out of the wilderness, I am confident that we will do so again—that what divides some of us at this moment is not nearly as important as what defines us as a people and brings us together."*

Once more, Yevir rose to applaud, as did several other vedeks, but as Pralon continued speaking with no pause, they quickly settled back down into their seats. *"No matter your beliefs as a Bajoran—"* she said, and she walked out from behind the podium, as though seeking to underscore what she would next say. *"No matter whether you subscribe to a traditional view of the Prophets or to the assessment imparted by the texts of Ohalu—"*

Voices buzzed in the Great Assembly, and then somebody shouted something Kira could not hear clearly. A second voice rang out as though in answer to the first, the words it yelled equally impossible to distinguish. Pralon did not raise her voice as she moved back behind the podium and continued her address, dismissing the interruptions by giving them no attention.

"No matter if your faith or lack of faith falls under some other label, or no label at all, you recognize the existence of the Prophets. There is little doubt that through the ages, They

have bestowed Their attentions upon Bajor. Even if some of us disagree on the particulars, we can all understand talk of the Prophets' majesty, of Their mystery."

The words impressed Kira. The kai worked hard to include the Ohalavaru in her speech, while neither espousing nor repudiating their beliefs. By the same token, she did not run from traditional religious viewpoints, nor did she insist upon their acceptance.

"More than two years ago," Pralon went on, *"renegade forces of the Typhon Pact attempted to generate an artificial wormhole and link it to the Celestial Temple. As the Emissary led a Starfleet crew to stop the aggressors, another individual, traveling aboard a much smaller vessel, helped save the day. That vedek vanquished a Romulan warship and made it possible for the Emissary and his crew to escape the temporary closure of the Celestial Temple."*

Kira found it uncomfortable to listen to what sounded to her like hyperbole. The kai said nothing untrue, but her account bordered on the spectacular. *Thank the Prophets she doesn't know about everything else that happened.*

"We rejoiced when the Celestial Temple reopened several months ago," Pralon said. *"It demonstrated what many of us never doubted: that the Prophets not only endured, but that They would continue to play a role in the affairs of Bajor."*

Kira briefly wondered if the Ohalavaru might take exception to such a characterization. She realized, though, that even if they believed in the mortal nature of the Prophets, that didn't mean they wished Them to come to harm. For that matter, just because the Ohalavaru branded Them as "wormhole aliens," it didn't follow that they didn't find value in the Prophets' interest in Bajor.

"When the Celestial Temple reopened," the kai said, *"many thought that Vedek Kira might materialize from within and return home."* Even watching on the comnet, Kira thought

she could discern a sudden anticipation in the Great Assembly. *"At the time of the Temple's renewal, amid a sense of reverence and excitement, the vedek did not emerge from it."* The declaration seemed to dash the hopes of the vedeks and ministers. *"The vedek did not emerge, but another individual did: a man named Altek Dans."*

Kira's mouth dropped open. In the chamber, at the rear of the stage, a still image of Altek appeared on a large viewscreen the vedek hadn't even seen. *What is the kai doing?* Kira thought.

"Like Akorem Laan more than a decade ago," Pralon went on, *"Altek Dans soared out of the Celestial Temple and out of Bajor's past. Unlike our great poet, Mister Altek—Doctor Altek—has apparently come from much further back in history, and he is here to stay."*

The kai continued to talk, but Kira only half heard what she said. As far as the vedek knew, up until yesterday, Altek wanted to live on Bajor, but as an everyday citizen. He wished to continue assimilating to the present and to seek a place among the current generation of his people. He hoped to determine his purpose—or the Prophets' purpose for him—but he had already begun to think about acquiring a modern education and resuming the practice of medicine. Whatever he did, though, he did not want to be an object of curiosity, a man out of the past who did not belong. With regard to his travel in time, he sought anonymity.

Did Altek know the kai intended to do this? Or did she blindside him by revealing his identity to all of Bajor? It seemed unthinkable to Kira. She had known Pralon Onala for a long time and had followed her career for an even longer period, back to Pralon's days heading the Ministry of Religious Artifacts. Kira could not imagine her disregarding the rights of an individual to satisfy a political purpose. *Did she somehow change Altek's mind? Did she* pressure *him into changing his mind?* Again, Kira could not feature the current kai taking such actions. The vedek rejected the ideas, but she still wondered how and why Altek had chosen to allow himself to be put in the public eye. Pralon concluded her remarks about him by speaking of his humble desires, although any hope he had for privacy had just been undermined.

"As Doctor Altek set his sights on making his way back to Bajor," the kai said, *"attention turned once more to the Celestial Temple. Three days ago, a small vessel unexpectedly appeared from within it. This time, Kira Nerys did return."*

A startled hum rose in the Assembly. Behind the kai, an image of Kira—taken at the Vanadwan Monastery before her disappearance in the Celestial Temple—replaced that of Altek Dans. Somebody in the audience clapped, and then so did several others. The applause built slowly, then rose in volume. A number of people stood up, and then so did others. In the front row, Yevir kept his seat until those on either side of him had risen to their feet. Kira wondered what the vedek thought of her return.

Once the ovation finally ended and the audience sat back down, Pralon said, *"Vedek Kira has been examined and found to be in good health. I have spoken with her, and she is in good spirits. She tells me that she looks forward to going back to her life as a vedek at the Vanadwan Monastery, but before she does, she will speak to the Bajoran people."*

As Pralon provided details about Kira's address the next day, the vedek thought about what exactly she would say. While she had no anxiety about public speaking—she had often talked to large groups of people, both when she'd served aboard DS9 and during her time in the clergy—she had never before had the population of an entire planet as an audience. The act of doing so did not concern her, but she had yet to figure out what she would say. She had no interest in talking about herself, but that was basically what the kai had asked of her. While Kira understood the power inherent in the tale of her extended excursion in the Celestial Temple, she did not know how to frame it in a way that would satisfy the kai's needs—especially given the vedek's sporadic memories of her time in the Prophets' realm.

As the kai completed her remarks in the Great Assembly, Kira thought about Altek Dans. Despite the kiss they had shared aboard the transport and the emotional resonance it had stoked within her, she could not yet contemplate the idea of them as romantic partners; she had not come to terms with the bizarre nature of their relationship—from its setting in history, to the confused nature of her identity during their courtship, to their disjointed perspectives on just how long ago they had been together. But she did ponder his story, as a man displaced from a world he knew to one only vaguely familiar. She wondered again why he had changed his mind about maintaining his privacy, and she decided that she would ask him.

Kira also would have to discuss the content of her speech with the kai. The vedek hoped that she could limit what she had to say, and that, sooner rather than later, she could contact the people in her life on Bajor. More than anything at that moment, she simply wanted to pick up where she'd left off at the Vanadwan Monastery; it seemed to her that, with the controversy about the falsework gripping the population, her work as a vedek would be needed more than ever. Kira did not look forward to giving her speech, but she hoped that Pralon was right that it would bring a measure of calm to Bajor.

iii

Quark approached the cockpit, making sure to walk loudly so that he wouldn't startle Laren. She looked up when he entered. "Hello, Quark."

"I can relieve you now," he said, working hard to keep his tone neutral. He didn't want the disappointment and hurt he felt audible in his voice, though he knew that he'd made his emotions clear.

"We can both watch the helm," Laren offered. Since he'd left her in the passenger cabin the previous night, they'd taken turns monitoring the ship's functions.

"That's not necessary," Quark said.

"I know it's not necessary," Laren said. "But I'd like to stay here."

"Fine."

"Good," Laren said. "I'm glad."

"When you want to be relieved," Quark told her, "just let me know." He moved back into the passenger cabin, headed aft for his bunk. He figured he would retrieve his padd and have a look at the Ferengi Futures Exchange. He had never really had the capital to invest heavily in the FFE, but business at both of his establishments had been solid lately, even brisk. If he could recover his lost funds from Mayereen Viray, it might just be time to—

"Quark." Laren almost barked his name. He thought about just continuing on into the sleeping quarters, but he heard her get up from the console. He stopped and turned, and she appeared in the doorway. "You can't keep ignoring me."

"I don't know," Quark said. "I'd say you've done a pretty good job of ignoring me."

Laren raised her hands and let them drop against her thighs. "That's not true," she said. "I'm here now with you. You came to me for help the other day, and even if I was skeptical at first that I could do anything, I did listen to what you had to say, and I checked with the JAG office, and also with my friend at the Geopolis spaceport."

Quark said nothing.

"Let's not do this, Quark," Laren went on, her manner earnest. "We've known each other for so long, and we've had so many enjoyable times together."

Quark still didn't react—at least not visibly. He could not help but recall some of those times. He relished those memories, but it also made him sad that they would not make any more of them together.

"Do you remember when we went out to the Ovarani Valley to tour the vineyards?" Laren asked. "When I had a little too much wine, but when we went hiking, it was you who fell in the creek." Laren took a step forward into the passenger cabin, a smile lighting up her face. "I thought you might have 'slipped' intentionally, just to have an excuse to take off your clothes."

Even though Quark still said nothing, that three-day trip with Laren remained not only fresh in his recollection, but vivid. It had been during their time on Bajor after the loss of the old station, maybe halfway through the construction of the new starbase. Business had been surprisingly good at his bar in Aljuli, Laren's crew had settled into a routine at Bajoran Space Central, and there had been time for them to get away together.

"Or how about when I had that mission on Gavaria, and I met you afterward on Ferenginar?" Laren asked. "It rained the entire time we were there—wait. It didn't rain, it . . . it *choritzed* and *sneedered*." Laren seemed pleased with herself in using two of the one hundred seventy-eight words the Ferengi had for rain. "Why does it suddenly seem that we spent our relationship with one or the other of us getting wet?" She chuckled, clearly trying to draw him out.

Quark stayed silent, but he pictured that holiday they'd taken on Ferenginar, not long after Iliana Ghemor and the Ascendant fleet had attempted to wipe out Bajor. It *had* rained—*choritzed* and *sneedered* and *pradooshed* and *horrocked*—for their whole stay, but he had barely noticed. He couldn't recall ever having a better visit with his family—Rom and Leeta and Bena, Moogie and Zek, even his cousin Gaila—but showing Laren around Ferenginar had been the high point of the trip.

When Quark said nothing, Laren moved across the cabin to face him. "You know a time that I especially remember? It was after . . . after the dedication." Quark knew that she referred to the ceremony at which the Federation president had been assassinated. He'd staked out Laren's quarters until she'd arrived late that night. "You paid me a visit. We talked a bit, and then we just sat together on the sofa. You held me, and I fell asleep in your arms for a short while. It was the only peace I had that day, and you provided it."

Quark still didn't say anything. He didn't know what he could say. Everything Laren mentioned only underscored how good their time with each other had been, and how deeply she'd hurt him.

"I know you agree with me," she said, obviously misreading his silence for accord.

"Agree with you?" Quark said. "About what? That we had some fine times together? Okay, but when was the last time like that we shared? You mentioned the night after the dedication ceremony—which wasn't exactly what I'd call a date—but even that was almost half a year ago."

"What about last night?" Laren asked. "Before you walked out on me. We were playing fizzbin and having a wonderful time."

Quark scoffed. "I don't think you can peddle that interpretation of this trip even to yourself," he said. "I'll admit I was glad that you showed up at the dock to join me, but I know you're not aboard for me."

"I do want to help," Laren said.

"Okay," Quark said. He felt physically cornered, and so he walked past her, toward the front of the passenger cabin. "Okay, I believe you want to help. But you're not aboard this ship *just* for me." Laren started to protest, but Quark held up his hand to stop her. "Don't," he said. "You're mainly here because you're running from something. I'm not completely sure what, but I can tell."

Laren smiled with one side of her mouth and shook her head, as though in disbelief. "It is almost disconcerting how well you know me," she said. "You're right: I am running—not far and not for long, but yes, I needed to get away from Deep Space Nine for a little while." She crossed to the small table where the two of them had just the night before sat together, laughed, and delighted in each other's company. She sat down and appeared to gather her thoughts. "I know I hurt you last night," she said quietly, as though proceeding cautiously. "But you and I never talked about a long-term commitment."

Quark laughed, without humor. "What do you call a decade together?"

Laren opened her mouth to respond, but it took a moment before she said anything. "There have been long periods where we've gone without seeing each other." She stopped and inhaled deeply, then breathed out slowly. "You're right. Ten years is ten years, and even if we never actually discussed commitment—"

"But we did," Quark interrupted. He walked over and sat down across from Laren. "We talked about leaving . . . how neither of us belonged on Deep Space Nine, how we both felt like outsiders in the place we lived. We talked about how Bajor joining the Federation would be the right time to move on, and how we would do so together. What is that if not talk of commitment?"

"We didn't leave, though."

"Not because we didn't want to be together," Quark

said. "Because my simpleton brother granted me ambassador status and the *Enterprise* captain championed you in Starfleet. So we stayed on the station . . . *together*."

"Quark, I . . ." Abruptly, Laren stood up. "Why don't you take the watch?" she said. "I need some time to think." She didn't wait for him to respond, but headed into the sleeping compartment.

Incredibly, Laren had looked flummoxed, as though she credited every point that Quark had made, and that she realized the failure of her own arguments. He didn't quite know what to think. He wasn't used to being so completely right—particularly in matters of the heart.

iv

Ro lay in her bunk, in the dark, listening to the thrum of the ship's warp engine. She could feel the vibration of the drive translating up through the deck, but more than anything, she felt numb. *How could I be so blind?*

Except that she hadn't been blind. That would have been preferable to the reality: she had been selfish. She had resisted doing the right thing because it had been easier to do nothing than to face Quark and tell him the truth.

And because of that, I hurt him. Ro would have hurt him anyway, had she revealed her feelings for Dans in a timely fashion, but instead, she'd strung Quark along, prolonging and compounding his emotional pain. She hadn't been quite so disappointed in herself in a long time.

On top of that, she realized that she had done to Quark precisely what had just been done to her. Ro and Quark had been in a relationship when she'd developed feelings for Dans, and she and Dans had been in a relationship when he'd developed feelings for Kira. The parallel seemed not just ironic, but karmic.

Except that's not really fair to Dans, is it? she asked herself. He'd previously been involved with Kira, and as best Ro could tell, neither Dans nor Kira had ever ended their relationship; it had been ended for them when the Prophets had sent each of them trekking through time. *And Dans and I only started seeing each other a month and a half ago,* she thought. *Quark and I were together for almost ten years.*

Ro felt ashamed of her behavior. She would try to make it up to Quark, though she didn't know what she could possibly do to mitigate how she had treated him with such disregard. More than that, she would need to engage in serious self-examination. She was no longer a child living beneath the bootheels of the Cardassians, no longer an angry young woman rebelling against everything the universe sent her way, no longer an inexperienced Starfleet officer disobeying the orders of senior officers who actually did know better than she did. Her life had almost reached the half-century mark, and while she took pride in many of her accomplishments, she could not tolerate the way she had treated Quark. She expected more of herself.

V

Nog finished a third complete circuit of the casino floor and returned to its large main entrance. He looked around for Candlewood but didn't see him. He hoped that his friend had met with more luck on his reconnaissance than Nog had on his. Part of the problem stemmed from their lack of solid data about Vic's situation. They needed information, and they needed it quickly. It had already been two days since they had entered Bashir 62 through Felix Knightly's programmatic back door, leaving them just five days before the code automatically reinitialized itself. Nog imagined he could hear each second tick off the clock.

The previous night, after leaving Cool Papa Owens, Nog and Candlewood had located the Silver Lode Hotel and Casino on their map of Las Vegas. That morning, they made their way there on foot, where they first explored and then surveilled the exteriors of the buildings. They took note of the arrivals and departures of several Eldorado automobiles, which were driven to and from a fenced-off, guarded section of the parking lot directly behind the hotel tower. None of the vehicles they saw bore the identification number Nog had noted on the Eldorado in which Vic had been spirited away.

After studying the outside of the Silver Lode complex, they had explored inside the hotel, from the lobby up to its penultimate floor. Both the elevators and the stairwells required keys to access the top story. Nog could easily have picked the locks, but he worried about breaching a secured location only to be caught, or even to once again take weapons fire.

Nog waited near the main entrance of the Silver Lode casino, beside a full-size exhibit of Ancient West transportation. A linked pair of open wagons, constructed of thick black metal and mounted on rails, carried mounds of glossy gray ore, presumably galena or acanthite or some other silver-bearing mineral. Nog had seen similar depictions of manual excavating throughout the casino, in large framed photographs on the walls, in smaller pictures and illustrations on slot machines and wheels of fortune, in miniatures hanging from the ceiling. Other displays contained rudimentary mining accoutrements: pickaxes and mattocks, shovels, helmets with headlamps, ventilation fans. In several places, wooden frames, comprising vertical posts and crowning horizontal crossbars, stood over walkways like skeletal tunnels.

Nog regarded the mine cars, as he had the other relics in the casino, with a sense of frustration. The objects and photographs held historical and perhaps even artistic interest, but they also represented something distinctly antagonistic. In some ways, Nog understood the setting of Earth's twentieth-century Las Vegas very well; the unrelenting materialism it embodied felt more like home than many modern-day worlds. But Vic's holoprogram no longer operated like entertainment; it functioned like a challenge, a game for which Nog did not understand the rules. That made it difficult for him to formulate a winning strategy, and yet he *had* to win; Vic's existence hung in the balance.

From around a row of slot machines, Candlewood appeared. Nog could tell from the expression on his face that he had found nothing of value to them in the casino, but the operations chief asked the question anyway. "Did you learn anything?"

"No, afraid not," Candlewood said.

Nog shook his head. "We don't know enough about what's happened to Vic," he said. "We need to take a more direct approach." Nog headed for the wide walkway that connected the casino to the hotel.

Candlewood hurried to catch up. "Wait," he said. "What are you going to do?"

"I'm going to see if we can speak to—" Nog stopped walking and turned to face Candlewood. He looked around to ensure that nobody would overhear them, then decided on discretion. "I'm going to see if we can speak to the man Cool Papa pointed us to."

"Nog, we don't even really know if Vic is mixed up with Bugsy Calderone."

So much for discretion. "Calderone's involved," Nog said. "Vic gave me a clue pointing to him."

"That's what we think, but we don't *know*," Candlewood said. "What if we're wrong, and you go marching in to accuse a major criminal of something he didn't actually do. We could invite more trouble than we already have."

"We're not wrong," Nog said, projecting more confidence than he actually felt. "But if we are, we need to know that as soon as possible. Our time in the program is limited."

"All right," Candlewood said. "Let's assume you're right. That could be even worse. What do you think is going to happen when you confront a mobster about one of his crimes?"

"Listen, John, I would prefer to be stealthy about this, but we just don't have time," Nog said. "We need to find out what we're up against and start doing something about it. We can't spend all of our days here figuring out Vic's circumstances."

"All right," Candlewood said. "I'm just . . . I'm just concerned."

"I appreciate that," Nog said. "Especially since I know you think Vic is just a hologram."

"It's not Vic I'm concerned about," Candlewood said. "It's you. I know you consider Vic a friend, and since you're my friend, I want to help as best I can."

"Thank you, John," Nog said. "I really think we need to take direct action now."

"Then let's do it."

Nog entered the large hotel lobby—to which the mining theme had been extended—and approached the concierge. The older man—thin, with silvering, perfectly coiffed hair, and dressed in an elegant black suit—looked up from his desk. "May I help you, sir?" A large, framed mirror adorned the wall behind him.

"Yes," Nog said. "We'd like to see Mister Calderone."

One corner of the concierge's thin lips curled almost imperceptibly upward, as though the man wanted simultaneously to both conceal and convey his amusement. "We should go," Candlewood said. He took Nog by the arm and lightly urged him away, but the operations chief held his ground.

"A meeting with us will be of financial benefit to Mister Calderone," Nog said.

"I'm afraid I can't help you, Mister . . . ?"

"Nog."

"I'm afraid I can't help you, Mister Nog," the concierge repeated. "Is there anything else?"

"Nog, come on," Candlewood said. "Let's go."

Nog ignored the advice. Instead, he stepped forward, placed his hands on the concierge's desk, and leaned in over it. He'd seen his uncle take such a pose before, in the face of some very powerful people. "If we walk out the door," he said, pitching his voice low, "we're never coming back." A bluff, of course, but one Nog thought he could sell. "Before we leave, you might want to tell Mister Calderone that we can provide him what Vic Fontaine can't." Nog reasoned that if Calderone didn't want something from Vic—or possibly *for* him, as in a ransom of some kind—he wouldn't have sent his thugs to abduct the singer; he would have sent them to kill him.

The eyes of the concierge squinted for just an instant, as though he had chosen to adjust his focus on the Ferengi. A moment later, he stood up in a long, languorous movement that suggested that he had no intention of assisting Nog. "Pardon me for one moment," the concierge said. He retreated through a door in the wall behind the desk, into what looked like a dimly lighted office. Nog realized that the mirror must be one-way, allowing observation of the lobby.

When the concierge closed the door behind him, Nog asked, "What do you think?"

"I think he might be contacting security," Candlewood said. "I think we might be getting escorted out of here shortly."

"Maybe," Nog said. "But I think he might be checking with his boss." They waited, one minute, then another, and Nog wondered if he had made a mistake. He started to consider what he and Candlewood should do next if they were turned away.

Then the door opened, and the concierge returned. "Mister Calderone has graciously agreed to squeeze you in to his busy schedule, tomorrow at six p.m."

"Tomorrow?" Nog said, painfully aware of the hours drifting away. "That won't do. We need to see Mister Calderone immediately."

The concierge smiled tightly. "I suggest that if you wish to see Mister Calderone at all, you will beat a hasty retreat."

Nog locked eyes with the man, trying to evaluate him. *A lower-level employee,* he thought, *but a gatekeeper when necessary for the big boss. He doesn't want to mistakenly chase us away, but he also doesn't trust that we have a legitimate reason to meet with Calderone.* Nog thought about the cash in his pocket and briefly contemplated the possibility of offering the concierge a bribe, but dismissed the idea as unlikely to work. Instead, he simply thanked the man.

The concierge leaned forward over the desk, as though wanting to impart confidential information. Nog moved closer, as did Candlewood. In a whisper, the man said, "You'd better not be wasting Mister Calderone's time, or you'll find yourself in a far worse situation than Vic Fontaine."

vi

Candlewood didn't care for the concierge's threat. The science officer wondered once again why the holoprogram had become so antagonistic. Back on the old station, he hadn't visited Vic's often, but the few times he had, the atmosphere had been rather . . . jaunty. The style of music didn't suit Candlewood's tastes, but he could still appreciate the musicianship of the band and the silky voice of Vic Fontaine.

Of course, we're not sitting in a lounge listening to a singer belting out songs, Candlewood thought. Maybe that change in setting had something to do with it. Still, he continued to believe that something had gone wrong with the holoprogram, presumably during its confinement to the simulation tester. Perhaps the code contained a bug— or more than one. Nog asserted that he'd run diagnostics verifying the program's normal ongoing execution, but the more Candlewood experienced it, the more it seemed somehow off.

Does it, though? he asked himself as he and Nog exited the Silver Lode hotel and started across the drive beneath the porte cochere. In truth, the historical Las Vegas setting impressed Candlewood with its level of detail and realism. Theoretically, the program could contain one or more bugs, either native to the original code or that had developed in the simulator, and they could be constrained to some portions of the projected environment—such as the run-down Fremont-Sunrise Hotel—or to some of the characters—or to just *one* of the characters. Candlewood feared that, if they did manage to find and free Vic, the singer would no longer be the friend Nog remembered him to be.

The two did not speak on their way across the parking lot. Candlewood worried that their conversation with the concierge had distressed Nog. Once they reached the sidewalk and joined the river of tourists strolling toward Las Vegas Boulevard, he stole a glance at his friend in an attempt to gauge his emotional state. To his surprise, Nog smiled. "His threat didn't upset you?" Candlewood asked, pointing back toward the Silver Lode.

"Why would it upset me?" Nog said. "We already know that Vic is in trouble, and this just confirms it. But it also confirms that we're on his trail."

"What do you plan on saying to this Bugsy Calderone?" Candlewood asked. "Cool Papa Owens told us he's a mobster. That doesn't make me think that he's just going to hand Vic over to us."

"No, probably not, but we can find out the reason he kidnapped Vic," Nog said. "Whatever problem Calderone has with him, we'll have to figure out how to resolve it."

"You make it sound so easy," Candlewood said, "but I'm not sure that—" He stopped speaking when he saw that Nog no longer walked beside him. He looked back and saw that the operations chief had fallen a few steps behind, his face a mien of concentration. "What is it?"

Nog quickly hurried to rejoin Candlewood. "Let's keep walking," Nog said, his voice tense.

Candlewood resumed his pace. Nog fell in beside him, his attention still clearly focused elsewhere. "What's the matter?" Candlewood asked.

"We're being followed," Nog said quietly.

Candlewood resisted the urge to turn and search among the crowd of pedestrians for whoever might be trailing them. "How do you know?" he asked Nog.

"I can hear the footsteps."

Candlewood listened, but he could not distinguish among the many pairs of shoes beating against the pavement. With the ambient noise, he could barely make out his own footfalls. He nevertheless trusted Nog's instincts—his instincts, and his ears. The operations chief had impressed Candlewood with his auditory abilities on more than one occasion. "How many people are following us?"

"Just one," Nog said. "Just one, but . . ." He tilted his head to one side for a few seconds, as though adjusting the position of his ears to better hear the object of his attention. "It's just one set of footsteps, but they're familiar."

"Familiar?" Candlewood said. He thought about whom Nog had interacted with enough that he could recognize a holographic character by their stride. *The concierge? Cool Papa Owens? Maybe the thugs Nog had seen abduct Vic?* "Who is it?"

Nog didn't seem to hear the question. Instead, he asked one of his own. "John, do you see the entrance to the next parking lot up ahead?"

Candlewood looked past the people on the sidewalk. To the right, automobiles drove up and down the roadway. To the left ran a tall manicured hedge, which ended at a drive where a large sign trumpeted the entry to the Desert Palm Casino. "I see it," he said.

"When we get there, turn left and go up the drive toward the casino," Nog said. "Keep walking and talking as though I'm right beside you."

"All right," Candlewood said, guessing what Nog had in mind, and being cautious enough not to ask about it.

When they reached the drive, they left the main flow of pedestrians on the sidewalk and headed toward the Desert Palm. Nog immediately ducked behind the hedge, while Candlewood kept walking and talking. "By the way, Nog, did you notice some of the dealers in the Silver Lode?" he asked. "There were some very handsome men in there." He felt a bit silly speaking to empty air. *Except that, with those ears, Nog can probably still hear me.* "I don't know the full capabilities of this holoprogram, but if we can save Vic, I might just have to come back here and—"

"Hey!"

Candlewood heard the feminine shout, and he turned to

see that Nog had emerged from his hiding spot behind the hedge to grab a woman by her arm. She wore a long green dress and an elegant beige hat. A handbag dangled on gold straps from her shoulder. She looked familiar to Candlewood, but he couldn't quite place her.

As he rushed toward Nog and the woman, she yanked her arm free of his grip. Candlewood expected her to dash away, but she didn't. Several people in the parking lot looked over, but Candlewood assured them they had nothing to worry about, and the woman waved onlookers away.

"What are you doing here?" Nog asked as Candlewood reached the pair. Up close, the science officer noticed the creases on the bridge of the woman's nose. Either something had gone terribly wrong with the holoprogram, or she was a real person who'd entered the holosuite after them.

"I just wanted to see what sort of progress you were making with Vic's program," the woman said, lending credence to her status as a user, not a character. "I told you months ago that I wanted you to bring me here. I guess I just got too anxious."

"Who are you?" Candlewood asked.

Before she could reply, Nog answered. "This is Ulu Lani," he said. "She works for my uncle."

"You're a dabo girl?" Candlewood asked.

"Waitstaff," Ulu said.

"And a spy," Nog charged. He spoke the words as though they tasted bitter in his mouth.

"Nog—" Ulu started to say, but the operations chief interrupted her.

"Don't try to deny it," he said. "I heard you last night outside the Shining Oasis. You followed us to Cool Papa Owens's place."

"Wait a minute," Candlewood said. "Who would this woman be spying for? Not Calderone; that wouldn't make any sense." The notion of a holographic character enlisting the aid of a real person sounded ridiculous. *Except isn't that essentially what happened when Vic Fontaine needed help with the jack-in-the-box threat?*

"No, not for Calderone," Nog said. "For my uncle."

"But why?" Candlewood asked.

"That's a good question," Nog said. "If I know my uncle, it's because he wants to prevent me from saving Vic so he doesn't have to dedicate a holosuite to the program around the clock. Is that it?"

"I don't know," Ulu said. "I don't think he wants to stop you from restoring the program. I think he's just anxious for the situation to resolve one way or the other. He would prefer to have Vic's lounge back, but he doesn't want to keep waiting. Now that his business is doing so well, he has a greater need than ever for the holosuites."

"Business before family," Nog said. Candlewood wondered if he had quoted a Rule of Acquisition.

"I don't agree," Ulu said. "You've been working on Vic's program since the new starbase began full operation, almost five months ago. Quark has let you do that."

"But he doesn't trust his own nephew enough not to spy on him," Nog said. He sounded hurt, which struck Candlewood as odd. Nog loved his uncle, and Candlewood assumed that Quark loved his nephew, but they lived very different lives. The elder Ferengi remained ensconced in the world of capitalism, while the younger had moved from there to the more idealistic world of Starfleet. Nog and Quark had a familial relationship, but from what Candlewood had seen, neither really expected much from the other.

"You say that about Quark," Ulu told Nog, "but you don't trust him either."

"Of course I trust my uncle."

"Really?" Ulu said. "Is that why you've had Vic's program running for a month and a half, but haven't told Quark yet?"

"Well, I . . . I . . ." Nog seemed at a loss.

"I think the words you're looking for are: I don't trust my uncle," Ulu said.

"I just didn't want him tampering with Vic's program until I could set things right," Nog said.

"I understand," Ulu said. "You didn't trust that Quark wouldn't tamper with the holoprogram."

Nog gazed down toward his feet, obviously abashed, but then he looked up at Ulu. "You lied to me," he said quietly to her. Candlewood didn't know to what Nog referred.

"I didn't," Ulu said. "I just didn't tell you everything."

"You lied," Nog said again, and then he looked to Candlewood. "She's been flirting with me from the night I started working to upload Vic's program from the tester— obviously so she could follow my progress and report back to my uncle." Nog appeared crestfallen. "I should have known better."

"What?" Ulu said, suddenly angry. "Why should you have known better? Because you think I'm beautiful, and you think a beautiful woman could never be genuinely interested in you? Maybe you should tell that to your father's wife. Maybe you should tell Captain Ro."

"Don't try to sell me your lies," Nog said.

"I'm not trying to sell you anything," Ulu said. "I'm telling you the truth."

"So it's just a coincidence that you flirted with me while you were spying on me," Nog said.

"No, it's not a coincidence," Ulu said more calmly. "Quark wanted me to check on your work, but he didn't ask me to flirt with you." She reached forward and took Nog's hands. "I flirted with you because I liked you. I *still* like you."

"Really?" Nog said in a tone that somehow mixed melancholy and hope.

"Really," Ulu said. "And I can prove it to you." She opened her handbag. "Yes, I've been observing your efforts in the holosuite, but I've also been doing what I can to figure out what's happened to Vic."

"You know about what's happened to Vic?" Candlewood asked.

"You two talked about it in the Replimat," Ulu said. She plucked a small device from her ear, tugged the attached wire, and pulled a box from inside the back of her dress. "Audio pickup," she said, "though this doesn't work as well as a twenty-fourth-century model." She stuffed the device into her purse, then pulled out a sheaf of papers and handed them to Nog. "Here's what I found out."

As Nog started to examine the papers, Candlewood stepped up to take a look at them as well. The science officer saw a lot of numbers, but when he began reading the terms next to them, he didn't know what they meant. Nog glanced at the second sheet, and then the third, and then he hurriedly paged through the rest.

"What are we looking at?" Candlewood asked.

"They're financial transactions," Nog said. "Mostly real-estate usage deals and monetary transfers."

"And why is that important?" Candlewood asked.

"Because," Nog said, holding up one of the pieces of paper and pointing at a name printed on them, "they were all executed by Vic Fontaine."

vii

The doors opened before Keiko O'Brien to reveal chaos. Some of the furniture within had been pushed aside, a chair had toppled, several articles of clothing had been strewn about, and a siren pierced the air. It looked and sounded as though a low-yield photon torpedo had detonated.

Yeah, Keiko thought. *A photon torpedo called Clan O'Brien.*

Keiko couldn't help but smile. Where in the past she might have complained about the noise her husband and son were making, or the mess they'd made of the cabin, she instead took it in stride. She loved the bond that Miles and Kirayoshi had formed, even though the pair typically displayed it in raucous fashion. The siren belonged to a traditional Cardassian game they liked to play. *Koris-tahn* combined tactical and strategic thinking with physical play that rewarded dexterity and athleticism. With his experience and adult frame, Miles enjoyed a natural advantage over their son, but Yoshi, just turned thirteen, had recently come closer and closer to defeating his father.

Keiko had initially tolerated the displaced furniture and the occasional blare of the siren because of how it brought her husband and son together. She grew accustomed to it pretty quickly, though, sometimes even watching as the two played the game. Molly despised it, but as a teenager just shy of her eighteenth birthday, she despised an ever-growing list of things.

"I'm home," Keiko said as she entered the cabin. Miles and Yoshi looked up from where they sat facing each other on the deck. Both of them had a wooden rod in each hand, spinning a metal hoop around it, but they set them down as soon as they saw her.

"Hi, Mom," Yoshi called as he jumped up and ran over to hug Keiko.

Miles followed, though it took him longer to haul himself to his feet. He wore dark slacks and a deep-purple shirt with a stand-up collar. His shift had ended hours ago, which explained the civilian clothes he wore, but not why his uniform shirt lay draped across the back of the sofa. "Hi, honey," he said as he embraced her. "How was your day?"

"Long," Keiko said. "We began studying the data the *Robinson* crew sent back from the first planet they visited." Captain Sisko had departed Deep Space 9 six weeks earlier, taking his ship on an extended exploratory mission into the Gamma Quadrant. As the starbase's chief botanist—a civilian position she began three months prior—Keiko would lead the research effort on the newly discovered flora. "We saw some interesting specimens, but our initial work involves classification and a lot of setup. It's time-consuming and pretty tedious."

"Well, you're home now," Miles said, giving her a quick kiss on the lips. "I've got a meal queued up for you in the replicator whenever you're ready to eat. A seitan wrap, cucumber salad, and brown rice."

"Great," Keiko said. "I'm starving."

"I'll get it for you," Miles said. He headed across the room, toward the replicator.

"How was school?" Keiko asked Yoshi.

"Okay. We started learning about clouds in terrestrial science and the Federation Charter in civics."

"And what about that calculus test?" Keiko asked.

"I don't know," Yoshi said with a shrug. "I think I did okay."

"Just okay?"

"Yeah." He motioned back toward where he and Miles had been sitting on the deck. "I'm going to go back to our game."

Yoshi bounded back into the living area. Keiko wanted to ask her son more about his mathematics exam, but she let him go—it really had been a long day. Instead, she moved to the dining table, where her daughter sat reading from one padd and making notes with a stylus on another. "Hi, Molly."

"Hi," Molly said without looking up, her voice flat. Even after almost three full months on DS9, she hadn't completely forgiven her mother for taking her away from Bajor for her final year of secondary education. Molly's attitude had begun to improve recently, but she still sometimes lapsed into sullen moods.

"How was school?" Keiko asked as she sat down at the table.

"Fine." Molly inserted her stylus into one of the padds, stacked one device atop the other, and stood up. "I'm going to study in my room." She stomped away from the table.

"Molly," Keiko called, but her daughter didn't stop. Miles came over to the table and set her dinner in front of her, along with dining utensils and a napkin.

"Don't mind Molly," he said. "She heard from Suzanne today, so she's feeling sorry for herself again." One of Molly's classmates back on Bajor, Suzanne had been one of her closest friends. "Would you like a glass of wine?"

"How about a bottle?"

"Now, now, it's not that bad," Miles said. He moved to the sideboard, retrieved a red, and peered at the label. "We've got a Kendra Valley varietal open already. Is that all right?"

"That sounds perfect." Miles collected two stemmed glasses from the sideboard and carried them over with the bottle to the table. "It's easy for you to say it's not that bad, because Molly doesn't blame you for taking her away from her friends," Keiko said. She paused and thought about that while Miles poured wine for both of them. "Why is it that she doesn't blame you, only me?"

"Because she knows who makes the decisions in this family," Miles said with a chuckle. Then he raised his glass and said, "To the evil matriarch, Keiko Ishikawa O'Brien."

"Very funny," she said, but she smiled anyway.

"Don't worry," Miles said. "She'll be off to university before long."

"That's what concerns me," Keiko said. "She'll leave for some distant college, and we'll never see her again." She spoke the words in jest, but they reflected a genuine maternal fear: that Molly would choose to attend school on the other side of the Federation, making it impossible to see her on a regular basis.

"Relax," Miles said. He sipped at his wine. "The other day, I saw her looking at information for the University of Ashalla and also Brintall Provincial College."

"Brintall?" Keiko asked.

"It's somewhere in Bajor's southern hemisphere," Miles said.

Keiko let out such a loud sigh of relief, it sounded comical. Miles laughed, and she joined him. Molly's resentment still bothered her, but she had to trust that their relationship would mend with time.

"Do you really think she'll pick a university on Bajor?" Keiko asked.

"Either that or one on Cardassia," Miles said. "Those are the two worlds she knows best, and even if she's still mad at us for bringing her here—"

"Mad at *me*," Keiko corrected him.

"Even if she's still mad at you, I don't think she'd want to go to school that far from the family."

"I hope you're right, Miles," Keiko said. "I hope—"

The boatswain's whistle sounded. *"Hub to Chief O'Brien."* The voice belonged to the beta-shift duty officer, Ensign Allasar. Miles gave Keiko a questioning look—*What's this about?*—and then responded.

"This is O'Brien."

"Chief, the Defiant's *shuttlecraft,* Sagan, *has returned to Deep Space Nine,"* Allasar said. *"It was carrying Odo, and you*

wanted to be notified when he came aboard." Keiko felt her eyes widen at the name of the shape-shifter.

"Has he been assigned guest quarters?" Miles asked.

"Yes, sir," Allasar said, and she read off Odo's cabin identification.

"Acknowledged. Thank you, Ensign. O'Brien out."

"Odo's back," Keiko said.

"I was going to tell you," Miles said. "I only just found out today."

"Does he know that Nerys has come back from the wormhole?" The O'Briens had not spoken to her yet, but the vedek had apparently attempted to contact them two nights previous. She had left the starbase for Bajor the next morning, but had asked Doctor Boudreaux to let them know about her return, and that she would be in touch with them soon.

"I don't know if Odo's heard," Miles said. "I figured I'd pay him a visit when he arrived and let him know in person."

"That's a good idea," Keiko said. "You should go."

"I will," Miles said, "once I've sat with my wife through her dinner."

Keiko smiled at her husband. It seemed impossible that they had been married for almost nineteen years. In some ways, it felt as though they'd just met. Of course, they had two living, growing reminders who demonstrated every day how long the couple had been together. Even after all that time, though, Keiko still loved to come home to Miles.

viii

O'Brien watched Odo's expression as the door to the shape-shifter's guest cabin glided open. The engineer thought he might see at least a hint of surprise on the Changeling's face. After all, Odo had been back on the starbase for less than an hour, and he probably had no expectation of any visitors. But the curiously blank features Odo wore in his guise as a humanoid didn't change at all.

"Yes, Chief?"

"Welcome back," O'Brien said. "I'm glad to see that you're all right." He knew that Odo had been injured in an altercation with the shape-shifting Ascendant life-form, and that it had taken nearly six weeks for him to recover.

"Thank you."

O'Brien waited a moment for an invitation to come inside. Odo said nothing more, though, forcing the chief engineer to speak up. "I was hoping I could talk with you privately," he said. When it looked as if Odo might refuse, O'Brien added, "It's important."

The shape-shifter sighed—a curious action for a being who didn't actually have to breathe, but doubtless one of the behaviors he had cultivated in an attempt to fit in with natural humanoids. For a moment, O'Brien thought that Odo still might decline, but then he stepped back and gestured inside. "Please come in."

O'Brien walked into the living area of the guest cabin. "I won't take up much of your time," he said. He sat down in a comfortable chair and waited for Odo to join him. The Changeling followed him inside and took a seat across from him, on the sofa. "I'm sorry to come barging in here without contacting you first, but I thought this was something I needed to—"

O'Brien stopped speaking. In just the few seconds since Odo had first opened the door, something in his face had changed. *Not just in his face,* O'Brien thought. *In his whole body.* He couldn't quite identify what had happened, but Odo looked somehow less solid, as though whatever physical capacity he possessed to maintain his shape had begun to flag. "Odo, are you all right?"

"I am fatigued," Odo said.

"Just fatigued?" O'Brien asked. "I hate to say it, Odo, but you look terrible."

"How astute of you to notice," Odo said, not without sarcasm.

"I'm sorry, I just meant that you look like you need medical attention." O'Brien got up out of his chair. "I can call for an emergency transport and have you in Sector General right away."

Odo held up a hand. "No, please, Chief, don't," he said. "I'm still recovering from my injuries. I've been holding this form for most of the day, and I just need to regenerate."

"Is that all it is?"

"Doctor Girani is satisfied that I'm in good health now, and that I'll make a full recovery. It will just take some more time before I regain my stamina." O'Brien stayed on his feet and continued to regard Odo, debating whether he should take action regardless of the shape-shifter's wishes. "Please, Chief, if you could just tell me why you've come, then you can leave me to regenerate."

"Yes, of course," O'Brien said. "Sorry." He sat back down in the chair, took a deep breath, and started. "Three nights ago, a small ship came out of the wormhole."

"A Jem'Hadar ship?" Odo asked, concern evident in his tone, and O'Brien shook his head. "Was it from the Dominion?"

"No," O'Brien said. "It was carrying only one passenger. It was Kira Nerys."

"Nerys," Odo said, rising quickly to his feet. The surprise O'Brien had searched for on the shape-shifter's face moments earlier finally materialized. He looked thunderstruck, and as close to ecstatic as the chief engineer had ever seen him. "Is she . . . is she . . . ?"

"She's fine," O'Brien said, and he stood up too. "I didn't

speak with her directly, but Captain Ro and Doctor Boudreaux did."

"Where are her guest quarters?" Odo asked, taking a step toward the door.

"Hold on," O'Brien said. "She's not on the station anymore; she left for Bajor yesterday morning."

"I was just there," Odo lamented. "The *Sagan* stopped at Bajor to disembark Doctor Girani. If I'd known Nerys was there . . ."

"I'm sorry, I just found out a short time ago that you were going to be back on the starbase," O'Brien said. "The captain is away on leave at the moment, otherwise I'm sure she would have notified you herself."

"Do you know where Nerys is on Bajor?" Odo asked. "Has she gone back to the Vanadwan Monastery?"

"I'm afraid I don't know," O'Brien said.

"I need to contact her," Odo said. "I need to get to Bajor."

"Pardon me for saying so, but don't you need to regenerate before you do anything else?" In just the time they'd been speaking, O'Brien perceived a degradation in Odo's . . . *cohesion*.

Odo regarded the chief engineer, and O'Brien could tell that he didn't want to regenerate; he wanted more than anything else to see Kira. In an attempt to prevent the shape-shifter from taking any unnecessary chances with his health, O'Brien said, "I'm sure that Commander Blackmer will be happy to schedule a pilot to take you on a runabout to Bajor in the morning." Under normal circumstances, Odo wouldn't require a ship to make the journey from DS9 to Bajor—he could take on the form of a spaceborne lifeform—but the Changeling's compromised stamina clearly dictated that he choose another mode of travel. "I can look into that for you right now, if you'd like."

Odo appeared to consider the offer. O'Brien knew that

the shape-shifter preferred to do things on his own whenever he could, but now was obviously not one of those times. "Thank you," Odo said. "I'd appreciate that."

"Good, then," O'Brien said.

"And Chief," Odo added, "if you could possibly find out Nerys's location on Bajor."

"Of course," O'Brien said.

"Thank you."

O'Brien headed for the door and left. He immediately walked to the nearest turbolift, which he ordered to the Hub so that he could check on the runabout and pilot rotation for the next day. He knew that Odo had waited a couple of years for the wormhole to reopen after it had collapsed with Kira inside it, and then had waited months longer once it had reopened, still plainly hoping for her return. Since that had finally happened, O'Brien could just imagine how sweet their reunion would be.

Thinking about it put a spring in his step.

Five

Reinvestment

Candlewood finished dressing, putting on beige pleated slacks and a green aloha shirt, one of the casual outfits he, Nog, and Ulu had purchased at a shop off the lobby of the Shining Oasis hotel. The science officer had slept well the previous night. After sharing a sometimes-awkward evening meal with Nog and Ulu, the three of them had returned to the Silver Lode, where one of them had staked out the parking lot, one of them the hotel lobby, and one of them the casino's main entrance. They all kept watch for any sign of Vic. None of them espied the singer, but Nog did spot the vehicle in which he'd seen Vic kidnapped, identifying the Eldorado by the number-and-letter code on plates mounted on the rear. The sighting provided further confirmation of Bugsy Calderone's involvement in the abduction.

Candlewood didn't know what to make of Ulu Lani. Her presence in the holoprogram, and her efforts to spy on them, seemed suspicious at best. Her easy admission that she worked for Quark sounded reasonable, but it also felt convenient. Moreover, she hadn't fully explained the legal documents she'd produced—where she'd gotten them, when, how—at least not to Candlewood's satisfaction.

Despite all of that, Nog's behavior around Ulu suggested that he actually liked her, though Candlewood could only imagine that any romantic feelings he harbored had been tempered by her covert actions. Still, the operations chief had not demanded that she exit the program, a decision he later justified by claiming that he thought she could be of assistance to them. From the way that Ulu spoke to Nog, and from the way she looked at him, it also appeared that she felt her own emotional connection. That made her willingness to invade his privacy confusing.

Candlewood quietly pulled open the bedroom door and stepped into the main living area of the suite. Nog had insisted that Ulu sleep in his room, while he would stay on the sofa. Candlewood expected to see him there, but he saw only a rumpled sheet and blanket. Nog instead sat at a large, round table by the window, a sprawl of papers spread out before him.

"Did you get any sleep at all?" Candlewood asked. When he'd gone to bed last night, he'd left Nog studying the documents provided by Ulu.

"I managed to lie down and get a few hours rest." Despite the declaration, Nog looked and sounded tired.

Candlewood strolled over to the table and peered down at the pages covering it. "Have you learned anything from all these records?"

"From what I can tell, Vic went from singer to financial mogul," Nog said. "According to these documents, he owned water rights across considerable swaths of real estate in and around Las Vegas."

"Is that unusual?"

"Not for a Ferengi," Nog said. "And not even for a twentieth-century human, but it just doesn't ring true. Vic didn't care about such things. He lived to sing, to entertain people. He didn't care about the acquisition of wealth."

Candlewood sat down across from Nog. "I hate to bring this up again, but this program ran in the simulation tester for two years. Maybe Vic's matrix degraded and he's no longer the character he once was."

Nog did not respond right away. Candlewood could see that even the chance that the operations chief had essentially lost his friend troubled him. Finally, Nog said, "I hope that's not the case, but I have to admit that it's at least a possibility." He gazed back down at the papers on the table. "There's something else that's bothering me, though."

"What's that?" Candlewood asked.

"It's me," said a woman's voice. Candlewood hadn't heard the door to the other bedroom open, but when he looked in that direction, he saw Ulu standing there. "You don't trust me." She walked over to the table, pulled out a chair, and sat down.

Candlewood waited to see whether Nog would confirm or deny Ulu's assertion, but he did neither. Instead, he dropped the flat of his hand to the center of the table, atop several of the documents laid out there. "Where did you get these?"

Ulu took a deep breath and exhaled loudly, as though deciding whether or not to answer the question. At last, she said, "I got them from account files here, at the Shining Oasis casino."

"But how would you know to search for these there?" Nog asked. "How would you know to search for them *anywhere*? Why would you think that these would be in Vic's account?"

"I didn't think they would be in Vic's account," Ulu said. "I don't even know if Vic has an account at the casino."

"Then whose account did you take all these documents from?" Candlewood asked.

Ulu looked from Nog to Candlewood and back to Nog before answering: "Morn's."

ii

"Morn?" Nog said at the same time as Candlewood. He heard the same confusion in the science officer's voice as he did in his own. Lani simply nodded.

"Hold on," Candlewood said. "Are we talking about the same Morn? The bulky, bald Lurian who was more of a fixture in Quark's than the barstools? Who owned a shipping business and could take two hours to tell one story? *That* Morn?"

"I don't know about him being a fixture in Quark's because I wasn't there back then," Lani said, "but yes, *that* Morn."

"I don't understand," Candlewood said. "Why would there be legal documents with Vic's name on them in Morn's casino account?" Nog asked himself the same question. He could think of several reasons, none of them good.

"I can only tell you what I know," Lani said. "I'm not supposed to say anything to anybody, but because you employed an expiring, one-time back door to reenter the program, circumstances have changed."

Nog snapped his head up toward Lani. "How do you know we used a back door?" he asked, already knowing the answer. Lani cast her gaze downward, reinforcing his belief. She said nothing, and so Nog replied to his own question: "You spied on me even outside the holosuite and the bar. You heard my conversation with Felix."

"I'm sorry," Lani said softly. With her head bowed, her long red hair hid her face.

He threw up his hands, then pushed back from the table, his anger and disappointment making it impossible for him to keep still. Nog issued a disapproving grunt, moved out from behind the table, and marched across the room toward the front door. He had no particular destination in mind, only the drive to get out of the suite. He had his hand on the doorknob when Candlewood spoke up.

"Nog," the science officer said, "if we're going to help Vic, we need to learn everything that Miss Ulu knows."

The desire to put distance between himself and Lani remained, but Candlewood was right. She might have information that could help them save Vic.

Nog let go of the doorknob, then walked over to the sofa and sat down heavily on it. A pillow flopped over and slipped to the carpeting. He left it there. "Tell us," he said.

"You both served on the original Deep Space Nine, and you knew Morn," Lani said, "so I'm sure you know that he liked frequenting Vic's lounge to listen to him sing."

Nog did know that, and apparently so did Candlewood. "I didn't visit Vic's very often," the science officer said, "but Morn was there most of the times I did."

"He loved the sound of Vic's voice," Lani said.

The statement seemed strange to Nog, and speculative at best. *Unless—*

"Morn also enjoyed gambling in the casino," Lani continued. "He did so quite often, using the small sum the program supplies to users. He could never win, though; in the end, he would always lose everything, and he would have to exit the program so that his funds would reset." The on-hand cash provided to users of Bashir 62 marked one of the few details within the holoprogram that would reinitialize upon reentry.

"Of course he always lost," Candlewood said. "There's a name given to the stochastic process that describes betting games like those in the Shining Oasis—like those all over Las Vegas, I'm guessing. When the probability of a player with a finite stake winning any individual round is less than fifty percent, it's called *gambler's ruin*, and the outcome in the long run is assured." Nog understood the science officer's description. On Ferenginar, they dubbed the mathematical process *bettor's folly*, and it served as the underpinning for the wagering rules of dabo.

"Over time, Morn got bored playing for low stakes," Lani said. "So he opened an account at the Shining Oasis and deposited the small sum the program provided. Then he went back every day for months, each time adding to his account. It still didn't amount to all that much, but it eventually allowed him to make larger bets. He continued adding to the account each time he entered the program. By the time he lost all of those funds, he'd established a basis for credit with the casino."

"Established a basis for credit?" Candlewood asked. "By

depositing money and then losing it all? That doesn't make any sense."

"Nog?" Lani prompted.

"It makes perfect sense, especially for a casino," Nog said. "Morn demonstrated the capacity over time to produce capital, as well as the predilection for eventually losing it all at the gaming tables. For the Shining Oasis, what could have been better?"

As Candlewood shook his head in apparent disbelief, Lani continued. "Morn opened a line of credit with the casino, which finally allowed him to gamble for high stakes. He had a great deal of fun, and for a while he even won more than he lost, but it didn't last. When he ended up losing everything he'd borrowed, with no means of repaying the debt in anything approaching a timely manner, he was faced with being banned from the Shining Oasis—or possibly even being charged with a financial crime."

"Okay," Candlewood said. "Being banned from a holographic casino or being charged with a crime in an illusory world seem like problems without genuine repercussions."

"Not in the real word, no," Lani agreed. "But Morn would not have been able to enter the program without being escorted out of the Shining Oasis or being arrested, even if all he wanted to do was listen to Vic sing. Also, all of the other establishments in Las Vegas—even in the holographic Las Vegas—shared information about what they called deadbeats. Morn would have been prohibited from entering *any* of the hotels and casinos."

"I guess that's unfortunate," Candlewood said, "but what does it have to do with all of this?" He waved his hand over the legal documents covering the table.

"Morn didn't want to stop visiting the program," Lani said, "so he convinced Vic to cosign on his line of credit. That allowed him time to pay off the debt."

"But how could he pay it off without the funds to do so?" Candlewood asked, but Nog already realized what had taken place.

"With the increased line of credit," he said, "Morn thought he could win back what he already owed."

Lani nodded. "And instead, he lost it all."

Nog stood up from the sofa. "So the Shining Oasis not only held Morn responsible for the debt, but also Vic."

"What does that mean?" Candlewood asked. "Vic vouched for Morn, and then Morn lost holographic funds in a holographic casino, so Vic was in danger of . . . what? Being sent to a holographic debtor's prison?"

"Vic would have been fired from his job, barred from similar employment anywhere in Las Vegas, and would likely have been charged with fraud or a similar financial crime," Lani said. "Morn didn't want that to happen, so he had to make good on the funds owed to the Shining Oasis."

"But how could he do that?" Candlewood asked. "I know a lot about computers and mathematics and the physical sciences, but I don't have much of a handle on antiquated financial systems."

Nog walked back over to the table, though he didn't sit. "There were a lot of things he could have done," he said. "Almost none of them leading to a positive outcome."

"Morn hired a forger in Las Vegas to produce real-estate water-rights documents and records of the transactions that provided corroboration of those instruments," Lani said. Nog peered into her startlingly green eyes as she spoke about finance; she'd never seemed sexier.

"Why would Morn have fake documents created?" Candlewood asked. He sounded befuddled. "Wouldn't that just make things worse?"

"It could," Nog said, jumping ahead, "but he probably just wanted to buy some time."

"That's right," Lani said. "He gave the documents to Vic so that he in turn could produce them for the casino as a demonstration of his solvency. The Shining Oasis would then allow them enough time to repay the line of credit before attempting to sell the bogus rights."

"What good would time do," Candlewood asked, "if neither Morn nor Vic had the capital to pay off the debt?"

"It gave Morn time to amass the funds," Nog concluded. "But how did he intend to do it? Surely not by gambling again?"

"Not exactly," Lani said. "Morn believed that he could rig the slot machines in holographic Las Vegas. He intended to build a device from the materials available in the program and use it all over town."

"If he won enough," Nog said, "that could also get him barred from the casinos."

"He knew that," Lani said, "but he still wanted to relieve Vic of the burden he'd placed on him. If he couldn't craft such a device, then he thought that he could borrow the cash from the criminal element in Las Vegas. That also would have made it difficult for him to return to the program, but at that point, he cared only about helping Vic out of the bad position he'd put him in."

"So which of those things did he do?" Candlewood asked.

"Neither," Lani said, "because Deep Space Nine was destroyed."

iii

Nog saw Candlewood gaze up at him, and the two shared a silent, sober look. "What does that mean?" the science officer asked.

"It means that Vic was in trouble with the Shining Oasis

when the program was executing normally, in a holosuite," Nog said. He sat back down at the table. "But since the program's been running in the simulator, without Morn to help him out, his problems have somehow shifted to Bugsy Calderone."

"What did Vic do?" Candlewood asked. "Did he try to sell the rights to a mobster?"

"That doesn't sound like a recipe for a long life," Nog said. "Vic's not stupid. He wouldn't try to sell something he didn't genuinely own—especially not to a dangerous criminal."

"He didn't know," Lani said.

"Who didn't know what?" Candlewood asked.

"Vic didn't know the documents were forgeries," Lani said. "When Morn gave him the water rights as collateral for the debt, he passed them off as genuine."

Lani's statement seemed to bolster Nog's earlier intuition, but he wanted to be sure. "How do you know all this?" he asked her. "Not from my uncle."

"No," Lani said. "Morn told me."

"Then he's alive," Nog said. "My uncle's been looking for him."

"I received instructions from him just before I entered this program," Lani said.

"Instructions?" Candlewood asked.

"I work for Morn."

"I thought you worked for Quark," Candlewood said.

"When the new Deep Space Nine began operation," Lani said, "Morn hired me through a mutual acquaintance on Bajor. He wanted me to take a job at Quark's on the starbase to find out about Vic for him. Morn didn't think there would be problems loading Vic's program into the new holosuites, but when I reported that there were, and that you—" Lani looked up at Nog with her beautiful green eyes. "—were working to fix them, he asked me to follow your efforts. Quark also hired me to keep an eye on you, which was very convenient."

"Why didn't Morn just do all of this himself?" Nog asked. "My uncle would have welcomed him back."

"Morn is . . . busy."

"Busy?" Candlewood asked. "Doing what?"

"After the first Deep Space Nine was destroyed," Lani said, "Morn couldn't stop thinking about Vic. He knew he'd given the singer worthless paper to prop up his outstanding debt, and he worried that, while the program ran in the simulator, Vic would pay the price for that. He waited anxiously for Quark to install holosuites in his place on Bajor. Morn wanted to reenter the program so that he could warn Vic about the counterfeit documents and find a way to pay off his debt to the Shining Oasis."

"But when Quark installed the holosuites half a year later," Nog said, "they were older models that couldn't accommodate Vic's complex matrix."

"And because the program was continuing to execute in the simulation tester," Lani said, "Morn knew that he'd put Vic's freedom in danger. If either he or the casino attempted to liquidate the water-rights holdings, the fraud would be revealed and Vic could easily end up in prison."

"Is that why Morn left Bajor?" Candlewood asked. "Because he couldn't face that?"

"He left Bajor because of the situation he'd put Vic in," Lani said, "but not because he couldn't face it. He went in search of a means of saving Vic."

"Why didn't he just steal the tester and install the program in some other holosuite somewhere?" Candlewood asked.

"Morn doubted he could find a place that would allow him the dedicated time he would need in order to build the device for the slot machines and then acquire enough wealth to resolve Vic's situation," Lani said. "He also worried about Quark's security."

"My uncle typically rigs his equipment to fail the instant it leaves his property," Nog said. "He had to disable it on the simulator when he evacuated the station, but he would have reset it afterward."

"So what is it that Morn's doing to try to save Vic?" Candlewood asked.

"For one thing," Lani said, "he's got me helping you."

"But what is *he* doing?" Candlewood asked.

"I'm not sure," Lani said. "I only know that he's been working on finding a way to save Vic ever since he left Bajor."

"For almost two years?" Candlewood said. "That sounds like an obsession."

Lani nodded. "I think it is," she said. "It's all he talks about. Morn seems very single-minded about it. As best I can tell, he's dedicated his life to this endeavor to the exclusion of just about everything else. He also seems extremely depressed."

"My uncle thought he was suffering from survivor's guilt," Nog said. "I know he lost a lot of friends on the original Deep Space Nine."

"I think that's why he's fixated on saving Vic Fontaine," Lani said. "Vic is a friend who survived the destruction of the station, and somebody who Morn might be able to help."

"But help how?" Nog asked. "He can't bring funds or a device to cheat the slot machines into the program. What is it he's doing?"

"I don't know," Lani said. "But he's definitely up to something."

iv

Kira sat on a bench, near the end of one of the two long tables that lined the refectory of the Shikina Monastery.

The polished marble of the tabletop perched on rough-hewn pedestals and felt cool beneath her touch. The early cloud cover over Ashalla had yet to burn off, leaving a chill in the midmorning air.

Kira speared first one and then a second *alva* with a fork and lifted the small fruit to her mouth. She had waited to eat breakfast until after the resident monks had completed theirs. She and Altek Dans had the dining hall to themselves.

The previous night had seen the news of Kira's emergence from the Celestial Temple, and of Altek's arrival from the past, dominating the Bajoran comnet. While a few strident voices cast doubts about the veracity of the kai's announcements, most commentary centered on the astounding nature of the events. That morning brought the first mutterings of partisan arguments, with mainstream believers pointing to the return of Kira—herself an adherent of traditional faith—as an act by the Prophets to confirm their divinity. By contrast, several Ohalavaru leaders noted Kira's part in making public the Ohalu texts, implying that her sudden reappearance supported their opinions about the Endalla falsework and the alien nature of the Prophets.

"All of this conflicting talk has me off-balance," Kira told Altek, who sat across from her. "If there was one thing during the Occupation that held Bajor together, it was our shared faith."

"Surely, there must be room for dissent," Altek said.

"Of course," Kira said. "I'm not talking about only the Ohalavaru. I mean, I don't understand them; I've read their texts, listened to their arguments about the falsework, and none of it compels me to relinquish my faith. But I support their right to worship—or *not* worship—as they see fit."

"Then what's troubling you?"

"It's the incendiary character of the rhetoric, and the growing risk of violence hanging over Bajor," Kira said. "It's got to stop."

"In my experience," Altek said, "people are never so threatened as when facts disagree with their deepest held beliefs—religious or otherwise."

"I can only hope that Kai Pralon is right in thinking that my presence in the public eye will help calm people's fears," Kira said. "My presence—and yours." Kira had not seen or spoken with Altek since the kai's address the day before, so she had no idea how he felt about the public disclosure not only of his existence, but of his identity.

"I hope our arrival on Bajor will help too," he said. When he added nothing more, Kira decided to put her question to him directly.

"Did you agree to allow the kai to reveal your name and likeness?" she asked. "I thought you wanted to remain as anonymous as you could."

"I did," Altek said. "But Kai Pralon spoke to me about how she believed I could contribute in a positive way to what's been happening on Bajor. I don't know if she's right, but her conversation with me made me think about my responsibilities as a Bajoran."

"Did the kai pressure you into letting her make you a public figure?" Even just asking the question made Kira uncomfortable. She reminded herself that Pralon Onala occupied the position of spiritual leader to the Bajoran people, not Winn Adami.

"I can say that the kai was determined to convince me," Altek said. "I don't look forward to the attention I'm probably going to draw, but I don't regret my decision. I've been thinking a lot about what I would do when I finally made it back to Bajor. At first, I just wanted to be here, to find a place for myself among our people, but after I saw you again . . . I started to think more about what all of this means. When I arrived on Deep Space Nine, it all seemed so random, but now . . . with you here . . . I don't know. It feels as though there must be some meaning to my being here . . . as though I was brought here for a reason."

"Will you make a public address?" Kira asked, knowing that she would be speaking to the people of Bajor later that day.

"No," he said. "The kai did propose that I make a speech of some kind, introduce myself to our people, but I demurred."

"And she let it go? She didn't insist?"

"She suggested that I at least allow members of the media to interview me," Altek said. "I'm not comfortable with that idea, but I did tell her I would consider it. These are difficult times, and if I truly want to make a home for myself on Bajor, I have a responsibility to its people—especially during this time of spiritual crisis."

"I understand," Kira said. As Altek continued eating his *milaberry* pancakes with *jumja* syrup, the vedek finished the fruit on her plate: a few more alvas, some wedges of *moba*, and a few slices of *pooncheen*. She thought about what Altek had told her, and as she sipped from a cup of *cela* tea, she watched him eat his meal.

Something else is on his mind, the vedek thought. Altek hadn't said anything in particular, but Kira could still perceive his preoccupation. The observation made her realize just how well she knew him, undoubtedly because of her experiences as Keev Anora. "Is something bothering you?" she asked.

Altek looked up from his plate. He sighed heavily. "I guess there is," he said.

"Do you want to talk about it?"

"I think I have to," Altek said. He set his fork down with

a metallic ring. "You know how shocked I was when I first saw you."

"How shocked we both were," Kira said.

"Right," Altek said. "I also told you that, after our time together in the past, I still have feelings for you—"

"Feelings for Keev Anora," Kira said quietly, "not for Kira Nerys." She spoke firmly, but not without kindness.

"Nerys and Anora are one and the same," Altek said. "It's strange, and maybe not completely explainable, but I don't think you can deny it."

"Maybe I can't," Kira said, "but we already talked about this. We can't just pick up where we left off. Back then, with you, that was my life as Anora, but now I have an entirely different life as Nerys. Our experiences are wholly different. You can say that we're the same person, but there's more to it than that."

"There doesn't need to be more than the emotions we feel," Altek said. "Except . . . except that there is more to it." He looked away from her and shook his head.

"We don't have to talk about this again," Kira said. "You even spoke about moving forward cautiously . . . about getting to know each other again. We can just let that happen without having to continue reexamining it."

"I know, I know," Altek said. "That's not it." He set his elbows on the tabletop and folded one hand around the other. He spoke from behind his hands, as though trying to soften his words. "You know that I was on Deep Space Nine for five months. The captain and her crew helped me overcome a lot—the shock of leaving my own time, of ending up in space, the sorrow of leaving friends and family behind."

"I can imagine how difficult it must have been for you," Kira said. "How difficult it still must be."

"It is, but it's also gotten easier thanks to the people on Deep Space Nine," Altek said. "Especially Ro Laren."

"Ro is a good officer," Kira said. "A good person."

"I agree," Altek said. "She's helped me a great deal, and I've gotten to know her well. We've gotten to know *each other* well." The tone in Altek's voice spoke more clearly than his words. Kira felt the pit of her stomach tighten. "We started a relationship . . . a romantic relationship."

Kira stared at Altek, but she didn't see him. Somehow, she saw herself, but as Keev Anora—working side by side with him to free Bajora from slavery in Joradell, being freed by him from the collapse of a tunnel beneath the Merzang Mountains, kissing him outside their gild's forest encampment. It felt like looking at herself in a mirror, but with the image not following the movements she made.

Kira blinked and refocused her eyes on Altek in an attempt to let go of a past disconcertingly not her own. "You should have told me," she said, not reprovingly, but gently. It occurred to her that, when she first encountered Altek in Ro's quarters, maybe she should have wondered why he was there with the captain. Of course, people visited the quarters of others all the time without matters taking a romantic turn. Kira recognized the peculiarity of the situation, and the suddenness with which she had come back into Altek's life.

"I know I should have told you," he said. "I was just so surprised to see you . . ." He didn't complete his thought, but he didn't need to do so for Kira to understand his perspective.

"That's why you wanted to step back, take things slowly," Kira said.

"Yes," Altek said. "It was going to be hard enough leaving Laren . . . Captain Ro . . . to go to Bajor, but now, with meeting you, I just needed time to take stock. The last thing I wanted to do was hurt anybody."

"Of course," Kira said. "And I have to tell you that I

have no interest in being involved in any sort of a love triangle." Kira didn't know if her discomfort stemmed from
her having genuine feelings for Altek, or from her residual
memories of Keev's emotions, or from the realization that
her initial interaction with Altek must have been difficult
for Ro. "Of greater import," she said, deciding to change
the subject, "you and I need to concentrate on dealing with
what's happening on Bajor—not just with respect to our
return, but also to the discovery on Endalla and everything
it has wrought."

"You're right," he said, and he dropped his hands from
in front of his face. "I'm sorry I didn't tell you sooner."

"It's all right," Kira said, seeing no point either in blam-
ing Altek or in dwelling on the odd sequence of events. "It's
done. Let's talk about Bajor instead. Has the kai asked your
opinion about the discovery on Endalla?"

"She's made reference to it in a couple of our conversations," Altek said, "but no, she hasn't questioned me about
my views on it—not that I actually have any."

"You don't?" Kira asked. "But you worshipped the
Prophets in your time, and I'm sure you've learned about
the Ohalavaru beliefs. I'd think that would be enough
for you to form at least a preliminary judgment about the
meaning of the falsework."

"Maybe," Altek said. "I'm inclined to think that what
the Ohalavaru found does not invalidate my beliefs, but I
also know that's dishonest. Wanting to cling to my convictions in the face of evidence to the contrary is the product
of ego, or arrogance, or possibly just fear. I know that I
should wait for more information before I draw any sort of
conclusion about what it all means."

"That sounds remarkably open-minded in dealing with
a matter of faith," Kira said. "Perhaps too much so. Faith
sometimes has to reach beyond facts."

Altek shrugged. "I'm a medical doctor . . . a man of science. I have faith, but I don't want to run from facts."

"According to the kai, we should know more soon," Kira said. "First Minister Asarem intends to send research personnel up to Endalla."

Altek chuckled. "It's still strange to hear Bajor's first moon called Endalla," he said. "The planet's name hasn't changed, but the landmasses, the oceans, and even the moons are all called something different here in the future."

"What did you call the first moon?"

"Orendes."

With the name, a memory floated up through Kira's mind like a half-remembered dream. She tried to reach for it, but it eluded her. "And what about the others?" she asked, and thought, *Callastra*.

"Callastra, Spelder, and Dunnin."

The recollection came again, and Kira held on to it: waiting in the shadows to spring into action to sabotage an Aleiran drilling operation that threatened the gild's ability to free slaves. She remembered the scene before her bathed in the light of three moons: Derna, Endalla, and Baraddo—*Baraddo, also known as the Prodigal,* as one grade-school teacher used to make Keev's class recite. *Except that wasn't Keev's teacher; it was mine,* Kira thought. *And the moons weren't Derna, Endalla, and Baraddo; they were Callastra, Orendes, and Dunnin.*

A wave of disorientation crashed over Kira. *Whose memories are in my mind?* Did she recall Keev's thoughts, and had Keev's thoughts used names provided by Kira's mind?

"Are you all right?" Altek asked, reaching his hand across the table toward her.

"I'm fine," Kira said. She picked up her cup of tea and

drank from it, working to steady herself. "I just got light-headed for a moment."

"The color drained from your face," Altek said. "Are you sure you don't need medical attention?"

"I'm sure," Kira said. She considered telling him that she remembered the names of Bajor's moons from back in his time, but she didn't want to cloud her identity for him any more than it already was. She opted to go back to what he had been saying in order to distract his attention away from her transitory vertigo. "You were telling me your names for Bajor's moons: Orendes, Callastra, Spelder, Dunnin, and . . . what was the last one?"

Altek wrinkled his brow in a perplexed look. "The last moon is Dunnin."

"So which one am I missing?"

"You didn't miss any of them," Altek said. "You named all four moons."

Once more, Kira's world seemed to tip. "Five moons," she said. "Bajor has *five* moons." Except that Kira recalled Keev's knowledge and memories, and she knew how Altek would react, what he would tell her.

He looked at her askance, and she could see him deciding whether or not she was joking with him. "Bajor has four moons, and *only* four moons."

Kira understood the reality of the situation. "You've come forward in time from an era when Endalla did not orbit Bajor."

"What . . . what does that mean?"

"It means that you can validate the Ohalavaru claims," Kira said. "Bajor once had four moons, and then Endalla was constructed around the falsework."

"But if the Ohalavaru are right about that . . ." Altek let the implication dangle.

Kira stood up. She knew what she needed to do next, even if she didn't know where her actions would lead. "We have to tell the kai."

V

Odo sat down in front of the desk in the captain's office. Ro Laren had taken leave, and so her executive officer, Jefferson Blackmer, acted in her stead. Just a short time ago, the commander had contacted Odo and requested a meeting.

"It's good to see you," Blackmer said. "I'm glad that you've recovered from your injuries."

Odo hadn't fully convalesced. He still tired easily after holding a form for an extended time, which necessitated a lengthy regeneration period. But he didn't bother to correct Blackmer, both because of the private nature of his health and because he wished to end the meeting as soon as possible. "Thank you," he said. "What is it you wanted to see me about? Whatever it is, I hope we can dispense with it quickly. Chief O'Brien set up passage for me on a runabout heading for Bajor, and it's departing in thirty minutes."

"As I understand it, the *New York* is currently on its way specifically to take you back to the Dominion."

"It still won't be here for several days," Odo said. "I can easily be back on Deep Space Nine before it arrives." Odo chose his words carefully; he could return to DS9 from Bajor in short order, but he also hoped he wouldn't need to do so. That would all depend on Nerys.

After Chief O'Brien's visit the previous night, Odo had attempted to reach Nerys at the Vanadwan Monastery, but he'd been told that she had yet to return there. He then contacted the Shikina Monastery in the capital, hoping either to find her there or to speak with the kai. The person he talked to—Ranjen Linsa Noth—would not confirm or deny Nerys's presence there, though he did promise to convey his request to speak with Pralon Onala at her earliest convenience. So far, Odo had yet to hear from either Nerys or the kai, but he had learned that Nerys would be making a planetwide address that afternoon. That being the case, he decided that he would make his way to Bajor so that he could see her in person.

"All right," Blackmer said. "I called you here because, yesterday, long-range sensors detected a ship in the Gamma Quadrant traveling directly toward the wormhole. It was too distant to identify, but tracing its course backward, we discovered that it appears to have set sail from Dominion space."

"That seems unlikely, Commander," Odo said. "As you know, the Dominion is in a period of virtual isolation. Its borders are closed in both directions. Your calculations may show that the ship came from the direction of the Dominion, but perhaps the vessel hasn't traveled that far; perhaps its flight originated in a star system between there and here. Or perhaps its course has not been straight."

"We considered those possibilities," Blackmer said, "but during delta shift, the ship drew close enough for our sensors to identify its configuration. It's a Jem'Hadar battle cruiser."

The news startled and disappointed Odo. He didn't know what possible reason the Dominion could have for sending such a heavily armed, heavily fortified vessel to the Alpha Quadrant. Of course, that also depended on who led the Dominion. If more Founders had returned, he doubted that they would want to engage with any humanoid societies beyond those already a part of their civilization. If not, if the day-to-day operation of the empire had fallen to other member species such as the Vorta or the Thepnossen or the

Overne, Odo similarly expected that they would shy away from venturing beyond their borders.

But what if Laas has chosen to take a more active role in leading the Dominion? he asked himself. Odo could readily envision the volatile, humanoid-hating Changeling launching a recon of the wormhole and the Bajoran system, or even authorizing an attack. It also occurred to him that the Jem'Hadar themselves could have evolved enough to take on a leadership role in the Dominion, in which case no planned assault would be out of the question.

"Have you tried to contact the ship?" Odo asked.

"All our attempts to communicate with its crew have failed," Blackmer said, "possibly because the signal is being jammed."

"By who?"

"Sensors do not show any other vessels in the region," Blackmer said, "so our best guess is that the Jem'Hadar crew are blocking any incoming transmissions."

"Why would they do that?" Odo asked.

"That's one of the things I hoped you could tell me."

"Commander, I haven't been back to the Dominion in nearly two and a half years," Odo said. "My knowledge of the Jem'Hadar is not current."

"I understand that," Blackmer said. "I was just hoping that, having resided there for more than seven years, you might be able to provide some insight into what this lone ship could represent."

"I'm afraid I can't," Odo said. "Although I think the fact that there is only one ship, rather than a squadron or a fleet, indicates that its crew probably doesn't intend to attack. The Jem'Hadar favor overwhelming an enemy."

"I would hope that the Dominion no longer considers the Federation its enemy," Blackmer said.

"The last I knew, the Dominion didn't much consider

the Federation at all," Odo said. "That also should be considered a positive."

"I suppose so," Blackmer said. "Still, I have a responsibility to ensure the safety not just of this starbase, but of Bajor as well. Since we've been unable to make contact with the crew of the Jem'Hadar ship, I want to send a vessel into the Gamma Quadrant to ascertain their intentions—and to do so while they're still far enough away to sound the alert to Starfleet, if necessary."

"That sounds like a prudent course of action," Odo said, "although I would suggest not attempting to intercept the Jem'Hadar ship on an offensive footing. There's no sense in assuming an antagonistic posture."

"Agreed," Blackmer said. "Our second officer, Lieutenant Commander Wheeler Stinson, is currently preparing the *Defiant* for the journey. Given your familiarity with the Dominion—with the Founders, the Jem'Hadar, and the Vorta—I would appreciate it if you would join the mission."

The request irritated Odo, in part because he found it disingenuous. "Are you sure it's because of my knowledge of the Dominion," he said, "and not because a Jem'Hadar crew wouldn't fire on a ship carrying a Changeling?"

"That occurred to me as well," Blackmer said. "But you think that the Jem'Hadar don't intend to attack, so I am sincerely hoping that your ability to communicate with them will allow us to swiftly determine their purpose."

"I see," Odo said. He didn't want to believe Blackmer. He wanted more than anything to make his way to Bajor as quickly as he could so that he could find Nerys and reunite with her. To his dismay, though, he did believe Blackmer. More than that, Odo actually thought it would be wise for him to accompany the *Defiant* crew to find out about the Jem'Hadar ship before it reached the wormhole. Even after such a long time away from the Dominion, he bore an obligation to the beings living under its aegis to help them develop a just society. A Jem'Hadar ship taking aggressive action against DS9 or Bajor would serve the Dominion no more than it would the Federation.

Odo opened his mouth and expelled a burst of air, a mannerism he had long ago refined for use in dealing with humanoids. The grumble, part sigh and part derisive laugh, signaled his displeasure in such a way that his meaning could be accurately interpreted by multiple species. In this case, he did not appreciate having to delay his reunion with Nerys. "I'll go," he said, "provided that, upon my return, you will have the *Defiant* or some other vessel take me immediately to Bajor."

Blackmer rose from his chair. "You have my guarantee," he said. "You can board the *Defiant* at Docking Bay One. Thank you."

Odo stood up as well. "You're welcome, Commander," he said. "But I'm not doing this for you. I'm doing it in the interest of keeping the peace—on *both* sides." He didn't wait for a response, but moved away from the desk and exited into the corridor that would take him to the turbolift.

vi

Ro piloted the Nexvahl vessel through the atmosphere of Mericor toward the lone spaceport on the planet's surface. The mud-colored landscape filled the forward port, a few tufts of cloud threading here and there through the sky. Ro followed the approach vector she'd received from Planetary Injection Control, an orbital facility that monitored and directed arriving and departing vessels. When the ship reached the designated altitude, she opened a channel directly to the spaceport.

"Nexvahl Scoutship Seven-Eight-One-Eight dash Seven-

Three to Mericor Anchorage," she said. "Requesting a landing berth."

"*Nexvahl vessel, this is Mericor Anchorage,*" replied a fluttery male voice. If Ro had to guess, she would have bet that it belonged to a Callandran. "*Targeting a navigational beacon to your position.*"

Ro worked the conn. "Confirming detection of nav beam," she said.

"*Proceed through the outermost shields,*" the voice said, "*then switch to antigravs and power down your engines. A tractor beam will set your vessel down in the Eastern Terminal, Berth Thirty-Five Triangle.*"

Ro acknowledged the directions by repeating them, then glanced back over her shoulder. "We should be landing shortly," she said.

"Good," Quark said from the cockpit's aft seat.

His voice carried no attitude with it, but the brevity of his response confirmed the ongoing tension between him and Ro. They had both largely been quiet since their dustup the previous night—not ignoring each other, but also not saying anything more than they needed to say. It made a marked contrast to the way they normally related to each other, talking with an ease brought about by familiarity and affection.

More than anything, Quark seemed sad to Ro, but he also walked tall—as tall as a Ferengi could, anyway—from which she inferred his satisfaction that he'd finally gotten to speak openly with her about what had obviously been bothering him for some time. Ro felt sad too, recognizing that even though she had been the one to end their relationship, it still counted as yet another loss in her life. In addition, she took herself to task for how she had treated Quark. She had apologized to him, and he had accepted it, but the dynamic between them had definitely changed.

Ro saw a blue flash as the scoutship passed through the outer hemisphere of shields that surrounded Mericor—both the spaceport and the adjoining city that it served. When the vessel jolted a moment later as a tractor beam took hold of it, she immediately activated the antigrav system and then shut down the drive. She peered through the forward port and spotted the twin domes up ahead. The closer structure, colored white and with a large circular opening at the top, covered the spaceport, while the more distant, sky-blue edifice protected the city proper. The two domes afforded a sharp contrast with the drab, undistinguished planetary surface on which they stood.

Wanting to move past the tensions that had grown between them, and hoping not to lose Quark from her life entirely, Ro turned her chair to face him. "I know that I've hurt you, and that you're upset with me," she told him, "but whatever other reasons I might have had for coming on this trip, I also wanted to help you. I still do. I hope you'll let me."

Quark stared at her for so long that she thought he had decided not to speak with her for the duration of the trip—or perhaps not to speak with her ever again. But then he said, "We'll need to go to the northern terminal. I got a contact from Lenk, an old . . . acquaintance . . . of mine. It's somebody he knows who works in spaceport security."

"What do you want me to do?" Ro asked, pleased not only to have Quark talking to her, but that he would allow her to help him recover his lost funds, something patently important to him.

"I won't know until we meet him," Quark said. "But it might be something like what we did at Farius Prime."

Ro recalled well her turn undercover as a dabo girl. Despite having to wear what she initially thought of as a degradingly skimpy outfit, she actually enjoyed the experience. Even with Quark so upset with her, she doubted even he would have the lobes to actually suggest a similarly outrageous plan. *Although I've often heard people use the word* outrageous *when describing Quark and the things he's done.*

"Whatever you need, Quark, I'm here to help." *Too little, too late,* Ro thought, *but something is better than nothing.* At the very least, it would mark the beginning of her making amends.

vii

In every direction, ships of various configurations, sizes, and colors stood on landing gear in berths delineated by low walls. From a begrimed Pakled travel pod barely larger than an individual Pakled to a massive Frunalian clipper that looked like a collection of tall, flame-red triangles intersecting at their bases, the spaceport comprised a wildly variegated collection of planetary landing craft. A circular grid of wide pedestrian thoroughfares, joined by radial segments, ranged among them, thick with travelers. Runs of small squarish buildings housed various concessions, purveying foods, goods, and services. Quark saw one stand that advertised tube grubs for a price he wouldn't pay if they were wrapped in latinum. He also spotted a stall that offered detective services, and he wondered if he should have turned down Laren's offer to join him, instead employing a professional to help him once he reached Mericor.

For that matter, I could just have brought Zirk along, Quark thought. *At least he wouldn't have crushed my lobes like Laren did.* Quark felt equal parts angry and sad about the loss of their relationship. In part, he directed some of that anger toward himself. He had sensed their bond slipping away ever since leaving Bajor for the new starbase— and maybe even before that. Laren claimed an overriding fixation with her expanding crew and the increasing size and scope of her duties, and while Quark could see truth in those assertions, he also willed himself to ignore the signs that her passion for him had waned. His sustained pursuit of her was like continuing to bid in an auction when nobody had yet topped his previous offer—not a question of diminishing returns, but one of no return for a greater and greater investment.

Multiple Rules of Acquisition rattled through his mind, but he mentally batted them away. He also sought to bury his emotions with respect to Laren. At the moment, he had a more important matter with which to deal: the recovery of his stolen latinum from the treacherous Mayereen Viray.

At an intersection of walkways, Quark turned down a spur marked NORTH 19 SQUARE. He heard Laren's footsteps behind him as she followed at a distance. Quark visually scanned the avenue ahead and spotted the security office set off to the side. Like others they had passed, the freestanding conic structure stood wrapped in a highly reflective finish, making it difficult to distinguish from its surroundings.

Quark moved to that side of the pedestrian thoroughfare and trod forward at a rapid pace. When he came abreast of the security office, he stopped and spun toward it. It took a moment for him to see the outline of the door. He raised a closed hand and rapped his knuckles on the polished surface.

The upper half of the door glided open, revealing a shadowy interior lined with control panels. An Andorian male—either a *thaan* or a *chan*—stood just inside and gazed down at Quark. Another man—a pale, nondescript humanoid who might have hailed from Earth—looked on from where he sat at one of the consoles.

"May I help you?" the first man asked in heavily accented Andorian, which Quark's universal translator interpreted for him.

"I need to report a security violation," Quark said, employing the precise language Lenk had given him.

The man's antennae moved subtly, turning ever so slightly outward before returning to their previous position. "What sort of violation do you need to report?" The response, word for word, which Lenk had told him to expect, sounded to Quark like the ring of latinum slips and scintillas in a child's savings box.

"I saw somebody outside my landing berth with a scanner," Quark said, following the script. While Mericor did not outlaw the possession of sensing devices, since virtually all ships carried them, it did prohibit the use of such instruments—as well as transporters—within either the spaceport or the city. The other security officer stood up and joined the first, listening to what Quark had to say. "He appeared to be taking readings of the ships in that area." At his waist, Quark surreptitiously made a motion with his left hand.

"We didn't pick up any sensor activity," the second security officer said, obviously suspicious. He did not speak Federation Standard, but Argelian.

"He's probably masking his scans," the Andorian said.

"Can you describe the man?" the second security officer asked.

"He's tall," Quark said, offering the first adjective all Ferengi generally used when discussing the characteristics of an alien individual. "He's bald, has wrinkled, grayish skin, a deep line across his skull and down his nose, medium-sized ears—"

"An Yridian?" the first man asked.

"Yes, yes, an Yridian," Quark said, as though the name of the species had until that moment eluded him.

"Damned information merchants," the Argelian said.

At that moment, Laren walked up beside Quark, responding to his furtive gesture. "Pardon me," she said in Bajoran, in a register higher than that of her normal speaking voice. "I can't seem to find the berth I'm looking for." She smiled alluringly, in a way that Quark desperately missed.

The Argelian man tapped at a control and the lower half of the door slid open. He squeezed past the Andorian and stepped out to face Laren. "What berth are you looking for?"

"Circle North Three," Laren said, intentionally misstating a proper berth designation. She took a couple of strides away from the security office and peered in both directions down the walkway, as though lost.

"Do you mean the Northern Terminal?" the Argelian asked. "Berth Three Circle?"

"Yes, that's it," Laren said, feigning excitement.

The Argelian leaned in close to her—too close, Quark thought—and pointed back the way they had come. "If you go back to the second intersection," the security officer said, "then turn left, follow the arc around to—"

"Wait, what?" Laren said, seemingly confused.

"Follow this back to the second intersection," the Argelian repeated, "then go left and make your way to the third . . ." His voice trailed off in the glare of Laren's bewildered expression.

"Would you show me?" she asked coyly.

The man sighed as though frustrated by the request for assistance, but when he peered back over at the Andorian, he did so with a visibly satisfied look. "Rethik, would you mind if I escorted this lovely lady where she needs to go?" he asked the other security officer in pidgin Andorian.

"You have to do your duty," the first man said with a grin. Quark watched as the Argelian took Laren by the elbow and strolled at a leisurely pace with her back down the avenue. Then he looked back up at the other security officer.

"Lenk sent me," he said quietly.

"If you'll step into the office for a moment," the Andorian said in a voice clearly calculated to allow passersby to hear, "I can take a report for you." Quark entered the hutlike structure, and the man followed, closing both sections of the door behind them. "What do you need?" Rethik asked brusquely.

"A Mizarian transport is traveling here from Janus Six," Quark said. "I want to know when it's scheduled to land and where."

"How much?" The Andorian clearly asked not how much Quark wanted to find out the information, but how much he would pay for it.

Quark reached into his bright, multicolored jacket, to an inside pocket where he'd placed a specific amount of latinum. He pulled out all the slips there and held them out in his open hand. Rethik leaned in and counted.

"That's it?" he said with forced indignation.

"All I'm asking for is information I could find out for myself if I had more time," Quark said.

"But apparently you don't have more time," Rethik said, "so that makes what you want not only information, but timeliness."

Quark nodded, fully expecting such a reaction after he'd spoken to Lenk about Rethik. He found a different pocket inside his jacket and retrieved three more slips of latinum. He added it to the others. When Rethik reached for it, Quark closed his hand around the shiny currency. "Information first."

Rethik didn't spend any time thinking about it. He crossed to a panel and quickly worked its controls. "There's a Mizarian freighter slated to arrive in . . . twelve days."

"Twelve days?" Quark asked, more than a little discouraged by the response. "Where is it coming from?"

Rethik checked the panel again. "Kobheeria."

"That's not it; Kobheeria is in the wrong direction," Quark said. "Check again."

Rethik operated the console once more. "You're right," he said. "A Mizarian transport arrived seven hours ago. It came in from . . . Khefka Four . . . and before that, it traveled from—" He looked over at Quark. "It traveled from Janus Six."

"That's it," Quark said. Rethik grabbed for the latinum, but Quark kept his hand closed. He instead reached back into his jacket, found a third interior pocket, and pulled out an entire strip of latinum. "I was told that you might have something more than information . . ." He let the implication dangle.

Rethik smiled, which had the odd effect of smoothing out some of the wrinkles around his mouth. "You mean like a scanner."

"I mean like an *undetectable* scanner," Quark said. "I don't need to end up in a Mericor jail."

Rethik moved over to a control panel, bent, and opened a cabinet beneath it. He pulled out a small device, easily concealable in a humanoid hand. "It's got good range— enough to cover either the city or the spaceport, depending on where you are," Rethik said. "But it can only scan for one or two search patterns, which have to be preprogrammed. I presume you know who or what you're looking for."

"A Petarian," Quark said.

"That's easy enough to encode," Rethik said. He made a circling motion around Quark's closed fist with the slips of latinum and the open hand with the strip. "I get all of it."

"All of it," Quark said. "And if the scanner works, you get to keep all of it. Otherwise, we'll both end up in a Mericor jail." Quark didn't typically care to threaten people, at least in a nonfinancial context, but his desperation drove him to it—that, and the fact that Lenk had told him that Rethik responded to such warnings.

The Andorian went back to the control panel, tapped in a sequence of commands, then checked the scanner. He held it up so that Quark could see its small display. He saw the emblem of the Petarian people, a jagged white streak that resembled a bolt of lightning, atop of pair of overlapping yellow circles.

"It's got one button, which activates and deactivates it," Rethik said. "If it locates what you're looking for, it won't flash or make a sound, but it will vibrate briefly."

Quark opened his fist, and he exchanged his latinum for Rethik's scanner. The strip and the slips quickly vanished inside the white jumpsuit the Andorian wore. Quark wedged the scanner in the fleshy region between his thumb and forefinger, then closed his hand around the device. He heard the door open behind him, and without another word, he exited the security office.

Quark didn't look back. He started for his rendezvous point with Laren. Halfway there, he saw the Argelian security officer heading back toward his post. Quark turned left at the second intersection, then met Laren at the second junction.

"How did it go?" she asked.

"I got what I needed," Quark said. "The subject arrived seven hours ago, and I have the help I need to find her." He resisted saying anything more, but couldn't help himself. "That security officer didn't give you any trouble, did he?"

"None at all," Laren said. "But we need to bring this situation to a rapid conclusion, otherwise I have a date tomorrow night."

"Sure, as long as it's not with me, right?" Quark regretted the comment even as it left his mouth. He waited for Laren to upbraid him, but she said nothing. Quark didn't risk even a glance over at her, but he thought he might at any moment hear her footsteps moving away from him.

That didn't happen. Instead, they walked in silence back to the western section of the spaceport, to one of the two pedestrian tunnels that connected with the city dome. They mounted the slidewalk there and let it carry them to their destination.

When they reached the city dome, its interior looked different from what Quark had expected. The blue of its inner surface had a much darker tone than that of its exterior. The pedestrian walkways that led off left and right along the inside of the dome resembled all the others they had so far moved along, but those that ran into the city widened and stretched away at odd angles. The buildings, which Quark had thought would gleam of steel and glass, and rise far up toward the dome, appeared constructed of less sophisticated materials, like thermocrete and fusion-stone. The structures reached two or three stories near the mouth of the tunnel, and not much higher even in the center of the city. The locale looked dark, even foreboding, an urban sprawl made for a transient, anonymous clientele rather than for an indigenous, permanent population.

"Nice place," Laren said. It pleased Quark to discover that she had not decided to stop speaking to him, even after his last remark.

"Thieves don't like to hide in brightly lighted areas," Quark said.

"Not unless they're stealing by using corporate resources," Laren said. "Then you just need to find the mansions in the force-field-enclosed communities."

Quark laughed. She wasn't wrong.

Stepping off to one side, Quark moved out of the flow

of pedestrian traffic, and Laren followed. He squeezed his thumb and forefinger together and felt the button of the scanner click. "Let me do a preliminary scan," he whispered to Laren. "We may have to move to the center of the city in order to—"

The scanner vibrated in his hand.

Quark's eyes widened. "What is it?" Laren asked. "Have you got something already?"

"Maybe," Quark said. He lifted his hand to scratch at his brow, taking a peek at the scanner's display as he did so. "I'm reading only a single Petarian," he said. "About a third of the way across the city and to the left."

"Then let's go," Laren said.

Together, they strode into Mericor City, on the trail of Mayereen Viray.

viii

Nog sat with Candlewood and Lani in the backseat of the taxi. The two men had changed back into the suits they had worn into the holosuite, and Lani had put on a dress. The operations chief felt anxious as the vehicle turned into the drive that led up to the Silver Lode hotel, but he reminded himself that they had more information about Vic at that point than when they had first entered the holosuite three days earlier. That left them four days to resolve the situation. While they still didn't know the precise nature of the trouble Vic was in, they at least knew who had abducted him—Bugsy Calderone, with whom they would soon be speaking.

In the real world beyond the holosuite, Nog would have utilized DS9's powerful computer system and its massive set of databases to learn everything he could about the mobster before meeting with him. Because he and Candlewood had entered Bashir 62 via a back door, though, they couldn't yet leave without causing reinitialization of the program. Lani had not "perished" in Vic's Las Vegas, but she too had used the back door, meaning they could not be certain about the effect of her departure. Since Calderone might not even have been a historical figure, but simply a character created by the code—in which case searching DS9's databases for information about him would have been futile—Nog chose not to risk sending Lani out of the holosuite.

Fortunately, the starbase's computer system had not been the only option available to them. Candlewood suggested that they visit a public library. They spent the bulk of the day combing through physical copies of old newspapers, many of them bound together in large tomes. More recent editions had yet to be collected and came affixed to long, flat wooden rods.

With the help of two librarians, the trio had scoured through archived copies of the *Las Vegas Review-Journal* and the *Las Vegas Sun*. They learned certain public facts about Bugsy Calderone—such as that he had moved west from Brooklyn, New York, two decades earlier—while other details came by way of innuendo or accusation—such as the reason for his relocation, namely to take control of an established crime syndicate. While he claimed to be a legitimate businessman, Calderone had a reputation as someone who either got what he wanted or spilled blood. Various articles suggested that Calderone carried numerous law-enforcement officers and judiciary officials in the city on his payroll. Although the criminal undertakings of his organization appeared generally known and widely reported, little had been done to successfully curtail its operations.

All of that had sounded exceedingly ominous to Candlewood, who had openly wondered if taking a direct approach with Calderone might be a bad idea. Nog told him no. In

Vic Fontaine's Las Vegas, avarice motivated the criminal element; in fact, avarice even motivated law-abiding visitors to the city. Growing up in Ferengi culture, Nog had no trouble understanding such impulses, and so felt suitably qualified to deal with the mobster.

The taxicab pulled up beneath the porte cochere of the Silver Lode. A pair of bellmen opened the passenger doors. Nog paid the driver, and then he, Candlewood, and Lani made their way inside to the hotel lobby.

A man stood behind the concierge desk, different from the thin, gray-haired older individual Nog and Candlewood had spoken with the prior day. With a smooth, bald head and a stockier build, he wore a similarly well-tailored black suit. He looked directly at Nog and greeted him by name, no doubt a testament to the surveillance measures in place.

"It is good of you to be on time," the concierge said.

"It is a basic sign of respect for Mister Calderone," Nog said. "We appreciate his taking the time to meet with us."

Without overtly changing his expression, the concierge conveyed disapproval. "Mister Calderone agreed to meet with one individual, not three."

"These are my business associates," Nog said. "Mister Candlewood and Miss Ulu."

"As I said, Mister Calderone is expecting to meet with you alone, Mister Nog."

The operations chief looked at Candlewood and Lani. Strictly speaking, Nog didn't need them to accompany him to his appointment with the mobster, but he wanted them there. They would serve as moral support, but of more importance, they would provide two more sets of ears and eyes to ensure that Nog didn't miss anything critical to accomplishing their goal. He opted to reiterate the type of argument he'd made to the previous concierge. "Please assure

Mister Calderone that meeting with me *and* my associates will redound to his financial benefit."

The man regarded Nog, then said, "If you will excuse me for a moment." As his predecessor had done before him, the concierge withdrew into the office behind him.

"What if Calderone won't allow us to come with you?" Candlewood asked under his breath.

"I'll see him by myself if I have to," Nog said. "We can't pass up this opportunity." Nog expected it would be a few minutes before the concierge returned, but the door opened back up almost as soon as it had closed.

"Mister Calderone will graciously allow Mister Candlewood to attend the meeting," he said. "But I'm afraid the answer regarding Miss Ulu is, and I quote, 'No dames.'"

To her credit, Lani did not argue. "I'll wait for the two of you back in our suite." She did not wait for a response, but immediately strode back toward the hotel entrance. At the same time, another man stepped up to the desk. Tall and wearing a suit that did little to mask his muscular physique, he wore dark glasses that hid his eyes.

"Mister Spinelli will escort you to your meeting," the concierge said.

"This way," Spinelli said in a deep voice. He walked ahead of Nog and Candlewood, who followed him to a bank of elevators, one of which stood open. Spinelli stopped in front of it and motioned inside. Nog and Candlewood entered to find a second large man in a suit. Once Spinelli had boarded the elevator, the second man inserted a key into the control panel and pressed a button labeled PENTHOUSE.

When they reached the top floor of the hotel, the doors opened to reveal yet another large man in a suit. He asked Nog and Candlewood to step out and open their jackets, which they did. The man carefully frisked them, clearly hunting for weapons of any kind.

As he consented to the search, Nog examined their surroundings and immediately recognized the corridor in which they stood. Wider than those on the other floors of the hotel, it featured lush, decorative carpeting, rich wood paneling on the lower meter and a half or so of the walls, and brilliant crystal chandeliers suspended from a high ceiling. It had been there that he and Candlewood had last seen Vic Fontaine, accompanied by a pair of brawny men who had opened fire on them with projectile weapons. Nog cast a sideways glance at the science officer, who responded with a single, slight nod: Candlewood also recognized their location.

Satisfied that neither Nog nor Candlewood carried any weapons, the man motioned ahead and said, "Follow me." They did, and Spinelli fell in behind them. Halfway down the corridor, they reached a wide set of ornately carved double doors. Without knocking, the man pushed them open and entered the room beyond, then stepped aside. Nog and Candlewood both stopped in the doorway. Spinelli stood behind them.

The large room ran lengthwise left and right. Floor-to-ceiling windows formed the outer wall, opposite the doors, providing a panoramic view of verdant grounds behind the hotel, ultimately leading to the dun-colored expanse of the desert. Various cabinets and credenzas, constructed of rich, radiant woods, lined paneled inner walls beneath gilt-framed artwork. An outsize conference table sat in the center of the space, its dark, fine-grained surface tying in with the furniture and the wine-colored carpet.

Two men stood in the far corners of the room, their suit jackets unbuttoned and their hands crossed in front of them—their location, concentration, and stance making them each recognizable as guards. Nog didn't doubt that they carried weapons. Their obvious charge sat between them, at the center of one long side of the table, facing Nog and Candlewood. Dressed in a charcoal-gray three-piece suit, he wore wire-rimmed spectacles with round lenses. He had a medium build and sat with his hands folded together on the tabletop.

"That will be all, Mister Spinelli, Mister Sperano, thank you," the man said. He had a thin, reedy voice, but he nevertheless spoke with confidence and authority. In response, the men who had led Nog and Candlewood to the conference room quickly exited, closing the doors after them.

Nog stepped forward, motioning to Candlewood to remain where he stood. The operations chief coolly regarded the man seated at the table, waiting to see if he would begin the conversation. When he didn't, Nog said, "You're not Bugsy Calderone." The operations chief had seen images of the mobster in the newspapers. He and Candlewood did not have time to wade through different levels of criminal hierarchy.

"I never claimed to be," the man said. "But I will offer you a piece of advice should you ever speak with Beniamino Calderone: he does not care for sobriquets."

"My apologies," Nog said. "With all due respect, though, my associate and I requested a meeting with Mister Calderone, not you, Mister . . . ?"

"My name is Herschel P. Steinberg," the man said. "I am Mister Calderone's representative in matters of business, and he has authorized me to speak with you, Mister Nog."

"That may be," Nog said, "but we have come here for a meeting with Mister Calderone, not an underling who claims to represent him."

Steinberg smiled, though his expression contained no mirth. "In that case," he said, standing up and buttoning his suit jacket, "I am happy to cut this meeting short."

Nog immediately regrouped. Though he wanted to speak with Calderone directly in order to expedite Vic's release, he could not throw away any chance to deal with the singer's abduction. Nog held up his hands in a placatory gesture. "Please, Mister Steinberg, I meant no offense."

"And I took none," the man said. "However, if you do not wish to meet with me, there is nothing I can do for you."

"Even though you represent Mister Calderone," Nog said, "it's not clear to me that you will be able to make the decisions that need to be made."

"Why don't you let me determine that?" Steinberg asked. He unbuttoned his suit jacket, sat back down, and motioned to two upholstered chairs across from him. "Why don't you and Mister Candlewood have a seat."

Nog peered back at Candlewood, who gave him a questioning look. The operations chief offered a quick nod, and the two men sat down beside each other. "Thank you," Nog told Steinberg. "It recently came to my attention that a friend of mine might have had some business dealings with Mister Calderone, and that my friend might have made some . . . uh . . . inadvertent transgressions." Nog didn't know what had transpired between Vic and the mobster, but it seemed evident from what he did know that the singer had somehow run afoul of the crime boss.

"Transgressions?" Steinberg said. "*Inadvertent* transgressions?" His words came wrapped in doubt. Nog knew that he needed to exercise caution.

"I know my friend," he said, "and I know that he would never intentionally try to take advantage of somebody of Mister Calderone's stature."

"But he would take advantage of somebody of lesser stature?" Steinberg asked. The question seemed calculated to unnerve Nog.

"No. What I am saying is that if my friend acted in a manner that damaged Mister Calderone in some way, it was accidental."

"And did you perhaps play some part in all of this?" Steinberg asked, making no effort to hide the accusatory nature of the question.

"No, I didn't," Nog said, and then to be absolutely clear, he looked at Candlewood and added, "Neither one of us did." He gazed back across the table at Steinberg. "But we are prepared to offer a solution in order to resolve the situation."

"I see," Steinberg said. He stood up and began slowly to pace along his side of the table. "I wonder what the name of your friend is."

Nog had been circumspect about Vic's identity to that point because it had seemed like the appropriate thing to do, but he saw no reason to continue avoiding the issue. "His name is Vic Fontaine."

"I see," Steinberg said again. He reached the end of the table and reversed his course, slowly walking back toward his chair. "I'm not sure that we know Mister Fontaine, other than by his professional reputation, of course."

Nog's lobes grew cold. If he had erred, if Calderone hadn't been behind Vic's abduction, then he had wasted three days. Nog felt the oppressive weight of time passing.

"In theory, though," Steinberg continued, "if a singer—or anybody, really—borrowed a large sum of money from Mister Calderone and then didn't pay it back in a timely manner, that would be a cause for concern."

Nog didn't appreciate the coyness of the response, but it at least indicated that the mobster had indeed kidnapped Vic. The idea of the singer borrowing significant funds didn't seem in character. *But then, his program's been running for more than two years in a simulator,* Nog reminded himself. *Who knows what's happened?* "If somebody owed Mister Calderone a lot of money," he said, "they wouldn't be able to arrange repayment without freedom of movement."

Steinberg stopped when he reached his chair and stared over at Nog. "Ah, but freedom of movement also means the freedom to abscond—which is more of a possibility since, over time, such a debt would grow considerably as interest accrues."

"What kind of sum are we talking about?" Nog asked.

"A loan of a hundred thousand dollars," Steinberg said. "And perhaps payments were made for a time, but if those stopped at some point, the loan would have increased to a million dollars. Theoretically."

From the time he'd spent in Vic's, Nog had some rough sense of the purchasing power of the dollar, and he recognized usury when he heard it. On one level, he couldn't help but admire such profitmaking abilities. *Except that Calderone hasn't made profit from Vic,* he thought. *Otherwise we wouldn't all be in the current situation.*

"I am willing to act on Vic's behalf and pay back his debt to Mister Calderone, plus interest," Nog said.

Steinberg laughed. "And who are you, Mister Nog, that you would have such reserves?" Nog could feel Candlewood's gaze on him, the science officer doubtless wondering the same thing.

"My own means are unimportant," Nog said. "Especially since Vic owns substantial water rights throughout Las Vegas." Nog knew that the singer's holdings did not exist, that the paperwork purporting otherwise had been forged, but he wanted to gather as much information as he could about Vic's existence during the period when his holoprogram had been effectively locked away.

Steinberg shook his head. "Oh, yes, we know all about Mister Fontaine's realty usage rights." He bent beside his

chair and retrieved a satchel, from which he pulled a stack
of documents. Steinberg tossed them onto the table. They
landed with a slap. The top couple of pages fluttered away
from the others, but most of the sheets remained in a pile.
Nog looked at the top document and saw a copy of one of
the water-rights instruments Lani had acquired. He didn't
need to examine any of the others.

"With a person of such limited earning potential as a
lounge singer," Steinberg went on, "Mister Calderone would
not have approved such a sizable loan if not guaranteed by
some measure of collateral. To that end, Mister Fontaine
provided the documents showing his water-use rights,
which satisfied me."

"Which satisfied you or Mister Calderone?" Nog asked.

"In this case, me," Steinberg said. "I am Mister Calderone's accountant, and so my approval on financial matters
translates to his approval. In any event, Mister Fontaine
made payments on his loan for a while, but when he
stopped, Mister Calderone moved to take possession of
his water rights—except that Vic Fontaine owns no such
rights. All of these—" He pointed to the paper on the table.
"—are fake."

Nog at last understood the broad strokes of what had
happened. Morn had provided the worthless water rights as
a stopgap measure to back up his gambling losses—losses
from a line of credit for which Vic had cosigned. When
DS9 was destroyed and Vic's program relegated to running
in the tester, Morn could not make good on those forged
papers. At some point, the Shining Oasis must have demanded repayment in full. They probably hadn't accepted
the water rights, or perhaps had even discovered their il-
legitimacy, though Nog doubted the latter possibility, because if Vic had known the ersatz nature of the documents,
he likely wouldn't have used them as collateral in seeking a

loan from Bugsy Calderone. Nog wondered why Vic hadn't attempted to sell the water rights himself, but suspected that he wouldn't have had enough time before needing to pay off the sum owed to the casino. *Or maybe he felt obligated to retain what he believed belonged to Morn.*

Steinberg walked the length of the table and came around the end. He took a chair beside Nog and sat down. "You can imagine Mister Calderone's annoyance in these circumstances," the accountant said. He spoke quietly, but not without menace. "Mister Fontaine made payments for a while—not enough to settle his debt, but enough to keep him alive. But when he stopped paying and it turned out that he owned no rights, Mister Calderone had to spend resources on trying to locate him. Mister Fontaine remained out of our grasp for longer than expected, but when we found him, we invited him to be Mister Calderone's guest. He has denied knowing that the water-rights documents were forgeries, and he has also promised to repay his debt. Of course, having lost him once before, we have no interest in letting him out of our sight. He has been attempting to negotiate with us, but I'm afraid that Mister Calderone is just about out of patience."

"That's why I'm here," Nog said. "I will pay back Vic's debt. I'll get you the million."

Steinberg smiled, his disbelief manifest. He reached into his suit jacket and pulled out a small piece of paper, folded in two. He opened and read it. "One million two hundred forty-seven thousand," he said. "For the next forty-eight hours, anyway."

"What happens after that?" Nog asked. "What will the amount increase to?"

Steinberg folded the piece of paper and put it back in his jacket. "Normally, the sum would increase," he said, "but in this case, Mister Calderone has grown weary of Vic

Fontaine—of his inability to pay his debt, of his going into hiding to avoid that responsibility, and of his continued but failed promises to make good on the money he owes."

"What does that mean?" Nog asked, wanting Steinberg to spell it out.

"It means that if Mister Fontaine's debt isn't settled within the next forty-eight hours, Mister Calderone intends his people to close out the account." Steinberg had made himself clear: if Vic's loan wasn't paid off within the following two days, Vic wouldn't live to see a third.

ix

Kira paced forward and back in her room at the Shikina Monastery, her body tense, her mind racing, her emotions volatile. After their revelatory conversation that morning in the refectory, Kira and Altek had gone to speak with the kai. They looked for her first in the office she kept in the priory. There, they found Veldis Reyn, a vedek who served as an aide and adviser to Pralon Onala. He informed them that the kai had left the monastery and would be unavailable until later, at the Great Assembly, just before Kira's address to Bajor about her return from the Celestial Temple. Kira insisted to Veldis that she and Altek needed to speak with the kai immediately about a crucial matter. He said he would contact the kai with their request.

That exchange with Veldis had taken place several hours earlier, and still there had been no word from Pralon. The time neared when Kira would have to depart for the Great Assembly, and she would see the kai there, but she'd wanted more time before her address to discuss the implications of their discovery. It also bothered her that Pralon had not reacted swiftly to her urgent request for a meeting. Kira had a long record of service to Bajor, in multiple roles, and while she had often enough sounded the alert about one matter or another, she had never been an alarmist.

"You're going to erode a path in the floor," Altek said. He sat at the room's lone table. Just a few paces away, Kira stopped when she drew closer.

"I'd tear the floor up stone by stone with my bare hands if it would bring the kai here," she said.

"That won't be necessary." Kira swiveled around to see Pralon Onala standing in the entry hall. "Please forgive the delay in seeing you," the kai said, entering the room. "Vedek Veldis contacted me shortly after you spoke with him, but I could not get away until now."

"I wouldn't have asked to meet with you as soon as possible," Kira said, "if it wasn't critical."

"There are a great many critical issues facing Bajor these days, I'm afraid," Pralon said. "I have just come from Lonar Province, from the town of Kenthira. This morning, a bomb detonated there."

"Oh, no," Altek said.

"Who planted the bomb?" Kira wanted to know.

"Law enforcement officers in the area are still searching for the culprits," Pralon said. "So far, nobody has claimed responsibility, but their motives appear certain; the explosion destroyed a statue of Ohalu." The notion that somebody would demolish a work of art intended as an object of commemoration simply because they disagreed with the ideas it embodied offended Kira deeply—more so because it seemed to have been done by somebody who shared the vedek's own beliefs.

"Was anyone hurt?" Altek asked.

"Fortunately, there were no fatalities," Pralon said. "The explosion occurred early enough in the day that there were few people out in the town, but a young man nearby was struck by a piece of debris. Doctors have him in surgery, but he may lose an eye."

"That's terrible," Altek said.

"It truly is shameful," Pralon said. "We must find a way to bring Bajor together . . . to end this escalating violence."

"I agree," Kira said, "but I'm not sure that what we have to tell you will help that cause."

The kai paused. "Perhaps, then, you should refrain from revealing whatever it is you wish to tell me. There is something to be said for plausible deniability."

The vedek couldn't tell whether or not Pralon intended her suggestion seriously—the kai possessed a dry sense of humor—but Kira did not consider it a viable option to keep their discovery a secret. "This morning," she said, "Doctor Altek and I were discussing Endalla." She recounted the conversation for the kai, concluding by telling her that, in Altek's time, only four moons orbited Bajor.

"What are you saying?" Pralon said. "Is that an indication of how far back in time you lived, Doctor? Before the birth of Bajor's fifth moon?" Even as she spoke calmly, the kai obviously grasped for some explanation other than the one at which Kira and Altek had arrived.

"No, we don't think so," Altek said. "Bajor's moons formed billions of years ago, long before the evolution of multicellular life on the planet."

Pralon regarded Altek for a long moment before she pulled a chair out from the table and sat down. The color drained from her face. She looked as though she might pass out.

"Are you all right, Eminence?" Kira asked.

Pralon gazed up at the vedek. "No, I don't think I am," she said. "Not if I understand what you're telling me—that Endalla is not a naturally occurring satellite . . . that between Doctor Altek's time and our own, it was constructed around the falsework in order to hide it from our people . . . that the Ohalavaru are right."

"That does seem to be the case," Kira said. "I mean, it appears that the Ohalavaru may be right about the falsework and about Endalla's construction, but it doesn't necessarily follow that the Prophets are not gods."

"No, no, of course not," Pralon said. "But that is what the Ohalavaru will claim. They will point to the doctor's story as just one more corroboration of their convictions, and there will be people who believe them."

"True faith can withstand doubts," Altek said.

"It can," Pralon said. "It often does . . . but for some, their faith will be shattered. Maybe for enough Bajorans that it will lead to a schism . . ." The thought, once voiced, seemed to horrify the kai. The idea shook Kira as well. "Maybe . . . maybe Doctor Altek has not come from Bajor's past, but from the history of some other world, perhaps in an alternate universe."

Kira took a seat at the table and faced the kai. "I imagine that, technically, that's possible, but . . ." She realized that she would have to reveal information she had yet to impart to Pralon. "But I also lived in that time."

The kai gazed at Kira in confusion. "What?" she asked. "What do you mean?"

"After I entered the Celestial Temple and it collapsed," Kira explained, "at some point, I ended up living in that time period on Bajor . . . alongside Doctor Altek."

"What?" Pralon asked. "How is that possible?"

Kira shook her head and shrugged. "I was sent there by the Prophets," she said. "I don't know how or to what end, but I spent months working with Doctor Altek and others to free Bajoran slaves from the Aleira."

"From who?" the kai asked. Her questions sounded like

automatic responses rather actual attempts to elicit meaningful answers.

"Another group of Bajorans who called themselves by a different name," Altek said. "People who did not believe in the Prophets and who enslaved the Bajora."

"From my perspective," Kira said, "I have no doubts that I was on Bajor—our Bajor—and that it once had four moons."

"And you did not think to share this information before now?" the kai asked, anger seeping into her tone.

"Honestly, I didn't remember about the number of moons until this morning," Kira said. "My memories of that time are . . . fluid. I am also reluctant to say anything because of the Temporal Prime Directive."

"Which is a principle of Starfleet, not of the Bajoran clergy," Pralon said.

"But it is a principle rooted in the practical objective of not altering the timeline," Kira said. "And isn't it a Bajoran tenet that personal religious events—Orb experiences, pagh'tem'fars, Orb shadows, dream whispers—are private, to be shared only if an adherent so chooses?" Although, immediately after her return from the Celestial Temple, Kira had struggled with whether or not to tell the kai everything, she found herself resentful that the kai proposed that she should have done so.

Pralon looked down at her hands, not chastened, but thinking. "Pagh'tem'fars and Orb experiences are most often confusing episodes, difficult to harvest clear memories from, impenetrable in terms of meaning." The kai raised her head and fixed her gaze on Kira. "Can you be sure about what you *think* you experienced?"

Kira could only view the question as a desperate attempt to discredit her ability to substantiate the Ohalavaru claims. "From my perspective, Eminence, there is no doubt that Bajor once had four moons," the vedek said. "And I understand how the Ohalavaru will try to make the case that the Prophets constructed a fifth moon, an artificial moon, to hide the Alpha Quadrant anchor for the wormhole. But that doesn't mean we have the right to hide the truth."

"We're not even certain what the truth is," Pralon said. "It will require a scientific effort to confirm or refute the role of the subterranean complex on Endalla with respect to the Celestial Temple."

"I agree," Kira said, "but even if the Ohalavaru are right about the falsework, it doesn't mean that the Prophets are not divine. I know what the Prophets have shown me in my life, and what They've caused me to experience. My faith tells me that They are gods."

"As does mine," Pralon said. "When you appear before the public today, do you intend to speak of your travels in time?"

"I don't plan to," Kira said.

"And what about your interpretation of the events on Endalla?" the kai asked.

"I don't know that I need to say anything about that today," Kira told her. "But I can't be silent forever about what we discovered. That would dishonor our beliefs, make a mockery of our faith."

"You are well known among our people for your efforts during the Occupation and then serving aboard Deep Space Nine. You are also highly regarded for your dedication in joining and contributing to the religious leadership on Bajor." The kai paused, and Kira had the feeling that Pralon chose the words she would say next with care. "But I would also remind you of your role in posting the writings of Ohalu to the comnet, and of your subsequent Attainder. If you are once again seen lending credence to the heretical views of the Ohalavaru, I am unsure if even my office can protect you."

The words sounded as though they carried a message of concern and a promise of support, but they seemed to Kira like a charade. She heard a political threat, and it took her aback. She would have expected such behavior from Winn Adami, but not from Pralon Onala. "What are you saying, Eminence?" Kira asked. "Are you trying to silence me because my beliefs do not perfectly conform to yours?" She had lowered her voice in an attempt to soften what she said, but the content of her question could not be mistaken. The kai reacted accordingly.

"I would remind you of your station, Vedek," Pralon said, standing up from her chair. "Not to mention my position as the spiritual leader of the Bajoran people."

Earlier in her life, Kira would have forcefully stood her ground. She would have reminded Pralon—probably in rising tones—that being the kai required responsibility and unimpeachable integrity, that it demanded that she be scrupulously honest with the people whose spiritual well-being had been entrusted to her. Instead, Kira remained steadfast, but understood that, while she could make her arguments to the kai about the proper course of action, she could not force Pralon to do the right thing.

"I know my place, Eminence," the vedek said, her manner humble. "And I know yours."

Before Pralon could respond, a chime rang in the room, signaling a visitor at Kira's door. The kai glanced at the companel in the corner, then said, "That will be my security staff come to fetch us. It is time to go to the Great Hall for your speech." When Kira stood up, Pralon took her by her upper arms. "Vedek Kira, as a general principle, I seek neither to lie to the people nor to withhold factual information from them. I will remind you that I did not vote to suppress the publication of the Ohalu texts, nor did I support your Attainder."

"I know that, Eminence," Kira said, and she again told herself that she was dealing with Pralon, not with Winn. She found it troubling that she had needed to do that several times since her return from the Celestial Temple.

"I am not advocating that we don't inform the Bajoran people of the four moons that existed in Doctor Altek's time," Pralon said. "But I am asking that you do not make that information public until we have had a chance to speak more about the issue . . . to study it. We still do not know from whence the doctor came, nor have the scientists and engineers begun studying the falsework and its relationship to Endalla."

The kai's request sounded reasonable to Kira. "I understand what you're saying, Eminence. I defer to your judgment."

"Very good," Pralon said. "Thank you." The kai started toward the entry hall to meet her security team, and Kira and Altek followed—although Kira knew that the doctor would not travel to the Great Hall with them, but go back to his own guest accommodations at the monastery.

As they headed out of Kira's room, the vedek again told herself that she could not force Pralon—or anybody, for that matter—to do the right thing. *No,* she thought. *But I can do it myself.*

X

Quark stopped just before the end of the alleyway, staying in the shadows thrown by the building at his back. He felt Laren's presence beside him in the confined passage, heard the hush of her breathing. She had broken his heart, and yet he still felt glad to have her with him—not just for her support in trying to recover his latinum, but for the joy of simply spending time with her. When it came to their romance—and they'd had such a relationship, no matter how hard she'd attempted to rationalize it away as something less—Laren made it painfully clear that she had already moved on. Quark would too—he had no choice in the matter—but she couldn't prevent him from enjoying one last adventure with her.

Laren leaned in over Quark's shoulder as the two hid in the alley. Night had descended as they'd made their way deeper into Mericor City, the interior of the dome darkening as the hour had worn on. When they initially headed toward the center of the settlement, amid swarms of other visitors, the routes widened and the buildings reached higher into the sky, promising a welcoming and vibrant urban core. But then, following the guidance of the scanner, they veered north, and the character of their surroundings changed. Structures dropped back down to one and two stories, pedestrian walkways contracted, narrow alleys appeared between neglected, sometimes crumbling walls. The crowds thinned too, and the figures they passed kept their heads down as they moved furtively through the cheapjack neighborhood.

"Do you have her?" Laren asked under her breath, in a voice so quiet that Quark doubted even a Vulcan standing beside them would have heard her. Over the years, she had learned how softly she could speak and still have him able to distinguish her words.

Quark held up the diminutive scanner so that she could see its display. Green blocks represented the buildings around them, and black segments between them designated the alleys and streets that ran through the run-down section of the city. A single flashing red pinpoint marked the location of the only Petarian the scanner had to that point detected, inside one of the nearby structures. A flock of yellow dots indicated motion and heat signatures around the object of their search.

"Where is she?" Laren asked. "In what type of building?"

The barkeep held up one finger, and Laren immediately quieted. He listened, concentrating on filtering out the ambient sounds that told him nothing he needed to know—voices in the distance, footsteps moving away, music from three different sources. When his ears told him he could do so safely, he stepped out of the shadows and into the yellowish light of a nearby streetlamp. Quark peeked from the alley and down the cross street, in the direction the scanner signaled. He saw numerous doors and windows on either side of the walkway, many sets of them accompanied by signage in various languages. He recognized Federation Standard, Cardassian, Andorii, Yridian, Denobulan, not to mention two placards written in Ferengi, one announcing a gambling den and the other a private communications hub.

Ducking back into the shadows beside Ro, Quark answered her question in low tones. "There are so many entrances into so many places, packed in so tightly, I can't tell from here which one she's in," he said. "I saw saloons, breathing bars, a comm hub, substance purveyors, a betting parlor, and other places I can't identify. She could be in any one of them; there's no way of knowing without getting closer."

"Then let's get closer."

"No," Quark said. "Viray knows me on sight, and she's not stupid, so there's a good chance she's looked at images of you as well. I don't want her to know we're on her trail until we're ready to deal with her, in a place where we're sure she can't run from us."

"But how do you know we're going to get that opportunity?" Laren asked.

"I don't," Quark said, "but I do know that trying to corner her in a place with an unknown layout, among a group of people, any number of which could be her coconspirators, will probably only send her into hiding. We need to—" Quark abruptly stopped talking, his attention captured by what he saw on the scanner cupped in his palm.

"What?" Laren asked. "What is it?"

"It's Viray," Quark said. "She's on the move."

xi

Ro exited the lobby of the inn, moving quickly across the avenue and down a side street, to a public house where Quark waited for her. She entered the dark, dingy establishment and hastened to the booth in the far corner, mostly out of sight from other patrons. She braced herself for Quark to be gone, either because something had happened with Viray or because he'd finally tired of being around her after the way she'd treated him. But as she reached the booth, she saw him sitting at the inner end of the table, a half-full glass of something green and frothy in front of him. She slid onto the long seat across from him.

"Is there any news?" Ro asked.

"No," Quark said. "She's still in the restaurant."

They had trailed the Petarian—presumably the private detective and likely thief—on her crosstown journey, staying out of sight on parallel streets and tracking her with the scanner. Viray left the dodgy section of the city for one at least marginally better, ultimately entering a hostelry. They briefly lost track of her there, but not long after the Petarian entered the inn, she exited, still alone, and visited a local eatery. Ro and Quark secreted themselves away in the public house and continued to observe her via the scanner.

Once it had become clear that the Petarian had entered the restaurant to have a meal, Quark had asked Ro to reconnoiter the inn. "You were right about the inn," Ro said. "It offers rooms with only one door and no windows. They're soundproof and resistant to sensors. The man at the desk tried to convince me that the law banning sensors on Mericor is only partially successful, and certainly we've seen evidence of that." Quark nodded and turned over his hand for a moment to reveal the scanner still in his palm. "My impression of the inn is that it can be a relatively effective place to hide. I booked us a room for the night."

Ro expected Quark to offer an arch comment, or even to give her a leering, lascivious look, but instead, he only asked about the cost. She had to tell him that she spent almost all of the latinum he'd given her, a response that caused him to roll his eyes. "Did you at least negotiate?"

As Ro recounted her back-and-forth with the man at the hotel—a Troyian—Quark again looked at the scanner. "She's moving," he said. "It looks like she's going back to the inn."

"What do you want to do?" Ro asked.

Quark thought for an instant, then said, "We need to follow her. We need to know if she's staying here on Mericor by herself. When she enters her room, we'll have a moment to scan inside to see if she's alone."

"And if she is?"

"What better time to confront her," Quark said. He pushed himself out of the booth, and Ro got up and went with him. Together, they hurried through the streets toward the hostelry.

Perhaps a block away from the inn, Quark stopped, his hand raised up before his face. "She just entered the building," he said. Ro peered around left and right, then behind her, to ensure that nobody had them under surveillance. After a minute or so, Quark looked up. "She just disappeared from the scanner, at the very end of the building."

"Is anybody with her?" Ro asked.

"When her life signs vanished, there were no movements and no heat signatures anywhere near her," Quark said. "She's alone."

"All right, then," Ro said. "Are you ready?"

Quark bared his sharp, slantwise teeth. "I want my profits back."

They strode to the inn and, after a quick check of the scanner to ensure that the Petarian had not left her room, they entered the lobby. Ro led the way, nodding an acknowledgment to the Troyian man at the counter. She and Quark entered the corridor that led to the rooms. They saw nobody else in the poorly lit passage.

To Ro's surprise, Quark raced ahead to the end of the corridor, reaching into his jacket as he did so. She saw him withdraw a small device, and by the time she caught up with him, he was skimming it along the wall near the access pad. At one point, a yellow light flashed silently on, and then a second, and finally three more all at once. Quark affixed the device to the wall, then tapped several times along a row of control surfaces. In rapid succession, four of the yellow lights turned green. When the fifth finally did, the door glided open. Before Ro could stop him, Quark barged through it. Concerned for his safety—and knowing they were committing a crime by breaking into somebody's room—Ro had little choice but to follow. She pulled the device from the wall and slipped inside. The door closed behind her.

Quark stood in the middle of the room, staring toward the right-hand wall. There, a Petarian woman sitting on the edge of a bed gaped at him, obviously startled. It was Mayereen Viray; Quark had shown Ro images he'd recorded of her. The private detective had dark eyes and golden skin. She wore black slacks and a purple tunic.

Ro stepped farther into the room. Viray stood up, and the captain watched for any movement that hinted the woman might draw a weapon or otherwise take action. The Petarian held her hands open and at her sides, as though aware of Ro's scrutiny. Despite her small stature, Viray displayed a strong carriage and a confident manner. She looked from Quark to Ro and back again. She appeared to rein in her surprise. "Why are you here?" she asked Quark. "You are jeopardizing all the funds you've invested in my efforts, and more even than that."

"I didn't 'invest' in you, Viray," Quark said. "I *paid* you to do a job, and instead, you *stole* my latinum."

"I haven't stolen anything from you, Quark," she said. "Given the amount of work I've done and everything that's happened with this job, you've actually gotten a bargain."

"A bargain?!" Quark snapped back, waving his arms, his voice rising. Ro didn't know if she'd ever seen him quite so angry. As much as the acquisition of wealth meant to him, she wondered if her ending their relationship contributed to his fury.

Unexpectedly, the door signal chimed. Before Ro or Quark could react, Viray said, "Come in." The captain wheeled around and crouched down, preparing to spring at whatever threat appeared. The panel glided open, and for one disconcerting second, Ro could not comprehend what she saw—*who* she saw.

Morn stood in the doorway.

Ro peered over at Quark, and she saw that his eyes had gone wide. When she turned her attention back to the stocky, no-necked Lurian, she saw that he looked as though he had aged much more than the nearly two years since she had last seen him, back on Bajor. More arc-like wrinkles underlined his deep-set eyes, and he had lost all the wisps of hair from his piebald scalp. He wore a bulky dark-green jacket with quilted sleeves, and a pair of brown pants with many pockets down the legs. Morn appeared as stunned to see Quark and Ro as she felt to see him. For a moment, the tableau froze, as though none of them dared move or make a sound—but just for a moment.

"Where have you been?" Quark demanded of his long-time friend and customer.

Morn opened his wide, frowning mouth to reply, but then two men suddenly appeared behind him. One of them pushed the Lurian hard. Morn hurtled into the room, tripped, and went sprawling to the floor. The two men— one Vulcan, one human, both dressed in casual clothes— stepped inside. As the door closed after them, they each drew a type-1 phaser and trained them on Ro and Quark.

"I know who they are," Quark said, pointing at the two armed men, but speaking to Ro. "I recognize the way they move. They were the ones who faked Viray's abduction—in other words, her accomplices."

Morn rolled over and started to scamper to his feet, but the human aimed his phaser at him. "Stay where you are," he ordered the Lurian. "Don't get up." Morn stopped on his knees, then sat back on his haunches, his hands raised, open and empty.

"You," the Vulcan said to Quark. "Move over next to the Bajoran." Quark did as he'd been ordered.

Ignoring Morn and Viray, Ro regarded the two armed intruders. She wanted to appraise their physical capabilities— both looked exceedingly fit—and their behaviors so that she could prepare to act when she saw an opportunity. If she could not incapacitate the two men, if she could not at least secure one of their phasers, she had another course of action open to her: though she hadn't told Quark, she had brought an emergency transponder with her, which she'd hidden inside her boot. She could trigger it at any time and it would signal Mericor law enforcement—such as it was— but she doubted it would function inside a room insulated against sensor contact.

"I am Agent Corvok," the Vulcan said. "My colleague is Agent Amadou Toulet. We're from Federation Security." He pulled an identification badge from a pocket and held it out so that Morn, and then Ro and Quark, could see it. She did not know whether to believe the man.

"Federation Security," Quark said with ample sarcasm. "That's marvelous, because we're on the same side. This is Captain Ro Laren of Federation starbase Deep Space Nine . . . in the Bajoran system . . . guarding the wormhole to the Gamma Quadrant. Perhaps you've heard of it."

The Vulcan arched an eyebrow. "We'll check on your identities shortly," he said. "For the moment, stay quiet." Quark looked as though he would say more, but Ro suggested with a glance that he keep his own counsel, and he did.

"Place your hands behind your back," Toulet told Morn. Ro watched as the agent stepped past the Lurian and secured restraints around his wrists. "Now, on your feet." Morn lumbered upward. Toulet holstered his weapon, then began patting down his captive.

Ro considered rushing at the Vulcan in an attempt to surprise him and wrest away his phaser. Her intuition told her to wait. If the two men were criminals and intended to do them harm, she reasoned that they would have done so already. If they truly belonged to Federation Security, then she needn't have any concerns.

Toulet pulled a number of objects out of the pockets running up and down Morn's pants. Ro saw several isolinear chips, a Cardassian isolinear rod, a comm unit, slips and scintillas of latinum, and what appeared to be several pieces of wrapped candy. He set them down on top of a dresser opposite the bed, then searched through Morn's jacket. Toulet reached into one pocket and stopped cold. He looked over at Corvok as he pulled out a wide silver bracelet—except that Ro saw that it would more appropriately fit around her biceps than around her wrist. Technological components covered the object. It did not look familiar to Ro.

"This must be it," Toulet said to his partner. "Morn, native of Luria with dual Federation citizenship, you are under arrest for the possession of restricted technology. Under Federation law, you have rights and recourse, including but not limited to representation by legal counsel, the opportunity to examine all evidence collected in relation to your alleged crime, and the choice not to speak." Ro had to stifle a laugh; she could not recall the last time she'd seen Morn quiet for more than five minutes—if she ever had. "We are in possession of an extradition order executed between the Federation and the municipality of Mericor. This order allows us to remove you to our vessel so that we can transport you to a Federation court to face arraignment. In transit, you will be provided with a full list and explanation of all your rights, and you will be permitted to contact legal representation of your choosing."

As Toulet continued to deal with Morn, Corvok addressed Ro. "Captain," he said, "I trust you will understand that we need to confirm your identity, as well as determine your exact part in all of this."

"I'm not even sure what's going on here," Ro said. "Quark and I have come to Mericor only to recover funds seemingly misappropriated from him by this woman." She gestured toward Viray, who had not moved from her position by the bed.

"You're Quark," Corvok said. "You hired Miss Viray to track down Mister Morn."

"That's *Ambassador* Quark. And there's no crime in hiring a private detective to find somebody."

"That depends on your intent," Corvok said. "We have neither warrants for your arrest, nor extradition orders to remove you from Mericor. We can detain both of you, though, based on your presence here with a suspected criminal—"

"With *two* suspected criminals," Quark said, throwing an infuriated look at Viray.

"Rather than formally holding you," Corvok went on, "I request that you accompany us to our ship for the purpose of aiding our investigation. If you have no part in this, then there is no risk to you."

"I'm not going anywhere with these men," Quark announced.

"Excuse me," Ro told Corvok. She turned to Quark, took his hand, and pulled him a few steps away, into the corner of the room. "I know you're not mixed up in this," she told him. "I know you only wanted to find your friend at first, and then to try to recover latinum you thought had been stolen from you—"

"It *was* stolen."

"We'll see," Ro said. "But we should go with them. We can find out what's going on here—with Morn, with Viray, with all of it."

"But . . ." Quark started, but he did not voice whatever objection had occurred to him.

"Come on, Quark," Ro said. "It's over." The moment she spoke her final two words, she knew she'd made a mistake.

It's over. Quark seemed to deflate in front of her. He could not hold her gaze. Instead, he stepped away from Ro and over to Corvok. She watched as, in more ways than one, he gave up.

xii

Nog stood at the window in the living area of the suite at the Shining Oasis. The brilliant, flashing lights of Las Vegas burned against the night, turning the city into a literal beacon for fortune hunters. Nog usually appreciated the Ferengi-like nature of Vic's human city, but at that moment, the glowing neon and the blinking bulbs seemed to taunt him. Despite being a Starfleet officer, despite serving as the operations chief and assistant chief engineer of Deep Space 9, he still knew the Rules of Acquisition by heart. In the final analysis, Vic's dilemma could be framed as a financial problem, meaning that Nog should have no trouble resolving it. And yet the solution eluded him.

He turned from the window. Candlewood and Lani sat quietly on the sofa. They obviously waited for him to lead them. Nog and the science officer had come back to the Shining Oasis after their meeting with Calderone's accountant, and they'd filled Lani in on what had taken place.

"So what are we going to do?" Lani asked.

"We could try a brute-force approach," Candlewood said. "If we can determine where Vic is being held—and we did see him at the Silver Lode hotel back when we got shot at—we could break him out. If we can find Vic, we could bring him some sort of physical protection to keep him safe as we free him."

Nog understood Candlewood's point, but— "That doesn't really work," Nog said. "Let's say we can forcibly free Vic from Calderone." Nog walked away from the window and over toward the sofa. He stood on the other side of the low, rectangular table there and continued to talk to Candlewood and Lani. "That wouldn't actually solve Vic's problems. There would be a price on his head, and even if he escaped Calderone's clutches, he would be reduced to living in the shadows." Nog thought back to seeing Vic in the decaying environs of the Fremont-Sunrise Hotel, at how much of himself the singer seemed to have lost. "No, we can't leave him a hunted man."

"So at that point, if he became a 'hunted man,' you could transfer Vic's matrix to another program," Candlewood suggested. "There are plenty of Earth holoprograms . . . even some historical ones. Or we could code something new for Vic. It doesn't even have to be Earth, it doesn't even have to be historical. Move him into one of the *Vulcan Love Slave* programs for a while, until we can create something else where he'd have a place—maybe as an entertainer on Risa or on Wrigley's Pleasure Planet. Who knows? Maybe he'd want to be the morale officer on a twenty-second-century starship."

Nog considered the general idea of transplanting Vic. "Maybe," he said. "But I'm not even sure Vic's matrix *can* be transferred, at least not for more than brief periods. Felix Knightly created the Las Vegas simulation to challenge Doctor Bashir, who's a literal genius. Felix coded Vic to be self-aware, and he enacted restrictions on how the program could be used and modified. Look at all the trouble we had reentering it after being 'killed.' I'm not sure if we can permanently transplant Vic's matrix."

"You could ask Mister Knightly," Lani said. "Even if it's not possible now, you could ask him to alter the code."

"I could," Nog said, "but I'd have to exit the holosuite in order to do that, and we can't leave until we solve Vic's problems." Nog paced back across the room and over to the window. He gazed out again at the glittering Las Vegas Strip. "The idea that makes the most sense is simply to give Calderone what he wants."

"It sounds right now like he wants Vic dead," Candlewood said.

"No," Nog said as he watched the giant shoe spinning around at the Silver Slipper, its lights pulsating. "Calderone wants Vic's loan repaid—plus the vigorish."

"And where are we going to get over a million dollars?" Candlewood asked. "Even if we could leave the program to replicate that sum, the code only allows period clothing and certain other items to be brought in."

"Right," Nog said. "We need to get it from a source within the program."

"How?" Lani asked. "By robbing a bank?"

"Or by executing a confidence game?" Candlewood said.

Nog nodded. "Or by dealing in real estate, or by investing," he said. "Any of those choices might work, but we just don't have enough time to plan something, and then to actually accomplish it, with a one hundred percent chance of success."

"Is there anything we can do?" Candlewood asked. "As I understand it, the entire reason that the real Las Vegas succeeded as a destination is that tourists thought they could become wealthy overnight. The reason it could sustain itself is that it was casino owners and mobsters making all, or at least most, of the profits."

"Look at Morn," Lani said. "He had the knowledge and a perspective hundreds of years beyond this place, and yet even he couldn't win in the long run."

"No," Nog agreed. "It's like John said the other day: with the odds in favor of the casino, it's impossible for any player to win in the long run."

"If only we could change the odds," Candlewood said.

Nog suddenly remembered something that Lani had told them. He sat down at the table by the window and grabbed the stack of Vic's forged papers. He grabbed a pen, turned the top sheet over, and started to sketch. "Maybe we *can* change the odds," he said. "According to Lani, that's what Morn was planning to do."

"That's right," Lani said. She stood up from the sofa and walked over to the table, and Candlewood came with her. "He wanted to create some sort of device so that he could control the outcome of playing slot machines."

"That's a . . . a scientific problem," Candlewood said as Nog continued to draw. "The machines here don't use optical grids, multitronics, or bioncural circuitry."

"No," Nog said. "They don't even use duotronics. They're electromechanical." He finished his rudimentary illustration, turned it around, and pushed it across the table so that Candlewood and Lani could see it. It depicted the basic internal mechanism and circuitry of a slot machine. "So it's a scientific problem, and an engineering problem," Nog said. He looked up at Candlewood. "Do you know any scientists or engineers, John?"

xiii

Pralon Onala sat in the Apex Chair, gazing out from the stage of the Great Assembly. As she had when she'd spoken there the previous day, she saw every vedek in attendance. The present crisis had motivated all of them to attend Kira's address so that they could be seen standing their ground for their beliefs, be they traditional or Ohalavaru.

That reality saddened Pralon. If ever she gave public voice to such an emotion, many would surely judge it peculiar for a spiritual leader to find disappointment in her people's firm display of faith. By itself, the show of the vedeks' devotion did not trouble her, but the fact of its context did. The kai understood it, of course; when worshippers faced adversity, it made sense for them to turn to their gods for guidance and solace. There could be no better example of that than the Occupation, during which the central role the Prophets inhabited in the lives of most Bajorans helped them through unspeakable horrors. For Pralon, that marked a selfish—or at least a self-involved—version of religious belief. She preferred to practice her own faith from the other side, using it not as a crutch with which she could navigate the bumpy path of her own life, but as an instrument of virtue and decency in order to bolster the lives of others.

But Pralon remembered all too well the tremendous opposition among the Bajoran people to providing aid to the Cardassian Union after the Dominion War. At a time of peace and prosperity for Bajor, its citizens should have been led by their faith to offer charity and forgiveness. Many were, but a significant and vocal minority fought against giving any assistance at all to Cardassia. Even though Bajor ultimately did become a vital component of the reconstruction efforts, the kai believed that the considerable objections still reflected poorly on their society.

To Pralon's right, Asarem Wadeen sat in the Premier Chair. The first minister had introduced Kira Nerys, who stood at the podium as she spoke not just to the vedeks and ministers present, but, via the comnet, to all the citizens of Bajor. Asarem, rather than Pralon, had announced Kira in an attempt to deflect criticism, preemptively leveled by some Ohalavaru, that the vedek would speak as an instrument of the kai and traditional orthodoxy. Pralon hoped and trusted that the vedek would strike an intermediate note that would placate—or at least not inflame—believers on both sides.

Kira had begun her oration by detailing the circumstances that had led her into the Celestial Temple more than two years earlier. She then talked more generally about what took place inside the wormhole once it collapsed with her inside it. The vedek did not mention traveling back in time or meeting Altek Dans. Instead, she invoked a faltering recollection, comparing her elusive memories to something many Bajorans could relate to: an Orb experience. She spoke reverentially about the abilities and benevolence of the Prophets, but without the heavy-handedness that could have upset the Ohalavaru.

Pralon approved of everything Kira had said, and she also appreciated the manner in which the vedeks and ministers had received her words. For the most part, they listened attentively and without interruption, treating the event more like a personal discourse and less like a political speech. When Kira reached a natural stopping point by expressing her gratitude to be back home on Bajor, everybody in the Great Assembly rose to their feet to clap, including the first minister and the kai.

Pralon waited for Kira to step back from the podium, but that didn't happen. Instead, as the applause eased, the vedek said, "Though I am happy to be home, it has been jarring to return to a world in conflict." The vedeks and ministers started to sit back down. In her peripheral vision, the kai saw Asarem tense, but then the first minister once more took the Premier Chair. The two leaders had discussed Kira's appearance before the Great Assembly, and while they both believed the presentation of her story could help ease the present religious strife, they had agreed that the vedek should not directly speak about the ongoing troubles. The kai had passed that on to Kira. Pralon considered stepping forward and thanking the vedek, and in that way putting an end to whatever other remarks she might make, but she knew that she couldn't; stifling Kira after she'd mentioned Bajor's spiritual struggle would only aggravate the situation.

"I have learned about what recently took place on Endalla," Kira went on. Pralon fought to keep her expression neutral as she sat down again. She worried not only that the vedek would end up enraging one religious faction or the other, but also that she would reveal Altek's claim of Bajor having only four moons in his time—a declaration that would surely rock the foundations of orthodoxy and bring even more turmoil to their world. "It is difficult to credit the perpetration of violence by Ohalavaru extremists on Endalla, but there is also no justification for traditional adherents to oppose an examination of their faith. It is just to condemn the terrorist attacks committed by people on either side of the issue." Pralon noted with some relief that Kira seemed dedicated to walking the line between the two rival camps, apparently wanting to give neither any sort of rhetorical advantage.

"I don't feel that the so-called falsework repudiates my belief in the divinity of the Prophets," the vedek continued. "But I am also not afraid to put that belief to the test. My views are traditional, but I have no wish to impose them on the Ohalavaru, or on anybody else. I can't support barbarous acts or attempts to bring the Bajoran religion or its opposition low, but I defend the rights of people to seek the truth—even if that truth would contradict my own." The kai listened to Kira with a mixture of anger and appreciation—anger that she had spoken at all of Endalla and the Ohalavaru, and appreciation that she did not contribute more ammunition to one side or the other.

"I must therefore pledge my support for the first minister's plan to send scientists and engineers to study the falsework," Kira said, sending murmurs coursing through the Great Assembly. Before they could grow into full-throated dissent, she added, "I also support the kai's proposal of sending along observers from the Vedek Assembly to oversee those efforts." More voices rose, and then applause began—slowly at first, but then rising, until it spread throughout the hall. Pralon felt like exhaling loudly; Kira had avowed her own faith while championing those who disagreed with her, and she had done both in equal measure. In accomplishing the delicate balancing act, she demonstrated considerable political skill.

Pralon waited for the ovation to end and for the vedek to conclude her remarks. Kira had said more than the kai had wanted her to, but to good ends. The approbation of her peers, both traditional and Ohalavaru, marked a worthy close to her speech.

But then Kira said more.

xiv

Kira knew she'd spoken about issues that the kai had wanted her to avoid, but she didn't feel she'd had much of a choice. Whether or not Kai Pralon had intended her own comments to the vedek as a political threat, they'd sounded like one. It surprised Kira so much that she initially discounted the idea of the kai pressuring her. After Pralon's decision to at least temporarily hide Altek's news about Bajor's moons, though, the vedek decided that she needed to take control of her own public narrative. She would not permit the kai or anybody else to use her time in the Celestial Temple, her Attainder, or any other part of her life against her.

"As all of you know," Kira said from the stage of the Great Assembly, "almost ten years ago, I posted the translations of Ohalu's texts to the comnet. For that act, I was Attainted. I didn't think that would happen, but I knew it was a possibility. I chose to do what I did because I was secure not only in my own beliefs, but in the moral conviction that it was wrong to hide such a discovery from the people."

Kira could have stopped there—perhaps *should* have stopped there—but she no longer fully trusted the kai. She did not *dis*trust Pralon, but Kira needed to ensure the integrity and openness of the Bajoran spiritual leader in the ongoing controversy. "Because of the importance of the research efforts going forward, I have accepted the kai's offer to visit Endalla as one of the religious observers." Pralon had made no such offer, but with Kira's public statement to the contrary, the kai would have to allow her participation. Perhaps Pralon would have done so anyway, but Kira wanted to be certain that she played a part in the study of the falsework—not just because of its significance, but because another possibility had occurred to her.

"Perhaps," she ended her address, giving voice to that possibility, "it is because of the events on Endalla that I have been returned to Bajor by the Prophets." As Kira finally stepped back from the podium, the Great Assembly erupted in applause, which did not surprise her. Because of the mainstream nature of her beliefs, the vedeks who subscribed to traditional views would believe her invocation of the Prophets returning her to Bajor meant Their will to demonstrate Their divinity. But because she had in the past acted on behalf of the Ohalavaru, those followers of Ohalu would think the Prophets wanted her to support the revelation of their powerful but prosaic alien nature.

For Kira's own part, she realized that maybe she still had more work to do as the Hand of the Prophets.

XV

Pralon filed rapidly through the anteroom, paying no regard to her assistant, Ranjen Linsa, rising from his desk to greet her. The kai entered her own office at the Shikina Monastery and stepped off to the side, allowing Kira to follow her in. Once the vedek had, Pralon reached for the handle and swung the old wooden door closed. Then she turned to face Kira.

"What have you done?" Pralon asked. Though she spoke quietly, and even though she'd had time to calm down, she could not entirely prevent anger and disillusionment from infusing her tone. After the vedek's speech, Pralon had followed her offstage and told her that they needed to talk. Kira did not appear surprised, nor should she have, given the content of her remarks to the Vedek Assembly, the Chamber of Ministers, and all of Bajor. They walked in silence to the Great Assembly's transporter room, from which they beamed back to the monastery.

"I'm sorry, Eminence," Kira said, though she did not sound contrite. "I did what I thought best."

"Just as your former reputation would have it," Pralon said. In the Resistance, in the Militia, aboard Deep Space 9, and even while serving in Starfleet, Kira had been known to have her own mind. That she had often been right in going off on her own, or even by disobeying orders, missed the point. "I believed that you had outgrown such behavior."

Kira inclined her head to one side, as though mystified by the kai's comment. "Pardon me, Eminence, but you believed I had 'outgrown' doing the right thing?"

Pralon's eyes narrowed involuntarily. "I believed that your entry into the clergy, and your rapid ascent from novice to vedek, had afforded you the maturity to know that Kira Nerys is not the final arbiter of what the 'right thing' is."

"I'm not saying that I get to decide that," Kira told her. "I'm saying that I have to follow my conscience . . . that even if it would be easier for me—or easier for you—I can't abdicate my responsibilities."

Fury and frustration welled up within Pralon and compelled her to move. She circled the vedek and marched past the sitting area—where a sofa and several comfortable chairs surrounded a square wooden table—over to her desk. She moved behind it, intending to sit, but the tension she felt kept her on her feet. "Your responsibilities, Vedek Kira, include supporting the kai—not maneuvering her to do your bidding."

"I'm not talking about my responsibilities as a vedek," Kira said, her own voice rising as she approached the desk. "I'm talking about my responsibilities as a Bajoran . . . not just as a person of faith, but as a citizen of our world."

"You make it sound as though you took action based on high ideals," Pralon said, "but all you did was disobey my instructions and manipulate me." A thought rose in the kai's mind, and she struggled with whether or not she should speak it aloud. She looked down at her desk and noted the position of the large mass of blond wood that stood between her and Kira—a symbol of the obstacles that had suddenly grown between them. She decided that she wanted the vedek to understand how far apart they were. "The actions you took," she said, "are grounds for Attainder."

Kira actually laughed. "Is that another threat?"

"It is not a threat; it is a fact," Pralon said. "And I have never threatened you."

"Haven't you?" Kira shook her head. "I thought I knew you, Eminence," she said, the honorific sounding contemptuous when she spoke it. "I supported your candidacy to become kai—I *prayed* for your election—fundamentally not because of what I saw in you, but because of what I didn't see: self-interest, ambition, political calculation. I witnessed those qualities firsthand in your predecessor, and I also saw the terrible damage she caused Bajor."

"This is not about my interests or ambitions, or about

politics," Pralon said. "It's about holding together the collective spiritual life of the Bajoran people." The kai leaned forward and put her hands on her desk. "The only reason I advised you to avoid mentioning Endalla and the falsework was that I didn't want you inadvertently contributing to the ongoing conflict. You've only been back from the Celestial Temple for a few days. You haven't been here to observe how the lines have been drawn, how one small act here or one minor comment there has magnified the divide. I wanted to ensure your speech didn't add to the discord."

Kira appeared to give the kai's words some thought. "I worked hard not to make the situation worse," she said, her tone no longer strident.

Pralon nodded. "I believe you," she said, and the realization diminished her anger. She pushed off of her desk and sat down, then motioned for Kira to take a seat as well. After the vedek had, the kai said, "In my estimation, you succeeded in not exacerbating the situation. You might even have helped to ease frictions, which is the reason I asked you to speak in the first place. I'm grateful that you agreed, but you took a risk by making the remarks you did—a risk I wasn't prepared for you to take at this time. If you had failed, if what you said today had aggravated the situation by supporting one side of the conflict over the other, I couldn't do anything about it. Even if I censured you, the people who agreed with you would have seen it as a partisan move on my part."

"With all due respect," Kira said softly, "this shouldn't be about your position as kai."

"And it isn't," Pralon agreed. "It's about me—or whoever holds this position—having the tools to hold our people together. If you had failed in what you attempted today, you would have tied my hands. There would have been nothing I could have said to the Bajoran people that would have undone the damage—not with the state of affairs as it currently stands."

"I . . . hadn't considered that," Kira admitted.

"I didn't think you had," Pralon said. "It's not your job to do so. But if you had trusted me, if you had spoken to me beforehand about what you wanted to say—"

"I did speak with you about it."

"You did," Pralon said. "But when I told you that the first minister and I didn't want you to talk about Endalla, you agreed. You didn't object and tell me why you thought you should bring up the falsework. You didn't tell me what you wanted to say or how you would say it. I probably would have counseled against it, but I would have given you the opportunity to convince me otherwise." Pralon rested her arms on her desk and leaned forward. "As it is, you convinced me today, in the Great Assembly."

"Did I also convince you that I should go to Endalla?"

"Honestly, no," Pralon said, sitting back in her chair. "I haven't heard your argument for why you should go, even though you've left me with no choice but to send you."

"But you have heard my argument," Kira said. "The Celestial Temple collapsed with me in it more than two years ago, but the Prophets sent me back to Bajor *now*, at this critical time."

"Which makes you think that your return has something to do with the falsework," Pralon said. "I don't know if I agree your conclusion is that obvious."

"Maybe it's not," Kira said. "But even if the Prophets haven't sent me back to Bajor so that I can contribute to what's taking place on Endalla, what harm would there be in permitting me to be an observer during the scientific expedition there? And if the Prophets *have* returned me to Bajor because of the discovery of the falsework, there's no question that I should be there."

As Pralon considered Kira's reasoning, a bell rang. "Come in," the kai called, and Ranjen Linsa entered the office. He walked over to the desk carrying a padd in his hand.

"Please forgive the interruption, Eminence," Linsa said. "Doctor Altek came by immediately after Vedek Kira's address. He left a message for you and requested that I deliver it to you as soon as you came back to your office. I wanted to wait for your meeting to end, but the doctor insisted his message was urgent."

Pralon held her open hand out over the desk. A focused, even-tempered man, Linsa Noth had served as an aide to the kai since her election to the post nine years earlier, and as her primary assistant for the past three. Among his many duties, he functioned as a gatekeeper, and so Pralon knew that he would not have interrupted her meeting with Kira had he not had a good reason to do so. Linsa handed her the padd, then immediately left, pulling the door closed behind him.

The kai activated the padd. Its display contained a short message. She quickly read through it. She chuckled and shook her head, then pushed the device onto her desktop. "Vedek Kira, you believe that the Prophets have conducted you back to Bajor at this time specifically so that you can be an observer on the falsework expedition. It turns out that you're not the only one who thinks that."

"Altek thinks I should go to Endalla?"

"Not you, Vedek," Pralon said. "He believes that the Prophets have sent him here, now, so that *he* can go to Endalla."

Six

Arbitrage

As the early-morning sun sent its warm rays into the suite at the Shining Oasis, Nog pushed the small box across the table. "It's done," he said, satisfied with his efforts, and hopeful for what they would be able to accomplish with it.

Lani raised her head from where she'd lain down on the sofa after getting up at dawn. Her eyes appeared bleary, but she quickly sat upright and shook her head back and forth, as though trying to clear her mind. Not far from her, Candlewood looked over from where he sat in an over-stuffed chair, leaning over the low table in front of the sofa. In his hands, he had a deck of playing cards, half of which lay on the wooden surface before him. The prior night, Nog had taught him the principles of counting cards. Candlewood already knew how to play the game of blackjack, as well as an understanding of the basic strategy required for optimal results—although that basic strategy did not guarantee victory, since the odds still tipped in favor of the casino. But paying attention to what cards had already been dealt, keeping a corresponding count, and adjusting both gambling and in-game decisions based on that count would, when done correctly, skew the probabilities so that they benefited the player. Candlewood had been practicing ever since waking that morning.

The science officer stood up and walked over to the table. "That's it?" he asked. Nog detected a note of skepticism. "It doesn't look like a device."

"It's not supposed to," Nog said. It looked like nothing more than a wooden box, too large to hide in one's pocket, but small enough to be carried easily in one hand. He reached over and plucked off its top, revealing the circuitry within.

On the previous night, sometime between designing the device and teaching Candlewood the "black seven" card-counting approach—both of which the casinos would have taken great exception to a gambler using—Nog had gone out into the streets of Las Vegas in search of everything he would need to bend the city's slot machines to his will. He, Candlewood, and Lani hunted through myriad pawn shops for both tools and components. They found both, although they had to cull many of the electrical and electronic parts from existing appliances: radios, televisions, thermostats, remote controllers, adding machines, a microwave oven, and a compact refrigerator. They also bought a small, used slot machine, which Candlewood took apart in order for Nog to study.

The science officer leaned in to examine the device. Nog peeked in as well. By the standards of the twenty-fourth century, the operations chief hadn't crafted a particularly elegant apparatus, but given the level of technological advancement inside the holoprogram—or the lack of it—Nog felt pleased with his efforts.

"Will it work?" Lani asked.

"Technically, it should," Nog said.

"What do you mean, 'technically'?" Candlewood asked.

"I mean I used materials contemporary to the period," Nog said, "but I cobbled them together in a far more sophisticated engineering design than was available at the time. Because of that, I'm not sure it will function as expected inside the program."

"Did you test it?" Candlewood asked.

"As best I could here." Nog waved toward the primitive ammeter and voltmeter that they'd purchased from a pawn shop. "It may need to be calibrated, but—" He turned the small box around, revealing a button on one lower corner. "—I found a way to do that easily."

"How are we going to get it next to a slot machine?" Candlewood asked. "It might not look like a device, but if we start winning jackpots, we're sure to draw some attention."

"That's easy," Lani said, and she disappeared into her bedroom. When she came back out, she carried a handbag with her. She set it down on the table, reseated the lid of the device, and loaded the box into the purse. It fit easily.

"That's it, then," Candlewood said. "Let's go see if we can win."

ii

Candlewood sat at the bar in the Shining Oasis casino. He, Nog, and Ulu had decided to split up for their first foray into cheating a slot machine. They didn't want all three of them associated with a single jackpot, in the hopes that each could then win ample prizes. Nog thought he could construct a second device fairly quickly, and possibly even a third, though if not, Candlewood would do the best he could at the blackjack tables.

The science officer watched Ulu as she sat down at a slot machine on the end of a row of the gambling machines. Off to her right, a wall of video monitors and tote boards dominated an area of the Shining Oasis casino called the RACE & SPORTS BOOK. On the screens, various uniformed players participated in a myriad of athletic competitions, and horses carrying jockeys ran around dirt tracks. Beside those displays, probabilities, payouts, and scores announced numerous gambling opportunities and outcomes.

After they had met with Calderone's accountant, Candlewood had suggested they earn the money they needed to buy Vic's freedom by wagering on sporting events. After all, Felix Knightly had coded the program to incorporate real historical data into its matrix. Candlewood reasoned that if Ulu could safely exit and reenter the holosuite—by no means a surety, because of her entry via the back door—she could look up the results of the games scheduled for that day and the next, then return to Las Vegas to tell them on which entries to bet. Morn, it turned out, had already tried such a scheme—and failed. According to Ulu, the Lurian found out by experience that, while the sporting events listed in the holoprogram reflected actual events, the code randomized the results. Apparently, Knightly wanted to prevent users of Bashir 62 from being able to amass financial winnings without actually gambling—and knowing the scores of athletic contests beforehand did not constitute taking any kind of a risk.

Candlewood sipped at the glass of orange juice he had ordered at the bar. At the slot machine, Ulu set her handbag down, then loaded a coin into a slot. She pulled the machine's lever, and the reels began to spin. When they all came to a stop, Candlewood saw a bar, the number 7, and a bell on the payout line. Because of his location, he could not see the fourth image past Ulu's head, but he could tell that she had won nothing.

With casual movements, Ulu reached into her handbag and pulled out another coin. Candlewood knew that she had also pushed the button on the back of Nog's device, recalibrating it for another attempt. She played the slot machine a second time, with the same losing result.

Ulu repeated her actions a third time, a fourth, and a fifth, all without success. By her ninth attempt, what sounded like a couple of coins dropped into the tray at the bottom of the machine. Whenever she ran out of coins, she retrieved another from her handbag so that she could again recalibrate Nog's device.

On Ulu's nineteenth try, the three reels that Candlewood could see lined up as three 7s. The lights on the slot machine began flashing, and a bell rang loudly. Coins clattered into the payout tray. A casino attendant went over to Ulu, and with his help, she collected her winnings and took them to the cashier, where she deposited them on account.

Candlewood headed back to the suite. By the time he got there, Nog had already arrived and had started work on a second device. When Ulu got back to the suite, the trio plotted out their strategy. Ulu would go from casino to casino with the device in her handbag, winning one or two jackpots at each. When Nog completed the second device, he would place it in one of the paper bags they'd received to carry purchases out of one of the pawn shops. He too would make his way throughout Las Vegas to collect jackpot winnings, though he would visit different casinos from Ulu. In the meantime, Candlewood would try his hand at blackjack and counting cards.

Ulu headed out first. As Candlewood followed her, he stopped at the door of the suite and looked back at Nog. "I can't believe I'm going out to gamble in an effort to accumulate wealth," he said. "I know this must be commonplace in Ferengi society, but it feels strange to me."

"We're not trying to make profit," Nog said soberly. "We're trying to save Vic's life."

iii

Kira stood by herself in the aft section of the vessel, between a transporter platform and a bank of replicators. A short time earlier, she had risen from her seat in the passenger compartment, where she'd sat with two dozen other vedeks. She had begun to feel claustrophobic—a result, she thought, of the attention paid to her. Of all the vedeks traveling aboard the transport, only Solis Tendren had done more than offer her a pleasant greeting, pulling her aside to say that he appreciated her address the day before and that he believed the kai wise in sending Kira to Endalla as one of the observers. But even though the other vedeks aboard the ship said nothing of substance to her, she could feel their collective awareness of her presence among them. She tried to calm herself, but the atmosphere felt oppressive. She eventually decided that she needed to move, to find some space for herself, if even for just a few minutes, so she slipped out of her seat and walked to the rear of the vessel.

Alone by the replicators, Kira felt the slight shift of the inertial dampers as the ship altered its heading. She peered through a lateral port and saw the receding blue-and-white form of Bajor. As best Kira could tell from reports on the comnet that day, the fear and mistrust that had spread across the planet in the wake of the falsework discovery had eased in the previous twenty-six hours. No issues had been definitively resolved, but there appeared to be movement in both factions toward a less divisive, more open dialogue. Only a few minor incidences of violence had been reported since Kira's address, with no casualties of any kind. The vedek did not credit herself for bringing a calming influence to the populace, but venerated the Prophets for returning her to Bajor at a time when doing so would have an impact.

"It's still strange to see the world like this, from out in space." Kira flinched at the sound of Altek's voice. "I'm sorry," he said. "I didn't mean to startle you."

"It's all right," Kira said. "I didn't hear you come in."

"I don't mean to intrude if you want some time to yourself," Altek said. "When you didn't come back to your seat . . . well, I just wanted to check on you."

"Thank you," Kira said. "I'm fine. I was just lost in my own thoughts."

"I know what that's like."

"Of course," Kira said, thinking of just how far from the life he knew Altek had come, by no design of his own. "This entire experience must be difficult for you."

Altek nodded. "For a long while after I arrived on Deep Space Nine, it was almost impossible for me to believe that what I was experiencing wasn't some sort of dream or Orb experience—I had one of those before leaving my time. But then I spent my energies acclimating myself to this new reality, and then working to actually travel back to Bajor—to my homeworld and to my people. Except that's only nominally accurate. Every settlement I ever knew is gone from this future face of Bajor, as are all the people I ever knew— save, in some sense, Keev Anora." Kira tried to conceal the discomfort she felt at the mention of her alternate identity. If Altek noticed her unease, he gave no sign. "On a very basic level, all I want to do is go home, but even though that's Bajor out there—" He pointed to the port, through which the receding form of the planet still showed. "—my home is lost to me forever." He smiled and shrugged. "I guess that's why, after struggling to be allowed to return there, I don't mind that I only stayed for three days."

"Surely you'll go back to Bajor after our time on Endalla," Kira said.

"Yes, I will, and I'll try to do the best I can with my life," Altek said. "But I think I'm always going to feel like an outsider."

"I hope that's not the case," Kira said. "It is a fool's errand to presume to know the will of the Prophets, but since They sent you here, I have faith that you belong. Maybe one day you'll feel that too."

"Maybe," Altek said, though he did not sound convinced. "I do have trepidation about involving myself in what's happening on Bajor right now. I don't really have any interest in supporting or refuting anybody's particular religious beliefs."

"This is a turbulent time for Bajor."

"Perhaps a little less turbulent today than yesterday, thanks to you."

"If that's so, then it's thanks to the Prophets."

Past Altek, through a port in the starboard bulkhead, Kira saw specks of starlight abruptly disappear, eclipsed by another object. She motioned in that direction and then crossed the breadth of the deck. Altek followed, and together they gazed out into space. Kira saw a great, lifeless rock hanging in the void, its inanimate surface a leaden mixture of grays and blacks. "Endalla," she said.

"Have you ever been there before?" Altek asked.

"Yes, a number of times," Kira said. "It used to be a world of greens and browns . . . a living place, ripe with vegetation. It was also home to scientific expeditions studying it." Kira paused, remembering Endalla as it had looked for most of her life—until Iliana Ghemor and the Ascendants had tried to attack Bajor, and Taran'atar had saved the day. The cost had been Endalla's ecosphere and the lives of hundreds of scientists and support personnel.

"Last night, I read about what's happened there in the last decade or so," Altek said. "First with the Ascendants, and then with the two attacks by Ohalavaru extremists." He turned away from the port and regarded Kira. "After you announced that the kai would be sending you to Endalla, that perhaps the Prophets had sent you back to Bajor specifically for that purpose, it made sense that the same might be true of me. But after I learned about what's happened there, I'm not so sure."

"For whatever it's worth, I think your participation on Endalla is important. I don't know what the scientists and engineers are going to find down there, and I don't know how we vedeks are going to interpret what we see, but you have ancient knowledge that just might allow you to shed light on all of this."

"Perhaps," Altek said. "But it could be that some people—maybe a lot of people—would rather be kept in the dark."

"The truth is the truth," Kira said. She looked back across the deck to the port there, to where a sliver of Bajor's resplendent globe remained visible. "I have faith not only in the Prophets," she said, "but in the Bajoran people."

iv

Seated beside Kira, Altek felt the vessel lift off from the surface of Endalla. The sensation unnerved him, though not more so than traveling by transporter. After the ship bringing him from Bajor had landed on the moon, he and the other observers had been beamed in groups of six onto smaller vessels for the final leg of their journey. Interference from the rock substrata made transport down into the crevasse, if not impossible, at least inadvisable. Altek and Kira had been the last two to make the transfer and consequently found themselves alone in a six-seat passenger compartment.

Altek sat at a side port, and as the vessel ascended, he peered out at the gloomy landscape. A smooth, black plain extended into the distance, the result, he'd read, of the first Ohalavaru attack on Endalla half a dozen years earlier. That group of zealots wanted to strip-mine the moon in the hope of uncovering evidence of the Prophets' mortal nature.

The small ship swept to port. Altek looked down and saw the long crevasse jagging away in both directions, cleaving the ebon expanse in two. The handiwork of the second band of Ohalavaru to launch an assault on Endalla, the chasm ultimately provided access to the falsework. The ship moved above it, then began its descent.

The stars in Endalla's black sky vanished as the vessel dropped into the crevasse. Light from below provided faint illumination of the chasm's steep, irregular walls. As he studied them, a swarm of blue points of light flashed on and off. "What was that?"

"Probably force fields erected to prevent the walls from collapsing," Kira said. "Some loose debris must have fallen and struck on that side."

Altek nodded, though he had no real comprehension of the technology at work. He understood the concept of a force field, but like so many other things he had encountered in his new life in the future—things like starships and space stations, like transporters and replicators, like alien beings—he still had trouble accepting it all. It had been almost five months since he had emerged from the Celestial Temple and been brought aboard DS9, but both his journey and the destination continued to astonish him.

The trip down into the crevasse proceeded at a slow pace. As they traveled downward, the radiance from below grew in brilliance. At one point, the ship appeared to pass through another force field, which flickered blue as they descended past it. When they eventually alit at the base of the chasm, they did so amid a field of other vessels, surrounded by powerful light standards. For all the darkness that characterized the surface of Endalla, it seemed bright as day down below.

Through the port, Altek saw a substantial number of armed Bajoran Militia personnel on patrol. They supervised the disembarkation of the vedeks from the other vessels, directing them farther along the chasm, presumably to the chamber that housed the falsework. The vedeks all wore the robes of their office, with many of them embellishing their appearance with supplementary vestments. Kira had dressed herself in what she described as a traditional robe, a loose-fitting, rust-colored wraparound garment, but she had forgone any additional trappings, including any coverings for her head.

The front door of the passenger compartment slid open, and the ship's pilot, Sergeant Callis Neve, entered. "We've been contacted by the security team down here," she said. "Somebody will be here shortly to escort you."

"Thank you," Kira said.

Altek watched through the port as the vedeks and security officers disappeared into the distance. He and Kira waited quietly, until at last they saw a Militia officer approaching. A few moments later, the compartment's rear door opened. The Militia officer stood in an airlock, its external hatch open behind her. She entered the compartment and introduced herself as Lieutenant Delevan Klatta. "The Militia has completed its efforts to seal the area around the falsework and establish a breathable atmosphere, heat, and artificial gravity. You can proceed outside without the need to don an environmental suit. This ship and the others will remain here, at the base of the chasm, to provide any services you may need: medical aid, replicators, refreshers, and the like. If you have any questions or require assistance of any kind, you can contact me directly." Delevan reached out and opened her hand, which contained a pair of Bajoran combadges. Both Altek and Kira took one and attached it to their clothing. They thanked the lieutenant. Delevan told them that she would escort them to the falsework, and they followed her through the airlock and out of the ship.

Altek immediately noticed a drop in temperature. The Militia might have heated the environment that they'd created, but they hadn't made it warm. Altek rubbed his hands together. "It's chilly out here," Delevan said, "but inside the chamber, the air temperature is comfortable."

They tramped past the other vessels and into an extended run along the bottom of the chasm. Altek saw a great deal of equipment on either side of the crevasse, none of which he recognized, but which he assumed helped create the artificial environment around them. Up ahead, he saw light spilling from the side wall. When they reached it, he saw a large, ragged hole, as though somebody had hacked their way through it with a pickax. A circular metal piece had been fitted inside the opening, which would prevent anybody passing through it from injuring themselves on one of the sharp edges.

"The chamber is through there," Delevan said. "The floor inside is two meters down, so a ladder has been affixed to the inner wall. I will go first so that I can help you enter." The lieutenant hunched down and stuck one leg through the opening, planted her foot on the ladder, then swung her other leg inside. "I'm in," she called back a moment later.

Altek looked to Kira. "After you," he said. Once the vedek had made her way through the hole and down the ladder, Altek followed. He turned from the ladder and beheld an enormous space whose farthest limits he could not see. The tremendous size of the place impressed him.

Ahead, numerous lights had been set up to illuminate the area, and he saw still more being erected. Along the visible portions of the walls, great metal girders formed an irregular supporting structure. Altek could dimly make out the roof of the chamber far above, though he could discern no details. In front of him, the level floor on which he stood extended away into darkness.

A short distance ahead, the vedek observers clustered together with a man in civilian clothing. Beyond them, scores of other people—presumably the scientists and engineers tasked with studying the falsework—labored to set up various equipment. Altek could hear Bajoran voices, but they reached him as though somehow muffled.

Although the chamber seemed more or less like a massive, empty place, it had the feel of age about it. *No, it doesn't just feel old,* Altek thought. *It feels ancient.* He wondered for a moment if it had been constructed as far back as his own time, but then remembered that Endalla had not existed in his era.

"Please follow me," Delevan said, and she led the way over to where the vedeks all stood. The man in civilian clothes saw them walk up, and he greeted Altek and Kira by name. "I'm Tef Noka," he said. "I will function as the liaison between you, as observers, and the teams who will be analyzing the falsework."

"What do you do, Mister Tef?" Kira asked.

"I am a professor at the University of Janir."

"What do you teach?" Kira asked.

Tef smiled. "Diplomacy."

Kira matched his smile with one of her own. "Well, that should prove a useful skill set to have down here."

"Indeed," Tef said, and then he addressed the entire group of vedeks. "Now that you are all here, I'd like to welcome you. In your roles as observers, you will be free to roam throughout this chamber. As you can see—" He waved his arm toward where people set up additional banks of lighting. "—we are still working to illuminate the entire space. For that reason, security has requested that nobody enter a darkened area. Similarly, since the entire chamber has yet to be mapped in detail, it is possible that you could run across doors or hatches or the like. Please do not open or enter them, but report your find to me immediately. The scientists have asked that you touch no surface other than the floor, and that you inform me if you encounter any writing or artifacts. Feel free to observe whomever you wish to, but please stay out of their way and allow them to do their work. At the end of every shift, we will meet back here so that the lead scientists and engineers in the various disciplines can provide you a précis of their most recent findings. If you have any questions or concerns at any time, please contact me directly."

A brawny man gestured to Tef. "I have a question."

"Yes, Vedek Sorretta, what can I—"

A bank of lights activated and cast its beams upward in the chamber. Altek saw several of the vedeks lift their gaze, and he did too. The dim recesses high above had been illuminated, revealing oblique angles, uneven surfaces, and strange textures. Mammoth structures hung down in complicated shapes that Altek could not describe, even to himself. In places, the formations contorted together in an amalgam of complex geometries that he had a difficult time perceiving. It felt like an attempt to view an optical illusion—something made to look real, but that could exist only as a concept. The spectacle caused tension in his mind. He found it simultaneously breathtaking, overwhelming, and frightening.

Peering upward, Altek was stricken with a sudden headache. He wanted to look away, but he found himself mesmerized. All at once, movement above caught his attention. He shifted his gaze to look directly at it, but he immediately swooned. His knees gave way and he fell toward the floor. His vision clouded as hands grabbed for him and eased him down onto his back.

Altek felt the hard surface of the chamber floor below him. He blinked his eyes, but he saw only a gray wash. He felt hands on his arms, and then on either side of his head. He heard Anora's voice call his name, once, twice, but then it faded into the distance.

Suddenly, the floor under him softened. His body drifted down into it. He reached to his sides for purchase, but the surface melted beneath his touch. He slipped inexorably downward, the floor swallowing him whole.

He could feel nothing in his hands, nothing below him, nothing around him. His consciousness floated in the totality of the universe, a white light comprising all the colors of the spectrum. And in the center of all that existed, all that had ever been or ever would be, a spark ignited. Altek no longer possessed a body, but with his mind, he sought to reach the lone ember that stood out in the center of everything. He swam closer and closer, until he began to comprehend the outline of a purplish blue flame. He glided nearer still, and the outline gained substance, a blaze that extended toward him in the shape of a hand.

In the shape of my hand, Altek thought.

He imagined reaching for it, striving somehow to touch his real hand to the phantom hand. He envisioned his fingertips closing in on the burning fingertips that matched his own. Altek sensed people trying to stop him, trying to pull him back from the sum of all realities, but he would not allow it. Even as he felt himself being dragged backward, he lunged ahead—and finally pushed his hand flat against the hand-shaped flames.

At the moment of contact, the universe exploded in a revelatory burst of awareness.

Altek stood in a field near his childhood home in Joradell and gazed up at the infinite night. Above the city, in a display that had lasted weeks, the spectacularly long twin tails of a comet decorated the dark sky—one tail curved and white, the other straight and indigo. He watched as the glowing mass entered Bajor's atmosphere and died in a dramatic, fiery display.

When the comet faded into blackness, so did Altek Dans.

V

Kira lowered Altek to the floor. He had glanced up at the newly illuminated roof of the chamber, as had many people there, including Kira. She saw a confusing tangle of structures she could barely perceive, let alone explain. She had to tear her gaze away, and when she did, she noticed several of the vedeks near her staggering, as though they had lost their equilibrium. Farther away, she spotted other people swaying on their feet, and then Altek lurched into her. When she looked at him, she saw his eyes rolling back in his head. She reached for him and eased him down to the floor, and she felt his hand grabbing for hers.

"Altek," she called to him, trying to prevent him from lapsing into unconsciousness. "Dans! Dans!" She looked around for help and saw that several of the vedeks had dropped to their knees, though she saw nobody that had passed out.

Professor Tef appeared at Kira's side. "What happened?" he asked.

"I don't know," Kira said. "He looked up and then . . ."

"I don't know what it was," Tef said, "but I felt it too."

"So did I." Kira pointed toward the vedeks. "So did a lot of us."

Suddenly, the illumination in the chamber dimmed—back to the level before the last banks of lights had been activated. Before she could stop herself, Kira peered upward. The roof of the chamber had receded into the shadows.

A hand closed around Kira's own. She looked down to see Altek's fingers in hers. His eyelids fluttered open.

"Are you all right?" Kira asked him.

"What . . . what happened?"

"They shined light on the roof," Kira said, "and when you looked up, it affected you."

"Am I all right?"

"I don't know," Kira said. "But you weren't the only one impacted." She explained what she herself had felt, and how she'd seen the others affected. Altek pushed himself up on his elbows, as though in preparation to stand. Kira put a hand on his shoulder. "Hold on," she said. "We should have a doctor examine you."

"The Militia have medical personnel with them," Tef said without being asked. "Let me get somebody over here." He walked a few steps away and tapped his combadge. "Tef to Major Lanser," he said.

While the professor called for medical assistance, Kira asked Altek, "How do you feel?"

Altek squeezed his eyes closed for a moment. "Sluggish, like I've been asleep for a while," he said. He flexed his arms and legs, turned his head left and right. "Otherwise, I feel all right." He paused, then looked Kira in the eye. "This place . . ."

Kira nodded slowly. "It's special," she said quietly.

"Like the Celestial Temple?" Altek asked, also keeping his voice low.

Kira thought about that before answering. "No, not like that," she said. "But I think I understand how the Ohalavaru who found this place—or anybody—could interpret the construction here as the basis for anchoring something as extraordinary as a wormhole. This place . . . it feels otherworldly."

"Yes," Altek agreed. "A monument not just to advanced science and technology, but to the impossible." Something seemed to occur to Altek. He looked around, as though to ensure that nobody would hear him, and then asked,

"Doesn't that confirm the Ohalavaru belief that the fifth moon is artificial? And doesn't that contradict what you believe?"

"You just characterized this place as a testament to the impossible," Kira said. "What better way to describe the divine?"

vi

"We are approaching the Jem'Hadar vessel," announced Slaine from the tactical console on the port side of the *Defiant* bridge.

In the command chair, Wheeler Stinson felt a surge of adrenaline at the prospect of taking his ship and crew into an undefined, potentially dangerous situation. "Put it onscreen and magnify," he ordered.

"Aye, sir."

The main viewscreen quivered briefly, and although the pattern of stars didn't change, a ship appeared in the center of the display. Stinson recognized the insect-like vessel at once, with its lavender lighting details and bow-mounted phased-polaron emitter. "That's definitely a Jem'Hadar battle cruiser."

Standing beside the command chair, Odo offered a noise somewhere between a laugh and a grunt. Stinson didn't quite know what to make of the Changeling. He knew that members of the crew had served with him aboard the original DS9, and some—Chief O'Brien and Lieutenant Commander Nog among them—considered him a friend. During the last two-plus years Odo had spent in the Alpha Quadrant, which had included occasional visits to the starbase, Stinson had interacted with him several times, but he hadn't been able to get much of a read on the shape-shifter. The second officer understood that some of the reason for that might have to do with Odo's oddly "unfinished" humanoid face. Stinson also had enough self-awareness to consider the possibility of his own unconscious racism after the Dominion War, but he worked hard to eliminate that as a cause. More than anything, he ascribed Odo's inscrutability to the Changeling's taciturn nature.

"Lieutenant Viss," Stinson said, "open a channel."

To Slaine's left, Viss worked the controls of the communications station. "Hailing frequencies are open, sir."

"Jem'Hadar vessel, this is Commander Wheeler Stinson of the *U.S.S. Defiant*," he said. "Please respond." He waited for a moment, and when he received no response, he tried again. "*U.S.S. Defiant* to Jem'Hadar vessel, you are on a direct course for the Anomaly and the Alpha Quadrant beyond. We would therefore like to speak with you regarding the purpose of your journey."

At the comm station, the helmet of Viss's environmental suit rotated an eighth of a turn left and right, the equivalent of a headshake by the aquatic Alonis. "We're receiving no response, Commander," she said. "It does not appear that they are receiving us. They appear to be jamming all incoming transmissions."

"Sensors are being jammed too," Slaine reported.

"Well, isn't that just dandy?" Stinson said. They had known back on Deep Space 9 that their attempts to communicate with the crew of the Jem'Hadar were being blocked, but they hadn't known the source. They hoped the interference originated elsewhere, and that by taking *Defiant* out to meet the ship, they could circumvent the issue. That left him with few options, and only one that did not put his ship and crew at risk. "Odo, what do you suggest?"

"Clearly you cannot inform the Jem'Hadar that I am traveling with you if they refuse to communicate," Odo said. "And if they're blocking sensors, it's likely that they can't scan the *Defiant*. The only way to let them know that a Founder is aboard is to show them."

"You'll be leaving the ship, then?" Stinson asked.

"Yes," Odo said. "If you bring the *Defiant* to a stop, I can disembark and make sure they see me as they approach."

"Lieutenant Tenmei, bring us out of warp," Stinson said. "Full stop."

At the wide arc of the conn situated just ahead of the command chair, Tenmei operated her panel. "Bringing the ship out of warp," she said. On the bridge, the tenor of the ambient noise changed as *Defiant* fell to sublight velocity. "Engines answering full stop."

"Time to arrival of the Jem'Hadar vessel: twenty-seven minutes," Slaine announced at tactical.

"You can leave the ship via the shuttlebay," Stinson told Odo. "We'll keep station near your position. If they do bring you aboard, we'll pace the ship. If not, we'll reopen the shuttlebay for you."

"They'll bring me aboard," Odo said confidently. "They're Jem'Hadar. They won't have any choice but to allow a Changeling on their ship."

Stinson nodded, understanding the genetically engineered imperative that guaranteed Jem'Hadar fealty to the Founders. *But what about Taran'atar?* he thought as Odo headed for the aft door. Stinson had never met the Jem'Hadar soldier sent on an observational mission to the original DS9, but after what had happened the prior month, he had learned all about him. *When he left the old station, he never returned to the Dominion. He ignored his biological programming.*

"Odo," Stinson said, and the shape-shifter stopped just as the door opened before him, "what if those are Jem'Hadar who are no longer impelled to obey the Founders?" Even as he asked the question, others occurred to him. "Or what if those aren't Jem'Hadar aboard? What if that vessel was sto-len from the Dominion, and that's why its crew is jamming communications and sensors?"

Odo didn't hesitate before answering. "Then that's something the Federation will need to know." Then he con-tinued through the door and off the bridge.

vii

As Odo entered the shuttlebay, he turned Stinson's ques-tions over in his mind. He had told the lieutenant com-mander that the Federation needed to know if a group of Jem'Hadar had gone rogue, or if one of their vessels had been hijacked, but in truth, Odo needed to know. He had been gone for so long, and he had left with so many variables in motion—the scattering of the Great Link, the sporadic leadership of Laas and the distrust and odium he felt for "solids," the irregular return of individual Founders, the isolationism of the Dominion—he could form no hy-potheses about what had transpired in his absence.

Once he had entered the shuttlebay and sealed the door behind him, he moved to a companel mounted on the bulkhead and contacted the bridge. He confirmed to Stin-son his readiness to depart the ship. The lieutenant com-mander told him that the *Defiant* crew would depressurize the shuttlebay, then open the external hatch. Odo acknowl-edged the proposed sequence of events, then signed off and prepared for his change.

In his mind, Odo coasted along the currents of exis-tence, passing through time and space in a continual state of potential. He rode the flows, buoyed by them, but he perceived within the great river of reality the vortices that defined every stable state, that captured the possible in its pull—not gravity, not electromagnetism, not the strong or weak nuclear forces, but something like them, or like some combination of them. He mentally circled the whirlpool of rotational motion, then searched for and found their intrinsic derivatives: the rates of change that defined every position and every moment, and by implication, those that came before and those that would come after.

Odo envisioned what he would become, intuited the course from his current form to his new form, though he had never traversed precisely that route. He found bliss in that originality, discovering the shape he would inhabit, but doing so anew, all his past incarnations mere wisps of memory. Being a Changeling meant being everything, all at once, and choosing one aspect for one moment and the moments that followed.

Odo shifted his shape. His lungs filled and melted away, becoming a solid mass of his true physical nature. As the shuttlebay depressurized around him, as the atmosphere disappeared, his corporeal form liquesced. For an instant, his humanoid figure remained, but in appearance only. Then he released his control, allowed the artificial gravity to pull him down. His fluidic body dissolved into a cascade of biomimetic flux. His perceptions remained, though, and his will.

When the round hatch in the deck split along its diameter, Odo spun upward. He gyred into a rising maelstrom of movement. The two semicircular sections of the hatch parted, revealing the inky depths of space beyond. Odo changed direction, arced over and down, and spilled out into the void.

Unencumbered by the confines of *Defiant*, Odo morphed once more. His body expanded into a conical form, the texture of his outer hide changing, the substance of his internal biology taking on the shapes of organs. A pair of barbed antennae extended from the narrow front of the great spaceborne beast, and a trio of flattened, finlike tentacles grew from its aft end. In his new physique, Odo felt gravity, measured its impact on the local continuum, and adjusted his mass and dimensions accordingly, so that he could navigate the curvature of space-time.

Defiant moved away, but not beyond the limits of Odo's new perception. Time passed, and he waited for the disruption to come with the passage of the Jem'Hadar vessel. He prepared for the moment, and when the warp field of the ship registered at the far boundary of his senses, he shifted again. His reality as the spaceborne creature altered, and he became the humanoid Odo, but in form only. He took on his faux-Bajoran figure, but at one hundred times the scale.

The Jem'Hadar battle cruiser neared. Odo could tell when his visage appeared on their monitors because the ship dropped out of warp. The vessel approached him at sublight speed, slowing as it did so, until it floated in space before him.

Odo sent a message by causing his body to shimmer in imitation of a Dominion transporter beam. Then he solidified and changed yet another time, assuming his normal humanoid form, sans lungs, shrinking to its usual size.

A moment later, he felt the sensation of dematerialization.

viii

Odo felt the transporter platform beneath his feet. More than that, the pull of artificial gravity tugged at his body, and he realized that his multiple changes of form had exhausted him. Out of habit, Odo established lungs in his chest and began to respire, but he vowed to himself to alter his shape no more before he had time to regenerate. He stood still for the moment, not wanting to expend any more energy than necessary.

Two figures stood in front of the transporter platform. Odo recognized them at once: Weyoun and Rotan'talag, the Vorta and Jem'Hadar with whom he had spent the most time during his eight years residing in the Dominion. Odo expected Weyoun to speak up and explain the situation; as a Vorta, his function aboard a Jem'Hadar ship, among a Jem'Hadar crew, would be to lead. Instead, Rotan'talag stepped forward. Of even greater note, he did not wait for Odo to speak.

"Founder," he said.

"Rotan'talag," Odo said. He saw that the Jem'Hadar had advanced in rank from third to second, but not to first, which made his appearing to take charge even more peculiar. The same search that had identified Taran'atar as not being dependent on ketracel-white had turned up three others of his kind, including Rotan'talag. Odo assigned him to Jem'Hadar Attack Vessel 971, a ship initially designated as a sentry and stationed in orbit of the world on which the Great Link had settled. Odo made frequent visits to the vessel, in part so that he could have contact with Rotan'talag and Weyoun in his seemingly futile attempts to cultivate their development, to help them mature into individuals unencumbered—or at least less encumbered—by their genetically engineered prerogatives.

"I am pleased to see you," Odo said, "and you as well, Weyoun." The Vorta bowed his head in obvious deference, though Rotan'talag conspicuously did not. "Why are you here, outside Dominion space?"

"The crew and passengers of this vessel have chosen to move on from the Dominion," Rotan'talag said.

"Passengers?" Odo echoed. Other than their crews, he had only ever known Changelings to travel aboard Jem'Hadar battle cruisers. "Are there other Founders aboard?"

"No," Weyoun rushed to say before Rotan'talag could reply. "We are graced only with your presence, Founder."

Odo did not care for the obsequious response, but he also did not find it unexpected. Based on his interactions so far with Weyoun and Rotan'talag, it suggested he should concentrate on speaking with the Jem'Hadar. "Weyoun, a Starfleet vessel, the *Defiant*, is stationed nearby in space. Contact its captain, Commander Stinson, and tell him that you are doing so at my request. Tell him that I am safely aboard your ship, and that I will talk to him shortly."

"Yes, Founder, immediately," the Vorta said, again bowing his head before scampering away.

Of Rotan'talag, Odo asked, "What can you tell me of the Great Link?" The communal sea of Changelings had disbanded nine years prior under extreme circumstances.

"Since your journey through the Anomaly, only a small number of additional Founders have returned," Rotan'talag said. "Until recently, those that had come back to the Dominion had aggregated in groups of two or three. Now almost all of those that have returned are together in a single link."

"Do you interact with the new link?" Odo asked. "Does anybody?"

"I have not," Rotan'talag said, "but there are Vorta and Jem'Hadar crews whose ships have been assigned to protect the new link, and the Founders sometimes communicate with them."

"And what about communicating with anybody else?" Odo wanted to know.

"As far as I know, the Founders predominantly stay linked, almost never emerging," Rotan'talag said. "Consequently, I believe that they have infrequent contact with any 'solids,' and only with the crews of the ships around their world."

None of that surprised Odo, though it did disappoint him. He had hoped that more Changelings would have come back to the Dominion during the time he'd been away. "What about the Dominion itself?" he asked. "Does it remain in isolation?"

"The borders are still closed," Rotan'talag confirmed, "both to incoming and outgoing vessels, for the most part."

"'For the most part,'" Odo repeated. "You are exempting your own vessel."

"Yes."

"And you have passengers aboard," Odo said, still trying to fathom that. "Why are you here?"

"As I mentioned," Rotan'talag said, "we have chosen to move on from the Dominion." The Jem'Hadar had indeed said that earlier, but Odo had been so focused on the radical idea of passengers aboard a battle cruiser that he had overlooked it.

"What exactly does that mean?" Odo asked. He stepped from the transporter platform onto the deck.

"Everybody aboard this ship has made the individual decision to seek a different way of life than servitude and subjugation," Rotan'talag said. "Collectively, we plotted to seize control of this vessel, debark the members of the crew unwilling to join with us, and leave the Dominion."

Odo stared at Rotan'talag in stunned silence. In the wake of the assault on him by the shape-shifting Ascendant colony, which had left him as close to death as he had ever come, Odo had never felt less like a god. He had never subscribed to the rhetoric of the Founders that equated their steel-fisted control over the Dominion with actual godhood, though he had long recognized the truth of the Changelings' role in engineering species like the Jem'Hadar and the Vorta. Odo could conceive of no circumstances in which he would consider himself a deity, but he felt genuine pride in learning that Rotan'talag and Weyoun sought to lead a group of Dominion citizens to a new and better way of life. He didn't know how much influence he'd had on the Jem'Hadar and the Vorta, but he had at the very least planted the seeds of self-determination. He could not have been more pleased.

"How many are aboard?" Odo asked.

"Three thousand seven hundred thirteen," Rotan'talag said. "Plus you, Founder."

"Are they all Jem'Hadar and Vorta?"

"No, we have members of numerous species on board," Rotan'talag said. "There are Karemma, Overne, Thepnossen, Bronis, and Ourentia."

Odo almost could not credit what he heard. The notion of the Jem'Hadar, the ruthless soldiers of the Dominion, working with other member races—besides the Vorta—seemed almost inconceivable. "What do you intend to do?"

Before Rotan'talag could answer, Weyoun reappeared. "Founder, I have spoken directly with Commander Stinson aboard the *Defiant*," he said. "I passed along your message. He told me that if he did not hear from you directly within fifteen minutes, he would have no choice but to open fire on our ship."

"A good Starfleet officer," Odo said wryly, understanding Stinson's stance, but not particularly appreciative of the threat.

"He wants to ensure your safety," Rotan'talag said. "In my time serving the Founders, I would not have given fifteen minutes of leeway."

"Then you don't serve the Founders anymore?"

"Not in the way we used to," Weyoun said. "With you here, of course, we are happy to serve, but we have discovered a new interpretation of our directives."

"And what would that interpretation be?" Odo asked.

"It is the interpretation you gave us," Rotan'talag said. "We serve the Founders not just by satisfying the purposes for which we were initially created, but by fulfilling the potential also bred into us." Interestingly, though the Jem'Hadar spoke to Odo with respect, he did so without reverence.

"What are your plans?" Odo asked, reiterating the question he'd posed before Weyoun had come back.

"We will take this ship through the Anomaly and into the Alpha Quadrant," Rotan'talag said. "There, we will seek an uninhabited world on which we can settle."

"Why in the Alpha Quadrant?" Odo asked, not sanguine about such a course. It would necessarily entail a Jem'Hadar presence in or near the Federation and other powers. "Why not in the Gamma Quadrant?"

"We wish to begin our new lives far from the Dominion," Weyoun said, "so that there is as little chance as possible of us being hunted down and either made to return or killed."

"We want to make our own choices," Rotan'talag said, "and to live our lives free from tyranny."

Tyranny, Odo thought. Even with their plans to leave the Founders and the Dominion behind for good, the single word marked the strongest sentiment yet about how Rotan'talag and Weyoun had changed—how they had *grown.* But Odo still foresaw trouble ahead, if not from the Dominion, then from the Federation—or from the Cardassians or the Klingons or the Romulans.

"Once you pass through the Anomaly, how do you intend to traverse Federation space?" Odo asked.

"Peacefully," Weyoun said.

"Yes, peacefully," Rotan'talag agreed, but then he added, "If possible."

The last sentiment concerned Odo, not just because of

what it could mean in terms of casualties on both sides of the equation, but because it could possibly spell the end of the amazing strides that Rotan'talag and Weyoun and the others had clearly made.

"I need to speak with Commander Stinson," Odo said.

"Of course," Weyoun said. "Right this way, Founder."

As the Vorta led the way to the communications station, Odo wondered just what he would tell Stinson.

ix

Ro paced alongside the conference table, feeling like a caged animal. *Because I* am *caged,* she thought. *Federation Security might have put me in a conference room, but it's not as though I can just leave this ship if I choose to.*

After appearing at the inn where Mayereen Viray stayed, the two Federation Security agents had escorted Ro, Quark, and Morn back to the spaceport, with the Lurian in restraints. Viray had come along as well, though Corvok and Toulet had not taken her into custody. The hike back through the city had taken place in silence, though Ro sensed the normally talkative Morn ready to burst from all he wanted to say; she assumed he didn't speak for fear of unintentionally incriminating himself.

Quark, on the other hand, seemed like he might never speak again—at least not to Ro. As tense as their journey from Deep Space 9 to Mericor had been, the barkeep's sullenness as they tramped through the city felt like something even worse. Ro didn't know if it had to do with Morn's arrest, or with discovering that his latinum had not been stolen and would therefore not be returned to him, or even with the dissolution of their romantic relationship. She also didn't know how she could help to bring him out of his choler.

When they had reached the spaceport, the Federation Security agents had led them to an auxiliary craft. The small Starfleet vessel, *Brinks*, took them into orbit, where they rendezvoused with the interceptor *Balju*. While Toulet ushered Morn to a holding cell, Corvok separated Ro and Quark—perhaps not the worst thing for either one of them—and asked them to wait, pending the confirmation of their identities. Ro guessed that they would also want to know about their relationship with Viray and Morn, not to mention why she and Quark had traveled to Mericor in the first place.

Eventually, the door to the conference room slid open. Ro stopped pacing as Agent Corvok entered. He held a padd in one hand. "Please forgive the delay, Captain Ro."

"You've confirmed my identity, then?"

"We have," Corvok said. "We've also verified Ambassador Quark's identity."

"Then you'll be taking us back down to the spaceport?" Ro said.

"Of course," Corvok said. "But we do have some questions for you, if you wouldn't mind staying aboard a bit longer." He gestured toward the conference table. Ro made a show of considering what to do, and then she took a seat. Corvok circled the table and sat down across from her.

"I'm happy to cooperate," Ro said, "but I have some questions of my own."

"Of course," Corvok said. Ro had difficulty reading the Vulcan's response. Did he mean that he would answer her questions, or did he mean simply to confirm that she had questions? "Do I understand correctly that you and Quark are traveling together?"

"Yes," Ro said. "We came here directly from Deep Space Nine."

"What is the nature of your relationship?"

Ro could not help but laugh. Off of Corvok's puzzled expression, she said, "We've known each other for ten years. We're . . . close."

Corvok nodded, and Ro thought he was debating whether or not to pursue the matter further. Instead, he asked, "For what purpose did you come to Mericor?"

"To track down Mayereen Viray," Ro said. She explained Quark's hiring her to track down Morn, and how the barkeep had become convinced that she had essentially stolen his latinum.

"Why did Ambassador Quark hire a private detective to find Mister Morn?" Corvok asked.

"Strictly as an act of friendship," Ro said. "Morn spent a great deal of time on the original Deep Space Nine at Quark's establishment there, and then after the destruction of the station, at his bar on Bajor. But Morn seemed to be depressed, and when he left Bajor without a word sometime after that, Quark was concerned about him."

"There was no business arrangement between them that motivated the ambassador to find Mister Morn?" Corvok asked. In truth, Ro didn't know, but despite her position as a Starfleet officer, she believed that Quark would have told her if she had volunteered to accompany him to Mericor on illegal business.

"No, they had no business arrangement," Ro said. "Quark will tell you that he was searching for Morn because he was the best customer he ever had and he wanted him back in the bar, but it was really an issue of friendship. When Quark thought Viray faked her own kidnapping, he decided to come after her to try and recover the funds she took from him under false pretenses."

"To be clear," Corvok said, "Ambassador Quark thought that Agent Toulet and I abducted Miss Viray."

"He did say he recognized you at the inn," Ro said. "He

obviously didn't know you were with Federation Security. But speaking of that, I'm assuming that you *didn't* kidnap Viray?"

"No, we did not abduct Miss Viray," Corvok said. He glanced down at his padd, activated it, then turned it so that the captain could see it. The display showed Ro's Starfleet record. "You have sufficient security clearance for me to give you information about our operation, but it is not to be repeated." Ro said nothing in reply, choosing not to dignify the implication that she might violate her security grade—though, of course, she had done so in the past. "Federation Security has been looking for Mister Morn for some time. Several months ago, we learned that Miss Viray was also searching for him, and so we placed her under surveillance, hoping that she would lead us to him. It is unclear how, but Miss Viray became aware of our efforts and worked to elude us. She did so several times, which required considerable efforts to locate her again. After the last time we found her, on Janus Six, we obtained legal authorization to take her into custody for the purpose of questioning her. We wanted to make sure that she played no part in Mister Morn's scheme, and once we did so, we requested her assistance in leading us to him. She agreed."

That explained to Ro why Corvok and Toulet hadn't arrested Viray, but it still left a lot of unanswered questions. "You told Morn you were arresting him for the possession of restricted technology," Ro said. "Did he steal something?"

"No, not precisely," Corvok said, which might have been the most equivocal statement Ro had ever heard a Vulcan utter. "We believe that Mister Morn cobbled together, from a number of sources, plans for a device based on the existence of certain classified technology. He then commissioned the construction of the device, and recently took possession of it."

"But you just arrested him on Mericor," Ro said. "Is the technology restricted here as well, or just in the Federation?"

"That is a legal question to which I am not prepared to respond," Corvok said.

"That's enough of an answer to suggest that Morn hasn't actually committed a prosecutable crime," Ro said.

"The issue will clearly need to be adjudicated," Corvok said. "The most important part of our operation was the recovery of the illicit device. A scientist we brought with us from Jupiter Station has corroborated the purpose of the object we confiscated from Mister Morn, though she has been unable to confirm if it actually functions as intended."

Ro wondered about the nature of the device, but she knew better than to start asking questions about a piece of restricted technology—particularly aboard a Federation Security vessel. "Is there any other information you need from me?" Ro asked.

"No, though as a matter of procedure, we will attempt to substantiate what both you and Ambassador Quark have told us."

"Then we're free to go?" Ro asked. "You'll take us back down to Mericor?"

"I'm afraid we can't do that just yet," Corvok said. "Because of the nature of Mister Morn's illicit device, we have been asked to secure your voluntary cooperation to stay aboard our ship until an agent from another Federation department has arrived to question you."

"What?" Ro said. "You want to 'secure' our 'voluntary cooperation'? That sounds like an oxymoronic concept." Ro pushed away from the conference table and stood up. "What if Quark and I withhold our 'voluntary cooperation'?"

"I am asking you not to withhold it," Corvok said. He

looked down at his hands, which he folded together, then back up at Ro. He seemed as emotionally uncomfortable as any Vulcan she had ever seen. "The agent coming to speak with you and Mister Quark is from the Department of Temporal Investigations."

Ro sat back down.

X

"They didn't kidnap me," Viray said. "They forcibly broke into my room in Geopolis and arrested me." She walked across the room to where Quark sat on the edge of the bed, then leaned down until her face was only centimeters away from his. He heard the click of her jaw in its socket as she spoke. "They *arrested* me." Quark didn't want to believe Viray, but he found that he actually did.

You're not thinking clearly, he told himself. *Too much has happened.*

After he and Laren had been separated aboard *Balju,* Quark had been taken to a small cabin. While not strictly speaking a holding cell, and while the door had not been locked, where could he go? The interceptor orbited Mericor, meaning that even if Quark somehow managed to get to an unguarded transporter room, he couldn't beam through either of the spaceport or city domes, and he couldn't set himself down anywhere else on the surface of the planet without first donning an environmental suit. The chances of him being able to make his way to the vessel's shuttlebay and commandeering one of the auxiliary craft seemed even less promising.

So Quark had waited. Agent Toulet had eventually arrived, informing him that Federation Security had confirmed his identity. He asked Quark questions about his visit to Mericor, and then about his business with Viray, and finally about why he had tried so hard to locate Morn. Even though the Rules of Acquisition preached that a good lie is easier to believe than the truth, he hadn't had enough time to fabricate a convincing falsehood, nor had he had the opportunity to coordinate it with Laren.

Oh, and also, I didn't do anything illegal, Quark reminded himself.

He answered Toulet's questions as best he could, and then he had tried to ask some of his own, to no avail. He assumed that, as a Starfleet captain, Laren would have been told more about the situation than he had. He resolved to ask her.

Not that she's been all that interested in telling me anything lately.

Quark had waited in the cabin for somebody else to appear and give him more information. He attempted to order some food from the replicator, but not only had it not been programmed for slug steak, toasted tubeworm, or beetle puree, it wouldn't even give him a simple bowl of tube grubs. He ended up settling for a plate of *lokar* beans.

Then the door signal had chimed, and when he'd called for the visitor to come in, Viray had entered. She told him that she wanted to clear up any misconceptions he had about the work she had done for him. She went into detail about her efforts to find Morn, and explained how, one day, the normal precautions she took during the performance of her job had revealed an unknown party surveilling her. She took steps to lose them, only for them to find her again and again.

When Quark had asked Viray why she hadn't told him about any of that, she'd said that none of it had concerned him. Even if the people watching her did so because of an interest in her finding Morn, she didn't feel that should impact whether or not she accomplished the task she had been hired to do. But then, according to Viray, Federation Security arrested her.

"On what charge?" Quark asked.

Viray stood back up. "Abetting the possession of restricted technology," she said.

"And?" Quark asked. "Did you?"

"Did I what?" Viray said. "Abet Morn? Of course not. I didn't know who Morn was until you hired me to locate him."

"And you didn't find him at some point and make some other deal with him?" Quark didn't think that Viray had done any of that, but his foul mood drove him to lash out at her.

"No," Viray said. "I'm a private detective, and I take pride in my work. I agreed to help Federation Security because it made more sense than having them follow me and potentially unravel anything I tried to do. But remember, they wanted the same thing you wanted: to find Morn. So I kept doing what you hired me to do."

"What is it Federation Security is after?" Quark asked. He knew that, for the most part, Morn operated his shipping business legally, with only the occasional transport of contraband. He could not imagine the Lurian doing something so serious that Federation Security would track him out of UFP space in order to arrest and extradite him.

"As best I can tell—and Federation Security doesn't know I've learned this—Morn traveled all over the quadrant visiting various scientists," Viray said. "Some of them operated on the fringes of the law, while others had been largely discredited. Still, Morn apparently managed to use them to formulate plans for a piece of technology—"

"A restricted piece," Quark said. "What was it?"

"I don't know," Viray said. "I haven't been able to find

out, but I do know that Morn hired an engineer on Tendarri Four to build the device. Federation Security arrested him and searched his lab. They couldn't find his creation, but they did find the plans, which they confiscated. In order to obtain a reduced sentence, the engineer admitted to constructing a single device, and gave up the identity of the person who provided him the plans and paid him to build it."

"Morn."

"Morn," Viray said. "I never tried to con you, Quark. In fact, I have done an exceptional job for you. I not only tracked Morn across the Alpha Quadrant—and twice into the Beta Quadrant—I ultimately got him to agree to meet me here on Mericor."

"And what would you have done if I hadn't shown up when I did?" Quark asked.

"I would have let Federation Security arrest him," she said, "then I would have told you what detention facility they had taken him to. That was part of my agreement with Corvok and Toulet: I would assist them in finding Morn, but they would tell me where he would be held so that I could complete my contract with you."

Quark had to give her credit. Trying to accomplish a tough task made even more difficult by the interference of law enforcement, Viray had still managed to fulfill her contractual obligations. Among other things, that meant that Quark had no recourse to recover any of the funds he had paid her.

And why should you get any of your latinum back? Quark challenged himself. *She gave you what you wanted: Morn.* Except that Quark had really wanted his friend back in his bar, planted on a stool, drinking like an Ophiucan five-bellied water lizard, and regaling all and sundry with his jokes, stories, and epic poems.

And it's not about him reestablishing his bar tab, Quark admitted to himself. He simply missed Morn.

xi

The night had grown long. Ro found the hum of *Balju*'s warp drive almost hypnotic, and as she sat in the interceptor's conference room for the second time that day, she thought that she could just fold her arms on the table, lay her head down, and fall asleep in no time at all. Ro still wanted more answers about Morn, and she thought she could get them, perhaps paradoxically, by replying to questions asked of her.

After her earlier conversation with Agent Corvok, at the end of which he'd told her that the Department of Temporal Investigations would be getting involved, she had been taken to the ship's mess, where she had been reunited with Quark. Over a meal, the two didn't talk much, other than for Quark to complain about the quality of the food aboard the ship. Ro tried to tell herself that they didn't speak much to each other because they both assumed that Federation Security would be listening in on their conversation, but she suspected it had more to do with everything that had happened between them.

Once she and Quark had finished eating, Corvok had asked them if they'd completed their business on Mericor. Since Quark had been wrong about Mayereen Viray taking his funds under false pretenses, he and Ro had no reason to continue their visit there. Corvok then offered to bring them back to Deep Space 9 aboard *Balju*, since the Federation Security vessel would be heading there anyway; they would all be met on DS9 by a DTI agent. Ro wanted to say no, not only because she dreaded having to meet with somebody from the Department of Temporal Investigations, but because she wanted a little more time alone with Quark so that she could begin repairing the damage she'd done to their relationship. They wouldn't resume seeing each other, but she wanted to try to ease the pain she'd caused him. Quark jumped at Corvok's offer, though, and Ro did not argue.

Agents Corvok and Toulet had then accompanied Ro and Quark back down to the spaceport aboard *Balju*'s auxiliary craft. Ro and Quark took *Quark's Quest* into orbit, with Corvok joining them aboard the small scoutship. Considering that Federation Security had confirmed their identities and supposedly cleared them of any wrongdoing, it disquieted the captain that Corvok felt the need to travel with them from Mericor back up to the ship. In orbit, they loaded *Quark's Quest* into *Balju*'s shuttlebay, and the interceptor set course for DS9.

Exhausted but still seeking answers about Morn, Ro peered across the conference table and regarded the woman seated opposite her. Dressed in bland, utilitarian clothing, she had dark hair, dark eyes, and a tawny complexion. She had introduced herself as Doctor Ceylin Remzi, a scientist from Jupiter Station, in the Sol system. As Ro looked on, the woman continued to consult a padd, then made a few quick notes on it with the tip of her finger. A small box sat on the table in front of her. Finally, she looked up at Ro.

"Thank you for agreeing to meet with me, Captain," Remzi said. She spoke with an accent that heavily emphasized each syllable. To Ro, her voice had something of a lyrical quality to it.

"Of course. We're all here to help Federation Security."

"Actually, in this case, Federation Security is helping us," Remzi said. "I'd like to speak with you about Vic Fontaine."

Ro felt her brow crease. Of all the names Remzi could

have asked about, Vic's would have been one of the last the captain would have predicted. "I'm sorry. You said that you're from Jupiter Station. What exactly is it that you do?"

"I am an associate director at Starfleet's Holographic Image and Programming Center," Remzi said—which lent at least a degree of sense to her asking about a character in a holosuite program. The issue of *why* anybody would be interested in Vic Fontaine was another matter.

"What is it you want to know?" Ro asked.

"How much interaction have you had with the hologram?"

Ro shrugged. "Some," she said. "Not a lot. I'm not much of a holosuite user."

"When was the last time you used the program that hosted Fontaine?"

"Uh . . . I don't know precisely," Ro said. "It's been quite a while . . . years, in fact. It was back on the original Deep Space Nine, so I'd say at least three years, maybe four."

"How many members of your crew use the program?" Remzi asked. The nature of her questions bewildered Ro.

"I honestly have no idea," Ro said. "I know that the program was popular. I can think of maybe ten or twelve of my crew who used it, but there were probably more than that."

"The program 'was' popular?" Remzi asked. "Am I to infer that it is no longer popular?"

"It's not that," Ro said. "It's that the program is no longer available."

"What?" Remzi asked, and for the first time, her even demeanor changed. She suddenly appeared anxious. "What happened to the program? I was given to understand that it ran continuously."

"Yes, it did," Ro said, "but that was aboard the original Deep Space Nine, before the station was destroyed."

Remzi wrinkled her forehead, showing her confusion. "Then the program was lost as well?"

"No," Ro said. "It was uploaded into a holographic simulation tester and executed there."

"But it wasn't uploaded to another holosuite somewhere?" Remzi asked. "On a ship, or on Bajor, or on the new starbase?"

"No," Ro said. "As I understand it, there were technical issues with uploading it to older holosuites, and when the new Deep Space Nine became operational, there were other compatibility issues with the new ones. I know that there's been some effort to resolve whatever the problem is, but as far as I know, the program is still running in the tester."

"How can that be?" Remzi said, though more to herself than the captain. She looked off to the side, but Ro suspected that she no longer saw the conference room around them. "That doesn't make any sense."

"Pardon me, Doctor Remzi," Ro said, "but none of *this* makes any sense to me. Why are you asking me questions about a character in a holosuite program? How do you even know about that program? And what does any of this have to do with Morn?"

Remzi refocused her attention on Ro. "The Federation Security agents didn't tell you? You have sufficient security clearance."

"I was told only that Morn had been arrested for possession of restricted technology."

"Twenty-ninth-century technology," Remzi said. Ro momentarily stopped breathing. The idea of people traveling through time and potentially wreaking indescribable havoc across the galaxy greatly disturbed her.

"Morn is a time-traveler?"

"No," Remzi said. "At least, not that I know of. But he somehow learned about a piece of technology brought to our time from the future. It employs materials and science unknown in our time, and it is therefore irreproducible—

or so we thought. Morn appears to have developed plans for such a device using contemporary technology, and then he hired a rogue Milvonian engineer named Bayal Sego to construct it."

"Construct what?" Ro asked. "What does this futuristic piece of technology do?"

Remzi reached for the small box in front of her, opened it, and withdrew the wide silver band that Agent Toulet had confiscated from Morn. The director held it up before her. "It is called an autonomous self-sustaining mobile holo-emitter," Remzi said. "When connected to a holographic character, it allows that character to exist independent of holographically enabled environments."

"What does that mean?" Ro asked. "That a hologram with this device could just walk out of a holosuite?"

"Yes, it means exactly that," Remzi said. The director placed it back in the box, which she then closed. "Although Morn had this device created so that a holographic character could also be downloaded directly from its source code."

"And . . . what?" Ro asked. "You think Morn had this device created so that he could take Vic Fontaine out of his program?"

"That is what Federation Security tells me," Remzi said. "Morn has refused to talk until he has consulted with his legal representation, but a search of his personal communicator revealed several messages he sent that referenced Vic Fontaine."

"Who did he send the messages to?"

"An individual aboard Deep Space Nine," Remzi said. "A Bajoran woman named Ulu Lani."

Ro nodded. "She's one of Quark's waitstaff."

"What is her relationship to Morn?" Remzi asked.

"None that I know of," Ro said, "but I really don't know anything about the woman."

"And has she ever entered Vic Fontaine's program?"

"It's possible," Ro said, "but she never lived on Deep Space Nine prior to its destruction, so I'm not sure if she ever had the chance. Perhaps if she visited the station at that time." Ro thought about the questions Remzi had asked her. "I understand why the Federation would restrict the creation, possession, and use of twenty-ninth-century technology, but why are you asking about Vic Fontaine? I mean, even if Morn wanted to use the device on him, it's Morn who's committing the crime."

"From what Federation Security has seen on Morn's personal communicator," Remzi said, "we have reason to believe that he might have been asked—or maybe even somehow coerced—to do all of this by Vic Fontaine."

"How would that even be possible?" Ro said. "Vic's a *hologram*."

"That's why I wanted to speak with you," Remzi said. "You're somebody who has had direct contact with Fontaine. Would you characterize him . . . would you say that he is . . . that he might be . . . conscious?"

"Vic? Conscious?" Ro said, unable to hide her incredulity. "I know that there are members of my crew who like spending time in his program . . . who enjoy interacting with him. And they say he talks about being a hologram, in a holosuite, but I always assumed that was just part of his programming."

"A great deal of work has been done in the field of artificial intelligence," Remzi said, "but it is still difficult in many circumstances to determine consciousness, or even sentience. An android or a hologram might be made to look humanoid, and they might be programmed to emulate self-awareness, but that doesn't actually make them conscious beings."

"But you think Vic might be a conscious being? And

that he wants to be freed from the holosuite?" Ro said. "How would he even know about the technology you're discussing?"

"Although the specific instance of twenty-ninth-century technology is restricted information," Remzi said, "the existence of autonomous holo-emitter tech is public, if not widespread, knowledge."

"What do you intend to do?" Ro wanted to know.

"That depends on what we find out," Remzi said. "We need to learn if this device—" She tapped the box containing the mobile holo-emitter. "—actually works. And both the Federation Security agents and I want to speak with Vic Fontaine."

"That may be difficult," Ro said, "considering that his program is stuck running in a simulation tester."

"Not according to Quark," Remzi said. "During his interrogation, he revealed that his nephew entered a holosuite weeks ago to use Vic's program."

Ro hadn't known that, and it made her wonder what else Quark had kept from her. In the next moment, though, she realized that, prior to their trip to Mericor, she hadn't given him much opportunity of late to talk to her about anything. "What is it that you expect to learn from Vic?" she asked.

"Federation Security wants to know how he learned about the mobile emitter in the first place, and whether or not he somehow persuaded or forced Morn to have one constructed," Remzi said. "And I want to find out if Vic Fontaine is a sentient being."

Seven

Balance Sheet

Candlewood picked up the final bundle of bills and set it inside the long canvas duffel, atop the rest of the money already piled there. He zipped the bag closed, then stepped back to stand beside Nog and Ulu. Together, they stood near the door of Candlewood's room in their Shining Oasis suite, gazing at the three canvas bags laid out on the bed. Each contained more than four hundred thousand dollars.

"We did it," Candlewood said. The three of them had spent the previous thirty-six hours all over Las Vegas. Ulu used one of Nog's improvised devices to win numerous slot-machine jackpots, while the two men traded off using the second device—at least in the beginning. He and Nog also played blackjack, but the operations chief enjoyed far more success counting cards than Candlewood, so at some point, they divided up the work accordingly.

For the most part, they'd stayed out of trouble by moving frequently from casino to casino, trying not to win too much in one venue. A couple of hours earlier, Ulu got escorted out of the End of the Rainbow Casino after winning a third jackpot, a mistake she chalked up to fatigue. In the end, they collectively banked more than one point three five million dollars.

Throughout their day and a half of almost nonstop gambling, they had each periodically returned to the Shining Oasis with their winnings. On one trip, Nog brought the canvas duffels, which he purchased at a sporting-goods store. The bills—some of them in twenty-dollar denominations, some in fifty, some in one hundred—fit easily within the bags.

The telephone rang, and Candlewood jumped—probably because he'd been thinking about what would come next. Nog crossed the room to the nightstand and picked up the receiver. "This is Nog," he said, and then he proceeded to have a brief conversation. When he hung up, he said, "That was Mister Arden, calling from the lobby. He's waiting for us downstairs."

It had been Candlewood's idea to hire a guard from a local security company to shepherd them on the taxicab ride from the Shining Oasis to the Silver Lode for their meeting with Bugsy Calderone's accountant. Although Candlewood, Nog, and Ulu could come to no harm in the holosuite program, they still had to protect against their funds being stolen from them. To that end, they had retained a man named Charlie Arden from Strip Security Services.

"How much are we going to take?" Candlewood asked. They had debated whether or not to bring the full sum required to procure Vic's freedom. Ulu thought that they should, simply to bring an end to the situation as quickly as possible. But after all that they'd learned about Calderone—some of the newspaper articles they'd read painted him as a vengeful man—both Candlewood and Nog had reservations about giving him everything he wanted without them being able to ensure that the mobster would release Vic.

"Just one bag," Nog said. "We'll bring Calderone a third of his money. That will be enough to demonstrate how serious we are, and it will leave him with enough to lose that we can insist on him releasing Vic."

"What if he doesn't care for that?" Ulu said. "What if he decides to take the money you bring him and then shoot you?"

"I don't think he'll do that," Nog said, "not with two-thirds of Vic's debt still outstanding."

"But should we even take a chance?" Candlewood asked.

He had initially agreed with Nog, but he thought Ulu did have a point.

"If we bring two-thirds of the money, or even all of it, we risk the same thing," Nog said. "I think doing it this way will provide us with the most leverage."

"What if . . . what if only one of us went to see Calderone?" Candlewood suggested. "That way, if only one of us is there and he does have his thugs shoot, there will still be two of us here to try to free Vic."

Nog did not immediately respond. He seemed to roll the idea around in his mind. Finally, he said, "You're right." He went to the end of the bed and hauled one of the duffels up onto his shoulder by its straps. The bag hung horizontally along his hip. "If I'm not back here within one hour, contact Calderone yourself."

Then Nog strode into the living area and toward the front door of the suite.

ii

With the duffel slung across his shoulder, Nog stepped away from the elevator at the Silver Lode hotel just as he and Candlewood had two days before: led by one thug named Sperano and followed by another named Spinelli. The operations chief proceeded down the wide corridor feeling vulnerable—not because he could come to any harm, but because Vic's safety and freedom remained in doubt. He had actually considered bringing along his hired guard—a mountain of a man with sandy hair and a stoic demeanor—but in the end decided that such an act would send the wrong message to Calderone's men. Nog wanted the mobster's representatives to understand not only his seriousness of purpose, but that he had no interest in any sort of violent confrontation.

The two thugs escorted Nog to the same set of elaborately carved doors, and Sperano again pushed them open. Once more, Calderone's accountant, Herschel P. Steinberg, sat at the long table in the richly appointed meeting room. He had traded his gray three-piece suit for one in pinstriped navy blue. Also as before, another pair of guards stood in the room, in either of its far corners.

"Good evening, Mister Nog," Steinberg said in his tinny voice. He waved a hand to one side, a seemingly nondescript gesture, but Sperano immediately moved to close the room's doors. Unlike in the meeting two days earlier, both Sperano and Spinelli remained inside the room, not far behind Nog. "What have you got for me?" The accountant smiled thinly.

Nog stepped forward and hoisted the duffel bag onto the conference table. "This is four hundred sixteen thousand dollars," he said. "One-third of the sum Vic owes Mister Calderone."

Steinberg's unconvincing smile faded quickly. "I am a certified public accountant, Mister Nog, and have practiced my skills for many years, but it does not require a person of my training and experience to know that one-third of the money owed to Mister Calderone is not the same as *all* of the money owed to Mister Calderone."

"No, it's not," Nog said, "but I do possess all of those funds." He reached for the duffel, ran its zipper open, then overturned the bag and spilled the packets of paper currency it contained onto the table. "I happen to be skilled with numbers myself, and with finances," Nog went on. "Maybe that's why I realized that if I paid the entire sum owed to Mister Calderone, I would have no guarantee that he would release Vic, and I would have no power to compel him to do so."

Steinberg wordlessly pointed to the heap of cash, and

Sperano immediately strode to the table beside Nog and began to stack it neatly, and also, presumably, to count it. "Mister Calderone's word is his bond," the accountant said.

"That may be," Nog said, "but you are not Mister Calderone, are you? You are merely his representative. I'd rather hear it from him."

"Hear what, precisely, Mister Nog?" Steinberg asked. "That Mister Calderone insists that the debt owed to him be repaid in full? No matter whether I or somebody else makes that claim, you can rest assured that it's true. Surely, you can see that."

"What I can't see is Vic Fontaine," Nog said. "I can't see that you actually have him, or that he is in good health. I can't see that, once I hand over one and a quarter million dollars, that Mister Calderone will consider the debt settled in full and release Vic."

Very deliberately, Steinberg stood up. He made another motion with his hand, but that time, Sperano did not move. Instead, he said, "What?"

"Pack it back up," Steinberg snapped, clearly frustrated that the meeting was not proceeding as he'd hoped. Sperano grabbed the duffel and righted it on the table, then began stacking the packets of bills inside it. "Mister Nog, I will take this money and apply it to Mister Fontaine's debt. If you bring the remaining sum, I will apply that as well, but as you know, you only have the rest of the day to do so. Otherwise, your business here is done." Steinberg looked past Nog and issued a curt nod. An instant later, Spinelli grabbed the operations chief by his upper arm. The man's grip felt like a steel band around Nog's biceps.

Nog flung his shoulder backward to break Spinelli's hold on him. It didn't work. Nog didn't care. "I am prepared right now to pay off the entire sum due Mister Calderone, but if I walk out of here, you're not getting it." It was a bluff, of course—Nog would do whatever he could to save Vic—but he didn't feel he had much choice but to negotiate hard; other than the funds he, Candlewood, and Lani had managed to collect, he had nothing else with which to bargain.

"I do not take kindly to threats, and neither does Mister Calderone," Steinberg said, his tone icy. "Remove this man, and do not allow him back in the building unless he is carrying eight hundred thirty-one thousand dollars."

Spinelli wrenched Nog's arm and hauled him back toward the doors. The operations chief tried to resist, but the strongman probably stood forty centimeters higher and outweighed him by fifty kilos. When they reached the doors, Nog opened his mouth to call back to Steinberg, to say that he would go retrieve the rest of the cash and bring it back—but then he heard a click, and after that, much fainter, metal curving easily around metal. He didn't hear it much outside of the holosuite and Vic's program, but he recognized it at once: hinges.

Nog whirled around so quickly, he spun out of Spinelli's grasp. In the middle of the right-hand wall, between a tall cabinet and a credenza, a floor-to-ceiling panel had swung open. A man stood in the suddenly revealed doorway:

Bugsy Calderone.

He cut an impressive figure. Tall and broad-shouldered, he wore an impeccably tailored black suit, with a ruby-colored tie around his neck and a matching handkerchief tucked into his breast pocket. He had sharp features and a deeply lined face. Drifts of white dusted his otherwise black hair. Smoke curled up from the smoldering end of a cigar sticking from one side of his mouth.

Spinelli grabbed Nog again, but when the thug saw Calderone, he froze. The mobster eased into the room with a dignity and grace that seemed to belie his reputation. He strode around the table and approached Nog. The operations chief could not help but think that Calderone intended to put the business end of a firearm against his head.

The mobster stopped a couple of paces from Nog. "I must tell you," he said in an oily tone, "that you are not in charge of this situation. You never have been." Calderone peered across the table at Steinberg, who stared back without saying a word. The fear in the room seemed palpable—not from Nog, but from the men who worked for the mobster.

Calderone took the cigar from his mouth and motioned toward where Sperano stood in front of the duffel of cash, which the thug had repacked. "You brought me a third of my money," the mobster said. "That's a good start, but it's not enough—not enough to settle Fontaine's debt, and not enough to save his life. Depending on how this conversation goes, it might not be enough to save *your* life." The guard in the far corner snickered, and Calderone threw him a look that suggested he had just earned a serious demerit in the eyes of his boss.

"Mister Calderone, I *want* to give you your money," Nog said carefully. "All I want in exchange is Vic Fontaine."

The mobster smiled, but Nog had seen such expressions before, and so he knew that it meant nothing but trouble. "I guess I'm not making myself clear," he said. "Either you produce the rest of my money right now, or I'm going to put a bullet in the head of Vic Fontaine."

With Calderone's mention of Vic's full name, two other people appeared in the previously hidden doorway: another of the mobster's henchmen—and Vic. The singer looked terrible. He wore the same clothes Nog had seen him in a week earlier, when Vic had been abducted. His face wore the scars of having been beaten: bruised flesh, bloodied scabs, and an eye swollen shut. The man behind Vic pushed him forward with the muzzle of a pistol.

"All right," Nog said to Calderone at once. "You win."

Calderone looked at him, then took a puff of his foul-smelling cigar. "So quickly?"

"You've made your point," Nog said. "There's no use dragging it out. I can get the rest of your cash and bring it back."

"Really?" Calderone said. "And you wouldn't take the opportunity just to put some mileage between you and Las Vegas, now, would you?"

"Why would I do that?" Nog asked. "You already have four hundred thousand dollars of my money."

"Of *my* money," Calderone corrected him. "And the answer would be that only money and Fontaine's life were at stake before. Now it's your life too." The mobster snapped his fingers in the direction of Spinelli, who reached into his jacket and pulled out a firearm. He pointed it at Nog. "Now then, let's all go get my money. If you're not lying and you to take us to it right now, then I'll let you and Fontaine go. If not . . ." Without looking, Calderone pointed back at Vic, his thumb and forefinger in the shape of a pistol. "Bang," he said, and then he aimed his pantomime weapon at Nog. "Bang."

"All right, all right," Nog said. "I'll take you."

"Then lead on," Calderone said.

Spinelli quickly moved to the doors and pulled them open. Nog headed in that direction, fully intending to take Calderone and his thugs back to the Shining Oasis and give the mobster the rest of the money. After that, he tried to tell himself, it would all be over.

Except that Nog had been trained on Ferenginar in the art of negotiation, and both his education and experience made one thing abundantly clear to him: he could not trust Bugsy Calderone.

iii

Kira walked beside Altek Dans through the immense chamber that lay deep beneath the surface of Endalla. The previous day, after the illumination of the roof of the chamber had caused vertigo in so many and an even stronger reaction in Altek, the work there had been briefly halted. Nobody knew exactly what had happened or why, though there had been no shortage of opinions—not among the scientists, who reserved their judgment for when they had collected more data, but among the vedeks present. Predictably, those in the mainstream faith saw it as some sort of message from the Prophets confirming their divinity, while the Ohalavaru viewed it as an indication of the significantly alien nature of the wormhole denizens.

Everybody impacted by the sight of the chamber roof had recovered quickly, though it had taken Altek longer than the others. Medical scans showed that, whatever had taken place, it left no physical trace in the brains or the bodies of those affected. Most compared the incident to an Orb experience, though exactly what that implied depended on the perspective of the speaker. Nobody recalled any precise thoughts or images during their periods of dizziness, but that did not prevent many of them from proclaiming their vertiginous moments as proof positive of whatever it is that they believed.

That morning, as they'd shared a meal aboard their shuttle, as they'd wandered the chamber and observed the work of the scientists and engineers, Kira had watched Altek for any lingering effects of his experience. He showed none. He had no real recollection of what he'd experienced beyond his initial swoon. The scientists had—wisely, in Kira's opinion—decided to leave the roof of the chamber only dimly illuminated until they could figure out how to brighten it in such a way that it could be studied safely. One idea had been to empty the chamber of people, but leave remote viewing equipment inside, or perhaps recording devices. The scientists would explore those and other options until they ultimately reached a decision on a course of action.

Beside her, Altek pointed. Kira looked in that direction and saw a man and a woman standing in front of a wall near the far reach of the lights that had been set up in the chamber. The vedek nodded, and she and Altek altered their path. As they walked, it felt to Kira almost as though they entered a tunnel. She reflexively glanced upward, then experienced a moment of anxiety as she recalled what had occurred the prior day. But when she looked up, Kira saw that the light in that part of the chamber faded before it reached anything solid—whether the roof of the chamber far overhead or some surface lower than that, she could not tell.

When Kira and Altek arrived at their destination, the two scientists did not look away from their work. Kira recognized the woman as Alavor Ment, an archaeologist who had participated in the study of the formerly lost city of B'hala, which had been rediscovered more than a decade earlier by the Emissary. Alavor and her colleague stood in front of an expanse of wall that, at first glance, appeared no different from the areas around it. The two scientists both carried padds, and they had set up what looked to Kira's untrained eye like an overly complex holographic recorder. She suspected that the device, which stood waist high and featured a pair of complicated control panels, had other capabilities beyond producing holophotos—perhaps spectroscopic analysis or the like.

Kira and Altek kept their distance from the pair of scientists, wanting to avoid disturbing their work. They positioned themselves off to the side so that they could see the object of Alavor and her colleague's attention. Kira initially detected nothing that distinguished that particular section of wall, but as she continued to study it, she began to perceive gradations in its surface. She thought that she saw some lighter and darker patches, which could have been slight differentiations in pigments, or perhaps subtle concavities and convexities in the surface.

"If you don't look directly at it . . . if you use your peripheral vision . . . you can actually see it better," Altek said quietly.

Kira tried to do as he suggested, gazing to the side of that section of wall. It made no difference, and so she eventually shifted her gaze again, peering past that area. At first, nothing changed, but then the variant patches appeared to pop, as though suddenly thrust into focus. "I see," Kira whispered, and she worked to discern the blotches or undulations or whatever they were. Though she could not tell how they had been formed, the shapes gave the impression of having been created deliberately; there appeared a loose structure, both to the individual colors or contours and to how they all related to one another.

"Are those . . . do you think those could be letters?" Kira asked quietly. "If not letters, then glyphs . . . writing of some kind?"

Altek didn't respond. Kira didn't want to look away, concerned that once she did, she would not be able to reestablish her view of the characters or pictograms. "Do you see it?" Kira asked. When Altek still said nothing, she could not help but turn toward him.

He was no longer by her side.

Kira spun around quickly, thinking that he might have

moved behind her or to her other side, but that hadn't happened. She looked past the two scientists toward the darkness, toward where the lights in the chamber could not reach. She took a step in that direction, worried that Altek had wandered into that blackness, and hesitant to do so herself.

Kira turned again to look behind her, back toward the larger, lighted part of the chamber. Movement caught her eye, and she looked in that direction, off to one side. Maybe fifty paces away, Altek stood facing an odd-angled corner, where several surfaces came together unevenly. He stared at the peculiar intersection, at the dark space it formed. As Kira watched, he raised both of his hands, fingers extended, palms out, as though he intended to push against the wall.

"No!" Kira yelled. She launched herself toward Altek, pumping her legs as fast as she could, as hard as she could. She called out his name, but he took no notice of her. As she drew closer, she saw two dark areas on the wall before him—uneven depressions, with rounded edges, looking like some random, fuzzy-edged flaws in the construction. But then the hollows began to glow, and Kira saw that each formed the shape of a hand—mirrors of Altek's own hands.

"Dans!" Kira cried out, desperately trying to reach him in time. She bent low and tucked her shoulder, preparing to strike Altek at the waist, to get low enough that she could tackle him and pull him away from the wall.

I'm not going to make it, she thought, even as she continued to race forward. She covered ground quickly, until only twenty paces remained between her and Altek. Fifteen paces. Ten.

Altek touched his hands into the indentations in the wall. They fit perfectly.

The chamber exploded in a brilliant coruscation of light. Kira struck Altek, and they tumbled to the floor together.

His hands came free of the wall, but still the chamber burned with brilliant illumination. A few steps away from where Altek crashed to the floor, Kira landed on her back hard. She instinctively slammed her eyes shut and raised her arms up before her face. For a moment, she thought that something—a power source, maybe even a weapon—had detonated, but then the bright glow began to recede.

Kira lowered her arms and opened her eyes. She turned to look at Altek, who lay on the floor beside her. The shape of his hands still glowed on the wall. He no longer appeared dazed, but in awe. He stared upward, and Kira followed his gaze.

Far above them, the twining structure of the distant roof had vanished, somehow replaced with the infinite depths of space. Familiar patterns of stars dotted the heavens, constellations that had for generations endured above the surface of Bajor. Kira saw the Chalice, the Runners, the Candles, and others—including the Flames, a stellar configuration that had grown in importance over the prior seventeen years, ever since the Emissary had found the Celestial Temple. Benjamin Sisko had been born on Earth, which orbited one of the lower stars in the Flames.

But the constellations could not hold Kira's attention. Among them, a great pair of streaks emanated from a single source. A line of deep purplish blue and an arc of brilliant white emerged from a glowing point. Kira recognized it at once: the impressive twin-tailed comet that had adorned the skies of her youth for a month. She had been in the Singha refugee camp at the time, where, despite the privations of her family, her father had mined emotional sustenance for her and her two brothers as he shared with them the spellbinding astronomical pageant night after night.

Kira marveled at the comet above her, in a sky where the roof of the chamber should have been, and she felt the bittersweet memories of lost family. She could not look away as the radiant ball of ice, dust, and gas plummeted into the atmosphere of Bajor. It brightened the heavens in its last moments of light.

Before it faded completely, Kira peered over at Altek. He continued to behold the spectacle, even as she saw the reflected light dying on his face. Past him, on the wall, the outlines into which he had pressed his hands also dimmed. When they disappeared, Kira looked back up. Not only had the comet gone, so too had the night sky, replaced by the shadowy roof of the chamber.

Kira struggled to stand, her balance off. Not wanting to waste time, she gave up, choosing instead to clamber over to Altek on her hands and knees. She saw his head lolling back against the floor, his eyes closed, his body unmoving. When she reached him, she grabbed for his wrist. She felt for a pulse and failed to find one.

She slapped at the combadge on her robe. "Medic!" she called.

iv

"The wormhole is opening," reported Ensign Elvo Minnar from the tactical station.

After receiving word from Wheeler Stinson aboard *Defiant*, Blackmer had stood up from the command chair and made his way down into the Well, where he faced the situation table. "Let's see it," he told Minnar.

"Yes, sir." The controls of the tactical console chirped in response to the ensign's commands. Above the sit table, the holographic display resolved into a swirling rush of blue and white as the wormhole terminus leaped into existence in the Alpha Quadrant. A bantam ship sailed from the heart of the turbulence, and Blackmer immediately recognized the lines of its hull. "The *Defiant* has emerged from the wormhole," Minnar announced needlessly, but the acting captain did not say anything.

Better too thorough than not thorough enough, Blackmer thought.

As *Defiant* altered course and swept toward Deep Space 9, a second ship appeared in the center of the spinning light. "The Jem'Hadar battle cruiser has also exited the wormhole."

"Thank you, Ensign," Blackmer said, suppressing the urge to smile at the young officer's earnestness. "Status of their weapons?"

"Powered down, sir," Minnar said, confirming not only the plan previously agreed to, but also the readings the DS9 crew had already received from the communications-and-sensor buoy in the Gamma Quadrant. "Once the Jem'Hadar vessel left the wormhole, it also lowered its shields."

"Commander," said Ensign Vigo Melijnek from the communications station, "we are being hailed by the Jem'Hadar vessel."

"Put it on-screen," Blackmer said. He stepped back and gazed up at the ring of viewers that hung above the sit table's holographic display. The screens blinked, and then a smooth, wrinkle-free face appeared. It filled the screen, likely indicating the sender employed the virtual-scanner headset favored by the Dominion.

"Odo to Deep Space Nine."

"This is Commander Blackmer." The first officer had spoken with Odo several times while the *Defiant* crew had chaperoned the battle cruiser to the Alpha Quadrant. Blackmer had listened to the shape-shifter's initial report of the situation with a considerable degree of suspicion—not of Odo, but of the proposition of nearly four thousand individuals seeking independence from the Dominion. It simply did not sound believable. Blackmer could certainly understand oppressed people seeking another way of life than in continuous servitude to the Founders, but he found it difficult to imagine the Great Link, which ruled with an iron fist, allowing such defections. Like many in Starfleet and throughout the Federation, the DS9 exec had viewed the Dominion's postwar isolationism as a positive development, but conventional understanding held that the Gamma Quadrant power had closed its borders in *both* directions.

"The crew and passengers have been eager to put as much distance as possible between themselves and the Dominion," Odo said. *"Now that they've made it through the wormhole and into the Alpha Quadrant, they would like to waste little time in finding a world on which they can settle."*

The emphasis on rushing the resettlement of a Dominion population to a location in or near Federation space concerned Blackmer, although such decisions would ultimately be made in the highest levels of the civilian government, probably in consultation with Starfleet officers far above the first officer's own rank and position. "I have contacted Starfleet Command," Blackmer said. "Admiral Herthum, the chief of Starfleet Operations, subsequently met with the Federation's External Affairs Council, and they quickly referred the matter to the Bureau of Interplanetary Affairs. The BIA has placed the director of their Displaced Persons Agency in charge."

Odo's already flat expression somehow became more dour. *"That sounds like a tremendous amount of bureaucracy,"* he noted, readily conveying his distaste for officialdom.

"I'm afraid I can't disagree with that," Blackmer said. "But I will point out how expeditiously the BIA was engaged. We just received word that the DPA is sending Director Barash and a support team to meet with you about the needs of the prospective émigrés."

Odo's eyes darted to one side for a moment before he responded. *"I do not speak for the people aboard this ship,"* he said.

"I am only relaying what I was told," Blackmer said. "I imagine that the BIA must think that you can handle the situation because of your familiarity with the Dominion and your role in determining the intentions of those aboard the Jem'Hadar vessel."

"I can discuss my experience here and what has been communicated to me," Odo said, *"but the people aboard this ship should be permitted to speak for themselves."*

"I'm sure that will be the case," Blackmer said. "They must have prepared to conduct diplomatic relations once they made it through the wormhole and into the Alpha Quadrant."

"No, I don't believe they have," Odo said. *"Their focus was on fleeing from Dominion tyranny. Their collective goal would not have been to then subjugate themselves to the will of some other power."*

Blackmer could hear the frustration in his words, which sounded like an argument against unfairness. The first officer did not know the Changeling well, but during the time Odo had spent on the starbase, Blackmer had read through the file Starfleet kept on him. From what the exec read, Odo had a well-deserved reputation for diligently pursuing the interests of justice.

"Odo, the Bureau of Interplanetary Affairs is asking that the battle cruiser remain at Deep Space Nine until Director Barash and his diplomatic team arrive," Blackmer said. "My understanding is that they want to work with the refugees to understand why they have fled the Dominion, what their status is, what they need, and how the Federation can work with them to find a peaceful resolution."

"Pardon me, Commander," Odo said, *"but that sounds a lot like the Federation deciding that it can't trust a group of people who only want to escape a totalitarian regime."*

Blackmer could see the Changeling's point, but he also remembered his time on the *Trieste* and his encounters with Dominion forces. "I don't think the BIA has made a choice to distrust the people aboard the Jem'Hadar vessel, but they do want to ensure that this is not some sort of plot by the Dominion, or, short of that, that it will reignite tensions between them and the Federation."

"The war ended more than a decade ago," Odo said. *"We shouldn't live in the past."*

While Blackmer believed the Changeling's interest stemmed from a genuine desire to help people in need, his last statement angered the first officer. Because of that, he took a beat before replying, taking care to steady his voice. "The war might be in the past, but its toll was more than a billion casualties; that means that there are many who are still suffering from those losses." He paused, then said, "Odo, the Federation just wants to talk before these refugees find a home in or near our territory. As long as we treat them fairly and with compassion, that's not unreasonable."

Odo took a long time to respond, and when he did, he sounded cautious. *"Very well,"* he said. *"I will speak to Rotan'talag and Weyoun and explain the situation. I will encourage them to wait. Shall we dock at Deep Space Nine?"*

Blackmer hesitated. "For now, it would be advisable for the *Defiant* to escort the Jem'Hadar ship to a place out of the regular space lanes," he finally suggested. "It might be wise to avoid stirring up public concerns before the Federation and the refugees even have a chance to talk."

"Of course," Odo said, though his tone made his disapprobation plain.

"I'll have Commander Stinson contact you," Blackmer said. "Deep Space Nine out."

Ensign Melijnek took the cue and ended the transmission. The viewscreens above the sit table went dark. Blackmer climbed the steps to the raised outer deck of the Hub and walked back to the command chair. As he stood beside it, he peered over to the communications console. "Open a channel to the *Defiant*," he said.

Ensign Melijnek worked his controls, but almost at once, he looked back over at Blackmer. "Commander," he said, "we're being hailed by Captain Ro."

V

Ro led Agents Corvok and Toulet, along with Doctor Remzi, out of the turbolift. As they swung from the radial corridor onto the wide outer walkway of Deep Space 9's Plaza, the captain noticed that, even though they headed for his bar, Quark had fallen to the back of the group. Ro worried about him. Beyond everything that had taken place between the two of them, she knew that he had no interest in Federation Security nosing around his business, though she also hoped that he had nothing he needed to hide from them—or, for that matter, from her.

The Federation Security interceptor, *Balju*, had raced from Mericor to DS9 at a speed far greater than *Quark's Quest* could have achieved, making the journey in just one day, rather than in two. Corvok and Toulet wanted to question Vic Fontaine, as well as inspect his code, all in an attempt to verify their understanding of events, to determine how Morn had learned of the existence of a mobile emitter, and to judge the singer's culpability in the Lurian's scheme. Remzi sought to interview Vic to learn the level of his advancement, and she also hoped to test Morn's bootleg mobile emitter—she carried it with her in a small box—though not on the singer, but on some random holographic character.

During the trip from Mericor, Ro had contacted Blackmer. He reported to her about a group of Dominion refugees seeking to relocate to the Alpha Quadrant, information that prevented her and the Federation Security officers from being surprised at the appearance of a Jem'Hadar battle cruiser keeping station with *Defiant* on the outskirts of the Bajoran system. Ro knew that she would have to deal with *that* situation just as soon as she finished with Corvok, Toulet, and Remzi.

And, of course, the Department of Temporal Investigations will be sending an agent to Deep Space Nine as well, Ro thought. She dreaded the hours of detailed questioning to which she would likely have to submit, as well as all of the documentation they always required to complete their investigations.

Already past the start of gamma shift, an evening crowd bustled about the Plaza. When she reached the bar, Ro saw past its outer half-wall that customers jammed all three of its levels. A great mix of sounds emanated from within, comprising mostly voices, but she could also make out the chirping spin of the dabo wheel and the many noises of the dom-jot table. Ro turned to ask the Federation Security officers and Director Remzi how they wanted to proceed, but Quark had already hurried from the rear of the group to face them.

"Welcome to Quark's Public House, Café, Gaming Emporium, Holosuite Arcade, and Ferengi Embassy to Bajor," the barkeep said. "What can I get everybody? A Warp Core Breach? A Finagle's Folly? A Scalosian Sling?" Though it might have seemed otherwise, Ro doubted that Quark offered the drinks for free.

"We told you what we need," Corvok said. "Take us to a holosuite and load the Vic Fontaine program."

Quark muttered something beneath his breath, but he dutifully marched into the bar. He expertly weaved his way through his customers, leaving Ro and the others bogged down as they tried to follow. By the time they reached the lustrous silver bar that dominated the establishment, Quark had already moved behind it, where he stood speaking with Treir. After a moment, he peered over at Corvok. "My idiot nephew and your science officer—" He pointed to Ro without actually looking at her. "—have been running the program continuously for the last five days. According to Treir, they haven't left."

"So they're in there right now?" Ro asked.

"Yes."

"Then let's go find them," Corvok said.

vi

As Nog walked down the corridor of the Shining Oasis, he tried to glance back to get a look at Vic. For his effort, he felt the barrel of a firearm jammed into his back. "Eyes front," Spinelli said. Nog obeyed.

Back at the Silver Lode, Bugsy Calderone had ordered three of his thugs—Sperano, Spinelli, and the man guarding Vic, whom he called Delvecchio—to accompany him, Steinberg, and Nog to retrieve the rest of his money. When they made their way out of the hotel and into the fenced-off parking area, another pair of large, muscular men in suits joined them. Nog recognized them as two of the three who had abducted Vic from the Fremont-Sunrise Hotel.

"Hey, Mister Calderone," the square-jawed thug had said. He had been in charge during Vic's kidnapping and had knocked Nog from his feet. "Dat's duh guy I was tellin you about. He was outside Fontaine's hotel room when we went to snatch him."

Calderone had nodded, but he'd said nothing. Sperano and Spinelli loaded Nog into the back of a long black automobile—an Eldorado, Nog noted—and then climbed in on either side of him. Square Jaw drove. Calderone took Vic, Steinberg, and the other thugs in a second vehicle.

Nog had given thought to directing Calderone and his men to some location other than the suite at the Shining Oasis, where Candlewood and Lani kept guard over the rest of the money, but he had seen no reason to do so. Without twenty-fourth-century technology, he couldn't overwhelm the mobster and his men, but even if he could, what good would it do? The only way to liberate Vic and allow him to resume his everyday life would be to buy his freedom from Bugsy Calderone. Nog only wished that he could have notified Candlewood and Lani of their impending arrival.

When Nog reached the door of the suite, he said, "This is it."

"Open it," Calderone said.

Nog took the key out of his pocket, but before he slid it into the door, he said, "Two of my colleagues are inside." He did not want Calderone or his men to be surprised to see Candlewood and Lani.

"They armed?" Square Jaw asked.

"No," Nog said.

"Then open it," Calderone said again.

Nog pushed the key into the lock, turned it, then pushed the door open. He saw Candlewood and Lani across the living area of the suite, sitting at the large round table by the window. As Nog stepped inside, Lani got up and started toward him. He held up his hands. "Stop," he said. "I've brought . . . guests."

Nog felt a hand on his shoulder push him forward. He

stumbled across the room, but Lani caught him and helped him to right himself. Candlewood stood up as though to do something, but Nog waved him back. When the operations chief turned around, he saw Calderone and his entourage entering the suite. Two of them, Square Jaw and Sperano, drew weapons from their suit jackets and moved to the two bedroom doors, where they looked inside and declared them empty. Nog looked at Vic, and for the first time that night, the singer made eye contact with him—with the one eye not swollen shut. Nog tried to read his expression, searching for any sign of energy or hope, but he saw only the reverse: fatigue and despair.

"Let's see the money," Calderone said, "and let's see it now."

"John, get the money," Nog said. "All of it."

"All of it?" Candlewood asked, and Nog nodded. The science officer crossed to the door that led into his bedroom.

"Hold it," Calderone said, and Candlewood wisely stopped. The mobster pointed to Square Jaw. "Go with him."

Together, Candlewood and Square Jaw went into the bedroom. They appeared again seconds later, each of them carrying a duffel. Candlewood walked over to the table and set his bag down. Square Jaw did the same.

"All right," Calderone said. "You three, step aside." He pointed at Nog, Candlewood, and Lani and waved them away from the table. Nog did as they'd been instructed, and Candlewood and Lani followed his lead. "Open them," Calderone told Square Jaw. The thug unzipped the first bag, peered inside, then held it open toward Calderone so that the mobster could see the bundles of bills inside. He repeated the operation for the second duffel.

Calderone looked to Steinberg. "Make sure it's all there," he told the accountant. Steinberg crossed the room to the table, where he began pulling the cash from one bag and stacking it up in piles. Everybody waited as he emptied the first duffel and tossed the empty canvas bag to the floor.

"Four hundred fifteen thousand," Steinberg said.

"Eight hundred thirty-one K," Calderone said. "Four hundred sixteen to go."

Steinberg began extracting money from the second duffel, stacking it up on the table in new piles. Even though Nog knew all the funds were there, that they would in just a few moments fully settle Vic's debt to Calderone, his lobes went cold. He knew he would not relax until the mobster and his men had departed.

Finally, Steinberg removed the last packet of bills from the second bag. He set it down with the rest of the cash, then dropped the duffel onto the floor with the first one. "It's all here," he said. "Four hundred sixteen thousand dollars."

Calderone turned his gaze to Nog. "You're a man of your word," the mobster said. "And I'm a man of mine." Calderone looked over his shoulder, to where Delvecchio held a firearm against Vic's side. "Let him go."

Delvecchio hesitated, and for an instant, Nog thought that the thug might just defy Calderone's order. But then he grabbed Vic by the upper arm and led him forward. Halfway across the room, Delvecchio stopped and shoved the singer ahead. He stumbled, and Nog reached out to steady him. They gazed at each other, and then Vic said quietly, "Thanks, kid."

At the table, Steinberg bent and picked up the two duffels. He put one on a chair and one of them on the table, where he began loading the bills back into it. "Sperano, Spinelli, help him," Calderone said. The two men rushed across the room and did as they'd been ordered.

When they finished, Steinberg zipped the two duffels

closed. "That's it, Mister Calderone," the accountant said. "We're done."

The mobster nodded, then looked at Nog. The operations chief waited for Calderone to say some final words or simply to leave. When he did neither, Nog said, "It's been good doing business with you."

Calderone took a single step forward. "We're not quite finished yet," he said, his voice low and menacing. Nog's heart seemed to stop in chest. "I have my money, but I also need my reputation."

"And how much will it cost us to restore that?" Nog asked. He knew that he, Candlewood, and Lani had ultimately won a hundred thousand dollars more than Vic had owed Calderone. Nog would gladly turn all of it over to the mobster. "Ten thousand dollars? Twenty?" He wanted to leave himself enough room to negotiate

Calderone smiled. "I will ignore that insult," he said. "That my reputation can be worth any amount of money, let alone one so paltry."

"I meant no insult," Nog said at once, understanding that he had miscalculated. "I just wanted to compensate you for whatever damage you feel your reputation has suffered."

Calderone slowly walked across the room. He picked up one of the duffels and handed it to Sperano, then picked up the other and gave it to Spinelli. He pointed back toward the front door, and the two men carried the bags of cash over there. Steinberg followed along after them, and then so did Calderone. Nog hoped again that they would just leave, but then the mobster spoke again.

"A reputation isn't something you can buy," he said. "It takes years to build up, and an ongoing effort to maintain. Me, I'm not a man known for being soft on people who cross me. That includes men who don't pay their debts."

Vic stared with his one functioning eye at the mobster, but he remained quiet, for which Nog felt grateful. "With all due respect," the operations chief said, "we have paid Mister Fontaine's debt to you in full."

"Yes, that's true," Calderone said, "but the debt was not repaid in a timely manner. If I don't do something about that, it will diminish my dignity."

"Where I'm from, Mister Calderone," Nog told the mobster, "it's said that 'Dignity and an empty sack is worth the sack.'"

Calderone laughed. "I like that," he said. "I suppose it might even be true, but I don't find the sentiment very satisfying." He looked back over his shoulder. "Mister Benedetti." The square-jawed thug came forward to stand beside Calderone, who regarded Nog once more.

"Your reputation is also based on your word," Nog said. "You told me that you wouldn't kill Vic if we paid his debt. We did that."

"Oh, I'm not going to kill him," Calderone said. "I'm just going to make an example of him. He paid me back, so he can live, but he paid me back *late*, so he's never going to sing again." Calderone reached into his suit jacket and pulled out something black that fit in the beefy fingers of his hand. He pressed a button with his thumb, and a blade sprung into place. He handed it to Benedetti. "Cut out his vocal cords."

vii

Ro stood in front of the door as Quark worked the controls of the holosuite. When the panel slid open, she strode forward into a large, carpeted room, presumably somewhere in 1960s Las Vegas. Remzi and the Federation Security agents followed her inside.

Ro quickly took in the scene. Directly in front of her, Nog stood with Lieutenant Commander Candlewood and Quark's employee on one side of the room, along with Vic Fontaine, who appeared to have been badly beaten. On the other side of the room, seven men in suits faced the quartet. The largest of them held a knife threateningly in one hand.

"Who the hell are you?" asked one of the men, while another asked where they had come from. At the same time, at least four of the men drew firearms.

Ro didn't hesitate. She had no idea what was going on, but she knew that the only one in danger in that room was Vic Fontaine. Ro turned to Remzi, grabbed the box from her hand, and pulled out the silver band inside. She opened the device and clamped it around Vic's arm, then hauled him backward and out through the door. She half expected the singer to vanish as he passed over the threshold, but he didn't. Ro saw Quark's eyes widen as Vic Fontaine stepped for the first time onto the deck of Deep Space 9.

viii

Nog didn't know what had happened or how it had happened, but he suspected it had to do with whatever plot Morn had hatched in his attempt to save Vic. Astoundingly, it seemed to have worked, with the singer actually leaving the holosuite but remaining intact. Across the room, Calderone and his men looked on in confusion, but then Nog saw the mobster turn his attention back to him, Candlewood, and Lani. "Kill them," he said, and his thugs aimed their weapons.

Nog grabbed Candlewood and Lani and pulled them bodily toward the door. "Computer, save and end program," the operations chief said.

As the suite at the Shining Oasis vanished, taking

Calderone and his men with it, Nog suddenly realized that he might have doomed Vic. When he looked down the corridor outside the holosuite, though, he still saw the singer. Nog quickly went to him.

"Captain," the operations chief said. "What's going on? How is this possible?"

Ro pointed to the silver band she had affixed around Vic's arm. "A mobile, self-contained holo-emitter," she said. Then the captain addressed the two other men with her. "What do you intend to do with Mister Fontaine?" she asked.

The Vulcan stepped forward and produced a pair of wrist restraints. "For the moment," the man said, "he is under arrest."

ix

He heard movement first, and then voices. They sounded distant, as though away in another room. He could not make out words, but he heard a tone and a way of speaking that he recognized.

Anora, he thought, and he knew that he missed her terribly. He didn't recall what had happened or where he was, but he remembered Anora—her lovely features, her flowing auburn tresses, her deep, dark eyes. He remembered her, and he missed her.

Altek opened his eyes. He lay on his back, and he saw above him a ceiling he did not recognize. *I'm not in my house, and not in the hospital in Joradell,* he thought. *And obviously not in the caves beneath the Merzang Mountains.* Altek turned his head and—

It all rushed in on him at once, the five months of his exile, the strange new world in which he found himself. Mourning his lost past. Acclimating himself to the future.

Falling for Laren. Suddenly finding Anora with him—Nerys.

And the falsework.

Altek pushed himself up, swept aside the sheet atop him, and swung his legs from the padded platform on which he lay. He was on one of the ships that had carried the scientists and the vedeks and the others down from the surface of Endalla. He could see nothing but darkness through the port in the opposite bulkhead, making him think that he hadn't been taken from the great chasm that led down to the falsework.

"Dans," a familiar voice said, and Altek looked to his left to see Kira Nerys in the doorway. She quickly stepped aside and allowed an older man to edge past her. He had a weathered face, graying hair, and an especially long column of folds on the bridge of his nose. He wore a Bajoran Militia uniform.

As the man reached for an instrument on a shelf beside Altek's platform, Kira said, "This is Doctor Rhyne Ashek."

"How are you feeling?" the doctor asked. He activated the device and worked its controls, slowly moving it around Altek's body.

"Like I just got run over by a Bajoran moon," Altek said with a chuckle.

The doctor smiled, but it appeared reflexive rather than genuine. "Seriously, young man," he said, "how do you feel?"

Altek took a deep breath and tried to assess himself. He flexed his arms and legs, shifted his body. "I've got some aches and pains," he said. "Nothing too bad, but . . . my energy is low. I feel almost like I've been electrically shocked. My thoughts are coming a little more slowly than usual, as though I'm a bit dazed."

Rhyne nodded. "These readings support that," he said.

"I'm detecting some unusual synaptic potentials in your brain, which suggests you might have had a pagh'tem'far, but most of what I see points to something approximating an Orb experience."

"Yes," Altek said, remembering back to his previous existence, when Veralla Sil had shown him the Tear of Destiny before Keev Anora had left to deliver it to Shavalla. "Yes, it felt very much like that . . . unreal . . . no . . . more like *hyper*-real. And overwhelming."

"We all felt it," Kira said. "Everybody inside the chamber. But, again, you were the only one who lost consciousness, and . . ."

"What?" Altek asked when Kira seemed reluctant to continue.

"And it was you who caused it," Kira said. "You placed your hands in indentations in the wall—"

"Yes!" Altek exclaimed, jumping to his feet as he recalled the event. "I saw the shapes of hands . . . *my* hands . . ." A wave of dizziness overtook him, as though he had stood up too fast. He teetered, and both Kira and the doctor helped him to sit back down on the platform.

"No quick movements like that," Rhyne said. "I don't think you need any medication or treatment, but I'd like you to get some rest."

"Of course," Altek said.

"I'll make sure he does, Doctor," Kira said. "Thank you."

Rhyne shut off the medical device and placed it back on the shelf. As he moved to leave, Altek thanked him. Once he'd gone, Kira sat down on the platform beside him.

"Do you remember what happened?" she asked gently.

He shrugged. "We were watching the two scientists examining that one section of wall, and then I . . . sensed . . . something. I felt something pulling me—" He touched a finger to the side of his head. "—in here. I wasn't being controlled, but I felt compelled to move. Maybe *im*pelled would be a better description. I walked to that oddly angular intersection of surfaces, and that's when I first perceived the imprints of hands there. They began to glow, and when I put my hands up, I saw that they precisely matched."

"I saw that too," Kira said. "It was as though they had been made specifically for you."

"It felt like that," Altek said. "Especially because the previous night, when I got lightheaded and fell, I saw a vision of glowing hands."

Kira abruptly stood up. "This is why you're here," she said. "The Prophets showed you that vision so that you would be drawn to the imprints of the hands . . . so that you would place your hands there and activate the display of the comet."

"But . . . what does it all mean?"

"I don't know," Kira said. "The imprints that you set your hands in . . . they're gone now. After what occurred, the chamber was evacuated, but a few of the scientists have returned now. Where you were standing when everything happened, they can find only flat, smooth surfaces. Other than you and me, apparently nobody else saw the imprints."

Altek shook his head. "Disappearing imprints of my hands, hundreds or maybe thousands of years in the future," he said. "And I've somehow been sent to this time so that I could set my hands there, but for what reason? To see a comet die as it plunged into Bajor's atmosphere? Why?"

"I don't know," Kira said again. They stayed quiet for a few moments, each lost to their own thoughts. Finally, Kira said, "There in the chamber, it seemed so realistic, almost like a holographic recording. I remember it so vividly. I was just a child, and we were in the Singha refugee camp, but my father let my brothers and me stay up late every night for a few weeks to watch it. They called it the Temple

Comet because it shined brightest each night with the constellation of the Temple behind it."

"Are you saying that you actually saw that comet in your youth?" Altek asked. His mouth had gone dry.

"Yes," Kira said. "I don't remember exactly how old I was, but yes."

"*You* saw it?" Altek asked. "Kira Nerys, not Keev Anora?"

"Yes, I saw it as Kira Nerys," she said. "A lot of Bajorans saw it. I spoke to some of the scientists about it after we got you medical help. We all agreed it was a re-creation, if not a recording, of when the Temple Comet disintegrated upon entering Bajor's atmosphere."

"I don't understand how that can be," Altek said. "I saw the same comet from the backyard of my childhood home in Joradell. But if I came from so far back in the past, how could that be?" Altek tried to wrap his mind around the implications. "The odds of two such distinctive but identical comets, in two different time periods, seem so unlikely as to be impossible."

Kira leaned heavily against the bulkhead, as though she had been winded. "Not two identical comets," she said. "The same comet, not in two different time periods, but in two different universes."

"What are you saying?"

"I'm saying that you're not from the past," Kira told him. "You're from a parallel universe. We witnessed the same astronomical phenomenon that somehow spanned both realities. That means that your childhood and my childhood were contemporaneous."

Altek had trouble even imagining what Kira proposed. "Even if that's true, I don't understand it, or what I have to do with any of this."

Kira pushed away from the bulkhead and walked back over to sit beside Altek again. "You arrived here from the wormhole," she said. "That means that the wormhole exists in your universe as well as ours. But since the Bajor in your reality had only four moons, since it had no version of Endalla, that means that the wormhole existed in your universe without a falsework upon which it was constructed. It stands to reason, then, that what the Ohalavaru uncovered here on Endalla is *not* a falsework for the Celestial Temple. Whatever it is, it has some other purpose."

"But what does that mean?" Altek wanted to know.

"It means that you have been sent here, from your universe to ours, to refute the Ohalavaru claims," Kira said. "Dans, you are a Hand of the Prophets."

X

Ro sat in a chair in the security office on the Plaza, facing a large viewscreen that showed images from all two dozen of the facility's detention cells. Nog and Doctor Remzi occupied the seats beside her. On the display, in the lower left-hand corner, Ensign Ernak gov Ansarg appeared, leading Corvok and Toulet into the detention area. Vic Fontaine stood between the two Federation Security agents.

Even though Remzi had told Ro about the mobile emitter, its operation still impressed her. It felt odd enough to see Vic in a setting outside his old-Earth Las Vegas lounge, but it seemed surreal to watch a holographic character walk about Deep Space 9. Ro wondered what implications the technology would have in the wider Federation.

On the viewer, Ansarg went to a detention cell and stepped aside, allowing Corvok and Toulet to escort Vic inside. Once they had, Ansarg activated the cell's force field. The agents released Vic from his wrist restraints, and the singer went over to the room's lone sleeping platform and sat down on it.

"Ventor, isolate the cell Ernak just activated," Ro said. At the security office's main console, Lieutenant Bixx acknowledged the order and worked the controls. A moment later, the view of Vic's cell expanded to fill the display.

The singer looked terrible. As Ro had led Corvok, Toulet, and their prisoner to the security office, Nog had explained the sequence of events that had resulted in Vic's injuries. He began with Morn giving the singer worthless financial instruments to prop up an in-program debt, and ended with a hoodlum ordering one of his men to cut out Vic's vocal cords.

After Nog had told his story, Doctor Remzi had asked a number of questions. She focused primarily on Vic Fontaine's personality traits, but she also wanted to know about the particular nature of the overall holoprogram. Remzi seemed less interested in the expansiveness of the code, which Ro considered impressive, and more about its constraints.

On the display, Corvok said, "Your name is Vic Fontaine?"

"Yeah," Vic said. He sat with his hands in his lap and his head down. "Who are you?"

Corvok and Toulet looked at each other in a way that suggested they had never even considered introducing themselves to a hologram. "I am Corvok," the Vulcan said, "and this is Amadou Toulet. We are agents with Federation Security."

"I figured as much when you handcuffed me and locked me in jail," Vic said. He sounded as though he could not speak normally because of the swelling on his face. "Don't I get a chance to make a phone call?"

Corvok and Toulet again regarded each other, that time in obvious confusion.

"*A phone call,*" Vic repeated. "*So I can contact a lawyer. Or doesn't the Federation allow people they arrest to have legal representation?*"

"*For the moment,*" Toulet said, "*you haven't been charged with a crime.*"

"*So then I don't need a lawyer because I'm free to go?*" Vic stood up. When he did, Ro again noted the battering his face had taken.

"*Please sit down,*" Corvok said.

"*Right,*" Vic said, slumping back down onto the sleeping platform. "*That's what I thought.*"

"*Your face,*" Toulet said. "*That isn't what you normally look like, is it?*"

"*I can't see my face, pallie,*" Vic said, "*but from the way it feels and the way my mouth is forming words, I'm guessing no, I don't usually look like this.*"

"*Why don't you change it back, then?*" Toulet asked. "*Reconfigure your physical matrix.*"

"*Because I need to heal for that to happen, Einstein,*" Vic said. "*I might be a light bulb, but even a light bulb can't just change the color it gives off.*"

"*By 'light bulb,'*" Corvok said, "*do you mean that you are a hologram?*"

"*Yeah, I'm a hologram,*" Vic said, sounding annoyed. "*What of it? I see your pointed ears, but I don't go askin if you're a Vulcan.*"

If Corvok took any offense at the comment, he hid it well. "*It is unusual for a character in a holographic program to know that it is a hologram,*" he said.

"*Yeah, so?*" Vic said. "*I can only speak for myself.*"

"*You are aware that you are a hologram,*" Corvok said, "*but you are now outside any holographic environment. That does not seem to surprise you. Why?*"

Vic made a fist with one hand and rapped it against the silver band circling his upper arm. *"I'm not surprised because I assume this is a mobile holographic emitter."*

"Then you know about the mobile emitter?" Corvok asked.

"You know, I'm not sure if it's because you're a Vulcan or because you're in law enforcement," Vic said, *"but you don't seem to have much of a grasp on the obvious."*

Apparently undeterred, Corvok said, *"But the mobile emitter is restricted technology."*

"Hey, I'm not the one who put this on me."

"But did you want somebody to put that on you?" Toulet asked.

"So you're interrogating my desires?" Vic said. *"Should I confess to the dreams I have about Ann-Margret?"*

"I will be more direct," Corvok said. *"Did you hire Morn to acquire a mobile emitter for you?"*

"Me?" Vic said, and he rolled his eyes—or at least he rolled his one eye not swollen shut. *"First of all, how could I possibly hire anybody outside a holosuite? I don't have any cash or belongings that have any value outside my program."*

"That isn't a denial," Toulet noted.

"Fine," Vic said. *"Then I'll deny it outright: I didn't hire Morn or anybody else to dig up one of these things for me."*

"But you knew of its existence," Corvok said, more statement than question.

"Yeah, I did," Vic admitted. *"But it's not like I'm the only one. The emitter might be restricted technology, but it's not like its existence is top secret. My program has access to public files—at least, it did back on the old bicycle wheel."*

"On the what?" Toulet asked.

"Sorry," Vic said. *"On the old Deep Space Nine. I used to monitor public files, keep up on what was goin on out in the big, wide universe."*

"Are you claiming that you know about the mobile emitter from public sources?" Corvok asked.

"Yeah," Vic said.

"I don't think that's true," Corvok said.

"I'd tell you I'm not programmed to lie, but that'd be a lie in itself," Vic said. He shrugged. *"Look, I can't tell you if it's been publicly reported directly—I didn't monitor everything—but it's certainly been evident by implication. There's an emergency medical hologram who's walking around out there. He was first installed aboard a Starfleet vessel called* Voyager, *but he later joined a think tank, he testified at a rights trial for an android, and then he worked for the Federation Research Institute. It doesn't take a genius to know that there weren't holographic projectors installed in all the places he's been."*

"So you inferred the existence of a mobile emitter," Corvok said. *"Did you want one for yourself?"*

Vic lifted his hands as though offering his wrists to the agents. *"Ya got me,"* he said. *"I have to admit that the thought did cross my mind."*

"Did you hire—did you ask*—Morn to obtain one for you?"* Toulet asked.

"I might've mentioned in passing once or twice that I'd love to have one," Vic said. *"But no, I didn't ask him to get a mobile emitter for me."*

"How strongly did you convey your wish?" Corvok asked.

"Look, I don't kn—" A buzz emanated from the view-screen in the security office, cutting off Vic's sentence.

"What was that?" Ro asked. "Is there a problem with communications?"

"—to him," Vic continued, *"but it wasn't—"* Another buzz filled the air, and Ro saw Vic's image jump.

At the security console, Bixx worked his controls. "I'm not reading any malfunctions with the comm system, or any interference," he said.

"*—didn't make him think I wantzzzzz—*" Vic's image scrambled for an instant, like the effect of noise on an open channel, but Ro saw that the rest of the display remained steady.

Beside the captain, Nog leaped to his feet. "It's Vic's matrix," he said, and he raced over to the main security panel. Ro went with him. "Where are the sensors for the detention cells?" Nog asked Bixx.

The lieutenant pointed. "I've got a subpanel configured here."

As Nog operated the controls, Ro peered back at the display. Doctor Remzi had also risen to her feet. On the viewer, the edges of Vic's holographic body blurred, then snapped back into focus. The two agents watched, clearly unsure what to do.

"Captain, I'm reading power fluctuations coming from within Vic's cell," Nog said.

"It has to be the emitter," Remzi said.

"I'm also detecting a transceiver signal," Nog reported.

"A transceiver?" Ro said. "Broadcasting to where? Receiving from where?"

Nog continued working the sensor controls. "To and from my uncle's bar. It's got to be a link to the holosuite computers."

"The emitter's not a truly autonomous unit," Remzi said. "That makes sense. We haven't been able to make one work."

On the display, Vic stood up. He held his hands out in front of himself and studied them. As Ro looked on, the singer flickered, disappeared for an instant, then glowed brightly before returning to normal. "*What's happening?*" Vic asked, fear lacing his voice. "*This thing issss—*" The top half of his body skewed right, the bottom half, left. His form grew hazy, then righted itself completely. His face suddenly showed as fully healed, then resorted to its wounded visage.

"Ventor," Ro called out to the security officer, "tell Corvok and Toulet to stand by." Bixx stepped away from the tumult and tapped his combadge.

"Vic's matrix is destabilizing," Nog said, a note of panic in his voice. "We could lose him."

"What can we do?" Ro asked, looking to Remzi.

"Get him back to the holosuite, back into his program," Remzi said.

"We can't," Nog said. "Bugsy Calderone wants to cut out his vocal cords."

"Nog, one problem at a time," Ro said. "Doctor Remzi, can we transport the emitter without losing Vic?"

"I don't know."

"Captain, his matrix could lose coherence at any time," Nog said.

On the viewscreen, Vic's image vanished entirely before reappearing. *"What'sssss—"*

"Do it," Ro said. "Ventor, lower the cell's force fields so that Nog can transport the emitter to an empty holosuite."

Bixx returned to the main security console and worked its controls. "Force fields are down, Captain," he said.

As Ro watched Nog call up a security tie-in subpanel to the starbase's transporter system, she activated her combadge. "Ro to Quark." When she did not receive an immediate response, she thought that he might be ignoring her. She raised her hand to press her combadge again when she heard his voice.

"This is Quark."

"Quark, I don't have time to explain, but we have an emergency," Ro said quickly. "We are beaming Vic to an empty holosuite. I'll tell you which one when I know. We need to activate Vic's holoprogram."

"Should I charge the usage to Starfleet?"

"Yes, Quark, yes."

"Captain, transport is complete," Nog said. Ro glanced over at the viewscreen and saw Corvok and Toulet alone in the detention cell. Nog called out the number of the holosuite to which he had beamed the mobile emitter, and Ro relayed it to Quark.

"All right," the barkeep said. *"I'll go activate Vic's program. Quark out."*

Ro peered over at Remzi, then back at Nog. "Did we make it in time?" she asked.

"I don't know, Captain," Nog said. "I don't know."

xi

Nog stared at the closed door, thinking of all the time he had spent in a holosuite running Vic's program—not just in the previous five days as he'd attempted to rescue the singer, and not just in the previous weeks and months as he'd worked to upload his program from the simulation tester, but all the way back to the days of the old station. He still sometimes had nightmares about losing his leg in the Chin'toka system, but he also had important memories of how Vic had helped nurse him back to emotional health. Yes, Vic was a hologram, but that didn't matter; Vic was also his friend.

Nog operated the door controls, and the panel slid open. It revealed a seedy hallway with which the operations chief had grown very familiar. He had never been happier to see it, but as with his previous visits, he also worried what he would find there.

"This is it, Captain," Nog said. He walked inside, and Ro followed. The holosuite door closed behind them and faded out of sight.

Nog walked over to the door with the number *23* hanging on it. The last time he had visited, one of the door's hinges had been ripped from the wall. In the days since, it had been repaired.

Nog raised his hand and knocked. He expected to get no response, but the door immediately opened. Vic Fontaine stood there. His eye remained swollen closed, his face bruised, his flesh covered in scabbed-over cuts. To Nog, he had never looked better. "You're here!"

"Come in," Vic said, waving Nog inside. He gazed past the operations chief. "You, too, Captain."

Nog and Ro entered the shabby hotel room, and Vic closed the door. When Nog turned to face him, the singer held out his hand in front of him. The silver band of the mobile emitter sat atop his palm. "You can take this hunk of junk back," he said. "It almost killed me."

Ro reached over and took the device. "When I entered the holosuite, you looked like you were in trouble," she said. "The emitter seemed like the best way to get you out of harm's way."

"Don't misunderstand me, Captain," Vic said. "I'm grateful to you. But just because this thing worked as a life preserver, that doesn't mean it can work as a way of life."

"Are you all right now?" Nog asked.

Vic gestured to his face. "I've been better," he said, "but without your help, I could've been worse, too."

"I mean from the emitter," Nog said.

"Yeah, I think so," Vic said. "It was downright scary there for a few minutes. I felt like I was drowning and getting electrocuted at the same time. But everything seems back to normal now—which means I can't stay here long. Bugsy Calderone's hoods found me here once; it's a cinch they'll come looking here again."

"I'm sorry," Nog said. "I tried to resolve the situation in

a way that would clear your debt with Calderone and get your life back to normal."

"Not your fault, kid," Vic said. "Morn gave me those water rights to prop up his debt. I was skeptical, and he told me not to use them, that he'd replace them with something better, but he never showed up again."

"A lot has happened," Nog told him.

"I know," Vic said. "I figured there were big problems when everybody from the old bicycle wheel stopped showin up. When you managed to upload my program to the holosuite here, and then when your friend La Forge stabilized it, I accessed public files. I learned about what happened to the old station." He paused, then said, "Anyway, it's my fault. I shoulda known better than to go to a hard guy like Calderone for help."

"I think you're right," Nog said. "I think he'll send his men after you. Maybe if I can make more money, I can buy him off."

"It's no good, kid," Vic said. "You saw Calderone. You heard him. This isn't about money. It's about me diminishing his reputation, and him wanting to make an example outta me. That's why I can't stay. I'm only here because I figured you'd be comin."

"What are you going to do?" Nog asked.

"I don't know," Vic said. "I'm gonna start by going to ground, but that's probably not gonna work for very long this time."

"Why don't we just transfer your matrix to another holoprogram," Ro suggested.

"I don't think the code will allow that," Nog said. "When Vic or users are in jeopardy of any kind, the program won't allow them to escape like that."

"It's why I couldn't just avoid Calderone by heading to another program," Vic said. "Well, if any other programs had been runnin in the simulation tester, anyway." The singer paused for a moment, then added, "Besides, this is my time, this is my place. I don't want to live in the twenty-fourth century or the fourth century, on Bajor or Vulcan or anywhere else. I'm human, and I'm a singer."

"There have to be other holoprograms set on Earth in this time period," Ro said. "And even if you went to a different era or a different planet, wouldn't living then and there be preferable to dying in this time, in this place?"

"There's something else," Nog said. "Vic's matrix has been transferred to other programs for brief jaunts, but his code and memory core are in a constant state of self-examination and self-repair. It can't do that outside the context of his original program. If we moved him to another, it's likely that he would eventually fail."

"Fail how?" Ro asked.

"Holes could form in his memory, his personality could change," Nog said. "Even his physical parameters could suffer. In the end, he could just cease to function at all."

"Not really the way I wanna go," Vic said.

"Maybe I can figure out a way to delete Calderone from the program," Nog said.

"How long would that take?" Ro asked.

"Honestly, I'm not even sure it's possible," Nog said. "Felix coded this program with strict limitations against modifications. The way he explained it to me, he wanted to make this place as real as he could."

"Which makes this a great place to live," Vic said, "but also a place where it's possible for me to die."

A hush fell over the room. Nog regarded his friend and felt frustrated that he could not help him. After all Vic had been through, after all that Nog and Candlewood and Lani had been through, not to mention Morn, it seemed absurd that the singer's life would remain in such danger.

Then the captain spoke up. "Couldn't we delete Calderone from the program in a manner befitting his line of work?" she asked. Nog understood at once that she meant killing the mobster. "He's just a holographic character."

"So am I," Vic said.

"You're not *just* a hologram," Nog protested. "You're more than that."

"Yeah," Vic agreed. "But who's to say Bugsy Calderone isn't more than that too?" The singer paused for a moment, then added, "But even if he's not, killing him wouldn't take the target off my back. He's got a whole criminal organization around him. They won't stop comin after me just because he's gone."

"I actually thought about eliminating Calderone myself," Nog said, "but it didn't seem to me that it would solve the problem."

Vic shrugged. "Besides," he said, "that's just not how I roll, Captain."

"Then I guess, considering how realistic this program is," Ro said, "why don't you do the one thing that might actually save you?"

Nog and Vic asked the same question at the same time: "What?"

"Run."

Epilogue

Venture Capital

Kira Nerys regarded her sparsely furnished lodging at the Vanadwan Monastery. Her room had been kept intact during the time she'd spent in the Celestial Temple, and used by the only remaining "solid" Ascendant, a privilege granted to her by the vedek elders there. At the moment, Raiq attended services up at the Inner Sanctuary, beneath the Crown of Bajor, the historic edifice whose nine spired towers represented the Orbs of the Prophets.

Raiq had broken down when she'd seen Kira, dropping to her knees and uttering the vedek's name—the first word she'd spoken in the more than two years since the collapse of the Celestial Temple. The two, vedek and knight, had been through a long journey together that had begun when Captain Kira had prevented the Ascendant from ending her own life. Raiq had sought understanding for the apparent death of her race, for her own unexpected survival, and for the faith that she and generations of her people had clutched with extremist fervor. She had trusted no one, least of all herself, but somehow she had ultimately looked to Kira for guidance. The two had studied together, prayed together, looked inward together. It had taken many days, but they had both eventually found a peace within themselves that neither one of them had ever before known. They had greeted each other not like two long-lost friends, but like self-proclaimed sisters, joined together not by blood, but by faith and common experience.

Kira looked around the mostly empty space of her living quarters, which consisted of a single room and an attached refresher. Populated by only a few pieces of furniture—a dresser, a desk and chair, a bed—it contained few personal belongings. She saw her beautiful old copy of *When the Prophets Cried* lying atop the dresser, along with some framed photographs: the Emissary and his family, Kai Opaka, Odo. Though she couldn't see it, she knew that, under the desk, sat Odo's old bucket, in which he used to regenerate. The memory of him brought a smile to her face.

Growing up in refugee camps, and later living on the run as part of the Resistance, Kira had never kept much with her. When she joined the Bajoran clergy eight years earlier, she divested herself of most of her material belongings. Examining her surroundings, she realized that almost all of what she retained of her forty-two years was internal. Had she actually perished when the wormhole had collapsed, little physical trace would have been left of her existence. She could only hope that the value of her life would be measured by the impact she had on others.

Kira heard footsteps approaching, and she turned toward the open door. She expected to see the silver face and golden eyes of Raiq, but instead, Altek Dans appeared. He looked hale, fully recovered from his experiences far beneath the surface of Endalla the previous week.

"I hope you don't mind me visiting without contacting you first," he said.

"Not at all," Kira told him. "Please come in."

"It's good to see you," he said.

"It's good to see you too." Kira glanced around her room. "I'm afraid I can't offer you much in the way of hospitality. We could go for a walk, if you like."

"No, that's all right," Altek said. "I'm not going to stay."

"All right," Kira said. She walked over to the desk and pulled out the chair. "Have a seat." While Altek moved to the desk, Kira sat down on the edge of the bed. "You look well."

"Thanks. I feel good," Altek said. "I didn't really plan on coming here, but I was out in town for a walk, and when I passed a public transporter . . . well, the urge just struck me."

"I'm glad it did," Kira said. "So what town were you walking in?"

"I've settled in Forren," Altek said. "Do you know it?"

"No, I don't think so."

"It's a small town in Hill Province," Altek said. "Up in the mountains. There are a lot of artists up there."

"It sounds nice."

"It's quiet," Altek said, "and I like that."

Kira knew that he had wanted to flee the sudden notoriety he'd endured, before and especially after the events on Endalla. When news broke of what had taken place within the chamber of the falsework, some Ohalavaru loudly denounced the interpretation that Altek had come to Bajor from a parallel universe, rather than from the past, and a few even focused on his Bajor having only four moons as evidence supporting their claims. Mostly, though, the sect grew largely silent, at least in public. Though some mainstream adherents continued to have difficulties dealing with all that had transpired on Endalla, and all that had been claimed about it, an overarching calm settled over believers. Kira still hadn't finished processing everything that had occurred, but her faith in the Prophets had never wavered.

"So what do you plan to do up in Forren?" Kira asked.

"I've actually started to write," Altek said. "I decided that I wanted to record as much as I can remember of my old life, back before I traveled through the Celestial Temple."

"Is that helping you?" Kira asked.

"I'm not sure," Altek admitted. He spoke quietly, perhaps even forlornly. "It's hard right now, but I think it will help me down the road. I'm finding it more and more difficult to recall details from those days, and I don't want to lose it all. I want to keep what I can."

"I think I understand." It occurred to Kira that perhaps she should set down her memories of her time as Keev

Anora, no matter how few and fragmented they might be.

"I'm also thinking about attending university," Altek said, his tone growing enthusiastic. "I want to study Bajoran history, maybe with an eye to finding other parallels between where I came from and where I am now. I guess I'm just trying to put it all together in some kind of coherent context for myself."

"I'm a bit surprised," Kira said. "I thought you'd go back into medicine."

"Actually, I think I probably will," Altek said. "I'm just not sure when. I haven't been here all that long—not when compared with the decades of my life before now—and I'm still trying to figure it all out."

"That makes sense." Suddenly, she felt the need to say more. "Dans, I'm sorry if I hurt you. I don't doubt the truth of the feelings between you and Keev Anora, and I know that, somehow, I am Keev, or I was . . . but even though I sometimes recall flashes of that time, those days are fading fast for me. More even than that, there's your relationship with Captain Ro. Have you spoken with her since leaving Deep Space Nine?"

"No," Altek said. "I've thought about contacting her, but the way we parted, and her silence, tells me that it's probably best if I don't."

"I'm not so sure."

Altek shrugged noncommittally, then changed the subject. "What about you?" he asked. "What are your plans?"

"I'll be heading back to Endalla in a few days," Kira told him. "I'm still committed to observing the study of the falsework and assisting vedeks and scholars in interpreting what the scientists find. So far, there have been no further incidents."

"Will you be leaving the monastery?"

"No," Kira said. "I'll be splitting my time between Endalla and here. I want to contribute to the study of the falsework, but I also want to resume my life here at Vanadwan.

I'm grateful for all of my experiences, but it feels as though my time here has just begun."

"Well, I certainly know what that feels like," Altek said, though he did not sound wistful. He stood up, and Kira did so as well. "I just wanted to stop by and thank you for all the support you've given me, when I first came to Bajor and then on Endalla. I don't know if I could have gotten through it all without you."

"I wish you good fortune," Kira said, "and a happy life." She thought to say more, to tell him that they should stay in touch, that they should make sure to see each other from time to time, but she realized that she didn't know if either of them would want that.

"Good fortune to you too," Altek said. He started to leave, but then he stopped in the doorway. "I like the life that I'm starting to build here, and I'm excited about my plans, but some part of me is still unsettled because . . . well, I believe that the Prophets brought me here to act as a conduit for the message implicitly contained in the Endalla construct, but now I wonder what Their purpose is for me going forward."

"I can only tell you that you should have faith not only in the Prophets, but in yourself," Kira said. "If you do that, I'm certain that the Prophets will guide you along whatever path you are meant to walk."

Altek seemed to consider that. Finally, he nodded and left. Kira watched him go, and then listened as his footsteps receded.

She walked over to the dresser and picked up *When the Prophets Cried*. The texture of its deep-red binding felt familiar in her hands. She ran her fingers over the remnants of the gold-inlay letters of its title, which had been almost entirely worn away by decades of handling.

Kira carried the volume over to her desk and set it down. She sat and opened the book, flipping through pages she had read more times than she could remember. She flipped past chapter titles—"Home in the Firmament," "Seeds of Change," "Whispers in the Night," and others—until she came to the one she wanted to see at that moment: "Faith and Love."

Kira had only read a few lines when she heard footsteps approaching her door again. She waited, thinking that Altek had returned to say something more to her—perhaps to convince her that they belonged together after all. She steeled herself for a conversation that she didn't think would be easy for either of them.

Odo appeared in her doorway.

Since coming back to the Vanadwan Monastery, Kira had learned of Odo's return to the Alpha Quadrant after the collapse of the Celestial Temple, and that he had remained around Bajor afterward, refusing offers from Starfleet to carry him back to the Dominion. In her heart, she knew that he had been waiting to see if the wormhole would reopen and she would emerge from it. She knew that he remained in the Alpha Quadrant, helping the Federation in settling a ship of Dominion refugees. Kira had expected that she would see him again one day soon, though not whether it would be because he sought closure with her, or a second chance.

"Odo," she said, and the emotion in her voice seemed almost palpable. She stood up and took a step toward him, and his face changed. He did not shape-shift or alter his form in that way, but the line of his mouth wavered and his eyes sparked. She could see the love he still felt for her.

"I'm so glad you're all right," he said. "I've missed you."

"I've missed you," Kira said as she crossed the distance between them and embraced Odo. He wrapped his arms around her, and they stood that way for a long time. Then Kira felt his body soften, shift, change. His flesh dissolved around her into lambent light. She raised her arms over her head and spread them wide as the essence of his being curled around her in a warm, soothing display of love that she had ever only experienced with Odo.

For the first time since emerging from the wormhole back in her own time, Kira truly felt that she was home.

ii

Doctor Ceylin Remzi sat on the provincial, teal-covered davenport, just as she had done most days for nearly a month. She hadn't anticipated staying away from Jupiter Station for as long as she had; she'd initially joined Federation Security aboard their Interceptor for the purpose of verifying the existence of the mobile emitter, and whether or not the device actually worked. The events on Deep Space 9 with Vic Fontaine had allowed her to complete her mission with relative alacrity, but the holographic character, and the stories that Nog and others had shared with her, had motivated her to extend her visit to the starbase.

"Here you are, Doc," Vic said as he walked over from the kitchenette on one side of the small apartment. He set a cup and saucer down on the table, right beside her padd. "Cream and two sugars," he said. "Just the way you like it."

"Thank you," Remzi said. The dark aroma of the French roast drifted up to her.

"My pleasure," Vic said. He put his own cup of coffee down, then pulled over a linen-covered chair with a carved oak frame. "So what'll it be today?" he asked as he sat down opposite her. "My childhood in Philly? High school days? My on-again–off-again romance with Angie? On the road opening for Frank?"

"You make it sound like I've been interrogating you," Remzi said.

"Haven't you been?" Vic asked, though he did not sound threatened by the concept. "I mean, not like you're a cop or anything, but isn't that what headshrinkers do? Ask questions, dig for details, look for connections?"

"Yes, I suppose you're right," Remzi said. She had introduced herself to Vic as a psychiatrist, which had the benefit of being true. Remzi had earned her medical degree from the University of Kinshasa before finding her love and talent for the artificial intelligence side of holographic science. "But you've been through a great deal these last couple of years, and it's important to make sure that you're able to cope with all of that and get on with your life."

Vic held out his arms and looked left and right around the small apartment. "I'd say I'm doing a pretty good job of getting on with my life."

"Of course you are," Remzi said. "But how do you feel about it? You were isolated from your friends for more than two years, and your life was constantly in peril. That's a lot to deal with." During her previous sessions with Vic, Remzi had discussed his memories, from his childhood through to the present, but she had studiously avoided asking about how he felt about any of it; she had wanted to allow him to broach the subject of his emotional life.

"How do I feel about it?" Vic echoed. "It is what it is. I had a problem, and now I've solved it. There's no use crying over spilt milk."

"You didn't really like the solution Captain Ro proposed for you, though," Vic said. "At least, that's what she told me: that you didn't want to leave Las Vegas."

"Hey, nobody likes change, right?" Vic said. "But when the choices are change or never be able to sing again, it puts it all in perspective."

"That's a mature attitude," Remzi told him. "You don't feel any resentment toward the captain?"

"What's to resent?" Vic asked. "When it comes right down to it, she saved my life. Well, her and Nog."

"Tell me a little bit about that," Remzi said. "As I understand it, Nog stayed with you for a few days after you were returned to the holosuite."

"Yeah, he's a good kid," Vic said, with what sounded like genuine affection. "He helped me stay safely hidden so he could make arrangements—him and Johnny C. and Nog's new squeeze, Lani. They got me new I.D. and managed to get me outta town before Bugsy's goons got a holda me."

"And you feel safe now?"

"I do," Vic said.

"And do you feel at home here?"

"I feel alive and free and able to sing, and those are the most important things."

"I can't argue with that," Remzi said. She leaned forward and collected her pen and spiral steno pad, then stood up. "I'm pleased to have met you." She held out her empty right hand, and Vic stood up and clasped it with his own.

"That sounds like I'm gettin the ol brush-off," Vic said.

"That can't be a bad thing, right?" Remzi said. "You must be tired of talking to me all the time."

"Not at all, Doc," Vic said. "It's been a pleasure." He shook her hand, then escorted her to the door. "Will I ever see you again?"

"I don't know," Remzi said. " 'Ever' is a long time."

"Well, if you're ever around the new gyroscope again," Vic said, "feel free to drop in."

"Thank you, I will." Vic opened the door, and Remzi exited and walked down the stairs. At the first landing she came to, she said, "Computer, exit." The door to the holosuite immediately appeared—not directly in front of her, as she'd expected, but to her right. She stepped out into the corridor and headed for the nearest turbolift.

Remzi hadn't wanted to say anything to Vic for fear of undermining what she hoped to accomplish, but she fully intended to visit him again. *Perhaps in six months,* she thought. *Or maybe a year.* She would have to study the contents of her conversations with the singer and consult with her colleagues, but she thought he was exactly what they were looking for.

iii

"So what you're telling me is that they're dropping the charges," Ro said. She looked across the desk at the two visitors to her office.

"Yes," said Commander Desjardins, who had asked to speak with the captain regarding the investigations conducted by both the Federation Security Agency and the Department of Temporal Investigations regarding the mobile holo-emitter. He placed a padd on her desk and pushed it toward her.

Owing to Ro's incidental role in the entire affair, she had endured a great deal of questioning over the prior month by both the FSA and the DTI—especially the latter. As the captain understood it, she had never been a suspect herself, but that hadn't prevented the various investigators from thinking she might be able to offer them useful observations or insights. As far as Ro knew, she had been able to provide them with neither.

"Both agencies have completed their inquiries," Desjardins continued, "and they submitted their final reports in tandem this morning. Federation Security could find no evidence that Morn ever entered UFP space with either the plans for the emitter or with the device itself."

"But he intended to," Ro said. "He planned on using it to free Vic from the holosuite."

"Morn freely admitted that," Desjardins said. "He also claimed to have no knowledge that he was dealing with technology restricted in the Federation. Not everybody believed him about that, and even if it was true, his ignorance of the law would not have been a legitimate defense. But since he dealt exclusively with scientists and engineers outside the Federation to develop and build the emitter, he technically did not violate UFP law."

"If Federation Security truly believed that Morn was going to bring restricted technology into Federation space," Ro said, "why didn't they wait until he had done so to arrest him?"

"If you read the report," Desjardins said, pointing to the padd he'd set on the captain's desk, "you'll see that Federation Security wanted to do just that. It was the Department of Temporal Investigations who pushed for the arrests of Bayal Sego and Morn as soon as possible." It took Ro a moment to recall that Sego was the Milvonian engineer Morn had hired to construct the mobile emitter. "The DTI agents were concerned about potential damage to the timeline if twenty-ninth-century technology made it onto the black market."

"But wasn't the emitter made from twenty-fourth-century processes and materials?" Ro asked.

Desjardins shrugged. "The original idea is from the twenty-ninth century, and you know how those DTI agents are." Ro absolutely did know how they were: annoying, unrelenting, and humorless. "Even a potential violation of their rules and they overreact."

"When will Morn be set free?" Ro asked. Desjardins had overseen the Lurian's arraignment. Morn had been kept in DS9's stockade ever since.

"As soon as you give the order, Captain," Desjardins said.

"What about the Milvonian engineer? Sego?" Ro asked.

"He was extradited from Stervon Four to Andor," Desjardins said. "He'll be released today as well. Which just leaves the source of all this trouble."

"Vic," Ro said. Once the singer had returned to the

holosuite and he'd been safely removed from the danger he faced there, Federation Security and Temporal Investigations agents had interviewed him on multiple occasions. They had also examined his programming.

"The reports show that neither agency could reach a consensus as to whether Vic actually intended Morn to obtain a mobile emitter for him," Desjardins said. "Regardless, since what Vic said to Morn instigated the development and creation of restricted technology, and since he did so in Federation space, Vic did violate the law."

"So Vic is going to be arrested and charged with a crime?" Ro asked. "How is that going to work?"

"No, he's not going to be charged," Desjardins said. "I'll let Doctor Remzi explain why."

Ro regarded the other visitor to her office, who had accompanied Desjardins. "Vic is not going to be charged," Remzi said, "because he's not sentient."

"What?" Ro said. "I find that hard to believe, and I haven't spent that much time in Vic's program. And I know without doubt that there are members of my crew who would argue the point with you. I've heard them talk about how much they enjoy spending time with Vic. I've even heard people talk about how much they've *learned* from him."

"People can learn from books, Captain," Remzi said. "That doesn't make books sentient."

"So you think my crew are wrong?" Ro asked.

"I'm sure that some of your crew probably do believe that Vic is sentient," Remzi said. "But as you know, this is my field of expertise, and I've spent the last month speaking with Vic. I have concluded that he is pre-sentient—that is, not truly responsive to sense impressions, but programmed to expertly simulate such responses."

"I'm not sure I understand," Ro said. "Isn't that a distinction without a difference?"

"I don't think so," Remzi said, "although I will admit that it is a difficult distinction to make. There isn't any concrete test for it, but I've reached my conclusion based on my interactions with Vic."

That surprised Ro, not based on her own minimal experience with Vic, but because of what people like Nog thought about the singer. On the one hand, Remzi's opinion meant Vic would suffer no consequences from Morn's actions, but on the other, she felt concerned about the scientist believing that a nonsentient hologram was capable of committing a criminal act, and that she would therefore recommend deleting Vic's matrix. Ro tried to walk the middle ground. "I'm not trying to change your mind," she said, "and it's not as though I think Vic really should be arrested, but some of my crew count him as a close friend."

"People anthropomorphize inanimate objects all the time, Captain," Remzi said. "How much easier to do so with an object that looks, acts, and communicates like a humanoid? It is my expert opinion that Vic has yet to achieve true sentience."

"'Yet'?" Ro asked. "Does that mean you think that he will become sentient?"

"I think it's quite possible," Remzi said. "In fact, I think that if he hadn't ended up isolated from interaction with real people for more than two years, he might well have become sentient by now."

"So you think that people visiting him in the holosuite could . . . well, essentially bring him to life?" Ro asked.

"That's a very hard question to answer," Remzi said. "We have identified androids and holograms that we have classified as sentient, but we're not sure exactly how that occurred. As I said, it's possible that humanoid interaction facilitates the process. And if it does, then leaving his program running could be of benefit."

"Is it possible that you're wrong, that Vic is sentient?" Ro asked. The captain assumed that even the chance of that would prevent the singer's matrix from being deleted.

"Yes, it's possible," Remzi said. "I'm not infallible, and there's more gray area here than black and white. But I do think you'll be hearing from Starfleet's Holographic Image and Programming Center. I'm going to recommend in my report that we periodically monitor Vic."

"I understand," Ro said, pleased at where the doctor's evaluation had ended. The captain asked if either Remzi or Desjardins needed to discuss anything more with her. When they told her that they didn't, the captain stood up and thanked them for briefing her.

Ro watched the scientist and the JAG officer exit her office. Once the door closed behind them, the captain's thoughts returned to Vic. Something else occurred to her that she hadn't mentioned to Remzi. *What if Vic is sentient?* she wondered. Could he have realized that Remzi was talking with him not as a psychiatrist to help with the traumas he'd experienced, but as a holographic scientist attempting to evaluate him? Did he know that if she judged him sentient that there would be repercussions because he had broken the Restricted Technology laws? Could he have interacted with Remzi in such a way that she would conclude that he wasn't sentient?

Maybe, Ro thought, *Vic fooled her.*

iv

Nog and Candlewood entered the smoky, dimly lighted room. Customers sat scattered about at small, round tables, mostly in groups of two or three. Candles flickered, their flames glittering off drinks in tall, slim glasses.

For a moment, Nog worried that they would not be able

to find a place to sit, but then he spotted an empty table off to one side. He navigated toward it through the crowd, with Candlewood following behind him. Dressed not in their uniforms, but in civilian attire specific to 1960s Earth, the two Starfleet officers took their seats, both of them facing the small stage at the far end of the room.

"Are you sure this is the right place?" Candlewood asked.

"Trust me," Nog said.

On the stage, a man walked out from the wings. He stood in front of a black curtain and addressed the crowd. *"Mesdames et Messieurs, bonsoir. Bienvenue dans Le Rêve."* Nog's universal translator interpreted the French words into Federation Standard: "Ladies and gentlemen, good evening. Welcome to The Dream."

A server carrying a tray suddenly stepped in front of Nog, blocking his view of the proceedings. "Pardon me," he said, but when he looked up, intending to ask the server to please move, he saw a familiar face: Ulu Lani. "What are you doing here?" he asked.

"I work here," Lani said. "Well, at least for tonight." She took two plates from her tray and set them down before Nog and Candlewood, then placed a covered dish in the center of the table. "I believe this is for you."

"I don't think so," Candlewood said. "We just got here. We haven't ordered yet."

"And I really don't like French food," Nog added.

"Are you sure?" Lani asked, and she whisked off the cover from the dish to reveal an elegant arrangement of snails. She put linen napkins down on the table, along with tongs and snail forks.

"Wow," Nog said. The food looked delicious.

"And it's on the house," Lani said.

"Really?" Nog asked.

"Well, it's on me, anyway," Lani said. "Enjoy the show."

Without another word, she expertly weaved her way back through the tables.

Nog returned his attention to the stage, where the man continued to speak. *"S'il vous plaît accueillir à Paris un Américain qui chante avec l'âme d'un Français."* Again, Nog's universal translator provided the words in Federation Standard: "Please welcome to Paris an American who sings with the soul of a Frenchman." The man held his hand up toward the side of the stage and said: "Victor Printanier."

Just before the lights went dark, Nog spotted a familiar profile at a table just in front of the stage: Morn, looking more than a little silly with a beret perched jauntily atop his head. Then a spotlight winked on, picking out a man with silver hair sitting on a stool onstage. Curls of smoke wafted through the shaft of light. Polite but enthusiastic applause floated up from the audience.

"Merci, merci," Vic said, with an accent that obviously marked him as a nonnative.

It felt good to see him again, back in his element. His face had healed, and he looked like his old self again. Nog had been concerned for so long about his friend, from Vic's time confined to the simulator, to the problems in uploading his program to the new holosuites, to his troubles with Bugsy Calderone. The operations chief felt grateful that all of that lay in the past, but he still worried about the effect on Vic of his forced relocation from Las Vegas.

And then Vic began to sing: *"Non, rien de rien. Non, je ne regrette rien."* His voice sounded as smooth and velvety as ever, and his choice of song and the translated lyrics told Nog everything he needed to know about his friend: "No, nothing at all. I do not regret anything."

Acknowledgments

It requires more than the efforts of just a writer to publish a novel. Somebody must acquire the potential book in the first place. Somebody has to evaluate the story—beginning, middle, and end, character arcs, overall themes—and work with the writer so that they can produce a narrative outline (at least in the case of *Star Trek* works, so that both the publisher and the license holder can read and approve it). Somebody has to negotiate terms, then send out a contract and get it signed by all parties. Then once the novel has actually been written, somebody has to edit the manuscript, somebody has to copyedit it, somebody has to typeset it. Somewhere along the way, somebody has to create a cover, and somebody else has to pen cover copy. Once the writer has worked through all of those steps in concert with all of those people, the folks in production still have to go through the process of physically producing the book and sending it out into the world—printing it, binding it, shipping it.

Obviously, that's a lot of work, and yet it's not even an exhaustive list of all the steps involved. I want to thank everybody who took part in the publication of *The Long Mirage*. I particularly want to single out the people in production, who never get enough appreciation for all that they do.

Of course, somebody has to oversee the entire enterprise (in addition to doing much of the actual work). For me, those people are editors Margaret Clark and Ed Schlesinger. Without the two of them, this book would not exist. For all their hard work, I thank them.

On the personal side, there are so many people who support me. I'm very fortunate to have a host of caring, encouraging, and loving friends in my life. I'm grateful to each and every one of them. I especially want to thank Kirsten Beyer, her husband,

David, and their wonderful daughter, Anorah, for their steadfast and generous friendship. *Aloha me mahalo e ke ku'uhoa.*

And then there are my rocks, the people in my life who have been the steadiest and who have been there the longest. Walter Ragan is a Navy man—a submariner—who also knows his way around electricity. He has always been kind and loving to me, providing me with tremendous encouragement. He is like a father to me, and I am grateful for that.

Colleen Ragan and Anita Smith are technically my sisters-in-law, but in real life, they are more like actual sisters to me. They are both kind, loving women who make everything better just by being around them. I thank each of them for welcoming me into their family.

I am also privileged to have an amazing woman for my actual sister. Jennifer George is a brilliant and accomplished person who lives a wonderfully happy life that stands as a shining example for all of us. I am grateful for the many ways in which she helps and supports me, and I could not be more proud to be her brother.

I am also thankful to have Patricia Walenista in my life. A world traveler, a voracious reader, and a woman of eclectic tastes, she is also a skilled researcher and historian. She has taught me so much, and I continue to learn from her all the time.

Finally, as always, there is the incomparable Karen Ragan-George. My wife's talents know no bounds. Whether she is acting, writing, directing, dancing, painting, or taking part in some other art form, Karen always impresses (most recently onstage as Senator Emily Green in Charlie Mount's brilliant political thriller *The Leather Apron Club*). She also constantly astounds me with her lively intellect; dazzles me with her beauty, both inside and out; keeps me laughing with her sense of humor, by turns raucous and droll; and makes all the moments of our shared lives well worth the living. Karen is my sunshine!

About the Author

The Long Mirage is David R. George III's seventeenth *Star Trek* novel, and his tenth in the *Deep Space Nine* series, following *The 34th Rule*, *Twilight*, *Olympus Descending* (in *Worlds of Deep Space Nine, Volume Three*), *Rough Beasts of Empire*, *Plagues of Night*, *Raise the Dawn*, *Revelation and Dust*, *Sacraments of Fire*, and *Ascendance*. He also penned the *Crucible* trilogy—*Provenance of Shadows*, *The Fire and the Rose*, and *The Star to Every Wandering*—which was set during the original series and helped celebrate the fortieth anniversary of the television show. Another of his novels, *Allegiance in Exile*, takes place during the final part of *Enterprise*'s five-year mission. David also wrote two *Lost Era* books, *Serpents Among the Ruins* and *One Constant Star*, which feature John Harriman and Demora Sulu, as well as an *LE* novella, *Iron and Sacrifice*, which appeared in the *Tales from the Captain's Table* anthology. He also contributed an alternate-universe *Next Generation* novel, *The Embrace of Cold Architects*, to the *Myriad Universes: Shattered Light* collection.

David first contributed to the *Trek* universe on television, with a first-season *Voyager* episode called "Prime Factors." He has also written nearly twenty magazine articles about the shows and books. Of his non–*Star Trek* work, his novelette "Moon Over Luna" is available on Amazon.com. A second novelette, "The Instruments of Vice," appears in *Native Lands*, the third volume in the *ReDeus* universe, which tells stories set after the return of the gods to Earth. A third novelette, "The Dark Arts Come to Hebron," is included in a genre anthology titled *Apollo's Daughters*. David's work has appeared on both the *New York Times* and *USA Today* bestseller lists, and it has been nominated for a Scribe Award by the International Association of Media Tie-in Writers. His television episode was nominated for a *SciFi Universe* award.

David loves to play baseball, and as a native New Yorker, he has long followed his beloved but often frustrating New York Mets. He and his beautiful wife, Karen, love to travel, watch movies, attend the theater and concerts, visit museums, and dance. They presently reside in sunny southern California.

You can contact David at facebook.com/DRGIII, and you can follow him on Twitter @DavidRGeorgeIII.